ASUNDER

ASUNDER

KERSTIN HALL

TOR PUBLISHING GROUP
NEW YORK

ASUNDER

Copyright © 2024 by Kerstin Hall

A Tordotcom Book
Published by Tom Doherty Associates / Tor Publishing Group
120 Broadway
New York, NY 10271

www.torpublishinggroup.com

Tor® is a registered trademark of Macmillan Publishing Group, LLC.

The Library of Congress Cataloging-in-Publication Data is available upon request.

ISBN 978-1-250-62543-4 (hardcover)
ISBN 978-1-250-62542-7 (ebook)

Our books may be purchased in bulk for promotional, educational, or business use. Please contact your local bookseller or the Macmillan Corporate and Premium Sales Department at 1-800-221-7945, extension 5442, or by email at MacmillanSpecialMarkets@macmillan.com.

First Edition: 2024

Printed in the United States of America

0 9 8 7 6 5 4 3 2 1

This one is for me

CHAPTER

1

The shore. Black sand as fine as powder, the slick gleam of washed-up kelp. Over the restless grey waters, rain clouds loomed low and heavy.

A lot of people died here, thought Karys. The sea breeze ruffled her dark hair, and she drew her coat tighter. *Died violently.*

Coren Oselaw was watching her, his hands buried deep in his pockets. His jaw worked languidly as he rolled osk around his mouth. He had been chewing the resin stimulant since they left Psikamit, and the crunching had frayed Karys' nerves to their breaking point. He noticed her scowl and raised an eyebrow.

"Well?" he said.

In all honesty, Karys had wanted to refuse the job. She had wanted—and still wanted very much—to tell Oselaw to take a hike into the sea. But that risked offending Marishka, and people who pissed off the Second Mayor usually found themselves floating facedown out on the honey reef.

Besides, the money *was* good; she couldn't deny that.

"It was here," she replied. "Something happened near the beach, something bloody. Probably within the last three days."

"Was it our boys, then?"

"Maybe. I can't tell from this distance."

He grinned, revealing red-stained teeth. "Then I guess we'd better take a closer look, eh? After you, deathspeaker."

The path down to the beach had crumbled. Fallowgrass and whiteblossom pushed up from the thin soil and rustled in the breeze. Salt glittered on the rocks. Karys moved with thoughtless assurance, picking her way along the steep track, her mind elsewhere. It had taken three hours to reach this stretch of the coast. Three full hours of Oselaw's prattling, and he still hadn't told her what they were looking for.

Some of the boss's people failed to make a delivery, he had said with an evasive shrug. *She wants you to find out why.*

Karys didn't like it, and with every step toward the water, her unease mounted. Over the hush of the waves, she could hear a deep, discordant droning—a sound like swarming wasps. The hairs on her arms and neck stood up. She did not know what the noise signified, but it felt like a living creature was trying to burrow into her ears.

She glanced over her shoulder at Oselaw. He was struggling down the track, sweat glistening on his forehead, eyes narrowed in concentration. Didn't seem like he could hear it. Which suggested . . . nothing good.

The path ended at a rocky scree below the base of the cliffs. Beyond, the beach stood desolate and untouched, and the sour stink of rotting seaweed hung thick in the air. Small copper-winged flies scattered in front of Karys' feet. No gulls, she noted. If there were bodies here, she would have expected scavengers. The grey cliffs hunched around the shore, forming a jagged cove.

"How late was the delivery?" she called back to Oselaw.

"Two days."

That fit. She walked a little further and then stopped, listening. Death pressed up against her skin like a wet cloth.

"How many people?"

"Five to ten? It can vary."

That, on the other hand, felt wrong. Too few. Frowning, Karys closed her eyes and listened deeper, seeking out the edges of the Veneer and the bitter-bright whistle of snagged memories. She found the seam, and eased open the surface of reality. Opalescent light oozed through her eyelids. Waves crashed on the shore, and the strange droning continued, relentless and unchanging.

There. The faint murmur of a woman's voice.

Are those lights? A pause. Then the memory reset, and it spoke again: the same words, the same tone of puzzlement. *Are those lights?*

Oselaw's boots crunched on the sand behind her. Karys kept her eyes closed, still listening, but that was all she could hear—that single thread of memory, the last words of a stranger.

"They were caught by surprise," she said.

"In the water?"

Sand flies whined around her legs. Karys shook her head. "I don't think so. Maybe in the shallows, depending on the tide. But not past the breakers."

Are those lights?

"It happened so quickly," she murmured. "There wasn't even time for fear, just . . . confusion."

"You can't tell what killed them?"

"No, not without a body." She let the Veneer fall closed, and opened her eyes. "What's going on here, Oselaw?"

"Getting spooked?"

"Getting tired of your bullshit. What were you smuggling?"

He folded his arms and continued chewing his osk with deliberate slowness. Karys stared at him flatly, but he remained unmoved. The barest hint of a smirk tugged at the corner of his mouth.

"Is this amusing to you?" she asked.

"Am I laughing?"

"People died. Your people, specifically."

He paused to spit a wad of soggy resin onto the sand. He took a fresh osk ball out his pocket and popped it into his mouth. Resumed chewing. "Keep your nose out, deathspeaker. I thought you were supposed to be a professional."

Nuliere alive, but he was getting under her skin. Karys forced herself to unclench her jaw. It wasn't even Oselaw, really, but the whole job: the secrecy, Marishka's refusal to speak with her beforehand, and the sense that something deeply wrong had occurred here. A gust of wind caught the sea spray and whipped it through the air. Oselaw was right, she *was* spooked. With effort, she moderated her tone.

"Look, all I'm asking is whether the cargo itself might have killed them," she said. "That's all."

Oselaw crunched a harder shard between his teeth. He raised his gaze in thought, then shrugged.

"I doubt it," he said. "Not based on what you're telling me. What else can you sense?"

Too many people for a routine smuggling job. Which meant that either Oselaw was lying to her—entirely plausible—or that someone else had lied to *him*. At least eight had died on this stretch of the beach alone. Karys pursed her lips and scanned the water.

"I think their bodies might have washed out to sea," she said. "But not everyone died here. Come on."

The cliffs grew taller as they walked down the shore. The dark sand was strewn with kelp, but no footprints, no sign of life apart from the flies. All the while, the droning in Karys' ears grew louder. Oselaw slouched along behind her, humming to himself, but even his nonchalance seemed a little forced.

You can feel something too. Karys' skin itched. She slowed.

"There," she said.

Ahead, the dolomite wall veered sharply inward, forming a bowl-like indentation at its base. Heaviness lingered over the stone-strewn sand: the weight of many deaths, the crush of memory. Tucked inside the curve of the rock was a dark oval. Kelp and driftwood choked the mouth of the cave, and a fringe of green slime hung from the roof. The droning was coming from inside.

"Well, look at that," said Oselaw. "You found our collection site."

"What?"

He gestured to the cave entrance. "The place where our boys usually leave the goods. The boss does a retrieval every few weeks; sends me out on a fishing boat to collect. It keeps us out of the port authority's—"

"You *knew* this was here?"

"Well, yeah, that's kind of my role, logistics and such. Makes you wonder if the boys managed to bring along any merchandise before they snuffed it." Noticing her expression, he raised both hands. "Kidding, kidding! Although I don't see what's wrong with making the best of a bad situation."

Karys gritted her teeth. "Why not bring me here in the first fucking place?"

"Because this place is need-to-know. You didn't. But seeing that we're here now anyway, want to take a look inside?"

"Absolutely not."

"Oh, don't be like that."

"I have no intention of crawling into that hole, Oselaw. Not in my job description."

"Sure, but you *are* getting paid to find out what happened. And there's more likely to be a body stuck inside, right? Harder for the sea to reach?"

Karys returned her gaze to the narrow opening. The waves rocked the shore behind them. Oselaw was, annoyingly, right.

"Coward." Oselaw ambled past her, grinning. "I'll even go first."

"How gallant."

He crouched and awkwardly manoeuvred his legs through the gap, sliding inside on his back.

"You'll find it interesting." He pushed himself forward and disappeared down the hole. His voice drifted out of the darkness. "It's not what you'd expect."

Karys looked back at the beach. There were still a few hours of daylight left, and the weather would hold until evening—even with the delay, they should be able to get home to Psikamit before the storm hit. She just couldn't shake her sense of foreboding.

"Hey! Deathspeaker!" yelled Oselaw.

She sighed and crouched. The sand was damp and fine under her hands, and the rocks proved smooth as polished metal. She crawled into the gap, and the temperature dropped sharply. The passage ahead only stretched about eight feet in length, but it sloped downwards at an uncomfortable angle, and she suddenly understood why Oselaw had tackled it feetfirst. She felt like she was going to fall on her face.

The perfect way to finish this job. She reached her hands out in front of her, groping her way forward. *By breaking my own nose.*

Oselaw's chewing sounded even louder in the closed space. Her outstretched fingers met a flat, glassy surface, colder still than the air. Floor tiles.

"Mind your head," said Oselaw affably.

Karys stood up. Judging by the light filtering through the passage and the way that noises echoed, they were inside a small chamber. She shivered. The cold cut straight through her clothing.

"The boys stumbled upon this place a few years ago." Oselaw walked forward. "Asked around town and apparently no one's heard of it, leastwise nobody willing to talk, except some crab-haulers down in Creakers. And they won't touch the place; they warn us off, don't even like speaking about it. Superstitious old bastards."

He snapped his fingers. Blue light bloomed across the walls, spiderwebbing outward along thin channels scored into the stone. In seconds, the whole chamber was illuminated.

"It was perfect for us," he said. "We couldn't believe our luck."

Karys blinked in the sudden icy brightness. The chamber was small, dank, and curiously shaped: the polished stone walls undulated like frozen waves. The light gleamed crisp and cold through the rock.

"That's hallowfire," she said slowly.

Oselaw flashed his teeth at her. "Worried your master will be mad?"

She couldn't help it; she flinched. "We shouldn't be here. This isn't the sort of thing you mess around with."

"The Lady is superstitious, who would have thought?"

"I'm being serious. Your people are all dead; surely that's a hint?"

He brushed aside her concern with a careless wave of his hand. "We've been using the place for years. Besides, you said that most of them died on the beach."

"I never said that."

"All right, fine, but you said that they were 'surprised' on the beach. Right? So it seems to me that the threat came from *outside* and our boys ran *inside* to hide. Whatever killed them just followed." He pressed on before she could object. "Trust me, there's nothing left to haunt this place. Let's just finish up here and head back to town, hey?"

Karys bit her tongue.

"Come on," he coaxed. "It'll be fine, you'll see."

She wavered, and then relented.

"Hazard pay," she said. "And Marishka owes me a favour."

The chamber grew brighter as they walked, the hallowfire reacting to their presence. Goldback crabs scuttled away from their feet, and water dripped and echoed all around. By the looks of it, the passage flooded at high tide; driftwood and sand gathered in mounds around the edges of the room, and the smell of decaying kelp was suffocating. Set into the far wall was an ornate stone archway, where the hallowfire converged like lightning drawn to a rod.

"We've only ever used the outer chambers," said Oselaw. "But it makes you wonder what it used to be like, back in the old days."

Karys made a noncommittal sound, and sought out the edges of the Veneer again. A panicked rush of whispering washed over her; unnatural colours swarmed her vision. Nothing clear, nothing but a distorted haze of fear, and the droning growing ever louder.

"It gets drier a little way further in," said Oselaw, oblivious. "And hey, look at this."

He gestured to the stones of the archway. Karys released the Veneer and leaned closer, then recoiled in disgust. Pitted human teeth studded the granite, flecks of pale yellow in the grey. There must have been hundreds of them, scattered in random, incomprehensible patterns—dice cast over a tekki board.

"Marishka said the Bhatuma's name was Lilikess," continued Oselaw. "Said that she ruled Psikamit's waters back in the day. Isn't that interesting? Must have liked teeth."

"Please stop talking." Karys stepped through the archway.

"Ships that sail this coast without her mark still get wrecked, you know."

"Give it a rest, Oselaw."

He sniggered. "I wonder how old Lili would feel about an Ephirite lackey trespassing on her Sanctum. My guess is unhappy. Maybe even mad."

"In her position, I'd be more annoyed about smugglers using my home as a loading bay."

"Heh. Maybe."

The hallowfire branched over the walls ahead, bifurcating and rejoining in streaks of silver-blue. A set of stairs led upwards into the cliffs, each step dressed in a layer of fur-soft saltmoss. Their footfalls echoed.

Am I making a mistake? Karys tucked her hands into her armpits to keep them warm. If Sabaster *did* uncover that she had been nosing around Bhatuma ruins, he would probably call her compact in a heartbeat. And then, in all likelihood, spend the next three hundred years knitting her skin into a quilt of penitence.

Even so, she could not entirely quell her curiosity at the blazing lines of the hallowfire. Remarkable, for a Sanctum this large to have survived the Ephirite's cleansing of the continent. Karys had read about Lilikess—not amongst the most powerful heralds, but far from inconsequential. Foul-tempered, vain, lustful, inclined to fits of jealousy—fairly typical for a Mercian Bhatuma. She had been slaughtered out on the reef by three Ephirite; her faithful and Favoured later called it the Day of Black Waters.

The stairs came to an end at a second archway. Beyond it, a passageway curved away to either side, the walls covered in large silver disks like the scales of a gigantean fish. Hallowfire rippled out across the floor and the ceiling, bright as the midday sun.

"The boys usually leave the goods here," said Oselaw, with obvious disappointment.

"They must have fled further in." Karys' teeth chattered, and she rubbed her arms. "Embrace, why is it so cold?"

"It's always like this. Want me to warm you up?"

"I'd freeze to death first."

"Suit yourself." He gestured to the left. "This way."

The walls continued their smooth, gleaming curve down the passage. By now, the droning had grown so loud that it drowned out the sound of Oselaw's chewing. A byproduct of the hallowfire? The Veneer here felt sodden with old power, heavy and difficult to penetrate. Karys didn't like it. Twenty feet ahead, the lights ended where the passageway opened up to a kind of cavern or hall. She slowed.

"What?"

She pointed to the floor tiles at her feet. "Blood spray."

Fine black flecks splattered the glassy surface. Oselaw crouched to study them more closely. He spat again, meditatively, then nodded and stood back up.

"That's a promising sign," he said. "Good to know the boys *did* come through here. We must be getting warmer."

"Oselaw."

He ignored her, and continued forward into the hall.

"Whatever killed your people, how do we know it's not still here?"

He snorted, and made a curt gesture over his shoulder. "No body, no payment."

The droning grew louder, and Karys rubbed her forehead. *This is a mistake,* her instincts urged. *Leave, get out of here.*

Ahead, Oselaw came to a sudden stop.

"Oh," he said, in a markedly different tone. "Well, that's disturbing."

She followed him out of the passage. Her impression had been wrong: the space beyond was not a cavern, but a kind of hollowed-out tower. Rings of hallowfire ignited in reaction to their presence, lighting up the floors directly above and below them. Beyond the circumference of the lights, the darkness appeared fathomless and infinite. Eight sets of intricately carved stairs folded around the perimeter of the chamber, connecting the higher and lower levels like cells in a beehive.

It looks like a stepwell, Karys thought. *But why build one right beside the ocean?*

Oselaw stood beside the low central balustrade. At first she thought that he was staring into the pit below, but as Karys drew closer she saw that he was actually looking at something on the floor.

"Ah," she said.

A human foot lay in a pool of blood. It still wore a fitted sandal and a silver anklet, but the flesh had been cleanly severed just below the calf. The yellow-white gleam of bone stood out from the dark gore.

"I don't suppose you can use that?" asked Oselaw.

His tone was idle, but Karys noticed that he was sweating in spite of the chill. She shook her head.

"We should leave," she said.

Oselaw leaned over the edge, peering down at the lower levels of the step-well. When he failed to reply, Karys took a step forward.

"Listen to me." Her heart beat fast. "I don't like saying this, but we're too far out of our depth here. This doesn't feel right."

Nothing from him. He kept gazing into the dark, acting like she wasn't even talking. Karys waited, her nerves strung tight, expecting him to move or speak, to do something. The silence dragged. Nothing.

"Oselaw? Coren?"

He seemed focussed; he was squinting a little, straining to penetrate the pit's darkness.

"There's something down there," he said.

His voice made Karys' skin prickle: he sounded absent, distracted. She shivered and backed swiftly toward the passageway. Enough of this. The droning burned her ears—it was like two white-hot needles drilling into her skull.

"I'm going," she declared. "If you want to stick your neck out, that's on you. I've seen enough to report back to Marishka."

"No, there's something . . . someone's down there." He leaned further over the edge. "They've got lights."

Karys was only a few feet from the passage when his words sank into her brain. She felt like ice water had been upturned over her head.

"Maybe it's one of the boys," Oselaw muttered. "They could have hid, laid low for a couple—"

"Oselaw, *get away from there.*"

Startled by the vehemence in her voice, he turned around. At the same time, an amorphous, translucent figure rose from the stepwell behind him. It moved silently through the air, liquid and softly shining and fast as quicksilver, and wrapped itself around Oselaw, enveloping him completely.

What happened next happened quickly, and was almost too horrific for Karys to comprehend. In the blink of an eye, Oselaw's skin peeled back and *inverted*. A snatched glimpse of organs, a single heartbeat, and then his flesh erupted with blood. The creature's body flushed scarlet.

Karys' thoughts ground to a dead stop. The creature hovered in the air, swaying slightly. Glowing gold pinpricks played across its skin, growing dimmer and brighter like waves lapping the shore.

Are those lights? Are those lights? Are those lights?

Karys drew a shallow breath. Her head spun. *What just . . . what just happened?* Oselaw had vanished like conjurer's trick, one second whole and human, the next a bloom of red. Gone. Dead.

She stood within the mouth of the passage, and the creature seemed yet to notice her. About thirty feet separated them, perhaps less. Probably less. Digging her fingernails into her palms, Karys slid one foot backwards. Her head felt like it was going to explode from the droning in her ears, and this . . . this *thing* was the source. Another step. She needed to retreat around the curve of the passage, out of its line of sight. The redness was slowly fading from the creature's body; it was digesting, she realised. It was dissolving Oselaw down to nothing. Another step. Embrace, all the smugglers, *this* was why she had not found bodies; there had been nothing *left* to find. The hallowfire shone down from the ceiling like a floodlight, leaving her devastatingly exposed. Could the creature see? Could it hear her heart pounding out of her chest? Another step. She willed the abomination to remain still, willed it like a prayer or a mantra: *don't move, don't move, don't move.* Her mouth tasted sour. Another step and the walls shielded her from sight.

Karys' limbs went weak. She trembled violently, clenching her jaw to stop her teeth from chattering. *Fuck, Oselaw!* He had been right in front of her, right there, and she had just . . . fuck. She drew a small, silent breath. He had been right there, and she . . .

No, she needed to keep it together. Not much further. Not much further, and she would be back at the stairs. Her mind burned with the vision of Oselaw's body disintegrating, like someone had ripped the stitches from cloth.

The first archway stood ten feet from her now. Karys could not help it—she moved faster, less quietly. They should never have trespassed on the Sanctum; from the start, she had sensed the quiet, watchful malice of this place. But she would claw her way back to daylight, and return home to Psikamit, and never take a job from the Second Mayor again. The stairs were slick and treacherous; she took them two at a time. *What am I going to say to Marishka? Oselaw was . . . I was—*

Like a floodgate bursting open, the droning suddenly amplified to a roar in her ears. But this time, it emerged from the darkness *ahead* of her. Karys stumbled to a halt, catching herself against the wall.

Where the hallowfire ended at the threshold of the tooth-studded archway, yellow lights rippled like stars reflected on the surface of a wave. A second creature.

Karys ran, heedless of the noise. Her boots hit the tiles, each stride loud as a drumbeat in the silence. Into the shining passage again, but this time she took the right fork, nearly losing her footing as she careened sideways over the smooth floor. She did not dare look backwards. Hallowfire blazed to life around her as she sprinted deeper into the Sanctum, and the droning dogged her steps.

The passage ended at a new set of stairs leading to a lower floor. Karys flew down them—too fast, too careless—and tripped. Her knees struck the tiles, and pain shot upwards through her right thigh. A heartbeat later, she was back on her feet. The walls here were different, darker, carved with strange spiralling designs, and the hallowfire had dimmed. At her back, the droning grew louder and louder; she was losing ground and all she could see was Oselaw's expression of surprise before his face collapsed, the twisting of skin and sinew and muscle, the way he turned inside out.

She reached another landing, and ran straight into something hard. The impact knocked the air out of her lungs. She staggered, gasping, and realised there was a person in front of her, an unfamiliar man, and then he grabbed her arm and yanked her sideways through a new archway.

CHAPTER

2

A brief sensation of intense heat swept over Karys' skin, like her whole body had passed too close to a fire. Then it was gone. The man still gripped her arm, and now he pressed a finger to his lips. Unthinking, Karys tried to wrestle free—the creature was right behind her, she needed to *run*—but he held tighter. His eyes burned with a feverish light.

Quiet, he mouthed.

She raised her free hand to punch him, and he caught her wrist. He was strong, stronger than her, but his expression twisted in pain when he moved his left shoulder. With both of her arms restrained, Karys tried to kick him instead.

"Will you stop it?" he hissed. "I'm helping you."

By now the droning threatened to split her head open, and she breathed heavily, far too loud. "Get fucked."

"I already am." The stranger dragged her further into the room. "Be quiet. It's going to hear you."

He would get her killed, torn apart like Oselaw. Karys lifted her head to glare at him, and the man met her gaze—equally desperate, equally afraid, but there was also a stubborn edge to the set of his mouth.

"Quiet," he whispered. "Or we're both dead."

Karys swallowed the impulse to spit in his face, and jerked her head to the side. She nodded once, stiffly. Wasn't like she had a choice now. Even though she had stopped struggling, the man maintained his tense grip on her arms. He transferred his gaze to the archway behind her, and Karys followed his eyes.

The stairs glowed pale blue in the Sanctum's light, an eerie, underwater hue that bled through the walls. The hallowfire dwindled in the distance, fading to nothing, and in that darkness Karys caught sight of the faintest hint of a golden shimmer. Her stomach clenched.

The creature wove from side to side as it descended to the landing. Although it had no clear face or features, the way that it moved suggested confusion. It clearly knew that she had come this way; it was searching for her. At the archway, it paused—a dog with pricked ears. Up close, its body was almost completely transparent; if not for the lights flickering across its skin, it would have been next to invisible. It drew nearer again and stopped, listening. There were barely six feet between them now; Karys could have reached out and touched it. The man's fingers crushed her arms.

The creature's skin shimmered. Then, as if reaching a decision, it flowed backwards out of the archway. Karys stayed frozen, not daring to breathe. The creature withdrew up the stairs again. Gradually, the droning in her ears faded.

For a minute longer, neither Karys nor the man moved.

I'm not dead, she thought, dazed. *It didn't see us.*

With a shiver, the man released her.

"Embrace," he muttered. "For a second there, I thought . . ."

To Karys' alarm, his eyes lost focus and he swayed. She stepped closer just as his legs gave way, letting him fall against her. He trembled, skin blisteringly hot through his clothing. Sour sweat dampened his shirt.

"Sorry." He tried to draw away from her, but his legs buckled again. "Embarrassing."

His voice was a strained whisper. The change in his countenance was jarring; in the low blue light, his skin appeared grey. It was as if fear alone had been holding him upright—in the absence of immediate danger, he could hardly stand. His teeth chattered.

"What's the matter with you?" asked Karys.

The man made a dismissive gesture in the direction of the stairs. For the first time, she noticed the blood on his hands. "Call it a disagreement."

"With one of those things?"

He nodded. Although slight, he was easily a head taller than her, and heavy. Karys awkwardly helped him to the ground. The left sleeve of his shirt was covered in blood; through a tear in the fabric she caught a glimpse of a deep gash cutting across his bicep to his shoulder.

"A violent disagreement," she said under her breath.

"I'll be fine, just give me a moment."

Karys found that difficult to believe; the stranger seemed worryingly close to passing out. A thin sheen of perspiration shone on his forehead, and by the light of the hallowfire filtering through the archway, his expression seemed pained. She glanced at the passage. They needed to leave before the creature returned.

"Don't suppose you're part of a rescue party?" the man asked, eyes half-closed.

She shook her head. "No."

"I didn't think so. A shame, really." The way he pronounced "shame" made Karys frown. He noticed. "What?"

"Going by your accent, you're Vareslian."

"Guilty as charged."

"Then you aren't a smuggler?"

He laughed softly. The sound had a hoarse quality, a dry rattle in his lungs. "No. No, I'm not a smuggler. Are you?"

She shook her head again. Now that she looked at him properly, she noticed that the stranger was well-dressed. Even though his clothing was bloodstained and streaked with grime, it seemed expensive: soft white linen and brass buckles, black cotton and tanned leather. He was probably in his early thirties: he had curling jaw-length hair, light brown skin, jewelled studs in both ears. No, not a smuggler, at least not of the type she was familiar with.

"Back there, that creature—why couldn't it see us?" she asked.

The man grimaced. He reached into the pocket of his trousers, and pulled out a small bronze medallion on a thin chain.

"This," he said. "It's called a Split Lapse. Bhatuma relic, family heirloom. Inside this room, we're suspended three days in the past."

He held it out for her to see, and Karys leaned closer. The surface of the disk crawled with tiny letters, cramped so close together that they resembled a solid mass. Even without opening the Veneer, she could recognise it was Bhatuma-worked—those authorisation descriptions appeared wildly, dizzyingly complex. Tiny rubies studded the rim of the medallion.

"We can watch real time passing outside the bubble, but it can't touch us." The man closed his fist around the device, and lowered his arm. "Not unless someone noticed the Lapse and tried to break inside, in which case the stasis dimension would probably shatter. Spit us out in the present."

Karys sat back on her heels. A relic to manipulate time, something that rare and powerful? She chewed her lip. It must be worth a fortune. "Then why should the creature hear us? If we're outside of its time?"

The man groaned and scrunched up his face. "I was *not* expecting a test on this. Something about proximity? 'Proximal overlay,' I think. Look, the thing has some flaws."

Karys gazed around the room, her mind still turning. The chamber was dim, and the blue light from the passage spilled their shadows long across the floor. Identical grey stone pallets ran in three rows along the length of the room. Sarcophagi, she realised. They probably housed the bodies of Lilikess' Favoured.

"Your relic, your Split Lapse," she said, turning back to the man, "is the dimension it generates fixed to one location?"

A faint smile, like he could guess what she was thinking. "I've got it fixed to this corner of the room for now, but it can be unbound and reinstated anywhere. If I turn it off."

Her stomach fluttered. "Then could we move toward the exit in stages? Stop and re-establish the Lapse if we came too close to those creatures?"

"In theory, yes. In practice . . . well." He gestured to the darkness around them. "This is about as far as I can go."

"What? Why?"

"Because I'm dying."

His tone was matter-of-fact and his expression perfectly serious, but Karys had the feeling he might be making fun of her—exaggerating, or telling a strange sort of joke at her expense. Yes, he looked sick, but . . . Her mistrust mounted as she scrutinized his face.

"You talk a lot for a dying man," she said.

He snorted. "One of my many flaws."

"What's killing you, then?"

"Like I said, I had a disagreement with one of those creatures. They're called Constructs, by the way." He gestured to his bloodied arm. "I wasn't fast enough, and it hit me. You've seen what they do to people?"

Karys nodded.

"The wound is . . ." A spasm in his jaw, a feeling swiftly repressed. "That's what's happening to me, but a little slower. The Lapse keeps me in a kind of stasis, but as soon as I return to the present, that protection falls away."

"You left the Lapse to grab me."

"Which hurt a lot. You're welcome." Using the wall behind him for support, the man sat up straighter. The effort obviously taxed him. "And that brings me to my proposition."

"Proposition?"

"Yes." He held out the Lapse, offering it to her. "Take it."

Karys did not move.

"You do want to live, right?" He let the medallion dangle by its chain, swaying it from side to side like he was luring in a cat. "See the sun again?"

She could recognise a trap when she saw one. "Why give it to me? You just said you'd die if it's turned off."

"Well, yes. I've had a lot of time to think about that, considering I've been down here two days. There's no reason to drag this out any longer."

Two days? The hair lifted off the back of Karys' neck. Two days, alone in the dark? And yet the stranger still appeared composed—in fact, he sounded almost cheerful. In her estimation, that made him either an exceptional liar or a fool, and she was not sure which was worse.

"And in exchange . . . ?" she said.

"In exchange"—the medallion stopped swinging—"I need you to deliver a message to the Vareslian embassy in Psikamit. Tell them that the ambassador to Toraigus has been assassinated along with her full entourage. If they want proof, they'll find the wreckage of the ambassador's ship in the sea caves outside this Sanctum. Tell them about the Constructs."

Karys studied the man, not offering an answer. Liar or a fool. Or both, maybe.

"Will you do it?" he pressed. "Please?"

The Split Lapse glinted in the low light. With it, she would stand a chance of escape; she could flee back to Psikamit, bribe the embassy, probably pawn off the device to the College. It would be serious money, far more than she could earn in a year. Shit, maybe more than she could earn in ten.

She took the medallion from the man's hand. He breathed out, a soft sigh of relief, and offered her another smile—this one more genuine. Karys did not return it.

"What's your name?" she asked.

"Ferain Taliade. And yours?"

She turned over the Lapse in her palm. "How much do you think your life is worth, Ferain?"

"Is that a philosophical question, or—"

"No. If you were ransomed, how much money?"

He appeared taken aback. "Er . . . hard to say? I guess it would depend on my father—"

"Five thousand cret?" she said, shooting sky-high to gauge his reaction. As she had anticipated, he scoffed at the number.

"I'd like to think he doesn't hate me *that* much," he said.

Karys had been about to suggest one thousand cret before his words fully penetrated her brain, and had to stop her mouth from falling open. *That's too low?!*

"Sorry." She recovered. "Fifteen thousand?"

"I've got to say, your interest in this hypothetical hostage situation—"

Screw it, she thought, and closed her fingers around the Lapse.

"I'll save your life for fifteen thousand cret," she declared.

A moment of silence.

Ferain blinked. "Uh . . ."

"Or I'll try. But you're going to die anyway, right? So you might as well take a chance on me." She held her hand out. "Your life for fifteen thousand cret."

It was his turn for silence. Karys waited with bated breath, trying not to betray her anxiety. But fifteen thousand cret? That was pure lunacy; with that money, she could probably buy all of Creakers and still have change to spare. *Who* is *this man?*

"You didn't tell me your name," he said at last.

"Karys Eska."

"Karys." He repeated it slowly, like he was committing it to memory. In his accent, the consonants sounded smoother. He nodded to himself. "Tell me how you would do it."

"Open the Veneer, re-establish the stasis dimension on the other side, then bind the Lapse to my body." She felt like a spring under too much pressure. "If I'm right, that would tether the time-locked space to me. With you inside it."

"Oh, you really aren't a smuggler." Ferain turned over the idea. "So you're a workings practitioner?"

"No, not really. But I can perform the basics if I have to."

"How would you access the Veneer?"

"I'm a deathspeaker."

A ripple of unreadable emotion passed across his face.

"Oh," he said. "I see."

Karys suppressed her irritation at the way his tone softened. "It might backfire hideously. But if it *does* work, I'll be able to get you to help."

"It sounds like you would be the one in danger, not me."

"For fifteen thousand cret, I'm prepared to take that chance."

He continued to stare at her, his expression inscrutable. Karys did not waver, holding her hand out.

"You're sure about this?" he asked.

"Certain."

Ferain glanced down. He hesitated a moment longer, then reached out and shook on it. His skin was fever-hot and his shivering worse, but his grip remained firm.

"All right," he said. "Deal."

The horror of the last hour receded, overtaken by a wild surge of hope: a violent, clamouring rush of feeling. Karys was struck by the insane urge to laugh. *It will be enough. More than enough.* Ferain watched her face, his expression curious, and she withdrew her hand.

"All right, then." Her voice emerged husky. She cleared her throat and brushed her hair back from her forehead, tucking the loose strands behind her ears. "In that case, let me see what I can do."

The Veneer inside the chamber hung heavy and dark, a forest of crushed-velvet drapes. Karys tried to shut out her feelings and draw apart the weave. *Focus, keep it together.* Her senses skimmed the rippling surface. Although the fabric moved reluctantly, it was quieter than the beach or upper passages; the air held none of the roiling terror she had experienced earlier. The Veneer flexed and then relaxed, and she drew it open. Unreal colours bloomed in her senses; the decayed power of the Sanctum settled on the back of her tongue, sweet and dry as pressed flowers.

"Okay," she murmured.

The fabric folded upon itself, drawing back and leaving an eerie empty hole behind, a deeper nothingness suspended in the air. She felt out its edges and moulded the absence, smoothing a space that would fit the Lapse: eight feet long, four wide, three tall. *A generously sized coffin.* She had never tried to leave something on the other side of the Veneer before, but it *should* work. Finding the object again might be a bit trickier—but if she tethered the space, then surely it would be feasible? Like dropping a stone into her pocket instead of the ocean. She guided the emptiness down to the tiled floor, settling it over Ferain.

"Okay," she murmured again, taking a steadying breath. So far, so good. "You'll need to stay still."

Ferain was positioned right in the middle of the void, and clearly couldn't feel a difference. He looked around, slightly sceptical, a little uneasy. "Sure. Got it. Anything else?"

"The sea caves you mentioned earlier—that's how you entered the Sanctum?"

He hesitated. "Are you thinking of trying to leave that way?"

"Well, my last exit was blocked by those things." Karys shook her head. "'Constructs.' I have to try something else."

"I guess, but . . . be careful." Ferain lowered his gaze. "We got caught between the sea and the Constructs while the tide was high. It was carnage."

She could feel those deaths, muted and dull through the walls of the Sanctum. A grim guiding star to lead her out of the place. "Are you ready?"

Ferain raised his eyes again, and Karys saw that he was afraid.

A liar, then, she thought. *You* do *want to live.*

"Ready," he said.

Karys bit the inside of her cheek and spat into her open palm. The most basic of Bhatuma-derived bindings, the simplest of workings. She pressed the warm metal of the Lapse into the blood and spittle, and clenched her fist shut.

"Hold fast," she whispered.

The medallion scorched her skin and she had to stop herself from crying out. Beneath her fingers, the metal softened and turned to liquid bronze, then vanished as it soaked into her palm. With a click like a key turned in a lock, the Veneer snapped closed. Ferain vanished; only the dim outline of her shadow remained on the floor where he had lain.

When Karys opened her fist again, all that remained of the Lapse was a stinging circular burn. The mark sheened gold when the light touched it. She flexed her fingers, then curled them inward again. For better or worse, the relic was physically tethered to her, and Ferain with it.

Now all she needed to do was escape the Sanctum.

CHAPTER
3

Karys moved cautiously. The Sanctum echoed with dripping water and the soft, regular rushing of the waves as they struck the cliffs outside.

She now knew that she possessed at least one small advantage over the Constructs—she would hear them before they heard her. Still, that offered little comfort as she crept deeper through the warren of passages. With each floor that she descended, the hallowfire grew dimmer, and the architecture became less regular, less defined. It felt as though the Sanctum possessed a more organic quality this far down, its corridors spreading like roots or feelers. Passages met abrupt dead ends, ripples and furrows marred the surface of the floor.

Although she could not pinpoint exactly why, the inconsistencies disturbed her. A series of grey bulges protruded from the wall, each slightly larger than its predecessor, like a form of arcane punctuation. The ceiling sloped at a subtle, drooping angle; the walls swelled at their bases. Individually, the defects appeared random, but Karys sensed that some obscure pattern or symmetry underlay their design.

And why a stepwell? The Bhatuma had built Sanctums according to their personal whims and preferences, unbeholden to the laws of nature, but it still struck her as an unfathomable choice. Why a well beside the ocean, where it would endlessly flood with seawater? It seemed pointless, uncanny.

The passages drew eastward, following the curve of the cliffs, and death cloyed the air. Karys was getting close to the caves, she knew it—the taste of brine burned in the back of her throat, and the wind keened through the stone corridors. Night would have fallen by now, and brought the late summer storm in with it.

She came to yet another set of stairs, these of deceptive, uneven height, and descended. *Nothing about this place makes sense.* As far as she could tell, the floors here should be underwater—based on the distance she had travelled, she should be miles underground. And yet she could not shake the inexplicable feeling that with every downwards step, she was in fact *rising*.

A faint buzz drifted out of the darkness ahead. Karys faltered. The droning was soft and steady—distant, for the moment at least. She held still, listening, but the noise remained constant: a low, ominous vibration.

She ground her teeth together. Although she could turn back and search for a different way out of this wretched place, she balked at the idea. Embrace, the thought of retracing her steps through all those shadowed passages, with their not-rightness suffusing every stone and tile and stairway . . . Karys exhaled. No. Slow and careful. She had to be close now.

The lingering weight of death gathered more thickly in the next corridor, and her bones ached from the cold. With the Veneer pulled partway open, the air swirled with veils of coloured light, sharp flickers of sound.

. . . *she's dead, oh help me, all of them—*

Embrace watch over me, guide me and protect me, lead me home.

. . . *have to be quiet, I don't know where it's gone.*

The voices blurred together, broken by hoarse screams, low gasps. Karys wanted to shut the noise out, but she hated the thought that doing so might dampen her awareness of the Constructs. Instead, she heard the final moments of desperate strangers, over and over again.

. . . *she's dead, oh help me, all of them—*

Did you see? Did you see what it did?

. . . *please, please, please, let me get out, please . . .*

Their fear and confusion bled through the air, and Karys found herself breathing quicker. They weren't her feelings, but their influence was real enough. She had never been surrounded by so much concentrated death before; she could not even tell how many people had been killed down here. Thirty, forty? Their voices ran over one another.

The sounds of the storm increased as she reached the end of the corridor. Wind whistled over rock, rain hissed. The hallowfire scarcely illuminated more than a few feet in any direction, but through the gloom she could make out a crumbling set of stairs, glistening with water.

Karys hurried forward. With each step, the Sanctum's chill retreated from her body. The storm was cold, but the wind didn't bite like the air of the passages, didn't slide knifelike into her flesh. When she breathed in the stinging salt spray, it tasted real and familiar.

The floor tiles ended at the base of the stairs, giving way to raw stone. To her right, the ground sloped down to a basin of churning black water; and she kept to the left wall, following the narrow bank of rock that hemmed in the pool. The roof of the cave was high and shrouded in shadow, but over the storm noise she could hear the squeaking of distressed seabats. Flotsam knocked against the rocks.

Although Karys had anticipated the problem, there was now no escaping it: she would have to swim out to the beach. The tide was too high, but she couldn't afford to wait for the water to retreat. No helping it. She let the Veneer close, then shrugged off her coat and stowed it against the wall. Her boots followed. She had only purchased the leather lace-ups six months ago, and that had been in a moment of rare, uncharacteristic decadence. Dark and supple, they moulded around her feet as if made for her, and the seller swore that they would last a lifetime. She reluctantly set them down. Should not have paid so much.

Behind her, the droning's volume surged. The Construct was on the move. Karys hastened down the bank and into the shallows. The seawater was warmer than the air, and the waves disguised the sound of her splashing. She ducked down and quietly waded deeper.

When she looked back, the Construct was at the base of the stairs. It swayed forward, body rippling with yellow light, and paused over her coat. It leaned down, curious—an animal sniffing at the back of a butcher's shop. Then it moved toward the pool.

Can it swim? Karys sank lower. Based on her earlier flight, she suspected that the creature's vision was limited. That seemed to hold true now, but the Construct also appeared capable of sensing that she was nearby. She held her breath as it neared the water's edge. For a moment, she was sure it would give up; it seemed apprehensive or unhappy. But instead it rose a little higher in the air and floated forward over the heaving water.

Shit!

Heart thumping, Karys inhaled and slipped below the surface. The howling wind fell quiet, and the world stretched dark and hazy. She swam forward. Around her, the sea roiled like a living creature. Although she could see almost nothing through the gloom, she kept her eyes wide open; irrationally afraid that the Construct might somehow rear up from the depths below. Debris littered the water.

She stayed under as long as she could, kicking hard against the current, and then slowly surfaced again. *Come on, come on, come on.* Karys turned and stared into the darkness, straining her eyes.

There. She caught sight of the Construct's glimmer. It looked like the creature had not strayed past the shallows.

It isn't following me. The realisation left her lightheaded with relief. *It doesn't know where I am.*

She ducked below the water and swam on.

When she came up for air a second time, rain whipped her face. The massive arc of the cave mouth loomed over her, scarcely distinguishable from the star-less storm sky—coal-black painted over deepest grey. She pulled the last few strokes to reach open water, and the cave fell away to the sea and the waves and the night. She was out.

If she had held to the old faith, Karys would have offered thanks to her herald in that moment. Instead, she just kept moving.

The shadowy bulk of the wrecked Vareslian ship hunkered in the jaws of the cave entrance. Between the surging waves and the darkness, she couldn't see much of the vessel, but she could tell its shape was wrong. Stunted and tilting, the gunwale curved inward like something had taken a bite out of its side. Waves crashed down on the deck.

Karys dove under the water again, fighting the current that sought to drive her right back into the Sanctum. It had been years since she had last swam in the ocean, but her body remembered. The surge swept over her. If she could make it past the surf, it should grow calmer; she would have the chance to catch her breath and gather her bearings. The water pummelled her, and for a few awful seconds she could not find the surface.

Then she was through and past the crest of the wave. The dark rolling plains of deeper water spread out in front of her, and she swam hard to escape the breakers. The rain hissed as it struck the sea. When the swell eased, she could see the glow of Psikamit's lighthouse. The green etherbulb winked as it rotated in place.

She allowed the tide to carry her a little way west down the shore, and then kicked toward the beach. She would have to walk barefoot for hours to reach the city—so be it. She had suffered worse, and she was alive. Her feet brushed the sand. That was enough, for now. That was more than Oselaw could say. She half-stepped, half-floated another few feet and then she could walk. The sea sucked hungrily at her limbs as she waded up the beach.

The water was at her waist before she noticed the Constructs. Two of them, then three, four: yellow lights hazy through the rain. They moved like sharks, drifting in slow, predatory arcs over the sand.

They were combing the beach. Karys curled her fingers into fists, digging her nails into her palms. Patiently waiting for her. She could see the path back up the cliffs, the same track she had descended only hours earlier. She could feel the swift, bloody shock of the smugglers' deaths. The creatures glinted like stars in the dark. There was no way she could evade them here; there were too many. It would be suicide.

A wave struck her lower back, and a part of her wanted to topple over, let the water swallow her up. Her limbs felt leaden.

There was, of course, another way back to Psikamit. One she had not allowed herself to consider until now. A very, very stupid idea.

Karys clenched her jaw, and pulled her clinging shirt over the top of her head. Her trousers followed; she let the current sweep them away. In only her underwear, she returned to the sea.

The distant green etherbulb pulled her like a lifeline. At first, she made good progress; she swam parallel to the shore, and let her movements fall into a rhythm, ignored the fear gnawing at her insides. Fatigue set in quickly, however, and her strokes began to lag. The beach ended at the westmost point of the bay; past that it was sheer cliff face all the way to Psikamit. She would have to swim the full distance or drown.

Rain slapped her face as she lifted her head. Had to be six miles or more. She was a strong swimmer, but this would have been a challenge even if the waters were calm. Now, tossed around like a sackcloth doll, it seemed beyond foolhardy. The wind howled ever louder.

One bad decision after another. She spat seawater.

Out of nowhere, a vertiginous sensation swept through her. Karys' body froze up in shock, and she slipped under the waves. A cold fist closed around her heart.

"Let me out!"

The voice rang with perfect and unnatural clarity through the water. Karys floundered, then fought back to the surface and emerged gasping.

"Where am I?" The voice was panicked, choking. "What's going on?"

The awful grasping cold spread through her chest, rippling over her shoulders and arms, and the accompanying dizziness threatened to drag her under a second time.

"Please, not the dark, not the dark anymore. It hurts so much. Please, I'll do anything; I'm drowning—"

"Ferain!" said Karys.

He fell silent. She struggled to keep her head up, and her voice came out rough.

"You're not drowning," she said. "You're safe; I'm trying to get you to help so just . . . just back off!"

After a second, the cold retreated from her chest. She shuddered, treading water. *What the fuck is happening?* She should not be able to hear him, he should not be here. Her heartbeat echoed in her ears.

"Where am I?" he whispered, a sound like the rain in the wind.

"Just let me get you to the city." The swell lifted her, then receded again. "You're going to be fine."

"It's so cold." His voice faded. "I . . . I don't know . . . tell Ilesha . . ."

Even though the dizziness was gone, Karys still felt shaken. "Hold on, all right?"

Ferain did not answer. She sensed that he had somehow drawn away or diminished; it felt as though she were alone once more. The wind swept across the water, desolate and heavy. The hissing rain stung her face.

"Hold on," she repeated under her breath.

Psikamit's misted lights clustered low above the black waves, dropping out of sight and emerging again with the movement of the water. Karys swam, and the lighthouse grew larger in her vision; the green light drawing into clearer focus through the falling rain. *Only a little further.* Her legs had turned to dead weights, but she repeated the words inside her head like a promise or a prayer. *A little further.*

She could not stop thinking about how, years ago, her brother had dropped a rat into the village's Penitence Pool. He had tangled it in old netting and weighed it down with rocks before throwing it in the water. Together, they had watched in silence as the panicked animal swam in circles. Scrabbling, squeaking in fear, hunting for any purchase on the algae-slick walls. Even burdened, it had taken a long time for it to tire—or at least it had felt that way to Karys. She had wanted to tell Oboro to let the creature out, but he had worn a razor-edged look on his face that day, and she had been unable to speak. So instead she had stood by wordlessly, watching the animal drown.

Karys gritted her teeth. *But I'm not a rat.*

Thunder rumbled in the south.

Psikamit's harbour squatted inside the bowl-curve of Sweetbay, sheltered first by the Bhatuma-gifted honey reef, and then by a complex series of break-waters and seawalls. A maze of docks and jetties curved from the mudflats of Creakers to the warehouses of Scuttlers, and during the day the place crawled with people: sailors, merchants, dockhands, port authority, all loud and cuss-ing and ruthlessly organised.

But when Karys finally dragged her battered body up the stairs of a pier, trembling with exhaustion, the harbour was near deserted. She hugged her arms around her chest and trudged forward. Inside the guard house, the lone night watchman stared at her in shock, mouth hanging open. She offered him a very tired salute, heading for the crude alley dividing two warehouses. He did not stop her.

The alley smelled of cat sick and urine, and the flagstones were greasy under her feet. Her body would still not stop shaking; now that she was out of the warm seawater, the wind chilled her through. An abandoned pile of brown sacking cloth lay on the ground beside the warehouse's refuse bins. She picked up one of the wet, stinking sheets—sending a cockroach scuttling out of the fold—and wrapped the cloth around her shoulders.

The opposite end of the alley opened onto Scrapper's Road. Rain gushed down the gutters and traffic was thin; a few covered awrigs trundled between the bars and dens of the district. Across the road, a single Hound huddled below the eaves of an old fishery. When Karys whistled, it stirred and shook out its coat.

"Kitha Street, Old Market," she said through chattering teeth, as she climbed onto the bowl of the creature's back. It bounced once in acknowledgement, and set off at a quick trot.

Karys drew her improvised cloak closer around her shoulders. The Hound's fur bristled beneath her bare legs, but for all the discomfort—the smell, the drenching rain, and the cold—she could not bring herself to care. She hunched lower in her seat. If anything, the weather served as something of a blessing; she didn't want anyone to see her like this.

Somewhere between the harbour and Old Market, she must have dozed off, because the next thing she knew the Hound was bouncing to get her attention again. She petted it unsteadily, and mumbled thanks as she stumbled off its back.

Her joints ached as she dragged her legs up the stairs to her door, fumbled open the combination lock, and let herself in. Twelve more steps and she had collapsed onto her bed.

Made it, she thought.

Exhaustion carried her under.

CHAPTER

4

Karys came groggily awake to the sound of loud knocking. She grimaced and cracked open her salt-crusted eyelids. Sunlight streamed into the room through the window above the kitchen stove.

"Fuck," she groaned.

Her flat smelled horrendous, which probably meant that *she* smelled horrendous. The sackcloth from last night lay in a crumpled brown heap on the floorboards. She could not remember discarding it, but at least she had not dragged the flea-ridden thing to bed with her.

Another loud knock.

She sat up, causing every muscle in her body to protest. From head to toe, her skin was covered in a sticky film of sweat and seawater. Her hair clumped together like a crow's nest—stiff as straw and hellishly itchy. She gazed around the room bleakly. The idea of getting up, of moving at all, let alone facing other people . . .

"Lady Deathspeaker!"

Mumbling obscenities, she stumbled out of bed.

"What do you want?" she yelled at the door.

"Marishka would like to see you," came the cheerful, muffled response.

She can damn well wait. "I'll pay her a visit this afternoon."

"Lady Deathspeaker, it is already afternoon."

Karys gave the door a foul look.

"Fine. Half an hour," she said.

The young messenger sniggered. "It would be her pleasure."

Twenty minutes later, damp-haired and scrubbed clean, Karys locked her door and dropped the offending sackcloth into the building's communal refuse bin. Carillo was busy sweeping the stairs outside, and he grunted in greeting as she passed. Karys nodded to him. He wasn't bad, as Old Market landlords went. His rates were fair, he kept on top of maintenance, and he minded his own business. He was also, as far as she could tell, utterly unfazed by her profession.

"Rough night," he remarked.

You're telling me. "I'll drop the rent by your office tomorrow, if that's all right."

Carillo grunted again, which she took as assent.

It was a cool, bright day; the clouds smooth and blindingly white overhead. Gulls squabbled over food scraps from the day market up the road, and the smell of frying eel made Karys' mouth water. The Second Mayor lived in Tomasia, only one district over from Old Market. She set off on foot, hoping to work some of the stiffness out of her legs. Awrigs and Hounds crowded the streets, and hawkers yelled out their prices. After the storm, everything appeared crisper, like the air itself had been washed clean. To the south, the sea gleamed dark blue over the red roof tiles of Scuttlers and Soresa Flats. Fishing boats dotted the harbour.

A lovely day. Karys tramped up the road. A pity she couldn't spend it in bed.

Her destination lay two streets off the main thoroughfare; a leafy cul-desac that looked up to the scale wall in the north. Marishka's house was the largest on the block, although not especially lavish. The building was double-storied and whitewashed, weathered with age and overgrown with flowering ivy. Honeysuckle draped over the eaves, humming with lazy bees, and rows of sunflowers formed tidy borders between fruiting persimmon trees. The Second Mayor liked her gardening. Karys unlatched the gate, letting herself in. A single white rabbit hopped across the well-tended path that led to the front door.

She rang the bell. A moment later, a large and extremely pale man appeared in the entrance.

"Ah, Deathspeaker Eska," he said, with a pronounced Toraigian accent and a polite smile. "So good of you to finally show up."

"Save it, Busin. I'm having a shit day."

"She's just finishing up with her earlier appointment." He welcomed her in with a slightly mocking bow. "Who I would wager is having a worse day than you."

As if to punctuate his argument, someone deeper inside the house howled in pain.

"Tea?" Busin offered. "She'll eat with you, but perhaps, while we wait . . . ?"

"No thanks. Who is the earlier appointment?"

"A mistake," he said dryly. "Tolaz, Tolatz? Something like that. He was shaving money out of the care fund, messing around with some of the kids."

Another shriek.

"Suspect he won't be doing that again." Busin led her into the kitchen. Oil sizzled in an old frying pan, and the air was rich with the smell of spices and tomato. "Sit, I'm sure they're almost done."

Karys winced as she lowered herself onto one of the kitchen chairs. The room was light and spacious, decorated in pale blue and white with paisley curtains and yellow ceramic crockery. Busin bustled about, finishing up the cooking, setting out plates and glasses. A second rabbit—white fur, pink eyes—sat in the corner. It blinked slowly.

"It's been a while," said Busin. "How have you been? How's money?"

She sighed. "Mostly the same."

"No big jobs?"

"Nothing that's paid out."

"Ah." He glanced at her sidelong. "If you asked, I'm sure Marishka—"

A muffled scream penetrated the walls.

"I'm not that desperate yet," said Karys.

No coincidence that the Second Mayor was holding Tolaz's appointment when Karys would hear it. Unsubtle, as warnings went. Karys leaned forward and poured herself a large glass of water. *This is what happens to people who cross me.* As if the reminder was necessary. She did not react as the man's sobbing apologies sounded in the passage outside. The front door opened and closed.

A minute later, Marishka appeared in the doorway to the kitchen.

"Hello, Karys," she said briskly. "Sorry for the delay."

Seventy, white-haired, and stout, Marishka stood amongst the most dangerous people in the city. She had deep-set black eyes and weathered walnut-brown skin, crinkled up under her brows and around her mouth.

"I trust you're hungry?" She crossed the room and sat down opposite Karys. The rabbit hopped over to her feet; she scooped up the animal and set it on her lap. "Busin, how's the food doing?"

"One minute."

"Excellent. What a storm last night, eh? First real screamer of the year." She settled into her chair. "A terrible night to get caught out in the rain."

Karys shrugged, noncommittal. Busin brought over a bowl of eggs poached in tomatoes, peppers, and white beans, and a separate plate of fried flatbread.

"The tomatoes are from my own crop; we had a real glut." Marishka leaned over to select a piece of bread. "You should take some with you. I can't eat them all and we're running out of jars."

"Thank you."

"Don't mention it. Eat up."

Karys' last meal had been yesterday morning, and she filled her plate without reservation. The cumin-spiced sauce let off small curls of steam, and the bread glistened with oil and salt from the pan. When she cut into an egg, the yolk ran bright and yellow.

Marishka watched her eat, smiling slightly. She stroked her rabbit's pale ears.

"I heard an interesting story this morning," she said.

Karys swallowed a mouthful of dipped bread. "Oh?"

"Apparently Scuttlers was visited by a Lure during the night. A naked woman rose out of the sea, tempting the good people of Psikamit to a dance below the waves."

Karys finished the last bite of her bread, and reached for another piece.

"I wasn't naked," she said.

At the stove, Busin snorted. Marishka tilted her head to the side like a quizzical bird.

"It's hard to swim in a coat," said Karys, straight-faced.

"What were you doing in the sea in the first place? I was under the impression that you and Coren planned to search the coast on foot."

Karys looked meaningfully at Busin's back. Marishka raised an eyebrow.

"One of those conversations, huh?" she said.

"I was just leaving." Busin transferred the pan to the sink. "Enjoy the food."

Marishka waited until he was gone, tapping her foot lightly against the leg of her chair. The undersides of her short nails were dark; from across the table, Karys could not tell if it was soil or blood.

"So," she said, "what happened to him?"

It felt, somehow, that everything had occurred a long time ago. Karys outlined the journey to the beach, her observations, the decision to search the Sanctum. She described Oselaw's death with terse precision, although within the sunlit kitchen the memory seemed hideous, newly profane. Marishka listened without speaking, mechanically stroking the rabbit's back.

"You believe those creatures also killed the others?" she asked when Karys finished.

"I'm certain."

"And you recovered none of their bodies?"

Karys pressed her lips together, then shook her head. "What were you thinking, using the Sanctum like that?"

Marishka leaned back in her chair.

"Convenient," she said. "The place was empty."

"Except it clearly *wasn't*."

The Second Mayor regarded Karys from under heavily lidded eyes. "So it would seem. But I was around in the years before the Ephirite's purge reached Psikamit. I know what Lilikess was like, and this doesn't sound like her work. Entirely too clean."

"Meaning?"

"Just not her style, I don't think. In Creakers, they talk about how she used her adherents as a type of living hourglass." An ironic half-smile. "The lower floors of that stepwell? They used to flood with the tides. Bind a worshipper to each floor, and you can count the hours by their deaths. That's how the stories go, anyway; I believe the practice was mostly reserved for specific festivals. Or when she needed to let off steam."

"Inventive."

"Theatrical. What you've described is not . . . ritualistic enough, I suppose. Besides, you'll have to forgive me for doubting that a Bhatuma ghost ate my people." Marishka's eyes narrowed. "So, what are you hiding?"

Karys took a measured sip of water.

"You don't believe me?" she asked.

"I believe that more happened than you're telling me."

"Well, if we're talking about *secrets,*" Karys leaned on the word, "then why don't you share what you're smuggling?"

Marishka's mouth widened into a smile, although her eyes never changed.

"All right," she said. "Ever heard of necrat?"

"No."

"It's something like a delicacy. Comes from Toraigus, and Vareslian high society is already mad for it. Word reached our own shores, created a demand."

"But what is it?"

"Oh, little yellow beads, a bit like caviar—Busin says it's been made to look just like the sacraments he had to swallow as a boy; that's how they're manufacturing the stuff without drawing the authorities' attention. My understanding is that the substance is derived from Bhatuma remains."

Karys sucked in breath. "What, pieces of their corpses?"

Marishka made an offhand gesture. "Sort of. It's hallucinogenic, apparently. *Very* pricey."

"Embrace, if the Ephirite ever find out—"

"I assure you, that's part of the thrill. That, and the inherent profanity of it all. Now, last night, what else did you *see?*"

Karys was struck by the absurd image of Vareslian nobility crowding around a rotting Bhatuma corpse, salivating, knife and fork in hand. She had long since severed ties with her childhood faith, but even so, she found the picture unsettling. She would have thought that, of all people, the Vareslians would be more reverential toward their dead emissaries.

"There was a Vareslian ship," she said, pushing the macabre vision out of her mind. "It was wrecked just off the shore, outside the sea caves. I think they were in the Sanctum too, before they died. I could hear the echoes of their voices."

Marishka chewed on the new information. "Interesting. Any idea what they might have been doing there?"

"I'm pretty sure one of them was an ambassador."

"Oh, someone important." Her hand stilled on the rabbit's fur. "I wonder if they brought the horrors with them. Or if someone sent the horrors *after* them."

Karys rolled her shoulders, loosening tension in her neck. "None of my concern."

"Aren't you curious?"

"I'm curious when I'll be paid."

"Ever the pragmatist, my dear." The Second Mayor smiled more warmly this time. "The money will be in your account by tomorrow morning."

"With hazard pay."

"I'll throw in a tip."

Karys glanced at the clock, sensing that the conversation was drawing to a close.

"There's one more thing," she said. "I need a discreet mender for a personal problem; someone not affiliated with the College or New Favour. Can you get me an appointment? Take it out of my tip."

Marishka's gaze bored into her, but Karys kept her face still and impassive. After a pause, the Second Mayor nodded.

"Sure, but it'll cost more than your tip. Twenty percent."

Karys smothered a scowl. "Fifteen."

The rabbit's ears quivered.

"Twenty," replied Marishka, implacable. "And that's a favour."

Karys gritted her teeth.

"Fine," she said.

"In that case, let me see what I can do." Marishka set the rabbit on the floor. She stood up with a groan, rubbing her back. "You should have an address by this evening. Excuse me for a moment."

Karys glowered at her empty plate while Marishka went off to fetch her tomatoes. Bad enough that the Second Mayor had knowingly involved her in Bhatuma business, bad enough that the job had almost killed her, but to take twenty percent? A *fifth* of her earnings.

The rabbit stared at her balefully, its little pink nose twitching.

"What are you looking at?" muttered Karys. "I'm not doing anything."

The animal scratched its ears with soft white paws, then hopped off toward the back door. Karys got up stiffly, her muscles aching. Well, if Ferain was good to his word, it would not matter anyway. Then she could be the one leaving Marishka a *tip*.

"Here we are," said the Second Mayor, returning with a wicker basket. "As promised."

"Thanks," said Karys, sullen. She reached out to accept the gift, but Marishka did not immediately let go of the handle.

"A small word of advice?" The Second Mayor's tone was genial. "When my people are keeping secrets? I tend to find out why."

Karys smiled thinly.

"Good thing I'm not one of 'your people,' then," she said. "Pass my thanks to Busin for the meal."

The streets of the district were no less busy than when she had arrived, although the sun had shifted across the sky, stretching toward Downside— the College and the schools, the public library and the banks, all the oldest parts of Psikamit. Karys whistled for a Hound, catching the attention of a grey-haired, bandy-legged creature. Walking had done nothing to loosen her muscles, and she was tired now, weariness from the previous day dragging her down.

Marishka had scarcely seemed to care that Coren Oselaw was dead. Not that Karys had expected an outpouring of feeling, but Oselaw had worked for the Second Mayor since he was a teenager. That should have meant . . . something. She set the basket of tomatoes on the Hound's seat, preparing to hoist herself up. On the other hand, Marishka wasn't exactly the emotionally expressive sort, so perhaps she would grieve him in private. It just made Karys wonder, if it had been *her* slaughtered by those creatures—

Without warning, a hot stab of agony knifed through her brain.

She jerked. White lights shot across her vision, her skin burned, and for a moment her awareness of the real world blinked out—she caught a glimpse of a crimson hallway: the walls billowing like they were made from silk, the floor shining like wet glass. The smell of burned sugar. Then the vision vanished with an elastic snap.

Karys squeezed her eyes shut and shuddered for breath. Not now. The pain was already receding to a prickly ache behind her eyes, and the noise of the street had returned. Her heart pounded like a drum. Not now, not now, not now. Why did he want to talk to her? Was it because of the Sanctum? But how would he know that; it wasn't as if—

"Hey, are you all right, sweetheart?"

Karys opened her eyes just as a tall, bearded man laid a hand on her shoulder. She flinched backwards.

"Get away from me," she said.

"No need to be rude, I was only—"

"I'm not your sweetheart." She turned away from him and climbed onto the Hound. Her skin was prickling; she felt too hot. The red tomatoes swam in her vision. "If I had needed help, I would have asked."

"What is your problem?"

Karys leaned forward and murmured her address to the Hound. The man shook his head, baffled and disgusted.

"Bitch!" he called after her, as the Hound trotted away toward Old Market.

Karys barely heard him.

5

The Old Market Bazaar was the largest of its kind in the lower city; a loose sprawl of walled boutiques and street stalls that covered four blocks of the district. Traders came and went, and goods rose and fell in favour as ships brought in fresh wares. Spices, wine, and perfume from Varesli, woven goods and ceramics from Toraigus, oil from Dulashe up north, worked tinctures out of the Fale heartlands. There was always something new for sale, and the streets were invariably packed—from sunrise to sunset, the market seethed with industry.

Karys hurried through the press. She had maybe an hour left until Sabaster arrived, although the time between the Calling and the Ephirit's appearance varied. Long enough to prepare, she hoped. She had already bought an armful of fresh carnations, a bottle of reef-wine, and a string of fine jasper beads. Put together, it was more money than she had spent in three months.

The Old Market blood-woman kept the same stall, one of the few permanent fixtures in the ever-changing bazaar. Psikamit had a high concentration of workings practitioners, and, with most Bhatuma derivations requiring blood as an imprimatur of divine authorisation, demand for her product never waned. She was a stooped old woman, permanently scowling and half-blind with cataracts. In spite of her age, however, her fingers remained deft. She filled wineskins from her canisters of blood: fish, ox, gull, dog, shark, and perhaps, if the right person named the right price, the contents of even more expensive veins.

Karys queued up behind a mousy-haired errand boy. He gave her a nervous smile, which she did not return.

"Let me shop first, and I'll give you a tenth," she said.

The kid weighed the offer, and might have tried to barter up, but Karys' wintery gaze silenced him. He nodded and stepped aside. She pressed a coin into his hand.

"What can I do for you?" the blood-woman asked Karys.

"Your cheapest. Two litres."

"Very good, very good." The trader's papery hand snaked out to accept payment, and she shuffled over to the ox canister. Karys resisted the urge to tell her to hurry up, and instead transferred her packages to the other arm, tapping her foot against the cobbles. From here, it would only take a few minutes to return to her flat. Enough time. It would be fine.

She glanced down the street, then grimaced. A woman in a grey and silver uniform was talking to the wine merchant. Hundreds of small metal plates studded the stranger's long coat; their surfaces sheened like dark oil on water. Half her head was shaven, and the skin of her scalp puckered with ridges of scar tissue. A New Favour saint. They seldom came down to Old Market.

"She's been here all afternoon," said the kid behind Karys.

Karys looked back at him. "Doing what, exactly?"

He puffed up a little at her attention. "Investigating. She's talking to all the traders, going from one to the next."

The saint made a curt gesture to the wine merchant, who looked uncomfortable. He shook his head.

"I overheard her earlier," the kid continued. "She wants to know if anyone's seen new reekers in town."

A creeping unease spread across Karys' shoulders. "Vareslians?"

"Yeah, that's what she said. 'Anything suspicious.' There's a reward."

Karys compressed her lips. "Suspicious how?"

"I dunno. Criminal, I guess. Shifty-looking." The kid scratched his head. "My Pa says they're all like that, though. Says New Favour should sink them in the harbour before they start getting comfortable again."

"Your father thinks a lot of New Favour, then."

"He says we should be grateful that they kicked the reekers out of Mercia. I don't think he likes the deathspeakers, though."

As if sensing Karys' attention, the woman glanced in their direction. Karys met her gaze without flinching, keeping her own face blank. The saint frowned.

"Here you go, cas." The blood-woman hobbled back to the counter with a bloated wineskin. "Two litres, ox."

Karys broke eye contact with the saint, and accepted her purchase. She could still feel the woman's eyes on her back.

"Thanks for the blood," she said.

The sun was setting over Old Market when she reached her flat, throwing the shadows long and thick over the pavement. Carillo had slipped the rent notice under her door. There was also a note from Marishka with the mender's address, and a form letter from Secured Dispatch asking her to collect outstanding mail. Probably New Favour recruitment again; no one else would pay to use the worked postal service. Karys locked the front door behind her, and shoved the papers into her drawer.

Her bedside reading light—sensing darkness—flickered to life as she drew the curtains. Karys moved quickly; she pushed her kitchen table against the wall to clear the floor space, and snatched up the bunch of carnations. Without ceremony, she began shredding their petals. Not much longer now. She scattered the red confetti on the floor, bit off the knot on the jasper string, and laid the beads on top of the ruined flowers.

The reef-wine had been her most expensive purchase; the liquor was distilled from the honey-sweet silver coral that grew out in the bay, a Psikamit delicacy. Two hundred years ago, one of the city's former heralds had altered the reef, transforming the beds of hard calcium to forests of edible, nectar-producing sponge. Karys removed the stopper from the bottle, setting it on the ground in front of her. The liquid inside the glass moved like pale smoke.

The hair on the back of her neck rose. She could sense Sabaster's coming, the way that the Veneer thrummed like the heart of a small animal. She kicked off her sandals and stripped down to her vest and shorts.

"Under control," she muttered. "All under control."

She picked up the wineskin of ox blood and knelt on the floorboards within the ring of petals and beads. Her hands shook as she fumbled with the plug. It came free with a soft plop. Closing her eyes, she raised the vessel and emptied its contents over her head. Cold blood ran in rivulets down her back and chest, soaking her in red.

"What the *fuck*?"

Karys almost screamed. The words sounded like they had been spoken an inch from her left ear. She cast around wildly, but there was no one else in the room.

"Why—why are you covered in blood?" Ferain sounded bewildered. "Where am I? Is this a hallucination?"

Him again. Her heart thudded. Why could she hear him? This was bad, very bad. Blood dripped from her chin.

"Sabaster likes red," she said faintly.

"What?"

Her shadow lay across the floorboards. Even though she was still, it moved. Her shadow-arms reached up to drag fingers through its hair.

"Red," she repeated. "The colour red. It pleases him."

"I have no idea what you're talking about. Is this some kind of deathspeaker ritual?"

No, not *her* shadow, not exactly. The silhouette seemed to drift, grow broader across the shoulders, taller, and then shrink back down to fit her again. As if it could not decide who it belonged to.

"He'll be here any moment," said Karys, and swallowed. "Whatever you do, don't move. Don't speak. Do you understand?"

"No, actually, not even a—"

"Shut up," she hissed.

The reading light guttered like a candle flame and her chest constricted. A flurry of hot damp air swirled through the room, lifting petals off the ground. Karys bowed her head and clasped her hands together in her lap, tight enough to crush her own fingers. A smell like machine oil and burned sugar rose up from the floor.

"You honour me, my lord," she said through gritted teeth.

Sabaster bled into existence. The Ephirit stood eight feet tall, even though his body curved over like the rim of a cup. He had three bone-pale faces— one on his head, one set in his chest, a third in his groin—and they moved independently, their expressions slack and infantile. The rest of his body was shrouded by waxy dove-grey feathers, the wings of hundreds of birds.

"Karys Eska," he whispered. All three faces spoke in perfect unison, although their tones differed: one fearful, one menacing, one seductive. The low chorus shivered out into the air. "Vassal of my will."

The feathers covering him trembled. Karys stayed still and prayed that Ferain would do the same. It had been a year since Sabaster had last called upon her, and she had half-forgotten the slippery feeling of dread that his presence wrought, like waves sucking at sand underfoot, like gravity slightly altered. It was hard to breathe around him.

"How may I serve you?" she asked.

Sabaster did not reply; he appeared distracted by the bottle of reef-wine. He stretched his body forward to peer at it more closely. Karys remained perfectly motionless, even as he came within inches of touching her. The Ephirit crooned.

"It's a gift," she said, voice strained. "An unworthy and humble tribute, my lord."

"It is . . . Disfavoured?" he whispered.

"Yes."

Sabaster's shroud of wings parted, and beneath it Karys caught an awful glimpse of shifting, glistening darkness, thick coils of flesh knotted together and sliding over one another like snakes. A mottled grey hand emerged from his stomach. No nails, each slender finger tapered into a single black needle point. With exquisite delicacy, he lifted the bottle and withdrew it back behind the feathers. She heard glass crunch.

"It is nothing and no more," he breathed, his voice like the splintering of bone. "But they lay their seed and tremble to be born. We watch for them, we search. We . . . prepare."

Karys closed her eyes for a second, trying to keep her composure. This close to Sabaster, she could feel the mad currents of his body's workings, the obscene logics that sustained him.

"May I support your preparations?" she asked.

He crooned again. The face in his groin drooled, yellow saliva dripping from his alabaster-pale lips.

"I would preserve you, Karys Eska," he whispered. "First of my vassals, I would honour you beyond measure. You shall provision me in glory."

"I fail to understand."

The jasper beads rattled on the floor. Karys did not dare look away from Sabaster, but out of the corner of her eye, she saw them rise into the air.

"You will be a tool to reshape the world," he said. "The culmination of our will wrought in flesh. I would have no other."

She still could not grasp his meaning, but she had a bad feeling about the direction of this conversation. The red beads had grown fluid and amorphous; they swam in rings around her and the Ephirit.

"You owe me no honour," she said carefully. "I have not yet earned that, my lord."

The beads drew into tighter loops. She could see that the stones had split open to accommodate small mouths, each filled with tiny red teeth.

"I would preserve you still," he replied. "Beyond the reach of the stain and the scourge, in eternal servitude to me."

The words slid like a cleaver into her brain.

"You would call my compact?" she whispered.

Sabaster leaned even closer. His second face hovered before her own, wide eyes bulging from their sockets.

"An honour beyond understanding," he breathed.

"I don't deserve it!" Panic threatened to overwhelm her completely. This was too soon, far too soon. If he summoned her now, all her efforts would have been in vain. "Allow me to serve you here, my lord. I will find and root out your enemies. Let me . . . let me earn my honour."

His body radiated sticky heat. Karys' breathing was shallow; she felt like she was going to be violently sick. She sensed the Ephirit was turning over equations in his mind, incomprehensible logical calculations and profane formulae. *Please,* she begged silently, *please, not now.*

"Be watchful, Karys Eska," he whispered. "Your honour awaits you."

And with that, he was gone. The beads clattered to the floor.

Karys slumped, burying her face in her hands. Her head pounded with the sound of her blood. Sabaster wasn't going to claim her yet; he had not called the compact. Relief turned her limbs weak. She had bought time. Hard to know how much—it could be years, or mere months. But time. She could still fix this.

"Karys?"

She started at Ferain's voice. He sounded like he was speaking from somewhere above her right shoulder. She lowered her hands to her lap.

"Are you all right?" he asked.

She could almost have laughed. "Do I look all right?"

"Honestly, the blood makes it hard to tell."

Her gaze settled on her shadow. A sensation of cold pressure lingered in her chest, an echo of the grasping vertigo she had felt last night. Although Ferain did not seem threatening now, she remembered that feeling all too clearly. He was dangerous. She clenched her fist, feeling the small ridges of scar tissue left by the Split Lapse. At least Sabaster had not perceived him. She could hardly imagine the Ephirit's reaction on discovering a Bhatuma relic bound to his favourite vassal's body.

"I'm fine," she said. "Normally I would have been better prepared, that's all."

"You can prepare for that?" Ferain's voice drifted to the left. He sounded a little breathless, his too-smooth foreign accent sliding across his vowels. "I mean, aside from writing a will? The way that it spoke—"

"He," she corrected automatically. "Sabaster is male. 'He,' not 'it.'"

"Do they distinguish?"

"The Ephirite? Yes, of course. And if it matters to them, it matters to me." She got to her feet, slightly unsteady. "The correct titles and honorifics keep him from removing my organs."

"Ah."

Embrace, she was tired. It seemed unfathomable that she had only left for Marishka's cursed job yesterday morning. She trudged over to her cabinet and collected her floor mop.

"And Sabaster is your, uh—" Ferain struggled for a tactful word. "Lord?"

"My compact-holder, yes. Most people would say 'master.'"

"He made you a deathspeaker?"

"He did." Karys crossed to the kitchen sink and turned on the water. The old pipes creaked and groaned under the pressure, and the faucet sputtered.

She closed her eyes briefly. Still here. She still had time. But for a moment back there . . .

"Why did you form a compact with him?" asked Ferain.

"That"—she turned off the tap, and thrust the end of the mop into the sink—"is a very personal question, Ferain Taliade. And on the subject of questions, what *I* want to know is how you are here, right now, talking to me."

She wrung out the excess water, and smacked the mop down on the floorboards.

"I'm not sure," he said.

"You're not sure," she repeated.

"It wasn't intentional."

Karys steadied herself. *Remember the money.* As much as she longed to tell Ferain exactly what she thought of his intentions, she was not going to risk fifteen thousand cret over it. She swabbed across the red pool of blood and petals, smearing the mess around. The cracked jasper beads rolled and collected in the grooves of the floorboards.

"Fine," she said. "It doesn't matter—I've got an appointment with a mender tomorrow morning anyway. They'll fix this."

"Have you been to the embassy?"

The mop's threads darkened with blood. Karys pressed it harder to the floor. "No. They're more likely to listen to one of their own. Better for you to talk to them directly."

Ferain did not argue. Karys washed out her mop, staining the water in the sink a dull pink, and returned it to the floor. She had avoided thinking about the matter, but a Vareslian ambassador killed in Mercian waters . . . well, wars had been triggered by less. And it was obviously personal for Ferain too; those had been his people murdered, his companions dead. Probably his friends. Of course he would want justice.

"Once you're healed, I'll give you directions to the embassy building," she said. "It's just . . . not something I want to be involved with. New Favour knows me; they might not like it if—well, it's better to keep a low profile as an independent."

"Of course," he said quickly. "I wouldn't want you to get in trouble."

There was tension in his voice, but no hint of resentment. Karys sluiced up the last of the blood, and pulled the plug out of the sink. The water drained away with a sucking gurgle; stray beads rattled around in the mesh filter. She wrung out the mop and returned it to the closet. Not that she should have to justify herself to him, anyway. What did she really know about the man? Back in the Sanctum, he would have agreed to whatever terms she proposed, told her exactly what she wanted to hear. She swept up the remaining beads and petals with a dustpan. Anything to ensure his survival. With a grunt, she pushed her table back into place, then walked across the room to open the curtains and windows. The sun had set, but the sky outside remained a pastel shade of orange. She leaned out on the sill, breathing in air that did not smell like Sabaster.

"You have a nice view," said Ferain.

In the north, the scale wall glowed in the evening light, glimmering coral and opal and dull platinum. Snatches of music carried on the breeze. Her shadow peeled out onto the windowsill.

"You know, I'd never visited Psikamit before," he said.

On the street below, an old man looked up and blanched at the blood-drenched sight of Karys. She flipped him off. "You weren't missing much."

"I thought it was supposed to be the modern heart of Mercia?"

"Guess that doesn't say much for the rest of the country, then." The breeze smelled of fish and salt. Her shadow leaned further over the window frame, distractingly out of sync with her own movements. Looking at it made Karys feel like she had drunk half a bottle of wine.

"What about the College?" he asked.

"What about it?"

"It has a good reputation. I heard that it's at the forefront of research into Ephirite derivations."

Karys shrugged. "Wouldn't know. I'm not a student."

If Ferain was put out by her stonewalling, he hid it well. Her shadow drew back from the sill, and when he spoke, his tone remained light.

"This might be a strange question," he said. "But after you closed the Veneer, did I—it's a little unclear in my head, but did you hear me speak?"

"You're talking about the part where you almost drowned me?"

"Oh." A pause. "Damn. I thought that might have been a dream."

Karys snorted. "No, it felt quite real to me."

"I'm sorry."

"What were you trying to do?"

"I don't know. I wasn't fully aware, I just felt—" He broke off. Her shadow twitched. "I remember water. Waves. It was dark, and I wanted to . . . to hold on to something. What were you doing in the ocean?"

"The Constructs blocked the beach, and I had to get back to Psikamit somehow."

"So you *swam*?"

"Yes."

"But that must have been at least six miles. In the *dark*."

"I grew up beside the sea. I can swim."

"Like a Lure, apparently." He sounded halfway between impressed and disbelieving. The comparison reminded Karys of her earlier conversation with Marishka, and she winced. She straightened up, causing her aching body to protest, and closed the window.

"The current favoured me," she said. "And the reef broke up the waves once I reached the bay."

"Even on a clear day, I would probably have drowned in the first mile."

She shrugged. Her shadow folded down to the floor.

"Karys, what I did?" he said. "It won't happen again. I swear."

He spoke with such absolute conviction that she instinctively mistrusted him. With the window closed, her flat felt stuffy and hot, and she was still covered in blood, and she really wanted to wash it off, but not until she was alone. So she wavered beside the window: exhausted, edgy, and unsure what to do.

"If there's nothing else . . . ?" she said at last.

A long pause.

"I don't think I can leave," said Ferain.

"Excuse me?"

The words sounded like they were being dragged from him. "It isn't under my control. Now that I'm here, I don't know if it's possible for me to leave again. I don't know how to."

Karys offered up a silent curse to the Lady of Brine and Urchins. "I see. Then you'll be present until tomorrow morning?"

Another pause.

"It seems that way."

She ground her teeth together. She was being stupid; it did not matter that some half-dead reeker would see her bathing. Or sleeping. In the larger scheme of things, it did not matter at all.

"It's fine," she said. "I don't care."

And yet, once she had filled her rusted bathtub, she still struggled to remove her clothes. Ferain had gone quiet, but she knew he was there, and her skin crawled as she peeled her shirt off her back. It shouldn't matter. She hunched down in the water. She didn't care.

When she glanced at her shadow, it stretched thin and far, an unnatural shape that hardly touched her at all.

CHAPTER

6

Karys slept badly. By the time the first rays of sunlight touched the dark sea, she was already locking her front door and setting off for the mender's.

Ferain had not spoken much since the evening before, but the feeling of his presence—a certain coolness, a kind of weight attached to her shadow—served as a constant, unwelcome reminder of his intrusion. Karys' self-consciousness left her irritable; she should not care, *did* not care, that this man had been inside her flat, seen her vulnerable, seen Sabaster. It didn't matter, and yet she was annoyed all the same, particularly because she received the distinct impression Ferain was both aware of her discomfort and trying to be sensitive about it.

Her appointment with the mender was at six o'clock, which left plenty of time for her to reach the address. Marishka had tracked down a woman from Upside, a freelancer named Balusha. She would be expecting Karys at her residence.

A thin fog rolled over the slick grey cobbles of Old Market, and Karys' footfalls sounded muffled and strange. It was quiet. In the distance, waves hushed into the harbour.

"Is that a Hound?" Ferain asked suddenly, causing her to jump. Her shadow lengthened as he peered toward the shaggy brown creature on the other side of the road.

"Stop moving like that," she hissed. "People are going to notice. And don't *talk*."

"No one else is around." Her shadow returned to its rightful place. "Besides, I'm pretty sure you're the only one who can hear me."

"What gives you that idea?"

"I tested a few things while you were sleeping. Hounds were made with Ephirite-derived workings, right?"

She scowled. "What did you do while I was asleep?"

Her shadow waved one hand. "I tried haunting the people who live on the floor below you. Either they're incredibly deep sleepers, or they can't hear me."

"You . . ." She took a deep breath. "Actually, never mind. I don't want to know."

"Right, but the point is that it's perfectly safe for me to talk to you. Probably."

"Don't feel obliged." She approached the Hound and patted its side in greeting. It stretched languidly, its hind leg twitching. Its fur radiated a damp, sleepy warmth. "In any case, I can't respond without looking like I've lost my mind."

"So the human-worked transport modifications are passed on as inherited characteristics in a living animal?" asked Ferain. A wisp of shadow reached out and touched the Hound's flank. "A whole new species, crafted by ordinary people. Almost like a Bhatuma-made creature. We have nothing like that in Varesli."

Karys sighed.

"What? You don't like Hounds?"

"They're fine," she said grudgingly, and clambered onto its back. "But the city is overrun with them. They'll soon outnumber the roaches."

"As infestations go, rogue transport workings don't seem the worst."

Karys made a noncommittal sound. When she gave the Hound her destination, it swayed and lumbered forward, apparently only half-awake.

"And there's no system? You can pick any Hound, and it'll take you wherever you want to go?"

"Mostly."

"Mostly?"

"They don't like leaving Downside, and they don't always follow instructions." She had learned the hard way that travelling near the harbour was perilous—Hounds loved to swim.

Her shadow drew closer, coiling up beside her in the seating bowl.

"Come on, don't you find them charming?"

"Yes, big headless furry abominations, very charming." Karys moved to the right, away from him. "Ask at the embassy, maybe you can take one home with you."

He laughed. "Tempting."

The Hound took Karys up through Tomasia to the base of the scale wall. The four-hundred-foot sheer cliff face gleamed with the pale light of daybreak: a muted, pearlescent white whorled with gold. The wall was a Bhatuma relic, a monument of the past. For forty years, the Ephirite had hungered to tear it down, while the city council sweated through countless negotiations with New Favour to stop them. Without the wall, Psikamit would be split in two: Upside cut off from the harbour, Downside from the inland. It was possible to traverse the cliffs on foot, but doing so was dangerous, awkward, and enormously time-consuming. Using the wall reduced the journey to mere minutes.

Karys climbed down from the Hound's back with a murmur of thanks. It nudged her hip gently, then wandered off in the direction of Scuttlers.

The faint hum of death pressed up against the Veneer, a low vibration at the back of Karys' mind. The commons below the wall was cold; the deep shadow of the cliffs soaking the chill permanently into the cobblestones. Up against the wall itself, nine giant hands lay palm-up on the ground, pale as exposed fish bellies. As it was early, no one else was using the arcane Bhatuma elevators, and she could travel alone.

Well, mostly alone.

"As an adherent of the Ephirite, do you ever worry that one of those hands might just . . ." Her shadow tilted its own hand sideways in demonstration. "Make an example of you?"

Karys thought very hard about fifteen thousand cret, and did not reply.

The scale wall was not made of stone nor metal, but near-seamless planes of extremely hard shell. In sunlight, the surface grew blinding; visible from miles offshore, it haloed the whole city in reflected light. While the hands were of a similar colour, they were crafted from a much softer material, somewhere between fresh resin and rubber—a mimicry of flesh. Karys stepped onto the upturned palm of one of the platforms, and the hand's fingers curled inward to cradle her. Then, slowly and smoothly, it began to rise.

Although she had made this trip countless times before, Karys' stomach still dropped as the city fell away beneath her. Over the tight-packed rooftops of the low districts, the sea melded with the misted gloom, a blue so deep that it appeared black. Little lights flickered out on the ocean; the night-fishers drawing in their nets, sailing back to the harbour with the dawn.

"Do people ever fall?"

Her shadow touched the tip of the platform's thumb. Ferain's cheerfulness had faded; he sounded more sombre now, subdued. Above the dark expanse of the water, the stars were fading out.

"Sometimes," Karys replied. "If they're drunk. But less than you would think."

"Do many jump?"

She frowned slightly. The whisper of death faded as the giant hand rose. "Sometimes."

Her shadow shivered.

"Sorry," he said. "I don't know why I asked that."

Karys said nothing. There had been a small quaver in his voice, like the thinnest fracture in a pane of glass.

The sky had turned coral by the time she reached the summit of the scale wall. Newtown, the district sitting closest to the cliff edge, was awash with low birdsong. It was peaceful; there were more trees, larger houses, broader streets—although the neighbourhood was by no means the wealthiest part of Psikamit, it was worlds away from Old Market. Karys knew the area well. Most of her easy, steady work took place here; unlike jobs in Downside, there was rarely any danger or complication, and pay was reliable. The commissions seldom varied: conferring with the deceased to clarify the terms of unusual wills, offering final sentiments to the bereaved, settling inheritance disputes. The residents of Upside had fewer qualms about contracting New Favour than the older, poorer neighbourhoods below them, but even they sometimes preferred more discreet and personal services. Karys was only too happy to charge them for the privilege.

Balusha's house was a ten-minute walk from the scale wall, a single-storey building at the end of a quiet road. It appeared poorly maintained and unwelcoming; the shutters had cracked, paint peeled from the façade, and leaves stuffed the gutters. One of the windows was boarded over where the glass had shattered. Stubborn weeds poked up around the walls—yellow flowers and long tufts of knotgrass. Karys studied the exterior. If her house was any indication, it looked like Balusha might have fallen on hard times. As she watched, a light came on in one of the downstairs rooms.

"Seems like the mender is up," said Ferain.

"Hm." Karys straightened her hair, tucking the loose strands behind her ears. "Do you remember the terms of our agreement?"

"'My life for fifteen thousand cret.'" He sounded amused. "Eager to be paid?"

"I'm just making sure that there are no misunderstandings."

"That's fine. I won't cheat you; you'll get the money."

Which was what he *would* say, but Karys only shrugged. She consulted her rusted old timepiece, and then put it back in her pocket. Close enough.

The front door of the house needed a new coat of varnish; the fine wood had turned grey and dull with neglect. Karys rang the bell, then took a step back. She felt jittery, tense with repressed nerves. If this went well, if everything went according to plan . . . There was a long pause, and then the door opened.

Balusha was tall and heavily built, with precise black eyebrows and salt-dyed hair. Despite the hour, she was already impeccably made-up, her eyes lined in purple and green. She studied Karys down the length of her nose.

"You're Marishka's resident deathspeaker?" she asked, dispensing with greetings.

"Actually, I'm independent." Karys held out her hand. "Balusha?"

"I said six for the appointment." The woman turned away from the door. "You're early."

The small foyer was tiled in grey and brown, the walls painted duck-egg blue and decorated with ugly miniatures of seabirds and fish. It smelled strongly of cooking oil. Karys followed Balusha through to the examination room on the right, which was brighter and cooler than the entranceway. A large glass cabinet dominated the far wall; inside it, Karys could see tools of the mender's trade—sealed phials, worked metals, scalpels, tinctures, all neatly arranged and labelled. A bed covered in a yellow oilsheet stood on the right, a plain wooden desk and chair on the left.

"I've never treated a deathspeaker before," Balusha said, brusque and efficient. "My knowledge of what modifications your master might have applied to your person is limited; my practice is more traditional, Bhatuma-based. Even if I'm unable to assist you, there is a thirty percent upfront fee for this meeting, which will not be refunded in the event—"

"Marishka has already covered the costs," said Karys.

Balusha shook her head. "I'm sorry, cas, perhaps there has been a misunderstanding. Your employer only made a partial deposit."

Karys could tell the woman was lying; the mender's voice had jumped an octave. *Not a great start.* "I'm aware that you have been fully compensated, and I don't intend to pay twice. If there is any misunderstanding, you are welcome to take up the matter with the Second Mayor directly."

Balusha's expression soured.

"Sit on the bed," she said.

Karys sat. Balusha walked over to her desk, and pulled out a form from her drawer. She scrawled something at the top of the page, almost driving the pen through the paper.

"Age and family illnesses?" she said, not looking up.

"Twenty-nine, and none that I know of."

"Existing personal body modifications, Bhatuma-derived, Ephirite-derived, or Ephirite-applied?"

"Only permanently wrought changes from my compact-holder, nothing active."

"Those changes being?"

"He altered my mind so that I can perceive the Veneer and what lies past it. His workings were not attached to me, only applied to me."

"Please explain."

"The workings moulded me like clay, and the clay has set—but it's still the same substance, rearranged."

"Hmph." Balusha made a longer note. "Nonreactive, then."

The condescension of her voice grated on Karys' nerves. "Yes."

"Are you pregnant or experiencing sexual difficulties?"

"No."

"Do you have any venereal diseases, or—"

"This is probably all irrelevant, anyway," interrupted Karys. "The treatment I'm seeking is for someone else."

Balusha's gaze flicked up from the form, and she raised an eyebrow.

"And this person isn't here now because . . . ?" she said.

"It's a sensitive situation, and I first wanted to be sure that you can help them."

The mender huffed.

"They were injured by an entity known as a Construct," continued Karys. "The attack left them . . . poisoned, I think. I saw the creature swallow and kill another man; he was completely dissolved in seconds. Like he had been turned inside out."

Surprisingly, Balusha did not flinch. She chewed the inside of her cheek.

"But your friend's exposure to the toxin was less extensive?" she asked.

"I think they were just scratched," said Karys. "I halted the progression of the poison before it spread to the rest of their body. Would you be able to draw it out?"

The mender raised her eyes to the ceiling, thinking. She tapped her pen against her front teeth.

"It doesn't sound like a poison or venom to me," she said. "Too virulent, based on your description. More like a worked effect—a withering curse of sorts. Potent. You say this creature was called a Construct? I haven't heard of them before, but they sound political. It would be very difficult for a death-speaker to identify the perpetrator without bodily remains, correct?"

Karys nodded.

"A sophisticated way to disappear people," muttered Balusha. She set down her form on the desk behind her, dropping the pen on top of it. "Removing an effect of that nature would be extremely complicated, even if the exposure was minimal. Without examining the patient, I can't tell whether it's within the scope of my abilities. I would have to see them."

Karys had a sinking feeling in her stomach. "They're currently in a form of stasis. If I brought them to you, that protection—"

"Stasis?"

"I placed them inside a time-locked space beyond the Veneer."

The mender's eyes narrowed.

"I've already told you that my Ephirite-based knowledge is limited," she said. "But how do you plan to locate that space again?"

"I tethered the relic generating the time lapse." Karys lifted her left hand to show the scar covering her palm. "With the working activated, the stasis remains—"

Balusha went rigid. "You bound this person to *yourself*?"

"No, I bound the relic that generates—"

The mender crossed the room and snatched Karys' hand. Her fingers were cold and soft. Her eyes flicked across the impression left by the Split Lapse, and her face darkened.

"Oh, you stupid woman," she said. "What have you done?"

Karys jerked her hand away automatically. "It was only a base Bhatuma-derived binding, nothing permanent."

Balusha let out a short, vicious bark of laughter. "'Nothing permanent'? Deathspeaker, you've sealed your little 'stasis' dimension from *within*—you've got a locked door with a melted key. I can't help you. *No one* can help you, not unless they had the ability to counter any of the relic's working authorisations, which is impossible without being able to examine the device that you physically subsumed. Nothing permanent? You've tied another person to your body; you've performed human fucking binding."

There was a ringing in Karys' ears. "No, I didn't."

"As good as." Balusha shook her head. "You're lucky that your victim hasn't consumed you already. Get out. I want nothing to do with this."

"Consumed me?"

"*Out.*"

Karys held her ground, although her heart rate sped up. "Your services have been paid for."

"Then I'll refund Marishka." Balusha's expression twisted. "You're welcome to take the matter up with her directly, of course."

"I have given you *no* reason to—"

"I cannot help you." The mender emphasised every word. "Get out before I throw you out."

For a second, Karys considered refusing. Balusha might be larger than her, but . . . She grimaced. What would be the point? The meeting was over; that much was clear. She pushed herself off the bed.

"Make sure you return the money," she said coldly.

Balusha's lips thinned, but she said nothing. Karys walked out of the examination room to the passage. As she left the house, she slammed the front door hard enough to startle the birds from the trees. Sparrows flapped into the air, twittering.

She moved quickly, her head down, her stomach knotted. A waste of time. Coming here had been a waste of time. Balusha had clearly misunderstood the situation.

"Karys," said her shadow.

"Don't talk to me."

The mender had jumped to conclusions, that was all. She had said it herself—she didn't know Ephirite workings, didn't know how the Veneer functioned. Her theories were irrelevant. Karys had *not* done anything permanent; it had only been a simple temporary binding, and even an apprentice workings practitioner would be able to release—

"Karys, stop," said Ferain.

She was halfway down the road and breathing hard, her skin flushed. "Leave me alone."

"My father is a Bhatuma historian, and he studied the Split Lapse for years. If what the mender said back there is true, then his notes could be used to counter the relic's workings."

Her shadow's voice was controlled, pitched low and clear, but its quiet intensity brought Karys to a halt. She stood in the middle of the street, her hands balled into fists, eyes fixed on the ground.

"Balusha may be wrong about everything," said Ferain. "And even if she's right about the way the Lapse is sealed, that doesn't mean we're out of options."

The sun was ahead of her, but her shadow lay in front of her feet. The light reflected off the windows of the houses to either side.

"We need more information, that's all," he said. "We're no worse off than when you woke up this morning."

Karys nodded. Her heart slowed; the heat of her anger faded. No better— but no worse.

You're lucky that your victim hasn't consumed you already.

"All right," she said. "More information."

CHAPTER

7

Although the Psikamit College of Advanced Workings was the largest and most prestigious university in Mercia, the campus itself barely stretched three city blocks. The facilities were old; the buildings' brickwork overgrown with dead ivy, their roofs patched with different coloured tiles, the graffitied walls blackened with ancient grime and soot. Every few years, someone new would lead an effort to clean up or renovate the College, but their undertakings were invariably met with failure. Grunge had seeped and settled into the bones of the institution; it spread like a wild fungal bloom.

"You seem to know your way around," said Ferain.

Karys cut across the scorched grass commons to the main administration building. Students between classes lounged in the morning sunshine, chewing osk and smoking. Two women leaned against the trunk of a chestnut tree, kissing.

"Not really," she muttered. "I just use their library."

"It's open to the public?"

"No, but I have a card."

"Do a lot of reading?"

"Some."

Her shadow rolled along at her side, matching her movements effortlessly. "I would think that, as an independent deathspeaker, you'd be very popular at the College. Insights into the Ephirite and their workings, firsthand experience of the Veneer, a slightly better temperament than the average New Favour saint . . ."

"New Favour wouldn't like that."

"Well, I didn't intend it as a compliment."

"No. I meant me talking to the College about Ephirite matters." She climbed the steps up to the admin building doors, past a huddle of students who were all peering at some kind of luminous yellow caterpillar in a glass jar. "They'd regard it as disloyalty. Sharing our masters' secrets."

"Wouldn't the College offer you protection from them?"

Karys snorted derisively. She pushed open the murky glass door and walked inside, blinking as her eyes adjusted to the dim interior.

Thirty years ago, the entrance foyer might have been grand, but it had long since fallen into disrepair. A pungent odour of curried samp, sweat, and mothballs lingered in the air, and the patterned green carpets had worn so threadbare that Karys could see the grey foundations through the holes. A row of mismatched desks served as the reception area, where a pale, black-haired student sat, looking singularly unimpressed. A man in a grey uniform loomed over them.

"Speaking of New Favour," murmured Karys.

The saint was younger than the woman she had seen at the bazaar, little more than a teenager. Like her, his head was half-shaven, and his left arm was bare, proudly sporting livid burns like the coils of a snake. New Favour practised self-mutilation as proof of devotion; the organisation's Supremes preached that reshaping the flesh to resemble the appearance of particular Ephirite would earn adherents greater honour upon their final Summons.

"—reputation for deviance, which is why we want to be sure," the saint was saying.

The student behind the desk replied with thinly concealed impatience. "I already told you, the College doesn't maintain records of who visits the campus, and even if we did, we wouldn't be obliged to share them with your organisation."

"The Harvester Agreements clearly state—"

"New Favour's edicts are not binding at academic institutions. You have no authority here, as I'm sure you are aware." The student shrugged their shoulders. "And besides, the records don't exist."

The saint's jaw worked as he ground his teeth. He turned abruptly and strode toward the door, nearly colliding with Karys.

She did not step aside.

"Who are you looking for?" she asked.

The man's attention settled on her. He had dark eyes, strangely lightless and unreflective, and a heavy jaw. He regarded her like he was studying an obstacle, and deciding how best to clear it from his path. Karys offered him a tight-lipped smile.

"I heard from a friend that there's a reward," she said.

The saint nodded, although his expression retained the same unpleasant blankness.

"Criminal elements," he said. "We have reason to suspect that one or more Vareslians might have infiltrated the city with the intention of undermining Mercia's local authority."

Vague. "Do you know what they might look like?"

"We are still gathering information. In the meantime, anyone suspicious should be reported to our local Haven."

"I'll keep an eye out. Good luck with your search."

He nodded again. "Excuse me."

Ferain held very still as the saint left the building. Karys could almost feel his tension seeping into her. The door swung shut. She crossed over to the reception desk, where the student eyed her with wary scepticism.

"They seem to be casting a wide net, don't you think?" she said.

They shrugged. "I try not to get involved."

"I wonder what money they're offering."

"Oh, enough to tempt. It's an ugly business, riling up old angers against the reekers. Someone's going to get hurt." They shook their head. "Anyway, what can I do to help you?"

Once the student had told her where to go, Karys thanked them and headed back outside. Walking down the steps, she rolled her shoulders to loosen the tension in her back and neck. She never liked talking to saints. That boy had looked so young too—nineteen, maybe twenty. Barely any older than she had been when she formed her compact with Sabaster. A sour taste remained in her mouth: part fear, part anger.

"New Favour are looking for Vareslians in Psikamit?" Her shadow collected underneath her, dark and bunched in the midday sun. "When did they begin searching?"

"Yesterday at the latest," she murmured. "But it might be a coincidence. Could have nothing to do with you."

He sounded unconvinced. "Maybe."

The Department of Higher Biological Workings was on the sea-facing side of the campus. No one paid Karys any attention as she hurried down the weed-strewn paths of the College. A young lecturer hosted a tutorial on the lawns outside the Marine Sciences Department, demonstrating a Bhatuma-derived working to draw salt out of water. A crowd of bored undergraduates listened as he droned on about the history of the authorisation's origins, and a small mound of salt grew beside the tank.

"I've never heard the term 'reeker' before," said Ferain. "Seems unflattering."

"Not many people around here care to flatter Varesli."

He made an amused sound. "I'm sure. I just thought it was a strange term. 'Reek' as in to smell bad?"

"Because Vareslians wear too much perfume."

"Oh. Interesting." A short pause, as if he was deciding whether to be offended. "Descriptive."

Karys sighed heavily.

The Higher Biological Workings building stood three storeys tall, rickety and overrun with grey-leaved creepers. Beneath the vines, the plastered façade was a weathered yellow. Sweeping silver maples grew in the surrounding garden, home to a flock of cooing, flapping pigeons. Someone had strung a collection of bird feeders from the branches.

Karys was ten feet from the main entrance when she noticed the woman crouched behind one of the trees. The stranger was watching the birds with a singular, burning intensity, and mumbling to herself. Not wanting to startle her or the pigeons, Karys coughed politely. When that didn't work, she coughed louder.

The stranger looked around. Like Busin, she was Toraigian; she possessed the near-translucent paleness characteristic of the island nation's citizens. Her hair fell in a black shock around her narrow features, and she wore round glasses with delicate gold frames. They magnified her tawny brown eyes so that she looked slightly birdlike herself—an owl blinking in bright sunlight.

"Hello," she said.

"I didn't want to disturb the birds while you were observing them." Karys gestured at the pigeons. "Do you mind if I pass?"

The woman smiled and shook her head. She stood up, causing the birds to fly off to the building's roof.

"It wasn't going well anyway," she said. "I was trying to isolate the quality of their hover flight pattern. It's why the feeders are greased, so they can't perch."

"Right."

The woman brushed off her long patterned skirt. She wore a slim-fitting brown vest and traditional beaded corset. Gold bracelets slid up her wrist when she held out her hand to Karys.

"Winola Diasene," she said. "Pleased to meet you."

"Karys Eska." She shook the woman's hand. "I'm looking for Professor Ersthazen? I was told he might be able to answer some questions about bindings applied to living organisms."

"Oh, you just missed him." Winola rested a hand on her hip. Despite her foreign attire, she spoke without a trace of an accent; by her voice, she could have been Psikamit–born and raised. "Living bindings, huh? That's a fairly broad field. Forgive me, but I don't think I've seen you around before."

Karys shook her head. "I'm not a student. This is just a matter of personal interest."

"Were you looking for Professor Ersthazen in particular?"

"Not exactly. Administration pointed me in his direction, that's all."

"In that case, maybe I can help you instead." Winola's easy smile grew brighter. "My current research focuses on animal motion replication, but there is considerable overlap with more traditional workings theory. Do you want to come up to my office?"

Karys was slightly taken aback by the offer. "Are you sure?"

"Of course." Winola gestured toward the bird feeders. "As I said, my observations hadn't been going well anyway."

The office proved to be a tiny room in the loft of the building, with a desk crammed between the wall and an overflowing filing cabinet. A single greenish-white etherbulb hung from the ceiling, producing a persistent ticking sound, and a Toraigian sunburst shawl hung like a tapestry from the wall. Flowers wilted in a vase on the windowsill. The space was airless and warm; Winola cracked open the window, and offered Karys a battered old chair.

"No one in the department ever retires," she said apologetically, moving a box of papers off her own seat. "I'm hoping they might allocate me a downstairs office one day."

A worked device—something like a feathered spinning top—hissed across the desk. Winola caught it deftly and stuffed it into her drawer, where it continued to buzz around ominously.

"Karys, you said?" she inquired, manoeuvring her legs to fit under the desk. "That's a lovely name. What is it that you do?"

"I'm a deathspeaker."

"Oh?" The scholar's eyebrows lifted. "I would never have guessed. Not with New Favour, I take it?"

"Independent."

"That's unusual. I've always wanted to talk to a deathspeaker about their experiences; you must have some fascinating insights into the Ephirite. Who is your compact-holder?"

When people learned of her profession, usually their response was to pity, fear, hate, or shun her. Karys was not sure what to make of Winola's breezy curiosity.

"Sabaster, Prince of Scales," she replied, guarded.

The scholar gave a low whistle. "Oh, I've read about him—he's in the upper echelon. What is he like?"

"Absolutely terrifying," muttered Ferain.

"He's . . . imposing, I guess," said Karys. "I rarely see him; he has many other vassals."

"Doesn't he also hold the compact for the Supreme of Psikamit's chapter of New Favour? From what I remember, he's a kind of elected Ephirite royalty." Winola tilted her head to one side. "For how long have you been a deathspeaker?"

"Six years," Karys lied.

A flicker of feeling passed over the scholar's face. She fiddled with the bracelets around her wrist. "It must be difficult."

And there it was: the old, familiar pity. "I still have time."

"Yes, yes, of course." Winola smiled again, although with less conviction. "It's variable, isn't it? Sometimes up to fifteen years. Can I ask what made you form a compact?"

The same question, posed for the second time in the space of a day. It rankled.

Winola seemed to sense that she had made a mistake. "Sorry, you just don't look, well . . ."

"Like a raging Mercian nationalist?"

"That wasn't the impression I received."

Karys raised and lowered her shoulders once: careless, indifferent. It was common knowledge that almost all deathspeakers formed compacts in order to become New Favour saints. Some pledged their souls for the sake of knowledge or power, others saw the Ephirite as new, better heralds, but most were lured in by the stories of the organisation's past glories—the founders' success in calling upon the Ephirite to put an end to the Vareslians' twenty-year occupation of Mercia.

"I didn't do it for my country's sake, no," she said. "But I had my own reasons, equally stupid. It can't be undone now."

"Sorry. I shouldn't have asked."

"It doesn't bother me." *Much.* Karys nodded toward the shawl hanging on the wall. "That's pretty. Family design?"

Winola blinked. The question was abrupt, clearly meant to change the topic.

"Yes," she said. "Yes, my father's motif—it was a coming-of-age gift, back when I still lived in Toraigus. That was, oh, ten years ago?"

"What brought you to Psikamit?"

The scholar adjusted her glasses. "Well, bilateral workings practice, I suppose. I wanted to learn about Ephirite and Bhatuma derivations, and, at the time, Psikamit was the only place that offered a practical education in both."

"I'm not sure I've ever met a Toraigian workings practitioner before."

Winola gave a little laugh. "You know, I hear that all the time. Seems contradictory, doesn't it? Like the setup for a joke—'what do you call the job of a successful Toraigian?' 'Not working.' Still, the College gave me an office here, so I must have done something right."

Karys wondered whether she had offended the scholar. Winola did not look upset, but a weariness had entered her voice—the tone of a person accustomed to having to prove herself in order to be taken seriously. "No, not contradictory."

"No?"

"Passionate. If you gave up your home to pursue workings, I think you must care about them a lot."

Surprise crossed the scholar's face, followed by a hint of pleasure.

"I do," she said. She crossed her legs at the ankle, and leaned forward slightly over the desk. "So, you wanted to know about bindings on living creatures? What specifically are you interested in?"

Karys hesitated.

"It's a controversial topic," she said.

"Intriguing."

"I'd like to understand how human binding functions."

Winola's eyebrows drew together.

"I . . . see," she said.

"To *avoid* performing that kind of working," Karys added hurriedly. "A friend of mine is investigating the emergency applications of some experimental time-based workings, and I'm worried they might hurt someone. Accidentally."

The scholar was quiet. Karys cursed her own fumbling; she should have approached the conversation more carefully.

"They don't plan to bind two people together, of course," she said. "They explained it to me: they want to use a worked device to freeze time around the body of an injured person, and then bind that same device to a second person as a tether. That wouldn't constitute human binding, would it?"

Winola rubbed her jaw. Karys' nerves were strung tight as a wire. *Tell me that Balusha was wrong. Come on.*

"I guess it would depend," said Winola.

"Depend on what?"

The scholar sighed. She folded her hands on the desk in front of her.

"Before I answer," she said, "does your interest in this subject have anything to do with the binding scar on your left palm?"

Karys' shadow swore. Karys rose from her seat, but Winola quickly shook her head.

"Wait," she said. "I want to help, if I can. Tell me what happened."

"We should go," said Ferain tightly.

Karys wavered. Winola remained seated, her expression focussed but not alarmed. She held out a hand across the desk.

"May I see?" she asked.

The Split Lapse scar looked old; it had faded to a pale tracery of the original, the mirrored script written white into her skin. Winola's thin fingers gripped Karys' wrist as she peered down at the marks.

"Bhatuma authorisations," she muttered. "Almost certainly a Vareslian relic, for it to be this sophisticated. It . . . holds back time? Holds old time in place, separately? The inscription is only a summary of the working's nature, but the herald who made this must have been extraordinarily powerful."

"The man who gave it to me called it a Split Lapse," said Karys, who very much wanted to pull her hand out of Winola's grasp. "A device that generates a dimension of the recent past. He used it to conceal himself from the present."

Winola nodded, but her eyes were still fixed on the scar. Without shifting her gaze, she reached into her desk drawer and found a compact mirror. She held it beside Karys' hand to read the inscription more easily in its reflection. Her lips moved slightly, like she was sounding out workings invocations. Her skin felt cool and smooth against Karys'.

"It's remarkable," she said. "If this description accurately summarises the device's function, it would have been one of the most powerful time-manipulation relics ever made. There's no way the workings could ever be fully derived by human beings; this is . . . I've never seen anything like it before. Do you know the progenitor?" She shook her head. "No, not the point, of course. So you bound this 'Split Lapse' to your body with someone inside the active time-locked dimension?"

"In order to get him to help," said Karys, biting back her impatience. "I tethered him beyond the Veneer inside the Lapse. Once I find a suitably qualified mender—"

"Is there any way you could manipulate the Veneer to forcefully sever that tether?"

"Now, in your office?"

Winola nodded. "You need to break the connection as soon as possible."

"But if the Lapse collapses, he'll die."

"And if you fail to remove the binding, you both will, horribly. Trust me. Break the connection before he wakes up."

Karys stared at Winola.

"But he's already awake," she said.

CHAPTER

8

The problem, Winola explained, was that two people could not coexist with only one body. At least, not for very long.

Karys let the scholar's explanations wash over her. Ferain remained wholly silent, and her shadow pooled darkly below the chair.

Attempts at human-to-human binding had been made since the earliest days of derivative workings, even in the centuries before the discipline had existed as a widespread formal practice. Back then, the power to reshape reality had resided almost exclusively with the Bhatuma, who were conferred their authority by the Embrace herself. The teachings that the heralds had gifted their adherents, often methods to work minor miracles of heat or light or sound, were scattered and poorly recorded, or else jealously guarded by the individuals who had received them. Nevertheless, even in those days, humans had experimented with the crude tools at their disposal.

Workings of any kind posed significant risk, that was obvious, but something about tying *people* together generated especially grotesque results. The Bhatuma had often been cruel and perverse, but even the most inimical among them avoided conjoining human beings—there was something in the act that they abjured, something insidious in its results. While the heralds had only acknowledged a small handful of true working sins—mind manipulation, soul retention or obliteration, and apotheosis—human-to-human binding stood out as an odd, out-of-place sort of taboo for them.

Perhaps because of their censure, very little information about the practice was available; just a scattering of fragmentary records and warnings. Most researchers seemed compelled to destroy their notes, as if to scour away any evidence of the horrors they had observed.

What Winola *did* know was that the bound individual would steadily grow in power, and seek to gain possession of the host's body. Depending on how the binding had been performed, this could occur extremely rapidly, or over the course of several hours. Days, at the most. In the best case scenarios, this simply resulted in the death of the host body, which the bound party would then inhabit and animate like a rotting flesh-puppet. In more unfortunate cases, well . . .

"It's been called 'contestation,'" said Winola. "The bound individual meets sufficient resistance from the host that they are unable to seize complete control."

Instead, the body would literally tear itself in two, with both parties fully conscious, fully capable of feeling, and fully able to understand what was happening.

Karys showed her teeth in an approximation of a smile.

"Delightful," she said.

In other instances, particularly those involving the physical meshing of multiple human bodies, the results varied even more gruesomely. More explosive, in a lot of cases, although the *implosive* incidents were certainly memorable additions to the corpus in their own—

"At least that's not my situation," said Karys.

"Yes." Winola had the grace to look abashed. "That's some comfort. Sorry."

Karys rubbed her temples. "But if the bound party knows they could get ripped in half or—I don't know, turned into a corpse puppeteer, why try to take over in the first place?"

The scholar hesitated, and then gave a shrug.

"It might not be a choice," she said. "It's theorised that the bound individual would be in pain, and desperate to return to something like their own body. In those circumstances, resisting might be like thrusting your hand into a fire and trying to hold still while you burn."

Wonderful. "Well, it's been two days. There's been no contestation, and I'm not dead. That has to mean I didn't perform human binding, right?"

"It's . . . promising. But not conclusive."

"Why not?"

"Because you can hear him. If he were truly contained within the Lapse beyond the Veneer, my assumption is that he would remain insensate and incapable of communication—he wouldn't be able to perceive the world outside, let alone interact with it. But if he can speak, then some part of his consciousness must extrude beyond those confines. While it's possible that the Lapse is dampening or slowing the usual effects of human-to-human binding, that doesn't necessarily indicate . . ."

"That I'm safe."

Winola nodded. "It's too early to be sure, that's all. Do I think you've performed human binding? No, not in the conventional sense—the relic seems to have formed a protective screen that divides you from this man. Is he nevertheless bound to you in *some* capacity? Maybe. If he can penetrate the Veneer, even partially, I believe he must have latched directly onto a part of you during the binding."

Karys envisioned an enormous leech affixed to her back, dark and hungry. She shifted on her chair, the hair at the base of her scalp standing on end. From the start, it had made no sense that Ferain could talk to her. Worse, she also had no idea how to sever the tether between them—and if what Balusha had said was true, if the simple binding she had worked now lay inside the Lapse . . . *a locked door with a melted key.*

"This is a misunderstanding," muttered her shadow.

Winola saw her disconcertion, and offered a little smile.

"The situation isn't hopeless," she said. "You said it yourself: it's been two days, and nothing has happened. You might be in uncharted waters right now, but there's no guarantee matters will deteriorate. If you can't disrupt the tether using the Veneer, then we'll find something else."

We? Karys tried to keep her expression neutral. "And what would that cost?"

Winola appeared briefly confused, then shook her head. "No, I'm not trying to charge you, don't worry."

"Then why help me?"

The scholar frowned. "Because I . . . want to? I studied workings with the intention of helping other people. It's a personal moral code, I suppose. Besides, your situation is very interesting and unusual, so I'm curious to see how it progresses."

"To see whether I explode or implode."

Winola laughed. "Not how I would have expressed it, but yes. Listen, if you give me a little time, I'll do some research into the matter. And if you think you owe me for that, there is one thing."

"Yes?"

The scholar sat back in her chair. She stretched her arms overhead, and cracked the tendons in her neck.

"Buy me dinner?" she said.

"Dinner?"

"I like that new bar in east Tomasia." Her cheeks had turned slightly pink. "I should have more information by tomorrow evening. We could meet there."

A meal seemed like a very small price to pay for her help. "That's all you want?"

Winola grinned. The expression made her look unexpectedly mischievous.

"It isn't every day a deathspeaker buys me a drink," she said. "Seven o'clock?"

When Karys left the Higher Biological Workings building, classes were ending, and the campus bustled with students. She kept her head down as she moved through the crowd. A warm evening. Overhead, a flock of cape petrels flapped and squabbled, their white-tipped wings cutting through the air. It was later than she had expected. She took the road past the administration block, down to the streets running parallel to the ocean. The air smelled sweetish and salty with the wind blowing off the docks, a mix of sun-dried fish and old blood. The Veneer prickled against her senses, whirring softly. The density of all the workings wrought on the campus produced a dull fizzing that seeped through the fabric and into her awareness.

Ferain waited until she had left the College grounds before he spoke.

"I think she might have it wrong," he said.

A Hound lay in the shade of the tea shop across the road. Karys whistled. The creature stirred and wagged its tail, but did not get up.

"Proximal overlay," said her shadow. "You remember how we could see the Construct outside the Lapse, how it could have heard us? What if that is what's happening now?"

The knotted tension in the pit of Karys' stomach eased a little. She exhaled.

"Makes sense, doesn't it?" said Ferain. "It's only a theory, but it fits."

"Maybe."

"Which would mean that I'm not a danger to you."

"Maybe," she repeated under her breath. She crossed the road, and the Hound's tail wagged harder. She crouched down beside it, and ran her hand over its flank at the ridge between the warm fur of its body and the hard horny slope of its seating bowl.

"I'm not going to hurt you," said Ferain.

"Are you in pain? Like Winola said, the part about contestation?"

"No. I don't feel anything, really."

She could not tell if he was lying. She did not know what to think. She straightened, and the Hound rose beside her. "You should have said something earlier."

"I didn't want to interrupt. Besides, I might be wrong—I know very little about workings."

"Still." Karys climbed onto the Hound's back. "Kitha Street, Old Market."

Her shadow grazed its fingers across the creature's fur, and then fell neatly back into her silhouette.

"It'll be fine," he said. "Tell Winola on your date tomorrow."

"Date?"

He seemed startled by her reaction. "Well . . . yes? You agreed to dinner."

"Because she was offering to help me." Karys' face warmed. "She said it was her moral code."

"You didn't realise she was flirting with you?"

"I—" She felt tongue-tied. "No. No, she wasn't."

He laughed. "You really didn't notice?"

"No one 'dates' deathspeakers. We aren't a good long-term investment."

"Firstly, that isn't how attraction works. Secondly, 'investment' is a tragic way of referring to yourself."

"She was not flirting with me."

"She was very pretty. In a bookish sort of way."

"Be quiet."

The journey back to her flat seemed to take an impossibly long time, and Karys was irritable and short-tempered when the Hound finally reached her street. An old man with a begging bowl hunched on the steps outside the neighbouring building. She dropped a coin to him without a word, and climbed the stairs up to her door.

"I don't know why you're so touchy," said Ferain.

She fumbled with the lock. "Maybe because there's a man who keeps following me around and commenting on everything I do."

"I don't comment on *everything*."

She got the door open and walked inside, tossing her bag onto the table. The room was soothingly cool, the yellow afternoon light streaming through the window onto her bare floor. Mail under her door again, another collection notice from Worked Dispatch, a request for a speaking in Tomasia—

"Wait," said Ferain.

The urgency in his voice brought Karys up short, and she went still. Her shadow stretched across the floor, quick and fluid.

"What is it?" she asked.

He stopped in the spill of sunlight beside her bedside table. "Your window. You left it closed this morning."

At the foot of her bed, the curtains stirred in the wind. The window stood slightly ajar, letting in the salt breeze.

"Does anyone else have access to your flat?" asked Ferain.

Karys shook her head. Her bed was made, but in the corner closest to the window, the coverlet was rumpled with the impression of someone else's hand. Her eyes travelled the room, itemising her limited possessions. Nothing missing, nothing that struck her as out of place—but someone had been here. Cold fingers crawled up her spine. "It doesn't look like I've been robbed."

"Maybe they were after something specific."

The books stacked on her bedside were as she left them; her shelves were undisturbed and tidy, a thin layer of dust coating them. She shook her head. "I don't think the flat has been searched."

Her shadow extended over to her closet, and slid under the door. It reappeared a second later. "No one there."

"Bathroom?"

He flowed across the room, losing shape, and slipped inside. "No, not here either. Whoever it was, they're gone now."

Karys glanced back at her front door. *Gone, but for how long?* The familiar space suddenly seemed alien and threatening, no longer a refuge. She had been robbed before, but this felt different, more invasive. Had the intruder expected her to be home? She imagined them padding across the floor, standing over her bed while she slept. Watching her. If Ferain had not said something, she might not have noticed the window.

"If they didn't take anything," she said slowly, "then maybe they left something behind."

"Such as?"

She motioned for him to be quiet a moment. The Veneer in her flat was smooth and thin, a curtain of gossamer on the surface of the world. She peeled it back, and her shadow breathed in sharply.

"What is that?" he asked.

She frowned. "The other side of the Veneer. You can sense it?"

"It's . . . amazing." He returned to her side. "So strange."

After over a decade of accessing the underside of reality, Karys was used to the preternatural sheen of the world past the Veneer: the shifting glaze of colour and texture and sound, the distortions that lacquered the air. She had not anticipated that Ferain would experience them too—probably not a good sign, but she could not afford to worry about it now. She listened, extending her senses outward, tracing currents of light and pressure.

The workings in her vicinity gleamed much brighter than their surrounds. A Bhatuma-derived working drew water from the heated cisterns in the basement, shining through the wall. She had personally wrought a simple Ephirite derivation to power the etherbulb in her reading light; it slowly revolved in place, emitting a gentle murmur.

"It's beautiful," said Ferain.

"Quiet," she muttered.

Her attention snagged on a faint mosquito whine coming from the gap between the wall and her bed. The Veneer bunched slightly over her blanket there, a tiny ripple in the otherwise inert surface. She walked over to the bed, and the sound grew louder. There was something there, something new. An inch at a time, Karys carefully pulled the blanket toward her.

Nestled in the coarse weave of the fabric was a tiny striped tick. Its forelegs twitched. A tight string of workings were knotted around its legs.

"Tracking bug," said Karys, stepping back.

Sensing prey, the tick crawled toward her, moving in an irregular zigzag over the blanket. Karys scowled, strode to the kitchen, and took a glass from the sink. She returned to the bed and trapped the creature.

"There might be more," said Ferain.

She shook her head. "I think I'd sense them. This is an Ephirite derivation: one of New Favour's. They're the only ones who could work this finely."

Below the glass, the tick walked in an unsteady circle. Karys' shadow coiled over the blanket, studying the worked parasite more closely.

"They know where you live," he said.

"Oh, they've always known. They've just ignored me—until now. Now they want to keep an eye on me."

Ferain made a frustrated noise. He flowed up to the windowsill, checking the street outside. "Do you think they could be watching the building?"

"Maybe. I don't know." She crossed to the kitchen again, and crouched before her cupboards. Her skin felt cold. Behind her mismatched collection of chipped bowls and plates, she found an empty glass jar.

"What are you doing?"

"With luck, wasting a saint's time." Karys walked to the bed, removing the lid. Deftly, she switched the glass and the jar, then flipped the edge of the blanket over so that the tick fell in. It landed on its back, tiny legs twitching. She screwed the jar shut again. "I can't stay here. If they suspect I might be harbouring the Vareslian they're looking for, then they'll be back."

"If they're watching and they see you leave now—"

"I can lose them in the city." She opened her bedside drawer, and took out her pen and a sheet of loose paper. In large block letters, she wrote: DO NOT OPEN, EPHIRITE MONSTER INSIDE, and then, below that: HOPE YOU ENJOYED THE SEARCH, SAINT, and then, for good measure: FUCK OFF. She bit the inside of her cheek, spat into her palm, and pressed the note to the side of the jar.

"Hold fast," she muttered.

Her saliva adhered the page to the glass like glue; the paper wrapped neatly around the vessel and stayed there. The same working she had used in the Sanctum. She raised the jar, checking that the tracking bug was still safe within it.

"Go to the embassy," said Ferain. "They'll shelter you."

She scoffed. "If New Favour's got a watch on anything, it's the Vareslian embassy. If I show up there, it's as good as confirming I'm involved with reekers."

"Then what's your plan?"

She pulled her safe out from under the bed, and pressed her thumb to the worked lock. The door opened. She took out her stash of emergency cret. Most of her money was in the bank, but paranoia always caused her to keep some on hand, just in case. "Lay low and consider my options."

Her coat was lost in the Sanctum, along with her good boots. Karys scanned her sparsely furnished flat. What else could she take, what else might she need? A small, childlike part of her lamented leaving: this had been a safe place, her own place, and she might never be able to return to it again. She quashed the thought. *Be practical.* If there was a chance that New Favour was watching the building, then she should take as little as possible, do nothing to arouse their suspicion. She tucked her flick-knife into her pocket, and fetched her light jacket and a change of clothes from the closet.

Someone knocked on the door. She froze, and her shadow tensed.

"Cas Eska?" called Carillo.

What did her landlord want? Karys did not move. Carillo almost never came up to her flat, not unless there was a problem. For him to call now . . .

"Cas Eska?"

"Who is that?" whispered Ferain.

She cursed under her breath, and strode over to the entrance. Her shadow made a sound of alarm. Karys ignored him, and opened the door.

Carillo stood on the step outside, hands buried in his pockets. His face was inscrutable behind the thick grey snarl of his beard. His eyes were small and black.

"Evening, casin," said Karys, keeping her expression neutral. She couldn't immediately see anyone else outside. Not that she expected New Favour saints to barge into her flat, but it still came as a relief to find Carillo alone. "What is it?"

"Your rent is late," he rumbled.

Of course. She had meant to pay that morning, but it had slipped her mind. "Sorry. I'll get the money to you, let me just—"

"You're never late with the rent," he interrupted.

"My apologies. It won't happen again."

He shook his head. "I'm not here to accuse you, Eska. I am making sure you're all right. You've been coming and going at odd hours."

She felt a little disconcerted. "I, uh . . . work. Sometimes the jobs are unpredictable."

"It's a hard occupation you've landed upon. People aren't always kind about that." Carillo shifted his hands in his pockets, gruff and unsmiling. Karys couldn't remember him ever having spoken this much to her before. "Not kind at all. But you always pay the rent on time. One of the best tenants I've had—so I wanted to make sure you haven't gotten into some kind of trouble."

"No, no trouble."

He studied her face, his own serious. He nodded.

"That's fine, then," he said in his deep, flat baritone. He turned to go. "So long as you're sure. And you know where to call if you aren't."

He was halfway down the steps when Karys spoke.

"I might be late with the rent next month too," she said. "Maybe the month after that as well. It could be difficult to find me."

Carillo paused. Then, without looking back, he gave a shrug.

"It's hard to attract tenants these days," he said. "Chances are, the flat could stand open a while, and I wouldn't notice. Goodnight, Eska."

"Goodnight. Thank you."

He carried on down the stairs. "Make sure you lock up."

Karys watched him go before stepping back inside. She picked up her bag and tucked the jar with the tracking bug under her jacket, then looked around the room one last time, struck by the sudden, strange certainty that the place would never be home to her again. This quiet refuge and its comforts were already lost. The yellow curtains fluttered in the breeze, shading the light over her old bed.

She closed the window, and left. The Hound was still nosing about the street; she whistled, and this time the creature came straight to her. It bent its legs, and she climbed up with a murmur of thanks, slipping the jar down to the floor of the seating bowl. She tried to look relaxed and cheerful as she gave the animal an address in Scuttlers.

Although it felt like she had left something important behind, when the Hound began to move, Karys did not look back again.

CHAPTER

9

Karys left the tracking bug in the first Hound's bowl, getting off the animal outside the busy dives of Scuttlers. She took a second ride by awrig to Soresa Flats, and then another Hound carried her to the border of Creakers. As far as she could tell, no one followed her. She made the rest of the way on foot.

It had been a year since she had last been down to Creakers. Death-speakers were tolerated in most parts of Psikamit, even grudgingly respected in the newer, wealthier districts—but here, people kept the old faith, and the Slaughter remained a close and open wound. Creakers' residents would have sooner kept the heralds, even if it meant the Vareslian occupation continued unopposed, even if Mercia was subsumed entirely. What difference was freedom to the starving? At least the Bhatuma had guided their souls to the Embrace.

As a result, New Favour saints steered clear of the district. Karys only ventured down occasionally, usually when Marishka wanted answers about a suspicious death in the neighbourhood. Seldom alone, though, and never at night. While the Second Mayor's reputation offered a degree of protection, the presence of a herald-killer's servant was still far from welcome.

The greenish, porous worked-paste shacks looked as drear as ever. Karys moved smoothly through the dark, damp paths, watching her step. Every year, seasonal high tides flooded the mudflats and collapsed half of the buildings, leaving whole streets submerged in grey silt. But come the springtime pilchard rush, new dwellings sprung up again like mushrooms. Bands of inland workers arrived in Psikamit to catch their share of the yearly surfeit—then left with the storm season, abandoning their temporary homes to wash away with the tides.

An easy place to disappear, or to be disappeared. She made for High Stretch, a small hill within the district. As it usually stood above the line of the tide, the area was cramped with sturdier shacks and permanent lean-tos, more established residents vying for space on the drier ground. Rough walkways of worm-ridden tinder crisscrossed the mud, and the platforms groaned loudly as the waterlogged earth shifted, the source of the district's name. Smells of woodsmoke, burning seaweed, and excrement hung over the hill, and feral dogs slunk along its narrow paths, dark eyes glinting in the purple twilight.

"I don't know about this," said Ferain.

"I'm making myself scarce," Karys replied under her breath, barely moving her lips. Two ancient crab-haulers looked up from their shared bucket of shells as she passed. Their eyes followed her, but they remained seated. "People here won't talk to New Favour."

"It just doesn't seem all that . . . hospitable."

His discomfort irked her; he was clearly unaccustomed to poverty. *Figures.* She spied the house ahead, Marishka's blue knotted flag hanging over the splinterboard door. Cheap grey etherbulbs hung off the rafters outside, which made the broken-down building appear curiously festive. A large, mean-looking man stood by the door. He made a face when Karys approached.

"Lady Deathspeaker," he said in greeting.

"Hello, Sav."

The man shifted his bulk to the other leg. "The Mayor send you?"

"I sent myself. Is there space tonight?"

His eyebrows rose. "Sure. If you want it."

"I do." She moved toward the door, but Sav stepped sideways to intercept her. He had a bright white scar that ran from his chin to his hairline, the product of an old bar fight.

"You need anything else?" he asked.

"I just want a floor to sleep on."

"You know that if you talked to the Mayor, she could—"

"Nothing's free with her. I'd rather not owe any favours, thanks."

He nodded with a smile that his scar turned into a sneer. "Right. At least take the good room, then; I don't want it said that I mistreated you. Back stall on the right. It stays warmer."

The dorm was a dingy hall that smelled of sweat and mildew. Plywood screens divided the space into cramped quarters, affording occupants the barest semblance of privacy. Children sat on the dirt-streaked tiles of the communal area, some holding strawdolls or blankets, bickering or playing pretend amongst each other. They fell quiet when she walked in.

"What is this place?" asked Ferain.

Karys could not answer without looking like she was talking to herself, so she silently crossed over to the stall furthest from the door. Within, a wood brazier burned and shed light on the screens; a rickety chimney carried its smoke up through the roof. No furniture, just a discoloured, scorched rug on the floor. She put down her bag, and lowered herself onto the ground with a stifled groan. Her body ached; she had still not fully recovered after the swim from the Sanctum. Getting soft, these days.

One of the kids, a boy with spider-thin legs and a long mop of brown hair, peered around the side of the screen. He had bright eyes.

"Who are you?" he asked.

Karys gave him a flat look. "A friend of Sav's."

"Sav doesn't have friends."

"A friend of the Second Mayor, then. Scram."

The invocation of Marishka was enough to chase him off, at least temporarily. Karys rubbed her hands together, hunching her shoulders. Although the worked-paste walls kept out the worst of the weather, the quick-setting foam wasn't as effective as natural materials. She leaned against the spongy surface, allowing her eyes to drift closed. It was going to be a long and cold night.

"Is it some kind of orphanage?" Ferain asked.

The communal area remained suspiciously quiet; Karys heard whispering as Spider-legs reported back to his friends. She covered her mouth with her hands, pretending to blow them warm.

"Safe house. A place for people with nowhere else to go," she muttered. "Often, that's the kids."

"Why 'lady' deathspeaker?"

"Just what people call me."

"There must be a reason."

She raised and lowered her shoulders in an exaggerated shrug. "Because they think I act like I'm better than everyone else."

"Oh."

Spider-legs' head appeared around the side of the screen again. Karys fixed him with a glare, but he only held out a single grubby bread roll to her. The boy had a vulnerable look about him; when he met her eyes, his expression was almost imploring.

"Thank you," she said.

He nodded, gave a shy smile, and scuttled off again. Karys held the roll closer to the brazier to check for weevils and mould. The bread felt rock hard under her fingers, which was a good sign. Softness usually indicated decay.

"I'm sorry that you can't go home," said Ferain.

"Hm."

"Sorry that you're in this position at all. I know it hasn't been . . . comfortable. Me being here, that is."

Karys bit into the roll. It tasted like beach sand. She chewed methodically, and swallowed. "What gives you that idea, reeker?"

"I'm grateful, that's all."

What am I going to do with gratitude, huh? She continued eating the bread, although she was not hungry, and it hurt her jaw. The fire in the brazier crackled and spat. Spider-legs returned, this time holding a tattered grey blanket. He thrust it out to her.

"Are you sweet on me?" asked Karys bluntly.

Behind the screen, children giggled. Spider-legs scowled, and shook his head.

"You're old," he said.

"Charmer." She took the blanket off him. "Are you sure you don't need this?"

"Yazi said you could borrow it."

No doubt another one of the kids currently eavesdropping on their conversation. Karys sighed.

"My thanks to Yazi as well," she said. "Now go away."

Spider-legs obliged. Karys wrapped the loaned blanket around her shoulders. It was too small to cover her properly and too thin to offer much warmth, but it meant something. She drew her knees in. *Marishka must be overstretched.* The Second Mayor expended a lot of resources keeping the children safe, but that didn't extend to keeping them comfortable. And there were always more: more kids, more risks, more hunger. An endless pit of raw need.

Her shadow pulled a little closer to her, its edges flickering in the shifting light.

"Do you have any friends who could conceal you?" he asked. "Somewhere better to hide?"

"No."

"And family? There isn't a cousin or—"

"No family," she snapped, and the words came out sharp and too loud. Behind the screens, the children went quiet.

"Okay," said Ferain slowly. "Got it. No family."

Karys brushed the breadcrumbs off her knees. The heat of the fire abruptly felt stifling; she shuffled further away from the brazier. After a few seconds, the children started whispering again, quick and secretive. She lowered her voice.

"We have a deal, Ferain," she said. "You don't need to be grateful, and you don't need to be my friend. All you need to do is pay me after I have fulfilled my side of the bargain."

"We don't know how long that will take."

She shook her head. "And?"

"And I feel responsible." Her shadow sounded collected, composed. "New Favour appears to want me dead, and now I've drawn their attention to you."

"I think Balusha was the one who drew their attention to me, actually."

"Most likely, yes. But the point stands."

She scowled and tucked her hands under her arms. "She probably would have sold me out even without the reward. Second-rate mending hack. I wish I knew what she told them."

"I'm sure she was well paid for the tip."

Karys was silent a moment. Night had fallen, and the dorm was growing darker.

"You think New Favour really is after you, then?" she asked.

"Seems that way."

"Do you know why?"

"No."

She gave a low huff.

"I don't," insisted Ferain. "But the timing of their search can't be a coincidence—clearly, no one was meant to survive that attack on the retinue."

"You think they were behind what happened in the Sanctum too?"

"Yes."

"And you genuinely want me to believe that you have no idea why New Favour tried to kill you there either?"

"I'm telling the truth."

Parts of it, maybe. "Balusha might have been a hack, but she was right about one thing: those monsters sound political. New Favour wouldn't assassinate an ambassador without good reason; they aren't stupid. You know more than you're telling me."

"What makes you think that?"

She drew the word out, imitating his accent. "'Constructs.'"

Ferain was silent. Karys' lips curled in a humourless smile.

"You recognised them," she said. "You knew what those things were."

He sighed.

"Well?"

He spoke reluctantly. "I'd heard about them, yes. I work as a diplomat for the Vareslian Foreign Ministry; last year, our intelligence community briefed us about a new weapon that had fallen into the hands of Mercian deathspeakers—some kind of failed Ephirite experiment, according to their information."

"The Constructs are Ephirite-made?"

"That's what we were told. The Ephirite discarded them, but New Favour managed to revive some of the creatures, and was looking for ways to harness their power. The saints seem able to compel the Constructs to seek and pursue specific targets, but only in isolated conditions. If they encounter other people, the creatures will attack them too."

Like Marishka's smugglers. "So you knew Constructs were a New Favour weapon all along."

He gave a nod. "Suspected it, yes."

"And when you met me inside the Sanctum, you didn't consider that I, as a deathspeaker, might be a part of that plot?"

His voice turned wry. "In my defence, I wasn't aware of your occupation when I first grabbed you. But no, I didn't think you were involved."

Karys brooded on that for a moment.

"Was I wrong?" asked Ferain lightly.

She ignored the question. "What were the Ephirite trying to create?"

"We don't know. According to the intelligence presented to the Ministry, New Favour had been sourcing corpses for some of their masters at around that time." Her shadow darkened on the floor. "Children's bodies, specifically. There's a theory that the Constructs are made from part of their remains."

Karys pulled the blanket tighter around her shoulders. "I see."

"All of this is confidential, of course. The methods that the Ministry uses to gather information are . . ."

Ferain trailed off as raised voices filtered through the walls of the dorm. The kids hushed, and Karys sat up straighter, her hand moving to the flick-knife in her pocket.

"Hey, Sav!" a man called. "You have the Ephirite bitch in there?"

Karys leaned a little to the side, looking around the edge of the screen. The children had melted away into the stalls; in the tense quiet, she could hear them breathing. Outside, Sav stood in silent sentinel. The glowing tip of his smoke-reed smouldered orange. He took it out of his mouth and extinguished it against the wall.

"Move along," he said, his deep voice carrying clearly.

"I'm just asking if the apostate is in there. Lorin said they saw her coming this way."

"And I said, 'move along.'" Sav tossed the reed aside. "You heard about Tolaz? Don't think Marishka won't do the same to you if she finds out you're harassing one of hers."

The stranger laughed. "I'm not scared of the old woman."

"Tolaz said that too, back when he had balls, and skin on his member. This is your last warning: *move along.*"

Karys retreated behind the screen, her fingers tight around the grip of the knife. A few stalls over, a little boy had started whimpering. Another boy shushed him. There was a sour taste in her mouth. Coming here had been a mistake. She should get up, she should leave before anyone else—

The man outside laughed again, false and forced. "All right, all right. I only wanted to talk with the bitch. No need to get hot about it."

Sav said nothing. Karys held her breath, straining her ears. She heard indistinct grumbling, the sound of creaking wood. Ferain slowly moved over the floor, stretching across the communal area to see out the door. He slipped back to her side.

"They're leaving," he murmured. "Two of them, I think."

She nodded tersely, and gestured for him to be still. A few seconds later, Sav sighed.

Karys got to her feet and walked over to the door, staying out of sight of the street. The waxing moon hovered above the scale wall in the distance. Sav heard her, and glanced over his shoulder.

"I'd stay inside if I were you," he said, dropping his voice.

"Do you think they'll come back?"

"Him? No. No, he's all talk. Nothing to worry about."

"I don't want to cause trouble here."

He made a contemptuous sound. "Everyone in Creakers knows where the power lies. There won't be trouble—and if there is, I'm paid to deal with it. Back inside, Eska."

She relented, ambivalent, and returned to her stall. The dorm felt more like a trap than a sanctuary now: only one door, the high windows too small to fit through. She should have known her presence here would draw attention. Careless of her. She sat back down, facing the brazier.

"Does that happen often?" muttered Ferain.

Karys folded her arms over her knees, and rested her chin on top of them. "Not often," she said.

He seemed unsure how to respond, and she smiled thinly.

"Deathspeakers are the Ephirite's door into the world," she said. "We let them in. Everyone knows it."

"I thought that Mercians would feel differently."

"Some do. For others . . ." Outside, a rusted hinge creaked in the wind, the sound forlorn. Sav coughed, and then cleared his throat. "For others, what the deathspeakers did was unforgiveable. Sacrilege. Even now, people want to believe that the heralds will come back, and they'll be rewarded for holding the faith. But if they can't have that, then they'll settle for whatever vengeance they can get."

Ferain was quiet. Karys tipped her head backwards, and rested it against the wall.

"I used to think that way," she said.

A shiver ran through her shadow where it lay on the floor.

"What changed?" he asked.

"I became a deathspeaker."

A long pause.

"It's similar in Varesli," said Ferain. "Not that people believe the Bhatuma will return, necessarily. Just that the Slaughter marked the end of history. Now it's only grieving that's left."

"They're not angry?"

"No, they are. At everything, I think. We're a nation haunted by the ghost of what we used to be. Always chasing the spectre of empire."

She shifted. "What is it like, living there?"

"In Varesli?"

"Mm-hm."

"I don't know. What is it like living anywhere?"

The answer felt evasive. "You don't like it?"

Ferain thought for a moment.

"It's many things," he said. "I grew up in the old capital, Eludia, and that's still home to me. Sometimes it just feels like the history of the place will drown it. Have you heard of the Singing Crescent?"

She had, but gave a tiny shrug.

"It was made by Ambavar, the Lord of Night. The story goes that he fell in love with a mortal girl and kidnapped her, spiriting her away through the veins of the Embrace. When she complained that she missed her family, he cut a crescent-shaped hole through the world so that she could see her parents again." He snorted. "It's a beautiful monument, if you can forget how it came to exist. That's sort of what it's like to live in Varesli."

Karys had read about Ambavar's Exchange in a long treatise on Varesli-Bhatuma interactions—although in that account the author suggested that the woman had tricked the Bhatuma into impregnating her, and Ambavar had subsequently felt honour-bound to care for her and his unborn progeny. Ferain's version of the story seemed much less forgiving of the herald. Her shadow stretched around the edge of the screen, checking the dorm.

"You should try to get some rest," he said. "I'll wake you if anything happens."

"Aren't you tired?"

"Not at all. I'm not sure sleep is possible for me, like this."

Karys wavered, then lay down on the rug, cushioning her head against one arm. She could feel every groove and rut in the floor beneath her. Somehow, she doubted she would be sleeping at all.

"Ferain?" she said.

"Yes?"

Maybe it was a mistake, maybe it was stupid. "I'll go to the embassy tomorrow. Tell them what happened."

He did not reply immediately. The fire weaved and banked behind the grating.

"Thank you," he said.

CHAPTER

10

The Vareslian embassy sat within the cloistered quarter of Yucreon, the wealthiest part of Downside, far enough from the harbour to escape the smell of rotting fish, but close enough to flee in case of trouble. Most of the city's tiny Vareslian population lived behind the walls of the adjoining compound. Their position in the city was precarious; a forty-year-old Sovereignty Accord meant little to Mercians who still felt the weight of the preceding twenty-year occupation.

Karys hunched within the one-seat awrig's chaise as it slid through the air, wishing she had chosen a vehicle with reflective windows.

This is a terrible idea, she thought.

She had blown a percentage of her emergency cret to ride the worked vehicle instead of whistling for a Hound. The painted carts were owned by a company in Soresa Flats; they hovered a foot above the ground as they roved through the city on Bhatuma-derived workings. Through the yellow-tinged windows, she could see the morning streets of the district: calm and ordinary, other awrigs passing sedately by.

"I appreciate that you're doing this," ventured Ferain.

She drummed her fingers on the armrest. "Just know that I'm charging for expenses."

The embassy building was situated next to one of the three major banks in Psikamit, and a long queue of people snaked across the street outside. Typical end-of-the-month traffic, nothing unusual. The awrig slowed, allowing pedestrians to move out of its way, and Karys steadied her nerves. After another near-sleepless night, she felt haggard and thick-headed. In all likelihood, New Favour had found the tracking bug by now, and she had no doubt they would be looking for her. But maybe, with so many people around, she would be able to blend in here.

The awrig cleared the traffic, and rolled up to the embassy gates. Beyond them loomed a double-storey building of rose-blushed yellow granite with arched casement windows and a grey gable roof. A fountain stood before the entrance, water falling in smooth sheets from a crescent moon sculpture and producing a soft, bell-like music. Lush green lawns surrounded the complex.

Karys breathed in. *Be quick, be inconspicuous.* She shouldered her bag, opened the door of the awrig, and stepped down. Outside, the sky was overcast, and a cool breeze blew off the ocean.

A narrow-shouldered woman was standing beside the gate. Her eyes quickly absorbed Karys' slept-in clothes and lank hair, but her smile remained impressively polite.

"How can I help you, cas?" she asked.

"I have sensitive information about a Vareslian ambassadorial retinue," said Karys tightly. "Please can I speak to someone? Inside?"

"Right this way, cas." The woman spoke with an air of perfect professionalism, like Karys had merely stopped for directions. "Please follow me."

Passing between the gates, Karys felt the Veneer stir as the embassy's workings brushed against her. She shivered, but the security derivations settled, and the fabric stilled once more. *So they weren't triggered by the Split Lapse binding. That's probably a good sign.* The woman led her inside the building, and shut the elegant brass and ivorywood doors after them.

"The complex is very secure," she said, turning to offer Karys a conspiratorial smile. "Quite safe."

The embassy's interior was no less refined than its exterior. The corridors were broad and wood-panelled, with sleek touches of silver around the light fittings. Huge glass-pressed collages of dried flowers hung from the walls, their compositions both effortless and perfectly balanced. Tiny studs of coloured glass glittered like drops of water on the dead petals.

"Thank you," said Karys, taking in the entranceway. "I was concerned—"

"That someone might see you?"

Karys nodded.

The doorwoman's expression was knowing. "Well, you're here now, and very welcome. I'll take you to casin Petresk. You can share your information with him."

Karys trailed after the woman, feeling distinctly unwashed. Muted voices drifted through the walls of the first-floor corridor, and footfalls sounded from rooms above. The embassy seemed curiously set apart from the rest of Psikamit; peaceful, clean, quiet. Karys suspected that the Mercian consulates wouldn't be half as well-appointed. Her eyes kept returning to the collages hanging on the walls; something about their careful simplicity drew her in.

"Do you like them, cas?" the woman asked.

Karys started. "Oh, I . . . yes. I've never seen anything like them before. They're lovely."

The woman smiled again.

"The series is called 'A Part Together.' A silly pun, but the theme is quite optimistic, really." She gestured to a work on the wall to her right. "I'm not sure if you're familiar with Vareslian floriography, but the flowers all hold different symbolic values. Selvea's Tears, for example, connote self-recrimination."

"Are those the blue ones?" The words sounded stupid and childish leaving Karys' mouth, and she winced. The woman did not appear to notice.

"They are, yes," she said. "But see, they're paired with rush poppies, which are typically associated with a desire for reconciliation. And then the golden climbing roses? A recognition of worth."

"So it's an apology?"

Now the woman definitely looked pleased. "Yes, exactly. An acknowledgement of wrongdoing, an entreaty for forgiveness, a token of respect. Or of love; the roses are contextual. As a whole, the series is a reflection on Varesli-Mercian relations, a message of sorts. Here, this is casin Petresk's office." She knocked on Karys' behalf, waited for Petresk's call of acknowledgement, then stepped aside and offered a small, polite bow. "It's been a pleasure to meet you, cas. I'll leave you in the counsellor's capable hands."

Petresk's office was much the same as the corridor outside, sleek and orderly. The man himself was built more like a blacksmith than a diplomat, and his bulk appeared out of place behind his small, antique desk. He had tanned white skin, a moustache peppered with grey, and a mane of thick black hair, and his clothes looked slightly too tight: a navy-blue waistcoat and a starched shirt.

"Good morning," he said in a rumbling baritone. He stood up to greet Karys, his movements smooth and confident. "To what do I owe the pleasure? I don't believe we've met, cas . . ."

"Eska."

"Cas Eska. Please, have a seat." He gestured toward an upholstered chair by the window. "Tell me what I can do for you."

She had not expected everyone to be this gracious. Karys crossed the floor, feeling wary. "I have sensitive information regarding a Vareslian ambassador."

"Information?" Petresk's thick eyebrows knitted together. "Which ambassador would this be?"

"Her name was Maret Corbain," said Ferain softly.

"Corbain." Karys lowered herself into the comfortable seat. She crossed her arms. "A few days ago—"

The sound of raised voices drifted through Petresk's door. He looked around in annoyance, and shook his head.

"A busy morning, apparently," he said. "I apologise. This would be Ambassador Corbain for Toraigus, correct?"

"Yes." She breathed deeply. "Yes, that's right. The ambassador and her retinue were travelling by sea. Their ship—"

A door slammed, and Karys jumped. The voices outside grew louder.

"What is going on out there?" grumbled Petresk. "Excuse me one moment, cas Eska; I'm just going to see what the commotion is about."

"Oh. Of course," said Karys. Petresk was already moving toward the door, and she felt a stir of unease, an itching anxiety. The voices were drawing closer, and sounded angry. She started to rise from her chair just as Petresk opened the door.

"Get down!" shouted Ferain.

Then the world exploded.

Karys' vision went dark, and she was thrown backwards. The air vanished from the room. Heat and sound and pressure; her senses overwhelmed, she briefly lost all sense of her own body within the roar. Then confusion—not fear, not pain, but terrible confusion.

What . . .

She could not see, but the pressure was fading now, and the sound turned to a shrill ringing. Light cracked in—the smell of dust and smoke in her mouth, blisteringly hot air—and a voice.

What happened?

"Karys? Karys, can you hear me?"

She moaned indistinctly. Her chest felt like it had been stomped on. She fluttered her eyelids open. A grey-brown fog covered the world.

"You're all right," said Ferain, and it sounded like half a question, half a statement. Her shadow was bunched close to her shoulder, formless and shifting as sea mist. "Karys, please say something."

Her tongue scraped the roof of her mouth like sandpaper. "What happened?"

"A bomb. It's taken out half the building."

Her face felt sticky and wet. Blood. She groaned, and struggled to sit up. Not her blood; she didn't feel any specific pain, only a cold, woozy heaviness spread throughout her whole body. She coughed on the dust, and pushed a splintered plank of wood off her legs. Through the haze, she could see that the explosion had torn through the wall to the corridor. Petresk was gone.

"Listen to me, okay?" said Ferain. "We need to get out of here. I don't know if the rest of the building is going to stay up."

The Veneer crackled with new death; shock seeping into the world like mud through a sieve. Over the ringing in Karys' ears, she could hear voices, screams, panicked sounds from elsewhere in the embassy, diplomats on the second floor calling out. She got to her feet unsteadily.

I should have stopped him from opening the door, she thought, and shambled toward the corridor. The opposite wall of the passage had also been blasted apart, and broken glass and rubble littered the floor. A few minutes ago, she had been standing right here, right in the centre of the storm. Blood, more blood, dark stains on the floor. Mangled body parts, unidentifiable gore, scorch marks. Karys moved toward the entrance, her legs unsteady.

The doorwoman lay flat on her back. She was clearly dead; her eyes had turned glassy, and the left side of her body was soaked in blood. Karys swallowed, and knelt at the stranger's side. She placed her hand on the woman's cheek, and drew the Veneer open.

"I didn't want to let him in."

The apparition bloomed into existence above the woman's corpse. Her body was translucent and her appearance changed like the surface of water, tangles of echoed feelings rippling and distorting her features. Where the woman had been bright-eyed and smiling, the lingering impression of her memories appeared worried. Tired.

"Hello," said Karys quietly. "Look at me."

The apparition's gaze shifted downwards. She did not seem to notice her own corpse, but her attention settled on Karys' face with a strange kind of relief, like someone offered unexpected shelter.

"I think I need to go home," she said, her tone ringing eerily flat. "This city is more than I can bear. They hate me here. They hate all of us."

"Is this . . . ?" Ferain started, and the ghost immediately flinched at the sound of his voice.

"Who's there?" she demanded. "Where am I?"

"Hush now. There's nothing here to hurt you." Karys coughed. The dust made her feel lightheaded. "It's just the two of us."

The apparition's flickering grew less erratic. "I didn't want to let him in."

"It's all right." Karys kept her voice soft and soothing, comforting. "I know you didn't. Can you describe what he looked like?"

"He was young. Tall. There was something wrong with his arm." The woman vanished for a second, and then reappeared. "Burned. The marks ran in a spiral, like a ribbon. I think he was a saint."

"How did he get inside?"

"He shoved me. I fell over, and he just walked through the gates. He was carrying a bag." Light swirled around the ghost. "I didn't want to let him in. That bag seemed wrong; he held it so close, and it seemed to move like a breathing thing. An unnatural thing. I thought the wards at the gate would repel him, but he passed right through. I couldn't stop him. The workings should have stopped him."

"You knew he meant to harm the embassy."

"I didn't want to let him in. The Mercian woman who came before was so much nicer. She looked at my art, and she said it was lovely. I told her it was safe here. But I didn't want to let him in."

"I know," Karys murmured. "It wasn't your fault; you aren't in trouble."

"I think I need to go home."

"You're going to be okay now." Karys let her fingers slide from the woman's still-warm cheek. "And your art was beautiful."

With a sigh like the wind settling amongst trees, the apparition faded. Karys brushed a hand over the dead woman's eyes, and got back to her feet. Around her, the walls creaked ominously. She could still hear movement and voices above, and an alarm bell ringing outside.

A part of her knew that she should be afraid, but instead she was detached, like the blast had knocked something out of alignment in her head. Still confused, a little sick, but mostly numb. She staggered toward the entrance. *The marks ran in a spiral, like a ribbon. I think he was a saint.* The same man she had seen on the campus yesterday. Dead now, dead like the woman and gracious Petresk. Karys coughed on the dust again, pressing her hand to her mouth.

"You're almost there," said Ferain.

Her body felt unnaturally heavy. Ahead, the front door stood open, and the grey haze turned white in the sun. She squinted against the light, fumbling forward through the scattered debris. There were dried flowers on the ground, blue petals under her feet.

Then a stranger, a woman, was helping her through the door. The lawns in front of the embassy were crowded with people.

"You all right, sweetheart?" asked the woman holding Karys' elbow. "We didn't think there was anyone left on the first floor."

People climbed down a ladder from the second storey; a few sat on the grass, pressing wads of cloth to small bleeding injuries. A man wearing a mender's sash moved between them, while a motley group of civilians stood just beyond the gate, watching with wide eyes.

"Fine," muttered Karys. "I'm fine."

"Just wait over here. The mender will help you in a minute, okay?"

Too many people. Karys felt the eyes of the crowd upon her as she emerged into the sunlight, saw them whispering. She pulled her arm free of the woman's grasp, and shook her head. "I have to go."

The woman looked confused. "You might be hurt. I really think—"

"Can't stay here." Karys backed away. "I'm sorry. I'm sorry, I can't."

She turned and pushed open the gate. The people outside automatically parted, stepping backwards as though they were afraid of touching her. Karys walked quickly through the crowd. Any of them could be with New Favour. She wiped her forehead, and her hand came away sticky and red. She shuddered. Not her blood. A row of awrigs stood outside the bank; she hobbled over to them, and fumbled for a handful of cret. Coughed again—all she could taste was plaster dust and salt. Someone in the crowd called out to her, concerned. She fed the money into the slot on the side of the vehicle, and the door popped open, and she hoisted herself up.

"Tomasia," she said, shutting the door.

The awrig hummed to life and slid forward. Karys collapsed onto the seat, breathing roughly. The dead woman's voice still echoed inside her head, and she was shaking so hard that her teeth clicked together.

She needed to talk to the Second Mayor.

11

As soon as Karys stepped down from the awrig, she knew something was wrong.

Marishka's gate stood open. The garden beyond looked ordinary—lush, well-tended, undisturbed—but a little bundle of white fur lay in the shadow of the sunflowers. Thin pink blood trickled from the dead rabbit's nose and ears.

"Shit," Karys hissed through her teeth.

"What is it?" asked Ferain.

The worked animals were meant to sense threats to the Second Mayor; they were specifically attuned to violent intent, entering a frenzied state when their mistress was in danger. Karys hurried down the path to the house, queasiness rising up from the pit of her stomach. *Someone attacked her.* The lock on the front door was shattered, like something had punched straight through the metal plate. The wood around the hole was scorched.

"Karys, wait," said Ferain urgently. "Hold on, this isn't—"

She shoved the door open.

"Marishka?" she shouted, her voice ringing through the house. "Busin?"

Her shadow produced a strangled sound. "Are you crazy?"

Her heart thrummed inside her chest. Pieces of glazed ceramic littered the floor; the coat rack lay on its side. There had been a fight here. She ignored Ferain, and moved to the kitchen. A second rabbit was dead beside the stove, its fur blindingly white in the shaft of sunlight cast through the window. More broken plates lay shattered on the tiles. A person had died nearby, she could sense it, but she was too afraid to open the Veneer. There was a tight, panicky feeling bunched up inside her—the house's silence oppressed her, pushing up against her breastbone. She stepped back into the hall, her eyes still upon the dead rabbit.

"Marishka!" she called again. "Answer me!"

"Quiet down, deathspeaker."

Karys whirled around. Busin stood in the doorway at the far end of the hall. The Toraigian offered her a wan smile. The right side of his face was heavily bruised, and his eyebrow split.

"Embrace, Busin." Her legs turned weak with relief, and she grasped the doorframe. "Were you trying to scare me to death? What happened? Where's Marishka?"

"We were a little busy, that's all. In here."

The Second Mayor was seated on a patchwork divan in the sitting room, mumbling an Ephirite-derived working over the quivering rabbit in her lap. She seemed unhurt, although rumpled and irritable; her hair askew and her expression stormy. Her foot tapped out a precise rhythm on the floor.

"She'll be with you in a moment," said Busin. "May I suggest sitting down? You look like you should."

Karys gave him an icy glare, but he merely gestured toward the couch opposite the Second Mayor.

"You're one to talk," she muttered.

"It's only a little scratch."

"You look like you got dropped."

Busin grinned. "Is it possible that you were worried about me, Death-speaker Eska? That feels like a high honour."

"Fuck off."

"As you wish, sweet lady." He bowed from the waist. "Refreshments?"

"Water. Please."

Busin retreated, still smiling. Karys sank onto the couch. She had never been in this part of the house before; she had always talked to the Second Mayor in the kitchen. The sitting room was also light and airy: the walls a cool mint-green, a collection of ferns and succulents decorating the windowsill and shelves. The furniture was worn, but well-made. Comfortable. She rested her head against the back of the couch, feeling dirty and exhausted. At least her shaking had stopped.

Marishka finished the working, and set the rabbit on the ground. She gave it an affectionate little push, and the animal hopped off toward the kitchen.

"I lost three of them," she said. "I'll have to talk to my contact at the College about acquiring more, but it'll be expensive. And I was fond of the old ones."

"Are you safe here?"

Marishka's gaze flicked up, taking in Karys' blood- and dust-stained clothing, her matted hair. "Not as safe as I believed, apparently. But I have absolutely no intention of losing face over it."

Busin returned and handed Karys a glass of water. She took it with a nod of thanks, and was surprised when he gently clapped her shoulder.

"The house is protected," he said. "There's nowhere safer in Psikamit."

"For all *that's* worth." Marishka gestured irritably for him to back off, and

Busin retreated to the wall beside the fireplace. "Doesn't say much for the rest of the city."

Karys drank from the glass. The water washed down the plaster dust in her mouth, and she grimaced. Tasted like chalk. She drained the rest in one go and wiped her mouth with the back of her hand.

"What happened?" she asked.

"A trio of saints paid an unscheduled visit. I encouraged them to leave." At her assistant's polite cough, Marishka rolled her eyes. "Busin was very encouraging too."

"But what if they come back?"

"Well, two of them won't—not unless New Favour's properly worked out necromancy."

"The Psikamit Haven had at least ten deathspeakers; they can send more."

"Then we'll be expecting them. Karys, this is hardly the first time someone's tried to kill me. It will be dealt with, and our Ephirite-worshipping friends might learn some manners in the process. Now tell me: what in the Embrace's unspoken name happened to *you*?"

Karys hesitated, then pressed her lips together and lowered her gaze.

"Are you hurt?" asked Busin.

She shook her head. She knew she needed to offer more than that, but there was nowhere to start; everything tied back to Ferain—why New Favour was after her, why she had gone to the embassy in the first place, why she needed help. Nothing came free with the Second Mayor; once her secret was uncovered, there would be a price to pay in keeping it.

Marishka let the silence grow stale, then leaned back on the couch and folded her arms, surveying Karys through lidded eyes.

"So, then. Karys Eska's little mystery." She drew out the word, breaking it into three distinct syllables, *mys-ter-y*. "Well, let's see, what do I know? I know that New Favour is looking for a Vareslian, a person who *might* have been part of a certain ambassadorial retinue, *might* be the only survivor of that retinue, and who is thought to be somewhere in the city. I know that, all of a sudden, Karys Eska is uncharacteristically willing to forfeit twenty percent of her pay in exchange for a private mender's appointment, despite her apparent excellent health."

Karys tried to interrupt, but Marishka held up one hand and went right on talking.

"I know that, after storming out of the mender's residence, she headed straight to the College, where she tracked down a scholar of Higher Biological Workings. I know that this scholar subsequently began researching, of all things, time manipulation and human-bindings." Marishka leaned her head to the side. "Must have been an interesting conversation, that one. And then—and this was the most mysterious part—I've heard that Deathspeaker Eska has started talking to herself in public."

Karys' face warmed in anger. "You had me followed?"

"Word travels, especially if you have as many friends as I do." Marishka clasped her hands over her knees. "Karys, look. I know you're in trouble, and I have a fair idea why. New Favour wouldn't be knocking down my door unless it was serious. Right?"

Karys dug her nails into her palms. She nodded.

"That being the case," said Marishka, "I'd like to make a suitable apology."

Karys instinctively glanced toward Busin, but he was as straight-faced and serious as his boss. She looked back at Marishka.

"What are you apologising for?" she asked.

"You asked for a discreet mender. Balusha was . . . not. I take full responsibility for that mistake, and have reimbursed you for the appointment."

"She talked to New Favour, didn't she?"

Here, something cold and frightening passed behind the Second Mayor's dark eyes. "Yes. I've already spoken to her, and she graciously explained the situation to me."

Karys looked at Busin again, rattled. This was not how she had expected the conversation to go; she had anticipated fighting tooth and nail for any scrap of assistance.

"Then you already know what I did?" she said.

"I can make an educated guess—but I do wish you had talked to me about it in the first place." The Second Mayor sighed. "Is this Vareslian dangerous?"

Her forthrightness felt like a trap, but Karys was too wrung out to be cautious. Her resistance crumbled.

"I don't know," she whispered.

Her shadow tensed beneath her, a movement too slight for anyone else to notice. Marishka made a noise somewhere between exasperation and sympathy.

"According to Balusha, you should be dead already," she said. "Which was the excuse she gave for selling you out, by the way. And yet, here you are. Mostly alive."

"What does New Favour want with him?"

"Unfortunately, I haven't been able to find that out. It's a strange situation. My sources indicate that orders are coming directly from the Supremes of New Favour, and the lesser saints are privy to almost nothing—they don't even know their target's name, but eliminating him has suddenly been made their highest priority. The Supremes seem to regard him as an existential threat."

Karys fought the insane urge to laugh.

"They blew up the Vareslian embassy this morning," she said.

A long pause. Marishka exchanged a glance with Busin.

"I take it you were present?" she said.

Karys looked down at the back of her hands. The dust had turned them ghostly pale. "They must have been watching the building; the explosion went off minutes after I arrived. Didn't want me talking to the diplomats, I guess. At least three people died, including the New Favour saint responsible. He was only a kid, there would have been years left before his master called his compact. I couldn't even tell where his body went; it was all . . ." She stopped, trying to get a handle on herself. Her voice still came out strained. "So they came here to ask about me?"

The Second Mayor inclined her head slightly in admission. Karys scraped her fingers through her hair.

"Sorry about your rabbits," she said hoarsely, which sounded stupid and clumsy and inadequate, but she meant it. Marishka gave a short, hard huff of a laugh, and beckoned to Busin.

"Which brings us back to *my* apology," she said. "As I said, I've already reimbursed you for the cost of the mender's appointment. But there's no question of you staying in Psikamit. You'll leave this afternoon for Miresse."

Karys felt like the wind had been knocked out of her. "I—"

"Sometimes I need to make decisions in my people's best interests— regardless of whether they approve or not." Marishka took an envelope from Busin. "New Favour will be watching the harbour and the trains, but I can get you onto the Silkess unseen."

Her stomach turned. "Not Miresse."

"You don't need to *stay* in the town," said Marishka impatiently. "Wait a few weeks, then take a train to Copata or Verlore. Somewhere remote, more conservative, somewhere New Favour is unwelcome. Lay low, find a new job—"

"And when people discover I'm a deathspeaker, I'll be just as unwelcome," said Karys. "I can't go back to Miresse. Psikamit is the only place I can find *work*."

"Right now, work is the least of your worries. You need to disappear, and you need to do it quickly."

But I don't have time to start over. There was a hot, painful tightness in

Karys' chest. It had taken almost a decade to establish herself in Psikamit, and she would be lucky if she had three years left before Sabaster called her compact. She could feel the time slipping away from her, like she was sliding into a sea of mud; her one slender lifeline pulled further and further out of reach.

Some of her despair must have shown on her face, because Marishka's expression softened.

"I do understand, Karys," she said. "Busin and I have talked about it, and we'll do what we can for you."

It's not enough. It will never be enough.

"Karys," murmured Ferain.

She shook her head.

"I know you don't want to go back," said Marishka. "Embrace, I don't blame you. But be smart about this."

She held out the envelope, and there was a light of pity in her eyes. Karys' mouth twisted in bitterness. *Don't look at me like that.*

"Varesli," she said.

Marishka's eyebrows drew together.

"I'll go to Miresse." Karys forced herself to reach out and take the envelope. "But from there, I'll cross the border into Varesli. Head east, make my way to Eludia. New Favour won't easily follow me, and if anyone can counter the Bhatuma workings I've entangled, it'll be a Vareslian."

Busin made a sound in the back of his throat. "If you think you'll be unwelcome in Copata . . ."

"I know. But I don't have much of a choice."

And it felt less like surrender.

Marishka gave another heavy sigh. She rubbed her forehead, and then made a small, dismissive movement of her shoulders.

"You won't get in at the border post," she said.

"No."

"Which means you'll need a guide."

"I can pay."

"Not with your savings, you can't." The Second Mayor scowled. "I have *some* influence in Miresse. Enough to ask for a favour, not enough to guarantee a free crossing. At best, I'll be able to lower the cost, but the rest will be on you. Are you sure about this?"

Karys nodded.

Marishka's mouth went hard. It looked like she wanted to say something more: to ask a question, or perhaps admonish Karys, tell her that this would all be a stupid, wasteful risk. She seemed angry. Karys did not shrink from the older woman's gaze, but, tired and aching, she sank lower on the couch.

"It might not work," she murmured. "But I have to try."

Marishka held silent a few seconds longer. When she spoke, her tone was brusque and impersonal.

"Very well," she said. "I'll do what I can. Go clean up your face in the bathroom down the hall. You'll leave in ten minutes."

Karys barely had time to rinse the blood from her hair and brush the worst of the dust from her clothes before Busin was bustling her out of the house. The dead rabbit's body had been removed from the garden, but its blood still darkened the earth, and the street was quiet. Karys glanced back toward the door, looking for Marishka, wanting to say goodbye, but the Second Mayor was nowhere to be seen. Busin swept her into the awrig waiting on the road, and climbed in after her. He gave an address near the harbour, and the vehicle hummed forward.

Karys slumped on the bench. Everything was moving more quickly than she could follow. It might have been the shock of the explosion at the embassy, but her head felt muddy and slow, her body drained. Committed, now, to this course. Her stomach turned.

The awrig stopped at the doors of an old warehouse in Scuttlers. Busin got out and spoke to the woman manning the entrance, then beckoned Karys inside.

"We're sending you up in one of our shipping crates," he said, voice low. "It might be a few hours yet, but I'll need to leave you here—other matters to attend to."

The warehouse's interior was dim, and smelled of brine. Karys blinked as her eyes adjusted. "Of course."

Busin briefly touched her shoulder. "You'll be expected in Miresse. And afterwards, when all of this has been dealt with, and your big job comes in . . ."

She nodded. "Thanks, Busin."

"Always a pleasure, my lady."

Along with the woman at the door, Busin helped Karys into one of the large wooden crates of delicacies bound for Upside; she crouched among bottles of reef-wine, tubs of iced oysters, and cold butter-baked sweetfish while they nailed the lid shut. As he left, Busin knocked against the side of the crate thrice for luck.

Then Karys waited.

It could have been two hours, perhaps three. Despite the tight, dark confines of the crate, she was not uncomfortable, and she dozed, snapping back awake with every loud noise. Her shadow was silent. Eventually, Karys heard voices, and the floor lurched underneath her as the crate was loaded onto a cargo vehicle. Between the gaps in the wooden planks, she saw white daylight.

Through Downside again. The crate was lifted from the vehicle at the base of the scale wall, and transferred onto one of the great hands. Karys hunched low and quiet inside, listening to the wind swirling up the cliffs. At the top of the wall, more movement, more voices. The lid was pried off the crate, and two of Marishka's people let her out, packing her straight into another waiting awrig.

The whole operation was smooth and seamless, perfectly coordinated. No one spoke to her.

Alone in the new vehicle, Karys stretched out her stiffened legs. To her left, she could see the curve of the bay and the sweep of Downside. To her right, rolling countryside. She felt like a stranger to the city already. The violent upheaval had left her hollowed out, numb to the world—in some oblique, unintelligible way, she had the sense that she was merely going through the motions of her own escape.

"Who was she?"

Ferain's voice was soft, her shadow melding with the darkness inside the awrig. They were the first words he had spoken since Marishka's house.

"The woman back there? Marishka? She seemed . . ." He paused. "She seemed to care about you an awful lot."

Karys shrugged.

"Are you related?"

"No." The idea was faintly ludicrous. "I've known Marishka for a few years, that's all. She runs most of the smuggling operations out of Psikamit."

"You told me you aren't a smuggler."

"Doesn't mean I can't be hired by one." Karys ran her thumb across her lips. "Marishka's . . . complicated. She keeps order in Downside, does a lot for those that no one else will help. People rely on her; that's why she's called the Second Mayor. But at the end of the day, everyone's expendable to her."

"I'm sorry."

"I don't lose sleep over it."

"No, not—I'm sorry. About today." Ferain's voice dropped. "About what happened at the embassy."

Karys shrugged again. She returned her gaze to the view out the window.

"Me too," she said.

To the east, the lighthouse's etherbulb revolved, sweeping a sickly green beam through the mid-afternoon sunshine. The Psikamit Silkess Station stood a tasteful distance from the edge of Newtown—near enough to be convenient, but not so close as to be visible, tucked into a small fold in the hills east of the district. She would be early; the first spider only arrived at four o'clock. Marishka had a contact at the station office, a man who overlooked the goods she regularly sent inland. He would not ask questions, even if Karys bore no resemblance to the Silkess's usual passengers.

The awrig coasted to a gentle stop in front of the station steps. The building had a heavy, industrial look; the windows were small, and the walls a flat, plastered grey. A sign over the front door bore New Favour's star-of-arrows insignia. The saints were not involved in the day-to-day running of the transport hub, but they had been instrumental in its founding, and still demanded a cut of the profits. Karys opened the awrig door and stepped down.

The doorman proved thoroughly uninterested, and waved her through without even a cursory inspection of her hastily forged identification documents. Inside, worked terracotta heaters glowed orange against the walls, and the air was warm and stuffy. The interior shared the same utilitarian quality as the exterior—New Favour had never cared about appearances. A lone man sat inside the ticket office on the far side of the foyer. He looked up from his novel, and raised an eyebrow.

"I'm in the spice trade," said Karys carefully.

For a moment, she was not sure the man recognised Marishka's phrase, but then he nodded. "Travelling light?"

"They're expensive spices." She handed him the envelope containing her ticket. He accepted it without even opening the seal.

"You've got about an hour's wait," he said. "The lounge is down the corridor on the left."

As she had hoped, she was one of the only travellers that afternoon. Karys adjusted her bag over her shoulders, and walked across the lounge to the benches on the far side of the room. A few merchants gathered around the windows, but none of them looked her way. Just as well—between her faded, rumpled clothing and her bleary-eyed fatigue, she felt painfully out of place. She lowered herself onto one of the empty seats, and set her bag down on the floor.

New Favour might not have seen her leave after the bomb went off. They might think her dead, Ferain eliminated, and their bloody task finished. There was a jittery feeling in Karys' teeth. She could not quite believe that, but it was possible. Maybe no one was hunting her at all.

It would be better once she had departed. She closed her eyes briefly.

Goodbye to Psikamit, probably forever. She never had paid Carillo the rent she owed. Back to Miresse, and then . . . and then Varesli. If everything went well. Thinking too far ahead gave her the same sinking-in-mud sensation she had experienced earlier. It was an insane risk. If Ferain had lied, if the deal wasn't real . . . well, she would be left with absolutely nothing, stranded in a country that despised her existence. Embrace, she barely knew the man. He could easily be stringing her along—in his position, she could hardly even blame him.

The idea made her feel cold. Karys wrapped her arms across her chest. *What are my alternatives? Wait for New Favour to find me? Hide in Copata until Sabaster comes to collect?* No, the damage was already done. And maybe contestation would rip her apart before they even reached the border. *That would simplify things, I guess.* She gazed around the room morosely.

The lounge's wall of glass windows overlooked the web outside, where the luminescent strands of the Veneer were visible to the naked eye—the places where the Ephirite had ripped unreality right into the mortal dimension, and wound it tight like spun yarn. Each thread was between three and eight feet wide, and they clustered down to a single mass at the centre of the tangle: a colossal, iridescent nest. The further from the core, the fainter the strands grew, until they faded from sight at the edges of the station grounds. Taken as a whole, it was pretty, but looking at the glowing mass for too long caused the hills to shudder and twitch in Karys' vision.

"Someone's coming your way," said Ferain. "Don't react."

Despite the warning, she automatically tensed and turned her head toward the door. A short brunette woman with olive skin was heading straight for the benches where she sat. The stranger walked quickly; she appeared flustered and out of breath, her messy curls tangled around her face. Over one arm, she carried a large shoulder bag. A couple of the merchants glanced at her with interest. Karys averted her eyes, trying to look unconcerned, even though her heart rate sped up. *That bag.* The doorwoman at the embassy said that the saint had carried a bag. It could not be happening again, not now, not—

The woman stopped right in front of her. "Karys?"

Karys blinked, and looked up. She had never seen the stranger before, but her voice was oddly familiar.

"It's me," said the woman. "I'm wearing a guise, that's all. Sorry. My appearance draws attention, so I wear it when I need to be more inconspicuous."

"Oh, you can't be serious," muttered Ferain.

Karys' mouth went dry. "Winola?"

"I was worried I would be late." The scholar sat down on the opposite bench.

She wore a brown tailored coat, cut in sharply at the waist, and a powder-blue blouse with silver embroidery at the neck. Although there were certain similarities to her real features, based on her appearance, Karys would never have recognised the woman beneath the worked disguise.

"What are you doing here?" she asked under her breath.

"I believe," Winola paused to consult a pocket watch from her breast pocket, "that I'm travelling to Miresse."

"Why?"

"Because that's where you're going."

"Do you remember this woman was harassing pigeons?" mumbled Ferain. "Because, in retrospect, that was probably a sign."

Karys hunched lower on the bench.

"What do my movements have to do with you?" she asked Winola.

The scholar leaned forward. Her hair looked newly washed, still damp, and smelled like lilacs. Her nails were painted a blushing pink.

"Because I think I can help you," she said, and then offered a quick, nervous laugh. "And you represent the most exciting research opportunity of my career."

Karys did not return the scholar's smile. "You don't understand the situation, and you shouldn't be here."

"You know, I spoke to Busin, and to his frankly rather frightening employer." Winola glanced toward the window. "They suggested I accompany you. Oh, and I'm supposed to give you this."

"What do you mean they—"

Winola opened her bag, and pulled out a cheaply made storm-grey coat. She handed it to Karys.

"'From Marishka,'" she said. "Nothing special. She said you wouldn't have much clothing for the journey, given that you're leaving in a hurry."

Karys turned the coat over. Copper-coloured fasteners ran from the neck to the waist of the garment. "What is—"

"Eludia has some of the best libraries in the world." The scholar seemed intent on talking over her. "Not all the material is accessible to the public, but when it comes to resources about Bhatuma workings theory, the city is incomparable."

"Keep your voice down!" hissed Karys.

"Give me a week there, and I'll be able to work out the exact nature of your predicament. In the meantime, maybe I can help you manage any . . . symptoms, I suppose. You haven't encountered any new difficulties since we last spoke?"

"No, but that doesn't—"

"Oh look!" said Winola, pointing. "She's coming in."

The strands of the nest glowed brighter, lighting up the valley with rainbows of shifting colour. The light was coalescing, gathering at the heart of the web. Then the whole mass *quivered*. A spear of darkness split the luminescence as the Silkess extended one leg into the web. A second leg followed, and the creature rippled into the station.

Karys had never seen one of the Ephirite's dimension-phasing spiders before, but she had read about them. None of those descriptions, however, had given her any sense of the sheer scale of the creatures. It dwarfed the building; each shadowy leg had to be at least forty feet tall, and the Silkess's body was probably a hundred feet long—although that was harder to see; its extremities seemed to phase and shift at a distance. Despite its size, it moved with a perfect, eerie silence. Once it had fully emerged from the Veneer, the spider lowered itself nearer the ground and then grew still again, awaiting its passengers.

"In all honesty, I've always been a little arachnophobic," said Winola, picking up her bag. She smiled brightly. "Shall we?"

CHAPTER

12

Boarding the Silkess proved simple. Karys followed the station attendants down to the rear entrance of the building, and was ushered along a covered pathway to the base of the creature's crouched body. Close to the web, the air crackled with arcane power, making her hair stand on end. The spider itself was still as stone, and Karys received the unpleasant impression that it was lying in wait for prey.

Winola, despite her stated arachnophobia, walked cheerfully toward it. The other passengers seemed similarly unperturbed, engaged in their own conversations and barely sparing the spider a second glance. Karys tried to act like them, pretending that the unnatural monster was unremarkable to her.

The Silkess's open mouth formed the entrance to the passenger lodgings, where the path cut between the spider's huge chelicerae. More uniformed attendants smiled and welcomed guests inside. The temperature within was a few degrees warmer, and the air held a faintly acidic odour. A tall, milk-skinned man escorted Karys and Winola down the tract of the Silkess's gullet. The flexible tissue of the creature's mouth gave way to polished burr walnut floorboards. Crystal chandeliers hung from the dark ceiling of the corridor.

"We should reach our destination by tomorrow morning," the man explained. "If there is anything you require, please don't hesitate to call on myself or one of the other attendants."

He explained the dining arrangements and safety regulations, which mostly prohibited attempting to leave the spider at any time after departure. Karys tried to pay attention, but she felt distracted, disorientated by the Silkess's strangeness. Within the confines of its body, the Veneer lay flat and inert; like the creature was a hole in the fabric of the world.

"And here are your quarters, cas," the man announced.

He opened a door off the main corridor. Beyond was a sumptuously appointed room; a large bed dressed in soft linen, plush red carpets the colour of new blood, woven tapestries hanging from the walls. A second door led to a private bathroom.

I'll be staying here? thought Karys.

"If you'd like to get settled, we'll be leaving in five minutes." The man turned to Winola. "Your rooms are just this way, cas."

Karys stepped inside the room and shut the door behind her. Covered-lamps coloured the walls in a mild, comfortable yellow, and fresh white roses stood in silver vases on each of the sideboards. The curtains were drawn over the window.

"It's so clean," she said aloud, without quite meaning to.

"Low standards."

She started, then glowered at her shadow. Ferain raised his hands.

"It's very nice," he said, voice too-smooth.

"You're mocking me."

"I wouldn't dare."

Outside, a bell chimed. They were leaving Psikamit. Karys sat down on the edge of the bed. The floor did not seem to move at all. She had expected to feel the spider's footfalls, but no. Not so much as a tremor. A crushing weariness settled over her limbs.

"I'm going to sleep for a while," she said. "Will you wake me if anything happens?"

Her shadow leaned toward the window, peering through the tiny gap between the curtains. "Sure. Of course."

Karys took off her shoes and her new coat, and lay back on the pristine bedding. The sheets were smooth and cool and soft—*like being hugged by clouds,* she thought—and she closed her eyes and immediately fell asleep.

She wasn't sure exactly how much time passed, but when she woke she no longer felt thick-headed. Her shadow pooled on the floor next to the bed, as if Ferain was sitting on the carpet there.

"Winola slipped a note under the door," he said. "Are you feeling better?"

Karys nodded, brushing her hair out of her face. With a groan, she stretched her arms above her head and cracked the joints in her shoulders. "I don't know why I was so tired."

"Last night can't have been comfortable."

"Even so. How did you know it was Winola outside?"

"I looked underneath the door. Don't worry, I was subtle about it."

Karys got up and padded across the carpet. She pulled back the Veneer a fraction. The folded sheet of paper on the floor had a little working stitched in; a Bhatuma derivation that caused the ink to sparkle. Nothing dangerous. She picked up the note and opened it. Winola's handwriting was small and neat, her signature an elegant, shimmering flourish.

Dinner is at eight o'clock. Meet me there?

"Hungry?" asked Ferain, reading over her shoulder.

She was. Karys put the note down on the pedestal table by the door. "I want to clean up first."

The bathroom was tiled in white and muted bronze, and the tub was surrounded by a ring of candles. A pitcher of wine rested on the basin, next to four crystal flutes. Before taking off her clothing, Karys checked her shadow. Ferain was already stretched right out the door.

For a Vareslian, his manners aren't terrible, she thought.

She stripped out of her dust-stained shirt and trousers, and stepped into the tub, turning the taps. It was easy to forget she was inside a living creature; the floor did not move, and hot water ran clear and steaming from the faucet. Karys had no idea what kind of workings allowed for that, but it seemed a ludicrous extravagance; her ticket must have cost a fortune. Of course, chances were that the Second Mayor hadn't actually paid the full amount in cret, but the fare still represented a whole host of favours and risks. It was uncomfortable: the idea that Marishka had gone so far on her account.

Unbidden, an image of the dead rabbits returned to Karys' mind. She shivered, and her eyes wandered back toward the entrance of the bathroom.

"Ferain?"

"Yes?"

"When the explosion went off at the embassy, why did I survive?"

He was quiet for a second, not moving. Then he asked: "What do you mean?"

"I was less than ten feet from Petresk. He was gone, completely, and I was—" She faltered, and her voice dropped. "I was too close. I think I should be dead."

Her shadow twitched, like a ripple cast by a stone on still water. "Sometimes it's just luck. Who lives, who dies."

She reached to close the tap. "This was different, I was too—"

She paused, her hand outstretched.

"What is it?" asked Ferain.

The Split Lapse scar that had previously sat squarely in the centre of her palm had shifted across the base of her hand, covering a little of her wrist crease. She drew her arm back toward her, studying the mark. It looked identical otherwise, the same ghostly impression of tiny glyphs and described permissions, but it had slid up half an inch. She wasn't sure when that might have happened.

"Karys?"

She shook herself and turned off the tap. "Never mind."

The dining room was small, but lavish. Painted wooden screens divided the tables, and rings of tiny copper lanterns hung above them. The chairs were shaped from solid blocks of wood, and the knotholes worked with bronze so that the tree rings shone. Winola was already seated at a table set out for two, swilling a glass of white wine between her fingers. She was wearing her earlier guise, but had changed into a different outfit: a black and mauve one-piece with a high neckline and shimmering gold beadwork across the shoulders. Karys warily sat down opposite her, conscious of her own shabby clothing. Winola replaced her wine glass on the table.

"Have you recovered since we left?" she asked. "You seemed exhausted earlier."

"I'm fine now."

"Good. That's good." The scholar paused as an attendant materialised with two bowls of amber-coloured broth. The woman set them down on the table with a small flourish, and then retreated. Winola waited until she was out of earshot before speaking again. "I think it would be wise to avoid discussing your condition in too much detail. The Silkess, after all, being owned by certain interests . . ."

Karys couldn't help smiling.

"I'm not stupid," she said.

The scholar coloured instantly. "I didn't think you were."

Karys dipped her spoon into the soup. She guessed it was some sort of seafood—but when she tasted it, the flavour was like rain and clean air, like she had placed something sacred on her tongue. She tried not to let her surprise show, carefully laying the spoon down again.

"So you're friends with Busin?" she said.

Winola's blush deepened by a few degrees.

"It's a terrible stereotype, really," she said, "but you know how Toraigians are all supposed to know one another? Everyone related to everyone else?"

Karys nodded. It was the subject of many crude Mercian jokes.

"Well, his uncle was my father's mentor about forty years ago, which makes us honorary cousins. Not that it matters much outside of home—and there aren't many Toraigians in Psikamit, so we all know one another anyway."

"And he told you where to find me."

"He contacted me unexpectedly after our conversation yesterday, and warned me to be careful around you. I found that disturbing, so I went to see him in person after today's morning lectures. One thing led to another."

Karys still struggled to believe that either Busin or Marishka could have suggested Winola follow her to Varesli—let alone that the scholar would actually do it. From the chamber next door, she could hear cooks moving around the kitchen. She picked up her spoon again and turned it over between her fingers.

"You look worried," said Winola.

Karys shook her head. "Mostly confused. I don't know why you're here."

"I told you: I think I can help."

"Well, I'm confused why you would want to."

"Because it feels like the honourable thing to do, I suppose."

"Right. Your moral code." Karys took another spoon of the broth. "You see me as some kind of charitable cause?"

"No." Winola moved her hand to the bridge of her nose as if she wanted to adjust her glasses, despite the fact that the guise wore none. "It's more that I need to live by certain principles in order to justify myself. On some level, my actions are entirely selfish."

"Justify yourself?"

The scholar had an ironic smile on her face, something slightly crooked. "It's complicated. But yes. If I have the power to use workings to help someone, I consider it my solemn duty to do so."

"Sounds exhausting."

"Most of the time, I find it fulfilling."

"So she's clever, pretty, *and* admirable," whispered Ferain, and Karys made a mental note to triple her travel expenses.

"I still don't understand what you mean by justifying yourself," she said.

Winola sighed. She looked down at her soup for a moment.

"I guess it's a displaced sense of obligation," she said. "I abandoned my home to pursue my ambitions. I want to believe the choice I made was right, so I need to . . . prove that. By my actions."

"You feel guilty?"

The scholar's gaze remained on her bowl. "It isn't so clear cut as that. I left Toraigus because changing it demanded too much and compensated too little, and I wasn't prepared to devote my whole life to the possibility of incremental progress. I *wanted* more, knew that I could offer more, but not behind the Wall. And there were other considerations, of course—it wasn't only about the pursuit of workings. At home, I would have been expected to marry a man in order to further my family line, and the thought of that was, well . . ." A small shudder. "Not for me. Staying in Toraigus meant sacrificing both my intellectual ambitions and my personal desires, and, in the end, I was unwilling to stomach either. So I left. It might not have been the brave thing to do, or the right thing to do, but it was the choice I made."

Her calm, level voice had gained a touch of defensiveness toward the end. Karys wavered for a second, then reached out and picked up her own wine glass.

"Suits me," she said.

Winola laughed, and looked up. "Good."

The attendant's reappearance with their next course halted the conversation. Steaming florets of young broccoli; a flaked pastry stuffed with white cheese, leeks, sage, and quail; cumin-spiced lamb with a dark, sweetish glaze; bright orange squash seasoned with cinnamon. Karys' mouth watered. The attendant smiled, apparently amused by the expression on her face, and returned to the kitchen.

"It looks good," said Ferain wistfully.

Karys tried to restrain herself, carefully cutting into the pastry.

"What is Toraigus like?" she asked. "I've always wondered."

Winola wiped her mouth with the corner of a napkin. She seemed more relaxed now, her posture less upright.

"Next to Mercia? Small," she said. "You can travel the length of the island in a day. The climate is a little cooler, and it's more difficult to grow crops with the sea on all sides, but people manage; they look out for one another. The community is very close, very insular and tradition-bound, which can be comforting on one day and suffocating the next. That's just the culture of the place."

"I've heard that once you leave, you're never allowed to go back."

The scholar nodded. "Yes. In Toraigian, the word for the act of departing home actually translates to 'self-banishment.'"

"No exceptions?"

"No exceptions." She paused to take a bite of her lamb. "Once you leave the shadow of the Unbroken Wall, you leave it for good. Theoretically, the inverse applies too—if an outsider moved to Toraigus, they would be permanently confined to the island thereafter—but that situation almost never arises. The restrictions are intended to preserve the Wall's sanctity; they're taken very seriously."

Karys pushed her food around her plate.

"Did you ever try to perform a working in Toraigus?" she asked.

"Never."

The quail inside the pastry was perfectly cooked, tender and pale pink. "Were you tempted?"

"I wouldn't have possessed the means, but no. The possibility that I might damage the Wall was always too frightening." Winola's expression turned rueful. "In all likelihood, I would have been far enough from the physical structure to avoid undermining the workings exclusion zone it generates, but there's no way of knowing where those borders lie from the inside. As much as I found workings fascinating in theory, I would never have risked my home's national security trying to perform them. Why the interest?"

Karys raised and lowered her shoulders, starting on her orange squash. "Trying to imagine what it would be like to live entirely without workings, that's all."

"Oh, it's easier than most people believe," said the scholar. "Besides, you seldom miss what you've never had."

They both fell quiet for a while after that, but the silence was comfortable. Karys ate everything on her plate; Winola did not quite finish her food. When the attendant returned to clear the table, the scholar thanked the woman, and told her that, although the meal had been lovely, she was too full for dessert.

"In that case, would you like us to package a serving for you?" asked the woman politely. "All food is included in the fare."

"If it's no trouble?"

"None at all."

"Could you do the same for me, please?" added Karys quickly.

"With pleasure, cas," said the attendant, again with a small smile. "I'll have it delivered to your room."

Winola finished the last of her wine, and they left the dining room together shortly afterwards. The scholar seemed thoughtful and a little distracted, toying with her bracelets absentmindedly as she walked. She did not appear upset, exactly, but Karys wondered whether talking about Toraigus had bothered her. Pressed against old wounds. They said goodnight in the long, wood-panelled corridor, and Karys returned to her own quarters alone.

While she had been at dinner, someone had lit the lamps on the bedside tables and rearranged the pillows. The room was warm and inviting; the walls radiated a subtle heat. Her coat hung neatly on a hanger in the wardrobe. Karys closed the door to the passage, and her shadow spooled out over the floor with a sigh.

"Before all of this, I really took food for granted," he said.

Karys crossed to the windows and drew the curtain back. The world beyond was a grey and silver haze, a nowhereland outside mortal dimensions. She could see the long, hairlike setae of the spider's abdomen, the thin black strands quivering in the grey.

"What do you make of Winola?" she asked.

Her shadow stretched like a cat, then fell back to her side.

"Well, I wouldn't underestimate her," he said. "The guise she's wearing is close to flawless. At the Foreign Ministry, they have been trying to produce similar temporary appearance modifications for years—from what I understand, it takes considerable skill to work something even half as effective."

Should you be telling me that? "You think she's dangerous?"

"I think she's very good at workings. That could be dangerous, and it could be useful." His tone turned arch. "What did *you* think of her?"

Karys let the corner of the curtain drop. "I'm not sure."

"Are you going to start talking about long-term investments again?"

She gave her shadow a withering stare, and then walked away from the window, sitting down on the bed and kicking off her shoes.

"I believe Winola wants to help," she said. "I just don't know if she can."

A knock on the door signalled the arrival of an attendant bearing her dessert, beautifully packaged in ivory card and bound with a cream-coloured ribbon. Karys took the box, and the man withdrew, bidding her pleasant sleep. She set it down on the sideboard, touching the end of the ribbon.

"Pretty," remarked Ferain.

"The Silkess fare must cost a fortune," she muttered. She carefully untied the knot and opened the flap. Inside were two perfect, identical tarts: golden pastry shells filled with segments of glazed tangerine half-submerged in a pale orange cream. Curls of yellow spun sugar domed the top of the dessert.

"Seems like they're trying to provide your money's worth," said her shadow.

Tiny beads of icing dotted the peak of each sliver of tangerine, bright white and shining. *Too lovely for me to eat,* Karys thought. She shook herself, and quickly closed the box again, feeling oddly flustered.

"If you were part of the diplomatic retinue, then you've seen Toraigus?" she said.

Ferain did not seem perturbed by the abrupt change of topic.

"Not exactly," he replied. "There's a meeting ground for trade in the Wall's shadow, where Toraigian representatives can talk to outsiders without banishing themselves. That's where we were docked."

"Stay long?"

"About a month. It's an interesting place: old, ceremonial. When we arrived, everyone in the retinue had to partake in a three-hour fellowship ritual before we were even allowed to speak to their delegates." His voice softened. "They treated us kindly, though. Invited us to return—this was only the preparatory trip; Ambassador Corbain intended to establish a permanent Vareslian office in the trading ground. Everyone was in high spirits when we left. Now . . . now they're gone."

Karys said nothing. Ferain shivered, and seemed to gather himself.

"Sorry," he said. "That wasn't what you asked, I—"

"Can you write your Ministry a letter?" she interrupted. "Or tell me what to write; I'll do it."

The angles of her shadow lost their tension. Ferain breathed out.

"You're willing?" he said.

"Nothing that identifies me, nothing that mentions me at all. We can send it from Miresse via Worked Dispatch tomorrow."

"Of course. No mention of you at all."

Karys dropped backwards onto the bed. Her shadow stretched and settled against the wall, completely at odds with the light in the room. The wrongness stuck out at her like a thorn lodged underneath her skin, irritating and faintly repulsive.

"It could start a war," she said. "What New Favour has done. I can see that."

"The Ministry will want to stop the situation from escalating."

"Out of the goodness of their hearts?"

"Out of the fear that Varesli would lose."

She snorted, but found herself glad that Ferain had not denied the danger outright. She knew that he held his own agenda, knew that he must be desperate to send word of the attack to Varesli—he had originally offered the Split Lapse for nothing but the hope she might carry his warning to the embassy. It was important to him. And yet he had not pressured her about the issue since, not once.

On the one hand, she respected his restraint. On the other, she had the sneaking suspicion he was simply getting better at manipulating her.

Getting softer every day, she thought. Well, if she couldn't go home, if Ferain was her gamble, and she was committed anyway . . . Karys scrunched up her face, and pressed her hand to her forehead.

"The scar moved," she said.

"Excuse me?"

Still flat on her back, she raised her other arm, turning it palm-side up. Ferain shifted closer.

"I hope you have a good theory about this," she said. "Because I don't."

He was silent for a few seconds. A finger of shadow touched the mark, and although Karys didn't feel anything, she still flinched.

"When did you notice the change?" he asked, drawing back a little.

"Before dinner. Seems bad, doesn't it?

"Seems . . . strange. Does it hurt at all?"

"No."

"Strange," he murmured again, like he was talking to himself. Karys dropped her arm back to the bed.

"You really believe your father can fix this?" she asked.

Ferain considered the question.

"I don't think we'll get the Lapse open without him," he said. "Or at least, not without his notes."

"But that's only half the problem. You'll still be dying."

"True. But solving half the problem's better than none of it, right?"

Karys sighed.

"Eludia is our best chance," he said, and it sounded like he was smiling. "I believe that."

Certainty would have been nice, though. Karys sat up again.

"All right," she said. "Tell me what to write to your Ministry."

CHAPTER

13

Miresse had not changed. The town was older and slower than Psikamit, scarcely a tenth the size, and it still possessed the same cold dustiness that Karys remembered—a taste in the air, a dry feeling on the back of the tongue, fine sand in the wind.

Eleven years ago, she had boarded a freight train bound for Psikamit, vowing never to return to this place. Yet, here she was. Right back where she had started.

They arrived at the Silkess station in the chill early morning. Attendants ushered passengers back out the spider's mouth and through the building; Karys followed the thin stream of people past the waiting area. New Favour's office stood empty and dark beside the ticket desk. No Haven in Miresse; there wasn't sufficient demand for deathspeakers in eastern Mercia, and so saints only came to the town when they were specifically commissioned. They had less influence here, less control. That knowledge should have been a comfort, but Karys didn't feel any safer.

No one is going to recognise you, idiot, she thought, hunching her shoulders. *It's been too long.*

Winola seemed in a comparatively good mood; she had purchased a map of the town from a vendor at the station. She studied it as she walked, unaware of Karys' discomfort.

"Did you know that there is a ruined Sanctum in the area?" she asked. "The heralds in this region were fairly obscure; I've never heard of 'Swask' before, but apparently he ruled a stretch of the Korasis River between the Lezas Basin in Varesli and the Mercian coast. According to this, his common aspect had twelve phalluses, which honestly seems a little excessive to me—but it's interesting that the less powerful Bhatuma often tended toward greater personal ornamentation. Compensating, I suppose."

Karys grunted.

"Twelve," Winola repeated, smiling to herself. "It's almost charming."

A row of dusty awrigs waited in the yard outside the station. The low, dun-coloured hills stood still and blank in the early light, and patchy thorn trees grew crooked from the dry soil on either side. Miresse lay ahead; the town's buildings gathered in an ugly sprawl around the river. Winola folded up her map, and they climbed into one of the vehicles. Karys spoke the name of Miresse's better inn, and the awrig hummed forward over the dirt track.

Once they were moving, Winola raised one hand to the space just in front of her left eyebrow, and adjusted something small and invisible. Her guise unravelled with a disturbing sound, like a seamstress ripping a bolt of cloth. Her appearance spiralled, the real and unreal splitting into two distinct layers, and then she was herself again. She lowered her fingers from the rim of her glasses.

"Much better," she said. "Wearing it for too long makes me itchy."

"Ask if she made that guise herself," said Ferain.

Karys folded her arms. "You'll stand out in Miresse too, you know. Probably more than in Psikamit."

"That's fine." Winola waved her map. "I'll tell people that I'm sightseeing. A historical tour of the Mercian countryside."

"Karys, ask her if she—"

Nuliere alive. "My reeker problem wants to know if you made the guise yourself."

Winola blinked. "Oh. I, uh, yes. I did. Is he here now?"

"Unfortunately, yes. He never leaves."

"Oh," the scholar said again, clearly disconcerted. She shifted in her seat. "So, the whole time . . . ?"

"Ever since he woke up."

"That seems intrusive."

"I'm still here," said Ferain.

"He wants you to know that he's still present."

Winola regained her composure somewhat. "Of course, yes. My apologies. I don't know why I never considered . . . but yes. How interesting. We should test your capabilities, work out the parameters of this situation. I'll give that some thought. The last few days can't have been easy for you either." She dug into her bag, fishing out a tattered notebook from the side. "Perhaps we should start with some basic questions."

By the time the awrig reached the centre of town, the scholar had filled several pages with cramped notes about Ferain's experience of disembodiment, which Karys had to recount sentence by sentence. He also demonstrated his ability to move her shadow—causing the scholar to yelp in alarm—and laid out what he knew about the Split Lapse and proximal overlay.

"Tied to your shadow," said Winola, head down and scribbling furiously. "Might flexibly align to the size of the dimension generated by the Lapse;

we'll need to test that. Seems like a projection, rather than a purely physical manifestation, so not genuine respiration but the expectation of it—an active mind warping reality to fill in the accustomed absences, while the body remains inert and bound. Oh, I didn't think of *that*."

"Is 'that' bad news?" asked Karys.

Winola shook her head, still writing. "Matters of perception can be radically reorganised."

Karys privately prided herself on her hard-won grasp of workings theory— but even she had no idea what that statement meant in context.

"Okay," she said.

The awrig grumbled to a stop on the commons outside the Orago Inn. The sight of the familiar double-storey building jarred Karys more than she had expected; it felt as though she had been doused in cold, dark water, tides pulling at her legs, dragging her into the past. She clenched her jaw. Winola stuck her notebook back into her bag, and opened the awrig door.

"There's an errand I need to run," said Karys.

Winola paused, and cocked her head to one side. "Alone?"

"It shouldn't take too long." Karys picked up her box of desserts and held them out to the scholar. "Can you keep this safe for me? I'll be back in an hour."

The awrig carried her over the dried-up canals of the town and down to the western side of Miresse. She got off the vehicle past the old tanneries, and went on foot from there. Seven o'clock in the morning, and the streets were quiet; only a handful of people wandered the grey-paved roads. A hollow-cheeked boy rattled his begging bowl from the corner. A cool day to mark the change of season—the sky had clouded over, and the breeze rippled clothing strung from lines stretched between apartment buildings.

Eleven years. Eleven years, and it all looked the same. Karys didn't know what else she had expected. While Winola had been chattering away about workings in the awrig, it had been easier to ignore the town, but now it all felt much closer. Unsettling. Every road, every worn-out building and tight alleyway, she knew them all; she could have traversed Miresse in her sleep. Even people's voices, the passing strains of their clipped rural accents, seemed strange, seemed to flatten and compress the world around her.

"Why don't you like it here?" asked Ferain.

Karys flinched, his voice yanking her back to the present. Her shadow matched her movements with mirror precision, falling in perfect step at her feet. She felt the uncanny weight of Ferain's focussed attention. While not unfriendly, it seemed uncomfortably acute.

"Ever since we left the Silkess, you've been nervous and angry," he said. "Why?"

"None of your concern," she muttered.

"I thought you might be in a bad mood because of something I did, but that's not it."

Karys turned up her collar against the wind.

"Do I need to be worried?"

"You need," she said under her breath, "to talk less."

Her shadow made an exasperated sound.

On first inspection, Temius Rasko's house was unremarkable. The drab little building stood apart from its neighbours; its garden cleared of everything but nettle and weeds. Most of the windows had been boarded over; if Karys had not known better, she might have assumed the place abandoned. Hundreds of lumpen wasp nests covered the underside of the roof's eaves, and a few insects flew lazy circuits around the property. When she approached the front gate, more crawled out of their holes, their jet-black bodies glinting in the sun.

There's no reason anyone would remember me, thought Karys. She pushed back her shoulders, and stood straighter. Miresse might have remained the same, but she had not. Besides, she had never even talked to Rasko. She rang the bell hanging from the gate post, and the wasps buzzed louder.

"Do you want to tell me what we're doing here?" asked Ferain.

The door of the house opened halfway, and a thickset, shaven man stared out at her across the porch.

"I want to talk to Rasko," called Karys. "He should be expecting me."

The man looked her up and down, and then snapped his fingers. In perfect unison, the insects ceased their patrol and returned to their nests. He jerked his head toward the door.

"Oh good," said Ferain. "We're going inside the wasp house. Excellent."

The interior of the building was less dilapidated, although an unpleasant musty smell hung in the air, and the rooms were dark and stuffy. Like Marishka, Rasko did not flaunt his power with ostentatious displays of wealth. There was no need; everyone in Miresse knew who the fixer was. When Karys walked into his parlour, he was seated with his shoes propped up on his desk, smoking osk. Somewhere in his late forties, his hair was thinning at the temples and his oiled reddish beard was starting to grey. He smiled like a shark— razor-thin lips peeling back from bright white teeth—and snuffed out his reed.

"Now, who might you be?" he asked.

"Temius Rasko?"

Rasko waved away his doorman, swung his feet down to the floor, and stood up. "You've found me. What can I do for you, cas . . . ?"

She held out her hand to shake. "Dasin. Marishka sent me."

"Ah, yes. Cas Dasin." Rasko took her hand and brought it to his mouth. Karys tensed. He kissed her knuckles, lips lingering on her skin, breath too warm. "A pleasure. I don't believe I've seen you around these parts before."

There was something slick about his voice: spilled oil on ice. Karys refused to pull her hand back; she waited for him to let go, and kept her expression blank.

"Did you receive the Second Mayor's message?" she asked.

"I might have."

"I have no papers, and I need to cross the border. I believe you could help me."

"Not one for idle conversation, are you? But I appreciate that." He gestured to the frayed divan opposite his desk, and returned to his own chair. Karys cautiously lowered herself down. The window behind Rasko stood ajar; through it, she could hear the coarse droning of the wasps outside. "Crossing the border, hmm? Dangerous business. Expensive. So, are you running to Varesli, or away from home?"

She shrugged evasively. "A little of both."

"Oh, a woman of mystery. You would need a guide to get through the canyon."

"Do you know one?"

"I might. But whether you could afford him is a different matter. What can you offer me, cas Dasin?"

"Did the Second Mayor not—"

"The old woman had a word, and I listened. But a man like me has to consider expenses."

Marishka had warned her that Rasko's help would come at a cost. Karys kept her voice light. "What are you looking for?"

Rasko smirked. "Four thousand cret?"

"More than I can afford."

"I suspected as much." His predatory sneer widened, and he rested his hands on the desk, interlacing each finger between the next. "Well, for the old woman's sake, I suppose I could find a way to reduce the price, if you were willing to render certain . . . services."

Karys gave the fixer a flat look. Out the corner of her eye, she saw her shadow darken on the divan beside her. Rasko laughed.

"A joke, cas," he said. "Where is your sense of humour? There's no need to look so worried—you aren't young or pretty enough to be saleable."

"Bastard," muttered Ferain.

Karys smiled blandly, and held her gaze steady.

"Hilarious, casin," she said. "Which services?"

A flicker of irritation crossed Rasko's face. He had wanted to rattle her. The expression disappeared again.

"I'd have to think on it," he said. "Tell me again, where in Varesli would you be headed?"

"Eludia."

"Ah, the old capital. Very scenic." He ran a hand over his beard, studying her more closely. "Yes, there might be something there. You're no beauty, but you've got a certain vulnerability about your eyes. It's hard to find people with that look in my line of business. Might be useful."

"Then you'll get me the guide?"

"I'll think about it." He rose once again, and snapped his fingers. A large yellow and black wasp flew into the room through the window. It landed on the desk, and rubbed its head with its forelegs. "But for now—a gift."

Karys watched the wasp. From antennae to the folded tips of its wings, it was the length of her little finger.

"Come, you're not afraid of a little sting, are you?" Rasko rotated his wrist, and the wasp obediently flew from the desk to perch on the back of his hand. "She'll mark you, that's all. It keeps the others from seeing you as a threat."

Face smooth, Karys tugged the Veneer aside. The wasp glistened with Ephirite-derived workings, wrapped tight like wires through its body. The walls of the parlour twitched with the hidden movement of hundreds more of the creatures, muted lights shining through the plaster.

"I'd prefer to just keep my distance from her friends," she said.

Rasko ambled over to the divan, self-satisfied and smiling. Karys kept her nerve as he sat down beside her, draping his left arm over the backrest, supporting the wasp on his right hand. She knew he wanted to fluster her. When he leaned in closer, reaching out to nudge the wasp onto the collar of her shirt, she could not quite stop herself from pulling away. Rasko tsked.

"You don't have to do this, Karys," said Ferain. "Walk out of here now; we'll find another way into Varesli."

Rasko smelled like osk smoke and unwashed skin. When he moved his hand again to place the wasp on her shoulder, Karys held herself still.

"A gesture of trust, cas," he said, warm and conspiratorial. "It's harmless, I promise. There we go."

The wasp climbed up the side of her neck, little legs scratchy on her skin. Karys swallowed. It took all of her self-control not to swat the fat-bellied creature off her throat as it crawled up to the triangle of skin between her left ear and her jaw. The feathery touch of the insect's wings felt hideously intimate.

Fifteen thousand cret, she thought. *Fifteen thousand cret, fifteen thousand cret—*

Rasko snapped his fingers again.

The pain was immediate and fierce, like a molten splinter driven into her jaw. Karys swore and reached up to crush the wasp, but Rasko caught her arm and forced it back down. After another agonising second, the insect withdrew its stinger. In a whirr of wings, it took off and disappeared back out the window. Karys breathed hard, her head spinning from the pain.

"Very good," said Rasko, releasing her arm. "I think I could grow to like you, cas. Say thank you for the gift."

Karys gritted her teeth. The bright stab of agony was already gone, replaced by a blunt coursing ache. She tentatively pressed her fingertips to the side of her jaw, but the skin remained smooth—no heat, no swelling.

"Thanks," she muttered.

It was a relief to leave the house. The morning remained cool, and the air tasted clean after the closeness of Rasko's parlour. Karys walked with her hands buried in her pockets, trudging back up the hill to the shuttered tanneries. More people were about, warehouse workers in stained overalls, old men talking on the street corners. None of them spared her a second glance.

Ferain was silent for a long time, her shadow slinking along the ground behind her.

"Sadistic pervert," he muttered at last.

Karys smiled, humourless.

"Could have been worse," she said.

A long pause. The cold wind bit through her clothing, whistling down the street and drawing up small whirls of grey dust. Loose window shutters rattled in their frames.

"I think," Ferain said, his voice unusually gruff, "that we might have lived very different lives."

Karys almost laughed.

"Yes," she said. "Probably."

She walked back to the inn instead of finding an awrig. By the time she reached the Orago, the clouds had darkened overhead, spitting thin rain on the bare clay brick buildings and the gravel roads. The inn's door stood open under the faded brown and yellow awnings. A few feet before the entrance, Karys slowed. Then she shook her head, and walked inside.

A few people sat at the bar, but the inn appeared largely empty. The entrance room smelled strongly of lavender soap and lye, and a large collection of framed artworks and posters covered the walls—yellowed gazettes, murky paintings of dour men, a handful of landscapes. During the occupation, the northern wing of the building had burned down, later to be rebuilt, and the ceiling beams still bore black marks from that fire. Karys talked to the owner behind the bar, and he directed her to a room on the second floor.

Winola was sitting at the dressing table when Karys walked in, stationery neatly arrayed across the surface in front of her. The room contained two beds, a pea-green armchair squashed into the corner, and a moth-eaten tapestry on the wall. The scholar brightened at the sight of Karys.

"You're back," she said. "I was just tidying up my notes. Have you finished your errand?"

Karys nodded. "Any trouble here?"

"No, not at all. Everyone has been very friendly." Winola turned over a page in her notebook. "If you wouldn't mind, I have a few more questions for Ferain, and then one or two experiments I'd like to try."

Karys dropped onto the armchair in the corner. "Go ahead."

The scholar's questions were varied and specific. Some seemed arbitrary to Karys: whether Ferain had consumed any food in the hours preceding the binding, exposure to certain metals and substances in the days before that, whether he wrote with his left or right hand. Others seemed more obviously pertinent: whether he possessed any body modifications that could interfere with the functioning of the Split Lapse, whether he could describe objects outside of Karys' field of vision, whether altering the shape of her shadow caused him discomfort. The last point seemed to particularly interest Winola, and she rephrased the question in several different ways—was it more difficult to mimic Karys' movements or produce his own, was the sensation of movement heavy or light, did he experience temperature? Could he discern texture through contact? Was he tired, was he hungry? What felt good, what felt bad? What hurt?

"He says he's fine," said Karys, after what felt like the hundredth question on the same theme. "It doesn't hurt. It doesn't feel like anything."

Winola pursed her lips.

"What?" said Karys.

"Hm. Just a suspicion." She wrote something down. "Right, circling back around to your answer on temperature, is the 'cold' you experience a persistent source of irritation?"

Ferain sighed. "I wish I could just *talk* to her."

"He says he wishes he could talk to you."

Winola glanced up, and her eyebrows drew together. Then she returned to her notes.

"Interesting," she said.

After that, she moved on to a series of small experiments, making Ferain distort his shape in various ways, asking him to spread or shrink. He proved unnaturally flexible; there didn't seem to be any limits on his ability to manipulate his form provided a small band of shadow still tied him to Karys' body. He could even cast himself upright, appearing as a murky darkness in the middle of the room, a translucent black silhouette cut into the world. Winola tentatively reached through him. Meeting no resistance, her fingers emerged unmarked out the other side of his body.

"Doesn't hurt," said Ferain, pre-empting the inevitable question.

Arms folded, Karys studied her upright shadow, feeling disturbed but intrigued. A small, childish part of her wanted to try sticking her hand through him too. She looked out the window instead. At any rate, they would have to take a break soon—Worked Dispatch opened at noon. Ferain had dictated his letter to the Foreign Ministry aboard the Silkess last night, recounting events calmly, as though they had happened to somebody else. He had not mentioned Karys or the Split Lapse, or his own wound.

Winola started on another test, crossing the room and opening the door to the long empty hallway outside. She told Ferain to stretch to the far wall of the passage.

It was probably still a terrible idea, the letter. Karys rested her chin on her hand, gazing down at the street outside. Hard to know what Ferain was really thinking. For all that he talked, for all his surface of candour and ease, she couldn't shake the sense that he was being . . . careful. He had a kind of self-possession or control that she was unable to penetrate, a quiet, cunning agility that became perceptible only in the moments when he seemed closest to relaxing his guard. It didn't strike her as malicious; she doubted that he meant her harm, or wanted to start a war between Mercia and Varesli, but—

A hard ache blossomed in her chest, and Karys made a strangled sound. Her ribs seemed to compress around her lungs; she could not breathe.

"Ferain," she gasped.

In an instant, he snapped back to her side. The pain diminished.

"That hurt you?" he asked.

She bent forward in the chair, nodding. Her pulse beat fast. "You?"

"Nothing."

"Of course not."

"Sorry," said Winola. She hastily shut the door. "Sorry, I had no idea—"

Karys waved off the scholar's concern.

"It's fine," she said. "Just caught me by surprise."

Winola looked unconvinced and uneasy. "Are you sure? You've gone pale."

Karys straightened, pushing her hair back from her face. "Yes, I'm fine. Could we take a break, though? I need to go to Worked Dispatch."

Winola stayed behind to collate her new notes, and Karys headed downstairs alone. More people had gathered at the bar since she had arrived—old men and women with weary expressions, most likely clerks from the magistrate's office down the road. Karys wound through their midst to reach the door. As she passed one of the tables, a curly-haired man in his early fifties frowned at the sight of her, then leaned over and said something to his associates.

I don't need any more trouble, thought Karys, and walked faster.

The Miresse branch of Worked Dispatch stood two blocks away from the Orago. Unlike most of the buildings in the town, it was not constructed from red brick, but rather a series of uneven mirror plates—it resembled an enormous lump of melted iron pocked with abscesses and cavities. The front door was uncomfortably low; although Karys was not especially tall, she still had to duck to pass through it.

Low-grade green etherbulbs illuminated the interior, casting garish light across the central island of cubicles. The walls and ceiling puckered around small irregular channels recessed into their metallic surface, tiny windows surrounded by tracts of glittering crushed ice. As with other branches Karys had visited, the space inside Worked Dispatch had a curiously underwater quality—its colours and lights seemed to diffuse and ripple, and sounds moved strangely between the walls. The private mail service had been founded over a hundred years ago, when a Vareslian herald had gifted one of her Favoured families a working that could be used to pass correspondence instantly over great distances. It only functioned while the sun was at its meridian, and the original family closely guarded the secrets of its operation, enabling them to charge exorbitant fees for anyone wishing to use the service. During the Vareslian occupation, Dispatches had opened in most of Mercia's larger towns, and continued to run after the Slaughter and subsequent signing of the Sovereignty Agreement.

There were a few other people in the room, sending or collecting their mail, but no one spared Karys any attention. *Not that New Favour should know I'm in Miresse, anyway.* She scanned the strangers' faces, peering through the Veneer for any sign of Ephirite-derived workings. Nothing.

"I'm watching your back," said Ferain.

Karys scoffed quietly, and walked over to one of the open cubicles. Although she had received mail via Dispatch before, she had never sent any. A faded board over the cubicle's entrance listed the price of transmission—ten cret per envelope. Easily enough money for a fortnight of meals. She stepped inside.

The orchid stood on the plinth against the back wall, growing from a thin bed of dark soil inside the reliquary. Its petals held a healthy, waxy shine; dark purple at their edges, snow white within. Karys counted out her cret and fed the money into the collection box beside the entrance. Then she took Ferain's letter out of her pocket, and wavered for a moment, fingering the bent corner of the envelope.

"I know you're worried . . ." began Ferain.

Karys dropped the letter into the tray underneath the reliquary, and pushed the drawer closed. "Do you want me to do this or not?"

"Trying to be reassuring, that's all."

She placed her left thumb on the tongue-like protuberance of the orchid's central petal. The plant warmed slightly, and then the outer sepals folded inward and kissed the skin above her nail. A faint click sounded from within the closed drawer. The letter had been accepted by the working.

"Done," she muttered.

Ferain gave a low sigh, hardly audible, and then made a small, self-deprecating sound of amusement.

"Sorry," he said. "That was . . . it was weighing on me. Thank you."

His gratitude felt oppressively sincere. Karys withdrew her thumb from the orchid, and rubbed her hand against the fabric of her trousers, skin prickling.

"I said I'd do it," she muttered.

With a little pop, the drawer below the reliquary slid open again. Inside the tray lay a new envelope.

Karys frowned. She picked up the letter. The outside was blank and smooth, no indicator of who the sender might be. Cheap, thin paper. In the past, when New Favour had tried to recruit her to the Psikamit Haven, their correspondence had always came stamped with an official seal—but this envelope only bore a circle of standard blue Dispatch wax. *Marishka?* The Second Mayor shouldn't have any reason to contact her now, not unless something had gone wrong. Karys turned the envelope over again. There was no danger; Dispatch's channels would accept nothing but unworked ink, paper, and wax.

She broke the seal.

The letter inside was not from Marishka. It was dated five days ago, and contained no signature, greeting, or address.

Oboro is dead. His send-off is next Saturday.

"Karys?" said Ferain.

She stood in the sickly gleam of the green etherbulbs, frozen in place. It felt as though the floor had dropped out from beneath her.

Her brother was dead.

CHAPTER

14

Karys sat alone in the darkest corner of the Orago's bar, and stared into the dregs of her drink. The letter lay on the table in front of her. Folded closed, but she could see the writing where the ink had bled through the cheap paper. Neat, practised, impersonal handwriting. Her limbs felt heavy. She did not want to move.

"I'm sorry for your loss," said Ferain.

Shouldn't she feel more sadness? Shouldn't she feel more . . . anything? She had last seen Oboro when she was fifteen. He would be thirty-one now. Would have been thirty-one now. She did not know if she would have recognised him if they passed in the street—for some reason, she could not recall his face at all, and the realisation chilled her. His voice, yes, and the way he walked, but not his face. There was a brother-shaped emptiness in her memories.

"No great loss," she muttered.

"Who was he? Family?"

Karys swallowed the remainder of her drink. Shrugged. She had no desire to talk. After leaving Worked Dispatch, she had wandered back to the Orago and ordered their cheapest spirit—an opaque barley wine that tasted like yeast. She didn't normally drink much, but it had seemed like the right thing to do. Like she should do *something*, even if it didn't matter, and she didn't feel anything. A gesture to mark the moment. Going through the motions.

"Is there any possibility that the letter is false?" asked Ferain softly. "A New Favour trap to lure you out?"

She shook her head.

"I realise it might sound unlikely, but if they faked—"

"I know who sent it," she said shortly.

One of the clerks at the neighbouring table looked over, and frowned. Clearly wondering why she was mumbling to herself. Karys hunched her shoulders. *Leave me alone. Everybody leave me alone.* On the wall to her left was a framed gazette from over a decade ago—the public notice of a child-killer's trial, the victim a little Vareslian girl murdered in Miresse. The edges of the paper had yellowed and curled.

"The letter is dated last Sunday," said Ferain, then paused. "Maybe you could still make it. How far away—"

"I'm not going to the send-off."

A long silence. Karys glanced toward the bar. Another drink, maybe. Something harder, maybe. That's what people did, wasn't it? Drowning grief. Except she wasn't grieving. Not really. She drew her finger in a circle around the rim of her empty glass.

"My brother," she muttered. "Oboro was my older brother. And I haven't seen him in fourteen years, so I'm not going to the send-off. It would be pointless."

"Pointless?"

She shrugged again. No, not "pointless," exactly. But saying that was better than "not worth the trouble." Besides, returning to Boäz after all this time? They wouldn't even know she was a deathspeaker. And if they found out, well. That would be bad.

"I think you should go," said Ferain. "Even if you weren't close to him. Take the chance to say goodbye."

Something white-hot and ugly rose inside her, and Karys shut her eyes. If she spoke now, if she even opened her mouth, she would lose control completely, and she could not afford that. Her head felt too light; the alcohol soaking in.

"Excuse me, cas?"

The timid voice was new. Karys grimaced and lifted her head. The same curly-haired man from earlier was standing in front of her table. He had medium brown skin and thick eyebrows, and his expression was curious.

"Is something the matter?" he asked. "You seem upset."

Nuliere help her, she could not handle this. Karys picked up the letter, and rose. Her chair screeched against the floor when she pushed it back, and other people in the bar looked around.

"Sorry," said the man, surprised. "I didn't mean to disturb, but you looked familiar. Did you perhaps once work at the court?"

"No." She brushed past him.

"Cas?"

Karys strode across the room and out the front door of the Orago. Hot blood pulsed against her skull, and her ears rang. *Leave me alone!* She kept walking. The chill air of the streets outside burned in her throat.

"Who was that?" asked her shadow, flowing after her. "Karys?"

The last of her patience gave way.

"Do not fucking *talk to me!*" she snarled.

Ferain recoiled, taken aback. She had spoken too loudly, her voice hoarse with anger, but she did not care—did not care what anyone in this miserable little town thought, or about Ferain's feelings, or about the send-off. The letter creased inside her grip, and the drizzling rain flecked her clothes.

Her feet carried her. Her shadow stayed quiet.

Karys had no destination, nowhere to go. She took the old bridge to the South Quarter, then followed the path alongside the canal. At this time of year, the Korasis River trickled by Miresse in a thin, drear stream; it would be months before the annual winter flood washed the walls clean, and swept the year's filth all the way down to the sea. Refuse and raw sewage collected along the banked slopes of the waterway, along with small dirty shrines dedicated to Swask. Fickle, demanding herald: ever jealous and quick to anger. People still worshipped him, after a fashion. The heaped offerings seemed fewer in number than Karys remembered, but they still remained—piles of river stones and knotted slipweed, strings of warbler eggshells threaded with silk.

She remembered arriving here, and seeing the bluish streetlamps scattered on the surface of the river, the close-packed buildings rising high above her head. It was scarcely forty miles from home, but it had felt like an entirely separate world at the time. It seemed so small now.

Up ahead, a group of kids were wrestling down at the base of the canal, all of them covered in mud and yelling. Karys slowed to watch them. A skinny dog growled and yapped at the children's heels, ears flat against its head. One of the boys threw a rock at the animal. It shied away, but continued to bark.

Funny, really. If she had not come to Miresse, she wouldn't be a death-speaker. No Sabaster, no compact. Down in the canal, one of the larger boys pushed a girl over, only to get kneed in the stomach for his troubles. On the other hand, she was still alive. That was more than could be said for Oboro, apparently.

How did he die?

One of the mud-soaked boys noticed that Karys was watching them. He yelled a crude obscenity. Expressionless, she flipped him off, then continued along the edge of the canal. With the heat of her anger fading, the world seemed greyer. She had left her coat at the Orago before she left for Worked Dispatch, and her bare arms prickled in the cold.

All it would have taken was one more sentence in the letter. A few words of explanation to say whether it had been sickness, or drowning, or . . . she didn't know. The omission felt deliberate; it would have cost nothing to include the cause of death, especially given the expense of sending the message via Dispatch. The absence seemed ominous; it tugged at her.

The buildings grew smaller and poorer, and the shrines to Swask increased in number as Karys drew nearer the edge of town. Where the canal forked, residents had erected a ramshackle monument of the herald: the figure of a barrel-chested man with his head thrown back to the sky in exultation, arms spread in challenge. It marked the site of Swask's death; during the Slaughter, two Ephirite had cornered the Bhatuma, and drowned him in his own river. They had then dismembered him, as if to share the trophy equally, and carried his halved remains back to their own domains. That was how it went with most of the weaker heralds; less a fight than an execution.

On the only occasion Karys had been summoned to Sabaster's domain, she had seen her master's collection of corpses. Swask might have been among them, she could not be sure; she had been too frightened to pay much attention. She did, however, remember the largest and most terrible herald amongst the Ephirite's trophies. The Bhatuma's enormous body had been distended by workings, so that their limbs could not be distinguished from the bloated protuberances of their flesh and sinew and bone—but Sabaster had left their face untouched. Masculine and beautiful, their skin like oiled bronze, their dead eyes the colour of moonlight. Karys did not know who the herald had been, but their face had haunted her nightmares ever since.

No creature, no living being, could be restored from that state. For better or worse, the Bhatuma were not coming back.

Karys slowed, and stopped. She had reached the border of Miresse. The afternoon was heading toward evening, and the scrub-covered hills ahead of her were shadowed. If she followed this road, kept walking into the night, she would eventually reach Boäz.

How did he die?

A cold wind swept over the street, and seemed to carry with it the faintest trace of sea salt. Maybe that was only her imagination. A gnawing, burning feeling had coiled up in Karys' chest; not grief, but something harder and quieter.

When she was ten, Oboro had lost his temper and hit her. Just that one time on the switchback above the boatyard, his twelve-year-old knuckles landing on her jaw and knocking her back. It hadn't hurt much, but he had *meant* it to hurt—she saw that on his face. Until that day, she had never perceived her brother's streak of viciousness, and it would be years before she realised it was in her too. But his fist had scarcely left her face before he went bone-pale and started apologising, then crying. Oboro never cried. She sat with him out on the windswept bluff, and he sobbed his heart out, and neither of them needed to say anything.

She had loved him, then.

"What would I tell Winola?" she asked.

There was a brief pause. When Ferain spoke, his tone was impossible to decipher; Karys could not tell if he was angry or hurt or indifferent.

"The truth," he said.

"What if she asks to come with me?"

"Do you want her to?"

Karys shook her head. The idea was awful. "No, that would be . . . no."

"Then tell her that as well."

"Do you think she'll leave? Run back home to Psikamit?"

"No."

"Too invested in her research?"

Ferain's voice remained flat. "She risked a lot to be here. To help us."

"Are you angry?"

"Why would I be angry?"

"I never know what you're thinking."

"I'm not angry." Her shadow sighed. "I'm . . . frustrated. It doesn't matter."

"Frustrated with me?"

"Karys, you're shivering. Please go back to the inn."

It wasn't that cold. But Ferain seemed weary, so she only nodded and turned to face Miresse again. The streetlamps were flickering to life; their lights shone glassy and pale blue, almost the colour of hallowfire.

By the time Karys reached the Orago, the clerks had all departed, replaced by the evening crowd. People were singing, and a fog of osk smoke hung around the building. A beggar sat in the alley opposite the side entrance, a teenage girl with a gaunt face and no shoes. A few coins lay in her bowl. She did not even look up when Karys passed.

Winola was waiting in their room, sitting on the edge of her bed. She quickly rose when Karys opened the door.

"What happened?" she asked, her brown eyes wide. "I was worried. You said you were going to Worked Dispatch, but that was . . ."

Karys took the letter out of her pocket, and smoothed the paper. Then she walked across the floor and handed it to Winola. The scholar's eyes flicked over the page, and her face fell.

"My older brother," said Karys. "Ferain thinks I should go."

Winola looked up. "Of course. I'm so sorry."

Her expression made Karys uncomfortable. "We hadn't spoken in years. It's unexpected, that's all. Bad timing."

"I understand. Will you need to travel far?"

"The village is about a day's journey from here, but I won't stay there long." Karys rubbed her neck. "Can you wait in Miresse until I get back?"

The scholar nodded seriously.

"Whatever you need," she said.

Karys turned away, fervently wishing that Winola would stop looking at her like that. At least she had not asked to come to Boäz; bad enough that Ferain would be there. Karys couldn't allow herself to think about that part too much. She walked over to the dressing table, and picked up her box of Silkess desserts from where Winola had left them that morning.

"Thanks," she said. "I . . . thanks. I'll be back in a minute."

Up close, the girl in the alley did not look any older than fifteen. She dozed, head bent to her chest. Her short hair was matted, her knuckles split over old scars. Karys reached into the waistband of her own trousers, pulled out a handful of sixths, then crouched and dropped them into the begging bowl with a soft clatter.

The girl started and woke.

"Embrace watch over you and her heralds bless you," she said automatically.

"Unlikely." Karys held out the dessert box. "I'm in liege with the enemy. Here."

The girl's eyes darted down the street, then back to Karys. "What?"

"Take it. It's for you."

The girl accepted the box, wary and unsure. She lifted the lid, and her eyes widened. "What is . . . why are you giving me this?"

Karys stood up again. She gave a small shrug, and turned back toward the Orago.

"I didn't want them anymore," she said.

CHAPTER 15

Karys arrived in Boäz as the storm rolled into the bay. Late afternoon, and the light over the sea was strange and red, the clouds bloated above the water. She had taken an awrig as far as Feln and hitched a ride on a farm wagon to Boreth before walking the last two miles on foot. With every step she took toward the ocean, her apprehension increased, and when she at last laid eyes on the village, all she could feel was dread.

"This is it?" asked Ferain.

Boäz rested in the gully between two sheer cliffs, like a marble lodged in a throat. Small, it was home to only a hundred or so people, most of whom could trace their family lineage back six generations to the village's founding. Every few months, a merchant vessel would arrive and exchange linens, spices, and sugar for Boäz's exports of dried fish, pearls, and brine-cryst. At all other times, the village existed apart and alone, governed by its own laws and vices.

"This is it," she confirmed. "Home."

"Seems quaint. Prettier than I expected."

She loosened the tension in her shoulders. "It is what it is. As soon as the send-off is done, we're leaving."

The slope down to the village was bordered with long grey grass and violet sea holly. Gulls circled above the jetty, their cries echoing over the low boom of the waves hitting the shore. By the look of the clouds, the storm would be an ugly one, and as Karys reached the outskirts of Boäz, people were already shuttering their houses. They looked up as she walked by, eyes narrowing in suspicion at the sight of a stranger.

She found their lack of recognition curiously satisfying. *Don't remember me?* She didn't smile at any of them, although she picked out a few familiar faces. Petrus, the roofer, now grey-haired and walking with a cane. Jashane, scolding a black-haired child that might have been her own. Ané, Nuliere's priestess, proud and cold as ever—her gaze lingered on Karys a little longer than the others' had.

The village temple overlooked the ocean. It was the largest building in Boäz, and the most richly decorated. The walls had been painted blue and orange, and the rafters strung with silver chains of pearls that clicked together in the breeze. A small bowl of blood stood in the offerings hold before the open timber and iron doors. Beyond, tallow candles burned on the floor of the main hall.

"Never thought you'd actually come."

Karys stilled at the sound of the woman's voice, a voice she would have recognised anywhere—at once rough and soft and clear. She turned, and found the speaker leaning against one of the temple's pillars. In the years since Karys had left Boäz, Haeki's bright red hair had grown long, and she had gotten broader across the shoulders. Harder-looking. There was a mean scar that stretched from her jaw to the line of her clavicle. Her ears were pierced at the lobe and along the upper ridge, and ringed with small gold hoops.

"Got rich, it seems," said Haeki. "Got important. It's so nice of you to grace us with your company."

Karys was lost for words. Haeki sneered at her.

"Forgotten me?" she asked. "I should have guessed."

Karys found her voice again, made it cool and indifferent. "Been waiting there long? I wasn't expecting a welcome."

Haeki's eyes darkened. She jerked her head toward the building. "I was with Oboro. No one here would wait for you, Eska; don't flatter yourself."

"I won't, then. If there's nothing else . . . ?"

Haeki lowered her chin and gave Karys a look of utter contempt. Karys met her gaze evenly—if they were to play at juvenile staring contests, so be it. But Haeki seemed satisfied; she straightened up and brushed past Karys, far closer than necessary.

"I hope you've got somewhere to stay," she said under her breath. "The storm's coming in tonight."

"I'm sure I'll manage."

Haeki scoffed, and carried on down the temple stairs, her steps loud and quick. Karys staved off the temptation to watch her go, and entered the temple without looking back.

"What was that all about?" asked Ferain, bemused. "Who was she?"

"Nothing and no one," muttered Karys.

Her shadow snorted. "Sure."

"Quiet."

The Boäz temple was dedicated to Nuliere, Lady of Brine and Urchins, Herald of Boäz. Despite the Slaughter, the village's adherence to the old faith persisted, undaunted and uncompromising. Hundreds of candles burned over the dark-tiled floor. Karys walked slowly between them, her breathing shallow.

Seeing Haeki again had flustered her, that was all. The echoing, heavy quietness of the temple pressed close. *Never thought I'd be here again.* It was in the past; she no longer kept the faith of her childhood; neither Nuliere nor this oppressive place held any power over her now. The mosaic murals on the wall gleamed, the glass tiles newly polished. The smell of salt water and iron seared her throat.

A young man stood before the door of the interstitial chamber, serving as temple guardian, and it took her a moment to identify him. Tion—when Karys left, Ané's son had been ten. Now grown, he had inherited his mother's severe jaw and narrow-set eyes, but his gaze lacked her sharpness. He spread his hands in an unsmiling welcome.

"Blessings of the Embrace and her heralds upon you," he said in a rumbling baritone. "Be humbled in the temple of the great Nuliere, most powerful of the Mercian Bhatuma, most beautiful and most righteous. Heed her voice in the waters, in the skies, and in the storms."

Karys inclined her head. "May her watch be peaceful. I'm here to see Oboro Eska."

A flicker of recognition. "Karys Eska?"

She stretched her mouth into a smile. "Hello, Tion."

The man's forehead wrinkled in consternation, and he rubbed his jaw. "Nuliere alive. You came for the send-off?"

"Correct. I won't stay longer than that."

"You look so different."

"That's the nature of aging, yes."

He still appeared perplexed, like she was an exotic and possibly venomous animal. His fingers fidgeted with the sleeve of his green tunic. "Did your Da send for you?"

Karys suspected that the man was not actively trying to needle her, but was simply dense. "No, he didn't. May I see my brother now, please?"

"Maybe I should call my Ma—"

"You're welcome to," she cut in, "but let me see Oboro in the meantime."

The resting chamber adjoined the main body of the temple; a windowless room twelve feet by nine. In the middle of the floor stood a large wooden bench, where all the dead of Boäz lay in state for eleven days before they were committed to Nuliere.

And there was Oboro: his eyes shut, his dark hair swept back from his face. A yellow quilt covered his legs, and boiled copper pennies had been laid across the exposed skin of his arms and chest. Sugar crystals frosted his lips.

Karys approached the bench, her heart beating against her breastbone.

Since she had last seen him, her brother's face had thinned, his shoulders had widened, and his jaw had gained a jut that looked sullen or stubborn. Fine wrinkles bunched around his eyes, a host of unfamiliar scars patterned his sun-darkened arms. But still, it was him. He looked like their father now. And like her too; she had the same heavy eyebrows and downturned mouth. Uncanny to see those features reflected on the face of a corpse.

And yet: no grief. She barely felt anything.

Karys glanced toward the door. Tion had left, presumably to summon his mother, and she was alone in the temple. This would probably be her only chance; she could not afford to deathspeak when anyone might see her. If the send-off was Saturday, then Oboro must have passed at least ten days ago—his death impression would be near-gone by now. It would push the bounds of her abilities to recall his apparition at all.

Still, she felt an odd reluctance to touch him. The man lying on the bench appeared unreal, somehow, despite his solidity. Oboro, but . . . not. She extended a hand toward his cheek, then hesitated, her fingers hovering over his face. *Do I truly want to know?* That was why she had come to Boäz, but this close to his body, this close to his death . . .

She lowered her hand and opened the Veneer.

The temple thrummed with the weight of old sacrifice and Bhatuma workings; generations of history stained the walls. Karys exhaled, sending her consciousness into the fog, sinking through the gossamer weave of the world.

Oboro's apparition no longer held its shape. The cluster of memory and feeling that comprised his ghost appeared only as a gentle silver haze haloing his body. Karys coaxed it toward her.

"Can you hear me?" she asked, pitching her voice low. "Oboro?"

". . . dark." Her brother's dry death rattle set her teeth on edge. "Never going to get out . . . the dark."

His apparition was fragmented; he had been dead too long already. There were no clear boundaries to his presence—Karys could feel him all through the room, all through the temple; he had dispersed like mist. She tried again. "Listen to me, Oboro. I have some questions you need to answer."

". . . to get away before . . . I am becoming . . ."

"I'd like to know about the last thing you remember seeing. Can you describe that?"

"The only option left . . . didn't want to turn into . . . the way I used to . . ."

Karys kept her emotions in check. She could make no sense of the apparition's stumbling half-thoughts, and she had a feeling it could not understand her either. "Were you on the water? Or in the village?"

". . . unless I ended it. What if . . ."

"I don't like this," muttered Ferain.

The effect was immediate. Oboro's ghost fell silent, and, like lightning, his scattered presence shrank down to a single point just above his body. An eye blinked open in midair. It stared right at her.

Fuck, thought Karys, and slammed the Veneer closed.

The eye winked out of existence. She stumbled back from Oboro's body, knocking coins off his shoulder. They hit the tiles with a sharp metallic clatter.

"Did you see that?" she whispered.

"Yes," said Ferain. "I think it's still here."

What was that? When deathspeaking, the apparitions were always aware of her; most seemed to draw comfort from her presence. This had felt different. When that eye had opened, it *recognised* her. Karys' nails bit into her palms. Even with the Veneer closed, she could still detect its presence in the room, a warm humming in the air over Oboro's body, a watchfulness.

A revenant?

Her shadow flowed over the floor and onto the bench, darkening Oboro's torso. It paused for a moment, holding stock still. Then it retreated to her side.

"We should go," said Ferain, calm and assured, but with no trace of his usual lightness. "Not too quickly. And don't turn your back on the body."

Her throat was tight. "Why not?"

"Call it a hunch."

Karys slid her feet backwards over the black tiles, the hair on her arms standing on end. She had heard the stories, read scattered accounts. Incidents when a deathspeaker had agitated or provoked an apparition, drawn them too far into the world, and the echo had turned into . . . something else.

"It's not moving," said her shadow.

"Can you see it?" she murmured.

"No, but I know where it is. Watch the step behind you; you're almost there. Don't knock over the candles."

She was in the main hall now; she could feel the breeze coming in through the open doors. The sea of candles guttered in the wind. Ferain was right; her sense of the apparition's presence was growing fainter as she moved away from the resting chamber. A hard knot of anger tightened in the pit of her stomach. He had done this. Oboro's apparition had only changed when her shadow had spoken. Ferain had woken it up.

"You're probably clear," he said.

She had reached the entrance. Karys breathed out slowly. The temple lay still and quiet and empty.

"That was me, wasn't it?" said Ferain quietly. "Your brother heard me."

Strings of pearls clicked in the cold breeze, and the crying of the gulls rang shrill between the towering grey cliffs. Her shadow was dark at her feet. His voice held a strange undercurrent, something almost like longing.

"My brother is dead," said Karys flatly. "The apparition is not him."

"Those things he was saying—"

"I shouldn't have come here." She shook her head, and the words spilled out before she could stop herself. "Why can you never just be quiet?"

"Karys—"

"No, just . . ." She pressed her hand to her forehead. "This was a mistake. If I leave now, I can still make it back to Boreth before nightfall."

"Not unless you run all the way."

"Then I'll run." She turned. "Leave now, and I can be back in Miresse before . . ."

She trailed off. Tion was climbing the stairs to the temple, shadowed by his mother and a second, older man.

Dayon Eska's hair was more grey than black, and his skin had weathered to a deep leathery brown flecked with age spots. Dark rings shadowed his eyes; his gaze had a haggard, slightly vague quality, like he wasn't fully present— but he walked upright, as straight and proud as ever. His blue mourning cowl hung loosely around his neck. When he saw Karys, he paused, and there was a small falter in his stride, enough to make Ané look at him. The priestess said something, and he shook his head, then smiled.

Karys remained rooted to the spot. She had known that returning to Boäz would mean seeing him again, but his appearance still hit her like a punch to the gut. How many times had she imagined this reunion? She had expected him to be angry, aggrieved by what she had done, but he was *smiling*. And now all three of them had reached the pavilion, and he had opened his arms, and she still felt frozen in place, and he walked forward and hugged her.

"Welcome home, Karys," he said gruffly.

She felt dizzy. Her father's arms were corded with muscle, but he held her gently. When he drew back, he studied her face, marking all the ways she had changed. No sign of resentment, no light of accusation in his eyes.

"Did you need to travel far to get here?" he asked. "You look tired."

Karys struggled for her voice. "Not so far."

"None of us knew you'd be coming for the send-off," said Ané, and there was the reproof that was absent from her father's voice. The priestess's tone bordered on scornful. "I could hardly believe it when Tion told me."

Karys had not experienced a tenth as much emotion when she saw Oboro's body. What did that say about her? *Get a hold of yourself.*

"Blessings of the Embrace, cas," she said. "It's been a while."

"Coming in with the storm too. A day later, and you wouldn't have been able to reach Boäz at all."

"Nuliere still offers me grace, despite my failings." Karys' words emerged more smoothly, and she inclined her head in a practised show of respect. "I give thanks for her blessing."

Ané bristled, and offered a sour little grimace. "May she bless us all."

"I'm so glad you're home," said her father. "It is . . . it is such a comfort, for you to return, after Oboro . . ."

He coughed, and gave a small shrug. Karys wished he would stop smiling. She wished she could be anywhere but here. Why had she let Ferain convince her to return to this forsaken place? "I heard the send-off would occur tomorrow."

Her father hesitated, and glanced at Ané. "If the storm passes. Otherwise we'll wait for calmer seas."

"Of course." She swallowed. "How did he—the letter I received did not say—"

Her father gestured toward the path back up the cliffs. "We can discuss it at home."

Karys shook her head quickly.

"It wouldn't be right for me to trouble you," she said.

"No daughter of mine will sleep out in the rain," he replied. "It has been so long, Karys. Come home."

What could she say? Tion and Ané were listening, one with curiosity, the other with disapproval, and no excuse Karys could offer would make any sense. She nodded mutely, and her father beamed.

As they descended the stairs, Karys noticed a glimmer of red hair below the sloping eaves of the skinner's house. Haeki scowled when their eyes met; Ané and her father were talking, oblivious, and did not see her. For a second, Karys thought that Haeki might say something. It seemed like she wanted to; her expression was angry, conflicted.

The moment passed. Haeki turned, and walked away.

CHAPTER

16

"Your father seems kind."

Rain lashed the windows in bitter sheets, and the wind screamed through the channel between the cliffs. Karys had not realised how deeply that noise had etched itself into her memories: that shrill animal keening. Even though the farm was a little way from the ravine, perched on the side of a hill half a mile above the village itself, the sound travelled.

"You take after him," said her shadow. "Same mouth."

Before, she had shared this room with Oboro—but her bed was gone now, and the space seemed too large without it. *Did he feel that way, when I left?* Thunder growled over the sea, and Karys glimpsed flashes of lightning through the pouring rain. Otherwise, the world beyond the window was a black void.

"Nothing like my father," said Ferain. Her shadow was spread like a thick carpet over the bare floorboards. "I can't remember him ever looking that happy to see me. As a boy, I was always running after him, trying to impress him, trying to get his attention. Even for a moment, just to get him to look at me. I think he found it irritating."

"Imagine that," Karys murmured, but without any real heat or conviction.

Dayon Eska had received plenty of grief-food from the village; his larder was full of cured eels and sugar-basted fish, jars of winter plums and flasks of home-brewed gin. Enough to last for weeks of mourning, although he would not observe the grieving period—without his attention, the farm would fall into disrepair. Walking up to the house, Karys had been struck by how little had changed. The kumquat trees remained upright and green against the grey sky, the long grass of the pasture fields rustled and swayed. The old barn had been patched up where some of the timber had rotted through, and the roof of the house was newly re-thatched.

They had eaten together in the kitchen, sitting where they used to sit, and her father had talked about his work and struggles and preparations for the fallow season. Nothing about Oboro, even though the subject hovered over the empty chair like a carrion bird. Karys had said little, eventually claiming that she was exhausted from travel, and slinking off to her old room.

"What happened in the temple was my fault," said her shadow. "I know that."

She sighed. "Leave me be, Ferain."

"I'm sorry. That's all."

He said it so simply. Without sentimentality, without shrinking. Karys listened to the rain hit the glass. The windowpane was cracked in the corner, and let in a cold stream of air.

"It wasn't him," she said quietly. "The ghosts, they aren't souls. They're just excesses of feeling. Footprints in the sand."

A lightning bolt briefly lit the bedroom in silver, throwing the walls into sharp relief. The space was bare; Oboro had left little behind. His clothing, a tackle box by the door, a blank book with dried flowers pressed between the pages, a pitiful stash of money and pearls in the hidden recess behind the skirting board. The last Karys had known to look for; Oboro had shown her the hole when she was seven. Their secret.

"What was your brother like?" asked Ferain.

She sat on the bed, leaned back against the wall. "Gentle, mostly. Quiet." *Angry.* "He kept to himself a lot. Liked stories; when he was younger, he was always pestering Ané to tell him tales about the other Bhatuma." *The violent ones.* "He was reckless, sometimes."

"How so?"

"I don't know. Ran too fast, jumped from places he shouldn't, swam out too far."

"And you missed him?"

She wavered, then nodded. "I did. He was a good brother; he tried to look out for me. Do you have siblings?"

"No, it was just me. But for what it's worth, I do have at least seventeen cousins on my father's side."

"Are you close to them?"

"Not particularly, but quantity has to count for something."

Karys smiled. She reached over and pulled Oboro's quilt around her shoulders. Lightning cracked the sky; she saw the darker pool of shadow where Ferain lay, a circle of midnight gathered on the floorboards. "You're not on good terms with your father?"

"No. Not really."

"Why not?"

Ferain's voice turned dry. Blithe. "I disappoint him, he disappoints me. Nothing unusual. He's cold, that's all."

"And your mother?"

A slight pause, hardly noticeable.

"She was warmer," he said. "But she died two years ago."

"I'm sorry."

"She had been sick for most of my life; it was inevitable. How about you? Related to many people in the village?"

He spoke with an unforced ease, but Karys did not miss the way that he shifted attention away from himself. She shook her head. "Not closely related. I only had Oboro and my father."

"No mother?"

"Left when I was five. I don't really remember her. Oboro was older; he took it harder, I think." She made a rueful sound. "He used to say she'd come back one day. Never did, of course. She could be anywhere now."

"You never tried to contact her via Worked Dispatch?"

"The branch in Boreth only opened a few years ago." She wasn't sure why she was telling him all this. "I probably wouldn't have bothered anyway; I doubt she would have replied. Oboro might have. Maybe he did. He was always the more sensitive out of the two of us."

"Really?"

"Yes. Why does that surprise you?"

"Because you're already so sensitive."

She bristled. "And you're basing that opinion on?"

Ferain laughed. "I meant it as a compliment. Just that your feelings run deep. The way you describe your brother, it sounds like the two of you were . . ."

He stopped speaking.

"What?" asked Karys.

"Be quiet a moment," he said, dropping his voice. "Something . . ."

He trailed off. Karys' skin prickled, and she tightened her grip around the edges of the quilt. Outside, the rain gushed. She could not hear anything unusual, nothing seemed out of place, but her sense of Ferain's presence was suddenly far more pressing. He was stretching out across the floor. She shivered, and slid quietly to her feet. The floorboards were cold.

With the next crash of thunder, lightning struck the sea, spreading white tendrils deep beneath the waves. The window rattled in its frame, and a gust of icy air swept through the room. A faint smell followed; something unpleasant, like burning fur and marsh lilies.

The door creaked open.

Karys pressed her lips together to stop herself from making a sound. Through the narrow gap between the door and the frame, she could see the light of the kitchen stove. The house was still. Ferain stopped at the threshold of the room.

"Karys."

The voice came from everywhere at once, seeping from the walls, welling up from the floor. Ferain pulled back, drawing her shadow close around her feet.

The door opened wider, but there was no one on the other side. Or at least, no one that she could see.

Karys took a shallow breath and peeled back the Veneer.

The presence in the doorway was indistinct, a dark red haze that pulsed brighter and dimmer in a slow, regular rhythm. It stood far taller than her, at least the height of her father, and hovered weightless as kelp beneath a calm sea.

"Why won't you answer me?" whispered Oboro.

She swallowed. It knew her, it knew her name. It had followed her home.

"It's so dark here," the revenant said, with a voice like velvet across skin. "I can't see at all."

The presence drifted forward into the room. Karys backed away from it, heart hammering. The air had grown very cold; her breath misted before her face. She could hear a soft sound now, a metallic clinking—the muted echo of copper coins striking the ground.

Without warning, the window behind her swung open. Rain swirled through the aperture, freezing where it touched her, and the sound of the storm rushed into the room. She gasped.

"Found you," breathed Oboro.

The revenant surged toward her. Karys brought up her hands automatically, but they offered no defence; the presence collided with her, and it was like being struck by a wave; she fell backwards and hit the ground. There was a crushing weight on her chest, bearing down heavier with every second. She clawed at the air.

A wall of shadow swept over her, and the pressure released.

"Back off," growled Ferain.

The revenant produced a pained whine, retreating across the floor. It swayed in the air, the edges of its form shimmering scarlet. "What was that, Karys? Karys, it hurt me."

She pushed herself up, her head thick. *Ferain can touch him.* She could sense her shadow drawn like a cloak around her shoulders. Her ribs felt bruised.

"Get out of the house," she said, voice ragged. "You don't belong here."

The revenant stilled and stopped whining. When it spoke again, its tone was no longer wheedling and pathetic, but altogether more sinister.

"Why him?" it asked.

"Don't talk to it," said Ferain sharply.

The haze jerked further away at the sound of her shadow's voice, as if startled, and then stopped in the doorway.

"It should be me," said Oboro. "I'm your brother. You should have let me in, not him."

"Get out," Karys whispered.

Like a whip crack, the revenant flew toward her again. This time, Ferain was ready. Her shadow collided with the haze, and where they touched a red mist blossomed in the air, spraying over the walls. Oboro howled, enraged, but Ferain did not relent; her shadow expanded and drove the revenant into the kitchen. His darkness blotted out the dim yellow of the stove; Karys could not see what he was doing, but her brother's curses rang louder than the storm, growing increasingly panicked. She knew it wasn't him, not really Oboro, but his distress still gave her a cold, sick feeling.

"Ferain, leave him." She stumbled out of her room. "Enough."

He didn't hear her. The revenant melted through the wall and fled into the rain, and her shadow pursued, slipping through the front window in a black river. Karys moved to follow. She was still winded and afraid, not thinking clearly. A part of her feared her father would wake up and demand to know what was happening, a part worried that Ferain might hurt Oboro—who was *not* Oboro, but it was his voice—

The violent wrenching sensation took her breath away, and she staggered drunkenly into the wall. Intense cold bloomed inside her chest cavity.

Gone too far, she realised. Ferain had stretched beyond their limits; it was Winola's test all over again. Her vision blurred. Embrace, it hurt. Worse than before.

"Ferain," she croaked. "You piece of shit, come *back*."

Another second, another heartbeat of searing pain. Then the sensation diminished as her shadow returned. Karys' muscles went slack with relief, and she folded double, bracing herself against the wall. The fire in the stove burned low and red, wavering before her eyes.

"Why did you—he was leaving," she whispered. "Why did you have to—"

"He was going to hurt you."

The unnatural cold remained, each breath stinging and sharp. Her head spun.

"I left Psikamit," she said hoarsely.

"Karys?"

"I left Psikamit. My life, and everything I had built over the years." Her voice grew stronger. "Gone. I threw it all away, I might have betrayed Mercia, and now I'm back here, and my brother has turned into a fucking revenant—because of *you*."

Ferain drew back from her slightly. "You said it isn't really him. You told me—"

"He was leaving!" she snarled. "He was already leaving, Ferain. You'd scared him enough, there was no need to go after him like that. You just wanted to hurt him."

She was talking too loudly, out of control, all of her tight, simmering resentment spilling over. She walked back into the bedroom, and snapped the door shut behind her. *Too loud.* The storm would cover most of the noise, but—

"Is that what you think of me?" asked Ferain.

"What I think?" The wind gusted into the room; she stalked over to the window and dragged it closed. "I don't even *know* you—so you tell me what I should think. That you've been using me all along? That you believe you're so smooth, so clever?" She fumbled with the latch, unable to stop speaking. "Binding the Lapse was the stupidest mistake of my life. I wish I'd never found you in the Sanctum."

She felt, rather than saw, Ferain flinch. The faint weight of her shadow veered heavier for an instant, as if unbalanced. Then he made a harsh, scornful sound.

"Ever considered that I might wish for that too?" he said.

Thunder boomed, loud and long, rattling through the house. Karys clenched her jaw. She bent and snatched the quilt off the ground, then lay down, throwing it over her body. She rolled to face the wall.

Rain poured down outside. The wind howled, the thunder pulled further out to sea. The bed sheets still smelled like her brother.

CHAPTER

17

The rain did not stop.

"Can't have the send-off today," said Dayon Eska. He had slept through the storm, hearing none of the commotion that had occurred beneath his roof. "The sea won't calm soon."

Karys nodded over the top of her pewter mug of eskelp tea. They were both in the kitchen; her father by the window, while she sat at the table. The old stove shed a pool of orange light on the raw brick hearth. The edges of the buckled pots and pans glinted silver where they hung from hooks in the ceiling.

"It'll be a long wake for Oboro," her father continued, staring out at the early grey sky. His broad shoulders were heavy. "I want to be finished with it all, and let him go to rest, but things must be done right. A few more days won't make a difference."

Except it meant that she could not leave. Karys sipped the sweet, slightly briny tea and tried to quell her swirl of paranoid thoughts. She still did not know how to ask her father what had happened to Oboro, and he seemed unwilling to volunteer the information. There was so much that felt unspeakable between them, silences she could not bring herself to fill. Being here again, she had the sense of her identity unravelling—all the things she had taken for granted slowly coming undone. The sooner she left, the better.

"I think I'll brave the weather." Her voice came out in a rasp, and she cleared her throat. "Pay my respects to Nuliere, greet the elders properly. I didn't have the chance yesterday."

"They would understand if you waited." Her father gestured to the clouds. "There will be enough time once the storm clears. More than enough time."

Does he believe I will stay after the send-off? Karys pushed down the tide of emotion rising up within her. "It would look better if I went now. I'm eating their grief-food, so it seems only right."

A slight pause. Then her father nodded. He turned from the window and took the seat next to her. "Yes, it would look better. Go to Ané, then; she can help you. I'd accompany you, but I need to check the trees after last night."

"Does she still live in the same house?"

"She does, with Tion. You spoke to him yesterday, didn't you?"

"Only a few words."

"He is a good man. Hard worker, very loyal. Ané sends him up here to help me with the heavier jobs." Her father smiled. "He would make a fine husband, don't you think?"

Karys tried not to wince. "I can't say."

"Oh, he would. A strong man like that isn't easy to find these days."

She made a vaguely affirmative sound, and took another drink of tea to cover her expression.

"Unless you are already committed?"

She lowered her mug, and spoke carefully. "Tion might not want me, that's all."

Her father's smile faded. He leaned back in his chair, and gave a weary sigh. Karys could not bring herself to meet his eyes.

"People here are willing to forgive you," he said. "Show them you've changed."

She nodded, although she knew Boäz would never accept her again. Too much water had passed under that bridge. Not to mention that if they uncovered her profession, she would be lucky to escape stoning. Karys gazed down at her reflection in the mug. She had no intention of making amends. No intention of staying.

"I'll try my best," she said.

"Let them all see that. Did you talk to anyone else when you arrived?"

Karys hesitated.

"Well?"

"I saw Haeki Maas," she said. "She was at the temple visiting Oboro."

Dayon Eska sighed again.

"That woman," he grumbled, shaking his head. "She walks around like she's a sea-blessed of old. Did she give you any trouble?"

Karys got up and placed her mug in the sink. "No."

"Well, stay away from her. She shouldn't be intruding on Oboro's rest either. It isn't her place."

The rain outside fell steadily, but the wind had calmed. Karys borrowed her brother's tattered old overcoat and trudged down the track with the hood folded low over her face. The coat had a clumsy working stitched into the seams, a Bhatuma derivation that repelled water. It kept her warm enough. Her shoes grew heavy with yellow mud as she walked. Frogs croaked from the green grass of the pasture field, and the rain formed an even hush; a numbing, relentless noise that made her feel slow and dull and empty, set apart from the rest of the world.

At the end of the farm track, before the path that led down to the village, Karys stopped and turned her head toward Boreth. She stood still. Rain dripped from her hood, and she squinted through the haze. After a moment, she continued down the road to Boäz.

The sheer walls of the cliffs loomed dark and flat on either side of her, and ahead the sea was near-colourless under the grey sky, the horizon indistinguishable. It would probably be calmer by the afternoon, although not calm enough for a send-off. A part of Karys wanted to turn around and walk the full, miserable, soaking distance to Miresse, but matters were tangled now. And she still wanted answers.

The houses in the village looked especially small and ugly in the drear light; slumping rough-plastered buildings cracked with age, roofs sagging over their rafters. Water gurgled over the hard-packed streets, and the caustic smell of burning sargweed carried on the wind. Karys kept south toward the sea. Although there were few other people outside, she felt watched and on edge. A mutt growled at her from behind a poorly mended fence, and she stomped, scaring it off. The rain pattered down on her shoulders.

The house sat at the very edge of Boäz. Smaller, more rundown than the others. Karys walked across the yard and up to the screen door of the kitchen. Through the walls, she could hear a woman singing—a dirge, gentle and slightly off-key.

"And they took my love to the sea, you see, and I heard the waves calling for me, for me. But I'll never walk more by the sea, you see, for fear of what's calling my name."

Karys shivered. *How things change.* She knocked, and the singing cut off sharply. She took a step back from the door.

Haeki had her coral-bright mane of hair bunched up on top of her head, and wore a brown shirt and loose trousers. There was soot smudged on her hands from tending a fire. When she saw Karys, her eyes went stony.

"What do you want?" she asked.

Karys shifted her weight to her other foot. "To leave Boäz as soon as possible. And answers. I think you're the only one who might talk to me."

"I wouldn't count on that."

"You sent me that letter."

"Letter?" Haeki folded her arms. "You think I'd walk all the way to Boreth for you? Don't make me laugh, Eska; I have better things to do with my time. And it's not like you ever wrote to me."

Karys reached into her waistband, and retrieved the ten cret she had counted out earlier. She offered it to Haeki.

"For the Dispatch fee," she said.

Haeki stared at the money like it might sprout fangs. "Don't insult me. You've got a lot of nerve turning up like this."

Karys shrugged and pocketed the money again. The rain was growing heavier; she pulled her hood further over her face. "One question, Haeki, that's all I'm asking."

Haeki spat onto the ground between them.

"One question," pressed Karys. "That's it. You won't have to see me again."

"If that's what it takes for you to fuck off, ask already." Haeki made a sweeping gesture toward the sea. "And then get out of my yard."

"How did Oboro die?"

Haeki flinched, and her eyes travelled to the street behind Karys. There was no one else around, and it would have been impossible to hear their conversation over the rain. Yet still she paused.

"Please?" said Karys.

Haeki exhaled. She uncrossed her arms and lowered her voice.

"His body was on the beach below the Penitence Pool," she said. "Yesha found him, ran back to the village in a state. Everyone thinks he fell from that cliff—maybe jumped, maybe stumbled. They patched him up with workings for the wake. No one wants to talk about it, at least not where they can be heard."

"And where they can't be heard?"

Haeki fixed her with a blank stare. "I'm not the most popular around here. Those conversations don't involve me."

"I'm asking what you think."

"That we'll never know for sure. Tell me, what difference will this make to you?"

It was Karys' turn for silence. The rain soaked through the shoulders of her coat; the working was not strong enough to repel the downpour entirely. After a moment, Haeki shook her head.

"There are some things that you should just leave—"

"It determines what I do next," Karys interrupted.

An even longer pause. A ripple of emotion crossed Haeki's face; apprehension and something harder to classify, a kind of frustration or anger. When she spoke again, her voice was softer.

"Be careful what you start here, Karys," she said. "No one's on your side."

"I know."

"Not even me."

"Not even you. I never expected otherwise."

Haeki frowned at that, and then lowered her gaze.

"Oboro talked about leaving," she said. "He was unhappy, and getting worse, but he couldn't quite seem to—" She gestured, not finding the words. "There aren't many reasons to go up to the Pool in the middle of the night. But the way I see it, someone can jump and be pushed at the same time."

"Or just be pushed."

"Or that. But don't say it too loud." Haeki gripped the wooden frame of the door. She looked up, and her jaw was tight. "I thought you'd ask to stay."

Karys smiled, a manufactured movement of her mouth. "I think I've asked enough."

"You're going to choke on your own pride, I swear. Just *ask*."

"Thank you, but there's no need for me to inconvenience you any further." She turned to go. "And I'm sorry I never sent any letters."

"Nuliere alive, you're insufferable. Watch yourself, then."

"I will." Karys nodded, not turning back. "I always have."

The path to the sea cut a straight line from the temple to the water. The sand here was coarse and grey, littered with crushed shells that crunched underfoot. A timber boardwalk led down to the tiny shipping yard, where small craft were housed out of the waves' reach. The wind spun the rain through the air, cold on Karys' face, droplets sliding down the side of her neck. She breathed out slowly.

So, probably suicide. Not an accident, not a disease, not a drowning. Oboro had fallen from the same cliffs where they had played as children, and now she needed to sort out what that . . . what that meant. Karys wiped the rain from her forehead. *He was unhappy, and getting worse.* It had sounded that way, in the temple. Had sounded like despair.

Why did thinking about him make her feel so empty?

She hunched her shoulders against the wind, and walked east along the top of the beach. The waves broke like a slow drumbeat beside her. White guano smeared the grey rocks, broad-leaved takgrass pushed up from the sand in yellow clusters. Everything was exactly as it appeared in her memories; this place had branded itself upon her. Further along the coast lay the sheltered cove where they had dived for spring pearls, her and Haeki, kicking down through the greasy kelp forests after oysters, cracking them open on the shore, sorting pale meat from shell. Always collecting, always saving, always making plans that led nowhere. Oboro sitting on the beach, eyes set to the horizon, mind elsewhere. Ever the dreamer.

"I didn't mean it," said Karys aloud.

Her shadow trailed along the sand next to her, a little way apart, not encroaching on her space. Careful, always careful.

"What I said—" she began again.

"You were right," murmured Ferain.

She slowed. When she glanced at her shadow, he gave a small shrug.

"I did want to hurt him," he said. "You were right."

Karys wavered. Then she resumed walking, trudging forward through the wet sand.

"Why?" she asked.

The waves churned white beside her. Ferain seemed to be grappling with how to express himself.

"It wasn't about your brother, really," he said. "It was . . . touch. I could touch him, could feel him. I was real to him."

Karys frowned, and said nothing.

"The fact that I was hurting him was . . ." He fell quiet for a few seconds. "It wasn't about pain. It wasn't about him. It just felt like being alive."

She held her silence. After a moment, Ferain laughed. It sounded painful.

"No excuse, is it?" he said.

"You haven't mentioned this before."

"Yes, well." Her shadow slipped her silhouette, losing shape. Returned to it. "I didn't really have the right."

"The right?"

"I don't want—look, I'm enough of an imposition already. We both know that."

She shook her head. "I told you, what I said—"

"Was nothing I didn't know. Trust me, Karys, I knew. You have a very expressive face; it's easy to read. I know what I've cost you. I know you never wanted this. I know you hate that I'm in Boäz almost as much as you hate being here yourself. So, under the circumstances, I figured that I could at least refrain from complaining."

While speaking, he had drawn further and further away across the sand, so that he almost touched the water.

"I scare you," he said, quieter. "And I hate it. I want so badly to be useful to you—more than anything. I'm so tired of feeling helpless."

There was a toneless quality to his voice, an emptiness laid open to the air. Something untouchable and lonely. Karys watched the wave pull back, leaving a border of grey foam behind.

"Do you really wish I hadn't found you in the Sanctum?" she asked.

Silence.

"No," he whispered.

She nodded slowly, and a tension inside her loosened. She tucked her hands under her arms to keep them warm.

"You don't scare me," she said. "So, how bad is it?"

For a few seconds, it seemed like Ferain might not answer. The takgrass swayed and murmured in the wind.

"It just feels cold," he said. "And . . . too light. Like I'm not connected to anything. It's difficult to describe."

"We've established that you're connected to me. Maybe too well. It doesn't hurt?"

"No. And it really isn't important. I won't lose control like that again."

"I know." Karys gave a small smile. "And you are useful, by the way. I've always got someone to watch my back."

Her shadow distorted, rippling across the ground in a shuddering wave. He made a harsh, choked sound, like a bark of laughter that was strangled in his throat.

"I'm sorry," he said.

"You don't have to be. But if anyone sees you right now, they'll probably stone me as an apostate, so if you could . . ." She gestured to the sand at her side.

Her shadow returned to its regular place.

The beach below the jut of the cliff was narrower than the rest of the shoreline; the sea hugged closer to the rocks. At high tide, the strip of sand was fully submerged, but for now Karys was afforded a few feet of space to walk. She shielded her eyes against the rain, gazing up the rough, craggy wall. She could not see the Penitence Pool from here, but she knew it was above her. A ten-minute walk from the farm to the cliffs. An easy distance to cross, even in the dark, and Oboro would have known the paths up there better than anyone.

"This is where they found him," she said.

Sea holly grew wild from clefts and recesses in the wall. A sixty-foot drop, easily. In her mind, she saw Oboro standing at the precipice, and she placed herself beside him, reconstructing the scene. Felt the pull of the wind, the lure of the fall. It would have been dark, the beach below swallowed by black waves. The sound of all that water, crashing down. The taste of salt.

"What are you thinking?" asked Ferain.

Karys continued to stare upwards through the rain. Saw her brother spread his arms wide.

"That he wouldn't have jumped," she murmured.

But even as she said it, uncertainty pulled at her. Because she had not known Oboro for over a decade. And maybe, maybe she just wanted to believe he would step back from the edge.

Her shadow gathered closer to her side.

"Are you sure you want to do this?" he asked.

It's what I came here for. "I owe it to him. It's probably been too long, but if anything remains beyond the Veneer . . ."

She left the sentence hanging. *Then what?* She had the obscure sense that learning the truth would bring her closer to Oboro, would let her feel . . . something.

"So it's not because you're trying to punish yourself?"

The waves broke on the shore behind her. Karys did not respond.

"Because it looks that way," said Ferain, then hesitated. His voice dropped. "I've been where you're standing. Sometimes it hurts less, accepting that you'll never know what drove them to it. You couldn't have stopped this."

Karys smothered a grimace.

"I owe it to him," she repeated.

The skin of reality parted easily; the Veneer was thin and pliant here. Empty. Peaceful. Other than the Bhatuma derivation in her coat and the binding on her hand, there were no workings nearby. No death impressions either, at least not within the shallows. Karys closed her eyes, and allowed her breathing to slow, delving deeper. Eleven days was too long, she knew that. Environmental impressions faded and washed away over time, faster even than the residue of emotions and memory that remained with the body. She sank further, and the Veneer's lurid colours began to bleed into her, bubbling and pressing at her ears and mouth.

There was the faintest breath of something. A sticky, pulling kind of whisper. It was out of her reach, fluttering and coming apart. Although she was already dangerously deep, Karys braced herself and extended her senses to touch the impression.

"He knew!"

The words were a short gasp of fear, a bright black burst of sound. Karys recoiled, and the Veneer swirled around her—thick and distorted, hungry—and she almost panicked; the way out was uncertain, her mind was beginning to blur. She breathed, and rose. The death impression fell away, and she emerged from the Veneer, back to her own body.

"What happened?" asked Ferain, shifting from side to side at her feet. "Did you find something? I could only see lights and colours."

Her stomach turned. "I don't know. There was a fragment. Something."

Her skin felt cold. The wind cut through her clothing in a sudden powerful gust, and she looked up at the cliff again.

"I don't know," she repeated under her breath.

Ferain made a frustrated sound. "Karys, enough. You're soaking wet, you're grieving, and you're not going to solve anything by standing around in the rain and staring at this cliff. Whatever you think you owe your brother, it's not this. Go home."

I don't want to go home. "I'm not sure I'm grieving."

"I think you are. It just takes different forms."

Karys gazed at the cliff a moment longer. The rain had finally eased off, but the sky remained dark, even at midday. Behind her, the waves drummed their slow beat.

"All right," she said heavily. "Home for now."

CHAPTER
18

Her father was not in the house when she returned. Karys stripped out of her sodden garments, hanging Oboro's coat beside the front door and placing a pan underneath it. The steady percussion of dripping water on metal seemed overly loud in the silent kitchen. She borrowed more of her brother's clothing—a woollen shirt, rough-cut trousers that she cinched in with a belt—and it left her feeling like a villain from the stories of her childhood; a skin thief come to devour his life. Stealing his clothes, his bed, his place in the house: a quiet imposter bent on wiping him out entirely.

She set about sorting through the grief-food, taking stock of what her father had received and arranging his larder. It seemed like that might be helpful. She also found a sack of tangled trawl lines under the bottom shelf; their hooks rusted and the threads snared up into a chaotic wad. With quick, practised fingers, she teased out the knots. Useless old skills, the stuff of second-nature and muscle memory, but she found that the task settled her.

Once the lines were straightened out and recoiled, she replaced the sack and shut up the larder again. Still no sign of her father.

The kitchen needed cleaning. She scoured the tiles before the stove and wiped old dust from hard-to-reach surfaces. Through the window, the trees in the orchard swayed, and the long wet grass gleamed darkly.

"What happened between you and Haeki?" asked Ferain.

Karys was busy scrubbing loose a decade's worth of sticky residue from one of the cooking pots, elbow-deep in soapy water.

"What do you mean?" she asked.

"Oh, you know." His tone was idle. "The part where she acts like you jilted her at the altar."

"That's what you're getting from her?"

"Did you?"

"No. Not exactly." She checked the base of the pot against the light. "I broke a promise we made as kids."

"That's it?"

"That's it. Around here, honouring your word is . . ." She gave it thought.

"Fundamental, I suppose. I betrayed Haeki's trust, so her talking to me at all is generous. Especially when it's going to reflect badly on her to the rest of Boäz."

"So you were friends, then?"

"Yes."

"Your father doesn't seem to approve of her much."

Karys hesitated, then returned to scrubbing.

"No," she said. "He doesn't."

"You missed a spot." Her shadow pointed to a blackened mark on the side of the pot. "I was wrong about him, though."

"Hm?"

"Just something I noticed. He talks a lot, but in all this time, he hasn't asked one question about *your* life."

Karys didn't say anything. She frowned at the water in the sink, the oily film of old grease on its surface. It was sliding toward evening outside, the light falling. When she looked up again, her father was climbing the path to the front door.

"Well, apart from whether you're in a position to marry that slack-jawed man from the temple," said Ferain. "But I'm not sure if that counts. Karys?"

She shook her head and set down the pot to dry. "Sorry. Thinking about something Haeki said. Quiet now, my father's back."

Her shadow flowed from the countertop onto the floor where it belonged. Karys dried her hands as the door opened.

"I didn't think you would be out for so long," she said with a smile. "How were the trees?"

Dayon Eska dripped with rain; his hair was plastered to his skull and his beard glittered. He took off his coat and hung it on top of Oboro's. His clothing underneath seemed just as wet. A pool of water formed at his feet, spreading slowly across the clean floor. He smiled back at her.

"They weathered the wind well enough," he said. "But there's always plenty of other work to be seen to."

"Let me get a towel for you." She crossed the room and opened the linen closet.

"The goats had gotten out again. I'll need to fix the fence. And one of the barn doors is stuck at the hinges too—water's swollen the frame. That will need sanding down once it's dried. How was your day?"

Karys fumbled and grabbed a large towel, then hurried over to him. "It was fine. The village was quiet, and I—"

He struck her across the face.

Karys' head snapped backwards under the force, and she staggered, knocking into the table behind her. Her ears rang from the blow, and she dropped the towel. At her feet, her shadow went rigid.

"Liar," growled her father. "You think to make a fool of me?"

Karys shook her head. He hit her again; her stomach this time. She doubled over, breathless. Ferain swore.

"I went down to see Ané," said Dayon Eska. "And what does she tell me? That my daughter never knocked on her door. Instead, she tells me, my daughter went to see Haeki Maas. So, I'll ask again: do you think to make a fool of me?"

"No," she gasped.

The third blow dropped her to her knees. Karys' vision swam. She looked up, and her father was looming over her.

"Running away in the middle of the night." He shook his head, face twisted with scorn. "Just like your mother. Do you have any idea what people were saying? Do you have any idea how you made me *look*?"

"I'm sorry," she rasped, tasting blood. She had cut the inside of her cheek against her teeth; its hot red salt spilled over her lip.

"Are you? And why should I believe a word out of your liar mouth?"

"Leave her alone," snarled Ferain.

"Well?" Her father gave her a contemptuous shove with his boot. "First your mother, then you, then Oboro. All of you ready to cut me loose at the first opportunity—rats from a sinking ship. How am I supposed to manage on my own? When I'm eighty and blind, who's going to take care of me? Do you ever think about that? No, no, you run off in the night, then come crawling back when it suits you. And now look what you've made me do."

Karys shrank. It was like being twelve years old again; nothing had changed. *Please stop. Please stop.* Her shadow swept over her shoulder as Ferain tried vainly to shield her, but in the dim, unevenly lit kitchen, her father didn't even notice. He grabbed hold of her by the arm, and hauled her upright. His grip hurt, his hands hard and cold. Karys automatically lifted her other arm to shield her head.

"You don't fool me!" His spittle hit her face. "Do you hear?"

"Yes," she whispered.

He shook her. "Yes, what?"

"Yes, I hear you. I'm sorry."

"Oh, you will be. Count on that. You're going to be sorry beyond—"

There was a very loud knock on the door. Karys flinched, and her father went deathly still. His gaze flicked to the entrance, then back to her. His fingers wrapped tighter around her arm.

"Not a word," he said.

Karys nodded. He held on a second longer, his eyes a warning, then released her. She backed away, clasping her throbbing arm, her breathing coming shallow and quick. Her shadow coiled in front of her.

Her father walked over to the door, and opened it a crack. Not all the way; he made sure his body filled the gap, concealing the kitchen and Karys from sight. When he saw the visitor, his shoulders went stiff, and his voice emerged rough and aggressive. "What do you want?"

The person outside sounded out of breath. "Ané sent me; you need to come quickly. It's Oboro—the temple, something has happened to the body—"

"What?"

"Ané said it was urgent. She said you need to come now."

Her father grew taller with anger. "What do you mean, 'something's happened to the body'?"

"Ané said you're needed. Embrace, we've angered Nuliere, and there's going to be a reckoning for it. I'm going back to see if I can help."

"No, you're going to tell me—wait! *Wait!*" By the swift sound of splashing footfalls, the messenger was already returning to the village. Dayon Eska swore, and cast a wrathful glare in Karys' direction. She stepped back again, knocking into one of the kitchen chairs.

"This conversation isn't over," he growled. "Wait here."

And with that, he grabbed his wet coat and strode out into the rain, slamming the door shut behind him.

Karys felt rooted to the spot. Her heart continued to pound, and her body ached fiercely where she had been struck. She reached up to touch her mouth. When she saw the blood on her fingers, she shuddered and sat down heavily on the kitchen chair. Her shadow moved in front of her, a darkness hovering in the air before her face.

"Easy, easy." Ferain spoke in a low hush. "He's gone now. You're going to be okay."

She shook her head. Her shadow reached out and touched her cheek: a strange, careful, gentle gesture. She could not feel it, and closed her eyes.

"I understand now," he murmured. "Karys, I'm so sorry."

"'He knew.'"

"Knew what?"

She shook her head again. The room was spinning beyond her squeezed-shut eyes, and there was a coarse droning in her ears. *Someone can jump and be pushed at the same time. Or just be pushed.*

"It's all right," whispered Ferain. "We're done here. We'll leave and head for Miresse, find somewhere to shelter along the way. Together, you and me."

She touched her mouth a second time. Ferain had seen. No one was supposed to see. This was meant to be in the past; she was not a child anymore, to cower and let her father hit her. Too afraid to even move. Why, after so long, had nothing changed?

Footfalls outside again, running. Karys' stomach clenched. She lifted her head, but before she could rise, the door was already swinging open.

Haeki was drenched to the bone. Her long hair stuck to her shoulders like curling vines, and she held the doorframe as she caught her breath, her skin flushed. Her eyes found Karys' face.

"He's going to be fucking furious," she panted.

The wind gusted into the kitchen. Karys felt immobile.

"I must have mentioned Ané about fifteen times. Figured that might get his attention." Haeki stepped inside, and held out a hand. "Come on, we need to go."

Karys stared up at Haeki, at her familiar features grown older and stronger and more solid, and felt the years dissolve around her. She was fourteen, standing before the Penitence Pool with Oboro, watching a rat flounder and drown. An offering, he had said, but it had not sounded like him, and she had not felt like herself, and she had stood there, just stood there. And then Haeki was there too, but yelling, yelling and rushing past with a net, yelling at Oboro while she scooped up the trembling creature, furious and bold and unassailable, yelling at him until he yelled back and the awful hard light left his eyes, and the rat shivered in the grass, and the world was set to rights. Karys' head was filled with a low buzzing, and her throat felt too tight to speak through. But she tried.

"How did you—" she swallowed. "How did you know to knock?"

Haeki's expression softened, even though her voice stayed the same.

"I've got ways," she said. "I'll tell you about them, and you can explain what's living in your shadow. But later."

Karys looked at Haeki's still-outstretched hand.

"I thought you weren't on my side," she said, and couldn't quite keep the tremor out of her voice.

"Then you're even stupider than you look. Let me help you."

Karys shivered, and took her hand. With no effort at all, Haeki pulled her upright. Her palm was calloused and warm, damp from the rain.

"You were meant to stay with me until the send-off," she muttered. "I had it all planned, but you always have to be so stubborn about everything. Grab your coat, let's go."

Leaving the house, Haeki appeared tense: her shoulders bunched, her eyes scanning the dusk fields and the path down to the village. The wind had picked up once more, thinning the clouds above the sea. Early stars glimmered amongst the blue. Ferain kept close to Karys, not bothering to conceal himself. She moved quickly to keep up with Haeki.

"What are you going to tell everyone?" she asked.

"Nothing," said Haeki.

"They're going to ask."

"And then? What are they going to do? Your father doesn't scare me."

The old track was flooded; they wound along the edge of the muddy fields. The trees in the orchard groaned in the wind. Karys' body felt heavy, her head too light. Where she had been hit, she could feel her skin bruising. There was a muted ringing in her ears. At any moment, she expected to see her father emerge through the rain; she could almost hear him shouting her name. The bright copper taste of blood remained in her mouth.

She didn't want to think about Oboro, but that whispered gasp—*he knew!*—haunted her. They were heading toward the cliffs now, following the path to the Penitence Pool.

"Haeki?"

Haeki did not look back. "It'll be safe up there."

"My father knew Oboro was going to leave Boäz."

Haeki's step faltered, and she went strangely still. After a second, she kept walking.

The old path was paved in shell and bone and brine-cryst, set with silver. It shone white in the last rays of thin daylight. Karys shivered as they climbed. Up ahead, the rim of the pool gleamed like the curved edge of a sickle moon. Before the Slaughter, it had been Boäz's custom to chain up sinners and throw them into the water, so that Nuliere could take measure of their remorse—the herald either dragged the condemned under, or dissolved their bonds. Approaching the pool now, Karys could feel its pull on the Veneer; taste the metallic presence of ancient ritual. The ringing in her ears continued unabated, and she stumbled over her own feet. If anything, the noise was growing louder: a harsh, vibrating drone.

"What's the matter?" asked Ferain.

"Nothing, my head just hurts," she muttered, trying to shrug it off. "I shouldn't be so . . ."

She trailed off as the sound became sharper still, an angry insect hiss that set her teeth on edge. Haeki glanced back to see why she had stopped walking.

"Karys?" she said.

The sound was unmistakable; she *knew* that droning. And it was getting closer.

"Oh shit," breathed Karys. Her words tumbled together. "Construct. There's a Construct. I can hear it."

"What are you talking about?"

It had followed her to Boäz. Ferain had said New Favour could compel the creatures to hunt their enemies. The saints had set a Construct on her.

"Are there transport workings in the village?" asked Ferain quickly. "Or even horses, anything fast you could steal?"

Karys raked her fingers through her hair. "I can't lead it down there; that would be a massacre."

"How about boats, could you—"

"The sea's too rough." Her heart thumped. "Is there a way I could hide from it?"

"Stop talking to yourself and tell me what's going on," said Haeki.

The droning grew louder. Karys' blood pounded against the wall of her skull, and she looked back toward the road. She could not see the Construct yet—the dusk light and the rain worked to conceal it—but it would not be long now. Through the misted air, she thought she detected movement. With a frustrated sound, Haeki snatched her wrist.

"Just tell me how to help," she demanded.

"You should leave," said Karys unsteadily. "Quickly."

The wind screamed through the channel between the cliffs. And there— her heart clenched. No telltale firefly lights, but where the main road met the cliff path, a dark figure was advancing. He strode up the switchback on his long legs. Although his face was shadowed, Karys could read the fury in his body: in the set of his wide shoulders, the curl of his fists.

"Ah, fuck," muttered Haeki.

Dayon Eska had seen them; he was moving fast, his hard-capped boots swift on the silver path. Haeki squeezed Karys' wrist, then pulled her onward, up toward the pool.

"You think you can run away again?" her father yelled.

The vegetation at the top of the rise was wild and fragrant; grasses as high as their knees, white chincherinchees and gum-bush. The pool, black-walled and wide, formed a dark mirror to the sky. The surface of the water remained preternaturally smooth.

"Karys, we're going to be cornered." Ferain veered back and forth across the ground, his voice urgent. "Turn back. If you keep going, there'll be nowhere to run."

Haeki's expression was grimly focussed; she kept going until she reached the wall of the pool, then released Karys' wrist. With a grimace, she pulled off her coat, baring her arms to the swirl of rain and wind.

At that moment, the Veneer *flexed.*

"Help me."

Oboro's voice rose from the earth, far louder than before, and the wind whistled with a new force. Neither her father nor Haeki showed any sign they could hear the revenant, but Ferain cursed, and Karys' shadow grew denser at her feet. Nerves prickling, she opened the Veneer. Up on the cliff top, the weave was slick with power, a tumult of bright sound and colour.

Oboro's revenant hovered ten feet from her. His form had changed; he appeared as a red cloud teeming with clusters of staring black eyes. Light strained tight around him, like he was sucking reality into himself.

"Karys." The eyes blinked and fluttered. "Do you see me now?"

"He's stronger," she whispered. "Ferain—"

"I won't lose control," her shadow replied.

"Don't leave me again." Oboro's tone was plaintive—not the tenor of a grown man. He sounded like a lonely boy. "No one else ever understood."

By this time, her father had closed the distance between them. His skin was blotchy and his collar loose; he looked hot with anger. He stamped up the path, ever closer to Oboro. Haeki put her right hand into the pool behind them.

"Far enough, old man," she called, her voice ringing clear.

Dayon Eska spat, still climbing. "I should have known you for a liar, Maas."

Karys' mouth felt bone dry. The Construct's droning grew ever louder, Oboro's revenant swayed and swelled with red light, her father . . . her father. He had that look on his face: that hard, cold fury, that same winter-sea viciousness she knew so well. Exactly as she remembered him.

Like struck flint, anger kindled in her too.

"Did Oboro jump, Da?" she demanded.

His mouth twisted and went thin, but he said nothing. Behind her, Karys could hear the water in the pool moving, seething like it boiled.

"You knew he was going to leave." Her voice came out high and tight. "You *knew.*"

"Quiet," he snapped.

"I'm so cold," said Oboro. "I had nowhere to go, and I couldn't take the step into nothing. He was always there. I didn't want to become him, Karys. Why did you leave me behind? Why won't you let me in? It was supposed to be—"

Her father passed through the revenant's clouded form. His face was briefly haloed in scarlet, and Oboro fell silent. The red haze rippled and compressed; Dayon Eska did not seem to feel anything, but now every one of the swarm's eyes locked upon his back, unblinking.

"We're going home," her father growled. "And Karys, if you ever, *ever,* think of—"

Oboro plunged forward, swirling around his father in a blur of eyes and colour, concealing him from Karys' sight. She took a step toward them instinctively, but Haeki raised one arm to stop her. Dayon Eska jerked to a halt, and produced a harsh, choked whimper.

"And now?" demanded Haeki.

He did not answer. The revenant drew closer and closer around him, emitting a sound like fire igniting: a low stream of guttural words spoken too quickly to be understood. The Veneer darkened the air surrounding them.

"It's trying to take over his body," said Ferain suddenly. "It's contestation, it's what Winola—"

With a crack loud as bones shattering, the red haze sank into her father's torso and vanished. Dayon Eska stood there, chest unmoving, face slack. Blood ran from his ears and nose.

"What was that?" Haeki muttered, and for the first time she sounded genuinely alarmed. "Old man?"

He's dead.

Her father was dead.

Karys had not realised she was moving until the small of her back hit the pool's wall. Her father, face devoid of any expression, leaned his head to one side. His lifeless gaze was directed at her, but there was nothing at all behind those eyes; she stared into a fathomless abyss where a person had been. And it was trying to speak.

"It is not . . . warm." His lips stumbled over the sounds. "I thought . . . it would be warm."

"Embrace," Ferain breathed.

The sight of her father's corpse, puppeteered on invisible threads, was hypnotic. Awful, fascinating—the way blood drained from his cheeks; the minute, searching quivers of his arms and legs, an uncertain force testing them for the first time. He lifted one foot, inched it forward, put it down again. The movement seemed to demand absolute deliberation and control. His head remained tilted to the side as if forgotten.

Karys was so transfixed that she almost missed the Construct's approach. A blur of yellow stars, a tidal-surge of droning, and the creature reached the crest of the hill. It advanced like a landslide; she shouted a warning just before it was upon them.

What happened next was unclear. Karys saw Haeki throw her head back—spine arching, skin gleaming pale blue in the dusk—and then Ferain was between them. A fraction of a heartbeat later, and pressure blasted outward from the pool. The long grass flattened, the flowers were ripped from their stems. Both Dayon Eska's body and the Construct were swept down the hill, and Karys' knees buckled as a violent weakness seized her.

What was that?

"That shining thing is your Construct?" Haeki sounded winded. She supported herself against the wall of the pool, bent over and clutching her chest. "I don't like the look of it."

The creature was far larger than any Karys had seen in the Sanctum. The Veneer around its body was scorched and distorted; it blistered the air. She could taste its presence in the back of her throat: a sweet, cloying, rotten flavour. It gathered itself with a shiver of light and advanced once more, cautiously this time.

"A plan, Karys?" said Haeki warily.

The droning in her ears made it hard to even think straight. Karys looked to the cliff edge. Ferain guessed what was on her mind; her shadow pivoted around, placing himself between her and the jump. As if that would make any difference at all.

"Don't you dare," he said fiercely. "Not that. Don't make me watch you do it."

"The Construct won't stop," she whispered.

"You've escaped before, you can do it again. We aren't giving up here."

Karys gritted her teeth, and turned to face the creature again. Even if she jumped, there was no guarantee it would save Haeki; the Construct was too close now. They were cornered, just as Ferain had anticipated. Her breathing came jagged. Her fault—she had drawn the Construct here, she had brought it down on Boäz. She should never have come back. But if this abomination was borne of Ephirite workings, then she, a deathspeaker of Ephirite-making, could stand against it. She had sold her soul for power. Let her fucking well *use* it.

With a snarl, Karys tore through reality and plunged into the depths of the Veneer.

The world eclipsed. The hillside vanished into grey fog, and her senses were subsumed by the violent force of workings. She dove deeper, pressing into the tumult. The Construct blazed with unnatural fire, and the Penitence Pool howled like an animal in pain. Weaker forces swirled around her father's corpse—red and wounded—and over Haeki, whose body was streaked with a shifting pall of hallowfire. When Karys inhaled, she felt her lungs might catch alight.

The Construct had reached the top of the slope once more. This time, however, Karys could *see* into it, like a body dissected on a slab. A tight knot of workings sat in its core, a web of bindings, and she felt their function; she knew how the Construct had been lashed together, melted and cauterised and remoulded by an unknowable will.

And just as she could sense those threads of function, Karys could reach out her own will and grasp them. Her body burned, her mind was flayed, but she was a child of Boäz, a child raised by the sea and tangled in nets, and she could unravel knots. The bindings loosened and, with a vicious yank, she pulled the creature apart.

The Veneer exploded. Her vision was obliterated; she could not see, she could scarcely feel anything but an intense burning cold throughout her body. Too overwhelmed for fear or thought, she remained suspended in the light and the sound and the roar all around her. There was no way to retreat, no way to pull back; the weave of the Veneer was gone, and with it all semblance of pattern and order. Sheer chaos rushed through her. She could feel her mind slipping; with nothing to grasp, she was falling ever deeper, ever further from herself.

"Karys!" shouted Ferain.

Amidst the storm, she could discern the fading yellow brilliance of the Construct as it collapsed. Even as it came undone, it was still moving; its body spread to envelop her. She observed its descent, detached from the world.

Only, there was a darker shadow between them now. A tall figure wreathed in red. A man, facing her. She could hardly see, but she thought he was smiling.

"I'm sorry," said Oboro.

Her father's corpse shoved her backwards as the Construct swallowed him. The force carried her over the wall of the pool; as her shoulders struck the water, she saw the creature bloom red. Then she was under the surface, and cold hands grasped her limbs and pulled her down.

CHAPTER

19

Lights, brilliant, flashing, whorls of obscene colour. The pool was screaming—Karys wanted to join in, but she could only choke. Cold water filled up her lungs, and it howled *inside* her, shrieking and clamouring to escape. She was sinking, she was sliding, she was drowning; the Veneer continued to dissolve in her senses, and there was no air. Instead she was dragged deeper, deeper, down into the Penitence Pool.

There was a voice—Ferain's, she still recognised it—but in her frozen, thrashing panic, she could not understand him. Bubbles streamed upwards, breath fleeing her mouth. Darkness, light, blue rioting against gold and black and orange, sinking, sliding, drowning—

And then air flooded her mouth. Karys' body convulsed, and her lungs emptied; water spilled over her hands as she clutched her throat. It burned, everything felt hot and cold at once. She was on her knees, bowed over and shuddering.

"Breathe!" Ferain's voice was frantic and unrestrained, unlike himself. She could hear him now, could decipher his words. "Come on, damn you, breathe!"

Another choking cough, more water, and she inhaled. The pain cut like razors in her chest.

"Ferain, I'm sliding," she gasped. "The Veneer—I can't get out. It's everywhere, I can't—"

"No, focus on me. You aren't going anywhere, Karys, just focus on *me*."

There's nothing to hold on to. Except her shadow. All was dark, all was bright, but she knew where her shadow lay. Ferain kept her anchored to the world by a slender thread, a single point of certainty in the writhing, sickening chaos.

"That's it," he said. "I'm here, I'm right beside you."

She could feel him, the subtle weight of his presence. Her shadow was draped across her shoulders, close and tense.

"Stay with me," he said. "It's going to be all right now."

Karys' lips felt numb. "My—my brother."

"There was nothing you could have done."

Karys concentrated on her shadow, and the howling around her grew quieter. The terrifying slickness of the world receded, and the blooms of light gave way to a more ordinary darkness. The Veneer remained open, but she could pull away from it, dragging herself back to her own body one painful inch at a time. Her breathing evened.

"Where am I?" she whispered.

"I don't know."

The ground beneath her knees was soft. Sand. She dug her fingers into it. It still felt as though she was underwater, or that she was suspended in something between water and air. Her movements met a slight resistance; a light pressure pushing against her skin. But she could breathe. She lifted her head. Nothing but darkness.

"Wherever we are, it's . . . strange," said Ferain. "I can't tell where it ends."

Karys let her head drop down again, and closed her eyes. She still felt unstable, as though she were clumsily stitched together and at risk of coming apart.

"Part of Nuliere's Sanctum," she said softly. "I think. The Bhatuma for Boäz; the Lady of Brine and Urchins. We threw sinners in the pool, and she judged them. There were two drownings when I was a girl. Temple thieves. It's forbidden to speak of them."

"That would have been after the Slaughter."

She nodded. The movement hurt. With effort, she pushed herself onto all fours, and then to her feet. Her hair floated around her face, and her clothes wafted. Not air. Not water.

"Ferain?" she murmured.

"What is it?"

"Stay close to me. Please."

The world remained black and quiet. Karys had barely walked ten paces before her foot came down on a hard, smooth object. It held her weight for a brief second, then cracked inward. She did not need to see it to know it was a skull. She removed her foot, and was still a moment.

"I am not afraid," she said, raising her voice. "Not of you."

The darkness held its silence. Karys waited, staring into the black. A faint change in the pressure around her: the suggestion of movement. Her hair rippled, touched by an invisible current.

"You should be," said a voice like frost cracking on stone.

Karys made a sound of contempt.

Beads of hallowfire bled to life around her; thumbnail-sized spheres that illuminated the darkness in unearthly blue. There were hundreds, perhaps thousands, stretching off into the murky gloom. Before her: a dark mass, a living hill glowing with rings of dull orange and circles of yellow. It was twice her height and about eight times that across, and its surface bristled with thick, curved spines.

"It can't be," whispered Ferain.

"Do you know," said Karys, addressing the hill, "that I tried to look you up? In the best college in Mercia, I sought your name. And do you know what I found?"

"Insolent apostate," hissed the hill. "You will address me with respect."

"Nothing." Karys made a sweeping gesture, encompassing the barren graveyard around her. "Nothing at all. Not a word, not a mention, not a passing reference. You are nothing, Nuliere. The world never even bothered to learn your name."

"That . . . that's a Bhatuma," Ferain breathed.

Nuliere's fury coursed through the space around her huge body. The herald rocked from side to side, stirring clouds of sea sand. Bones gleamed pale blue across the ground, the scattered remains of those who had drowned in the pool. Generations of the dead, generations of Nuliere's victims. But Karys was reckless now, and she spoke loud and quick.

"Throw your tantrums, I don't care," she said. "Embrace knows I wasted enough of my youth trying to make you happy, you poisonous coward of a slug."

The hill emitted a high-pitched sound, an incensed trill that cut into Karys' ears. She gritted her teeth and refused to budge.

"Is that your best?" she asked. "Is that all you can do, herald? Whine?"

"I could peel the flesh from your bones," Nuliere seethed. "I could choke you with blood. I could—"

"You could have done *something*!" Karys' own anger was like a noose pulled tight around her neck, and her voice cracked. "You could have saved me."

Nuliere's shrill complaint ceased. The hill went still.

"Where were you?" Karys trembled, not with fear, but with far stronger feeling. "You reveal yourself to me now? Now? Where were you when I begged for your aid in Miresse, when I promised you everything, anything—" She stopped, unable to continue, her voice trapped in her throat. One shallow breath. She swallowed. "How could that not be enough?"

"I do not hear the prayers of apostates."

"You filthy *liar*." Karys bunched her fists. "I wasn't an apostate, not until you left me with no choice but to turn to the Ephirite for help. *You* did this to me. And Oboro? Was his faith lacking? Get fucked, Nuliere."

A hard force knocked Karys backwards; she lost her purchase on the sand and went sprawling.

"I need not explain my choices." Nuliere's voice sliced through the liquid air. "I judged you unworthy, and that is sufficient. As for your brother, I do not interfere in the matters of my adherents. His fate was not mine to alter."

Karys sat up, clutching her side. "You're full of shit."

"I am your herald! You will address me—"

"Either I'm an apostate or your adherent. Not both." She dragged herself back to her feet. "You won't scare me, so why not just tell me what you want?"

Silence again.

"If you wanted me dead, I'd be dead." Karys shook her head. "So what is it?"

Nuliere did not move. The rash of orange disks covering her skin brightened and dimmed like a heartbeat. The sand settled around her. Seeing the invisible tyrant of her childhood at last, Karys could summon no reverence or wonder. She only felt contempt for the mound of boneless flesh lurking in this dark, forgotten place. It was like turning over a stone and seeing something hideous on the underside. This, this was the Lady of Brine and Urchins, perhaps the only Bhatuma remaining in the world. What a monument. What a joke. She had only survived by virtue of being utterly inconsequential.

"I want nothing from you," said Nuliere at last. "And although your death would please me, other considerations take precedence."

"Which considerations?"

Nuliere's lights dimmed; she seemed loath to reply to her former adherent's impudence. The hill stirred, then sagged like fat melting in a pan.

"Ambavar's progeny," she replied.

"What?"

But Karys' shadow had gone rigid, her silhouette turned to hard angles. "No, that can't—"

"I greet you, Son of Night," said Nuliere, and produced a curious whistling sound. "The Embrace favours our meeting."

Ferain seemed stricken. Karys looked up at Nuliere in confusion.

"You . . . what?" she said. "You mean Ferain? But how did you know—"

Nuliere acted as though Karys had not spoken.

"I have observed your suffering from afar," she said, and her tone was markedly different. The Bhatuma seemed warm, benevolent, even gentle. "I have seen how you have been persecuted, and feared for you. The usurpers have cast a wider net. You now fall within the scope of their hungers."

"Have you gone senile?" asked Karys.

"Silence, apostate! I shall remove your tongue."

Ferain's voice was gravelly. "This isn't possible. There's been . . . this is a mistake."

"No mistake, Son of Night. But do not fear, I mean you no harm."

She can hear him too? A chill ran down Karys' spine. *What is going on here?* Her shadow hesitated. "You . . . watched me? How? And why?"

"Where there is salt in the water, so am I," said Nuliere. "My influence diminishes at a greater distance from my Sanctum, but I may still exert some fraction of my power within the jurisdictions of other heralds. As to why? Because we are alone in this diminished world. I seek what kindred I can."

"Kindred!?" exclaimed Karys.

"No," said Ferain. "No, I'm not—you're not—"

Nuliere seemed vexed; her rings pulsed brighter. However, her voice remained even and conciliatory.

"No matter how thin the blood, you are of our line, Son of Night," she said.

"Stop calling me that." His voice grew more heated. "The Bhatuma don't have any claim on me."

"I do not seek to claim you. Only to protect you, to preserve what fragments of our grace persist in the world, to salvage what little remains of what we were. To shield you from the usurpers and their servants. You must see how fiercely the enemy pursues you?"

There was a long silence, before Karys' shadow made a strangled, tortured sound.

"You're wrong," he said. "This is all wrong. I'm nothing like you."

"But even now, the enemy hunts you. Surely you do not believe that is a coincidence? They mean to slaughter you, Son of Night, as they have slaughtered all others."

Ferain is . . . Bhatuma? Karys could not wrap her mind around the idea. Her shadow had lost coherence; it warped and distorted, flickering over the sand at her feet. She shivered. It felt like the ground had shifted; the realities she had taken for granted were no longer certain. *Explain,* she wanted to say. *Let me understand.*

"That is why the Embrace has brought you to me," said Nuliere. "You shall be alone no longer. I will accompany you, guide you—I can show you how to hide from them."

"New Favour is just trying to finish what they started when they murdered Ambassador Corbain," snapped Ferain. "It has nothing to do with—"

"Kindred, why do you believe they attacked your ship in the first place?"

Karys' shadow guttered like fire banking. His distress gave her a queasy feeling—if what Nuliere had said was true, then the ambassadorial retinue, his colleagues and friends, had been murdered simply because they were in his proximity. Not assassinated, but mere collateral damage. Incidental losses.

"Only I can keep you safe," Nuliere pressed, emboldened by his silence. "Varesli is a haven. I will direct your course, I will show you—"

"Enough," said Karys.

Without a sound, Ferain stilled. Karys gazed down at him. She did not know what was true, did not know how much he had hidden from her or why—but she mistrusted Nuliere. The Lady of Brine and Urchins had never been generous or gentle; she was a Mercian herald through and through. Ferain might not see it, but Karys could: right now, the Bhatuma was deliberately twisting the knife.

"You've said enough," said Karys, soft and clear. "Leave him alone."

"You *dare*—"

"If he's your kin, then let him choose. He can ask for your help if he wants it."

Nuliere hissed, but did not lash out. With shuddering effort, the hill contained its anger, and when she spoke again, her tone was satin-smooth and placating.

"I have no desire to pressure you, Son of Night," she said. "Would you prefer to think on matters?"

Ferain's voice was only just audible.

"Let Karys go," he said.

Returning to the surface was painless and swift. Karys' vision went dark, water streamed over her skin, she had the sense of rapid movement. Then light. She broke the surface of the pool. The sky above had deepened to dull violet, and stars glittered like tiny shards of crushed sea glass. She sucked in air—normal, cold air—and Haeki was there, pulling her up from the water with unnatural strength. They were alone. No Construct. No father. No Oboro. The waves cracked against the shore down below.

It was all unreal, suddenly, everything that had happened here. Haeki asked gruffly whether she was hurt, and Karys started to say that she was fine, then changed her mind and shook her head. She was alive. She should never have returned to Boäz, but she was alive.

"I'm cold," she said. "I'm going back to the farm."

Ferain was silent. When they started down the silver path, her shadow darkened the track ahead of her, falling against all natural order, defying the last bruised glow of daylight to lead her home.

CHAPTER

20

They stole into the village before daybreak. The air held a rare, near-impossible stillness, and the waves broke low against the beach. A clear day. Gulls and cormorants wheeled up high over the cliffs, their sharp voices travelling.

The temple was locked, but the doors swung inward at Haeki's touch. It would be an hour before Ané arrived to attend to the morning rites. Karys wondered how the priestess would react, discovering the building standing open and Oboro gone. At another time, the idea might have amused her, but now it scarcely seemed to matter.

They carried the pallet between them, along the empty street and down to the boardwalk, and from there to the boatyard. Haeki kept a small fishing boat; they dragged the vessel to the water, then set Oboro's body inside it. Difficult, heavy, awkward work. The dead were normally given to the sea by the whole village, but the two of them were enough. Karys sweated in silence. Warm seawater splashed up to her thighs, and she pulled herself aboard while Haeki held the boat steady. Oboro lay beside her, his pallet resting across both benches. She helped Haeki up, and they both took oars, and rowed out on the dark blue water.

There wasn't much to say. Haeki had stayed at the farm the night before, her presence both comforting and strange. Familiar things looked different with someone else to witness them. When Karys told her to go home, she had pretended not to hear, and, too worn out to argue, Karys had stripped off Oboro's wet clothes and gone to bed. Haeki had remained in the kitchen.

At some time during the night, Karys had woken to the sound of a door closing. In total disorientation, she started to get up, convinced her father had returned from tending the trees. Ferain spoke quietly.

"It's all right," he said. "Haeki left an hour ago; she's just come back now."

The bedroom door stood slightly open. Through the crack, Karys could see Haeki warming her hands before the stove. Her hair gleamed wet once more, though the rain had long since stopped.

"Go back to sleep," said Ferain.

When Karys woke again, Haeki was still in the kitchen, seated at the table

and eating a plate of clove-spiced quince and flatbread from the larder. The
room was cosy and warm, and it remained dark outside and very quiet. Haeki
looked up when she appeared.

"Will you help me with Oboro's send-off?" asked Karys. "Just us?"

Haeki nodded.

"That sounds like a good idea," she said.

The regular sweep of the oars through the water lulled Karys' thoughts
now; the soft smack of little waves against the boat. It felt like she could only
focus on one task at a time. When her mind turned to her father, or Nuliere,
or Ferain, she felt her sense of surety in the world slipping—the Veneer's fell
madness crept closer, and a fearful, suffocating pressure wrapped around her
chest. It would all wait, it all had to wait. She would untangle everything later,
but not before she had given Oboro his send-off. When she looked down at
him, her brother's face belonged to a stranger: remote and untroubled. The
sugar on his lips glittered like ice in the dawn, and, briefly, she could see a hint
of the person she remembered.

"I asked Nuliere last night. About what happened to him."

Karys raised her head. Haeki's eyes were fixed on the water, her hands tight
around the oars as she rowed.

"She's not usually forthcoming, but . . ." A shrug. "I asked. She told me that
he went up there on his own." Her oars dipped, came up again. "To request her
blessing. He meant to go, meant to leave Boäz like you. He was going to do it.
Planned to take me with him, if I'd agree."

"I see," murmured Karys.

Haeki's mouth did a complex thing, going soft and then hard.

"What I don't understand is how your father found out," she said. "Oboro
and I talked it over a hundred times, but never with anyone else."

"He must have let it slip."

"No, he was too careful—however your old man uncovered the plan, it
wasn't from him. But your father knew, and he followed Oboro up there. They
argued. And then, I guess . . ." Her hands clenched so tightly that the wood of
the oars groaned. "That's what Nuliere told me. That he didn't jump."

The white gulls drifted overhead. The sky had lightened, clear and empty
and pale. The sun would rise soon.

"I knew," said Karys. "Not with any proof or certainty. But I knew."

"For how long?"

"Since I got your letter, I think. This is probably far enough."

Haeki set her oars down. Her cheeks were wet, and she would not look at

Karys. The boat rocked on the water. Behind them, Boäz appeared small and dark.

"When they found him, I blamed you," she said. "Easier to put the fault on you for leaving, than on the person who might have done it. Easier than thinking I might have saved him myself. It has been so easy to hate you."

Karys didn't say anything. The still air pressed close, and the cries of the birds echoed like faraway voices. After a moment, Haeki set her hand on the edge of Oboro's pallet.

"Far enough," she agreed.

They placed pearls in his ears and silver in his fists, and laid white flowers in a veil over his chest. Karys said the rites—she knew them well enough—and Haeki tied weights to his feet and wrists. Together, they lifted him off the boat. Before letting the weights drop, Karys studied her brother's face a final time.

I'm sorry, too, she thought. *Goodbye, Oboro.*

The sun touched the edge of the horizon with gold, and they released him.

When they returned to the shore, Boäz had roused. Ané and a few other residents were already waiting, standing around and scowling. Haeki jumped out of the boat before it even touched sand, and strode forward to meet the crowd. Karys stayed with the vessel, pulling it up from the shallows on her own.

Ané had, for the first time since the Slaughter, been directly addressed by Nuliere. The Bhatuma had spoken to her that morning, and made certain facts known. The first was that she had deemed Dayon Eska unworthy, and his name was to be forgotten in Boäz—he would walk among them no more. The second was that Karys Eska was a deathspeaker, a servant of the abhorred usurpers, and was to be banished from the village. However, on the herald's mercy, she was not to be harmed. The third was that Haeki Maas was sea-blessed, one of Nuliere's chosen Favoured, and had an important task that required the cooperation of the village. They were to follow her instructions.

Karys hauled the rowboat up the beach and into the yard, and secured it in its berth. No one assisted her; the faithful would not lift a hand to aid an apostate. Across the beach, Haeki was arguing with Ané. The priestess looked deeply displeased, and kept gesturing toward the temple. Whatever their disagreement, it didn't seem like it required Karys' involvement. She followed the boardwalk back to the village, and started up the road to the farm. There wasn't much for her to collect: her bag and clothes, a few valuables, the money from the safe. It was early. She could easily make it back to Miresse by the end of the day.

"She didn't have to tell them you were a deathspeaker," said Ferain.

"I thought the slug was suspiciously generous, actually."

"We have a different understanding of 'generous.' Are you all right?"

Karys walked slowly. There were sparrows in the trees, and it smelled like wet grass. "Are you?"

"Well, I've been worse. And it's nice, us both still being alive. I feel that's a significant positive."

"Low standards."

"Trying to keep things in perspective."

She reached the farm gate. A few of her father's goats cropped at the lush green weeds along the fence. She let herself in, and closed the gate after her. "So, are you a Bhatuma?"

"Do you really believe that?"

"No."

"Good. Because I'm not."

"Part-Bhatuma, then?"

He groaned.

"Nuliere seemed very eager to adopt you." Karys walked lightly along the verge of the muddy track. "'Ambavar's progeny,' wasn't it? That would be the Lord of Night—the old herald of Eludia, the one with the stolen human bride?"

"I shouldn't have told you that story."

"I already knew it." She reached the house, unlatched the kitchen door, and walked inside. "Or a version of it, anyway."

Ferain grumbled.

"Yes," he said. "That Ambavar."

He was acting surly, but Karys thought that she detected something else underneath, a genuine discomfort. She picked up her bag from the shelf. "It's all right if you'd prefer not to talk about it."

"That wouldn't be fair to you." Her shadow settled on the counter, folding toward the window so that her silhouette looked out at the orchard. He sighed. "Especially after the last few days. It's fine, it's just history. So, let's see, Ambavar abducted my mother's grandfather's grandmother around three hundred years ago. This was a little after Varesli's secession from the Osiran Empire, when Eludia was still the capital. At the time, Ambavar was amongst the most powerful living Bhatuma, and he ensured the city's prosperity, which of course made him very popular. He also seemed to take an unusual interest in his adherents, adopting human aspects to walk among his people unnoticed, which is presumably how he met my ancestor. According to records, she was around fifteen when he spirited her away, but he kept her for a hundred and thirteen years after that, before returning her to Eludia without explanation. By that point, all of her immediate family was dead, and the world had changed—but she hadn't aged a day. She returned to a city where she was already a living legend: 'the mortal embodiment of Eludia's ties to the divine.'"

He paused.

"Accounts suggest that the experience left her mute; she never spoke a word after she returned. So it's a little ironic that the Temple of Elevation immediately appointed her as their Blessed Interlocutor—but on the other hand, maybe it was just convenient. Ambavar's priests wielded enormous influence back then; they functionally ruled the city. If they *hadn't* claimed her, any of her surviving relatives might have challenged the Temple's dominance by declaring themselves Ambavar's most highly Favoured family." He snorted. "Not to mention that you can put any words you want into the mouth of a girl who never speaks. She was the most honoured person in the city, and no one cared about her at all. Then, a few months later, it came out that she was pregnant."

"Oh."

"Suggestive, isn't it? The Temple went into a frenzy. Rare enough that a herald would sire a child, but for it to be Ambavar? Unheard of. If the girl was the embodiment of Eludia's ties to the divine, then her child would be the culmination of all favour: flesh proof of Ambavar's blessing. The Temple reported that the infant was his, and traipsed his former bride through the city for everyone to see. Made a festival of it. But there were two small problems." Her shadow, reflected on the wall beside the window, raised two fingers. "The first was that Ambavar himself was utterly silent on the subject; the herald refused to claim the child, and never acknowledged the girl again. The second was that the gestation period failed to line up. She gave birth *thirteen* months after her return to the city. Unfortunately for the Temple, ordinary people can count."

"Then it wasn't his?"

"Well, the Temple tried to sell the idea that a divine pregnancy might operate differently. Some people believed them. But more likely? One or more of the priests took advantage of an isolated, traumatised girl, and then tried to cover it up. No one openly challenged the order about the abuse, not even the girl's relatives. If people didn't *really* believe the priests, they were still willing to accept the story." He shrugged. "A year after that, she slit her own throat."

Karys knew that detail from the version she had read in Psikamit College's library. "So that's why you don't like Ambavar?"

"A part of the reason, I suppose. It's complicated. He granted Favour to my ancestors, and that . . ." He stopped, and shook his head. "I don't believe I'm related to him, no. Although my father does—I suspect it's why he married my mother in the first place. To get a little closer to history. If nothing else, there's a certain political capital in my bloodline."

Karys wasn't sure she had ever heard Ferain sound so bitter. She walked over to the larder, and crouched down to reach the lower shelves.

"Family is an ugly business," she said.

"It can be." His voice drifted out from the kitchen. "You never answered my question."

The preserve jars were neatly stacked up where she had left them yesterday. For a moment, Karys saw them shattered in pieces on the floor. Heard the ghost of her father yelling at her to clean up the mess. "You ask a lot."

"Are you all right, Karys?"

The safe sat behind three jars of cured squid; when she shifted them out of the way, her shirt sleeve pulled up. The scar from the Split Lapse now sat squarely in the middle of her wrist. The pale mark looked no different in size or shape; all that had changed was its location. Karys tugged her sleeve back down, and set the safe on the floor.

"I will be," she said. "Once I'm out of this place."

The lock on the safe, worked to recognise her father, now opened for her. Last in line. Inside was a small stash of cret and rough-forged jewellery; silver and pearls, meagre heirlooms. A thin chain bracelet with an ugly hematite setting. A blackened silver ring. She could pawn off the metal in Miresse, maybe earn thirty cret if she was lucky. *Some inheritance.* Still, she felt better, coming away with something. Karys tucked the cret into her waistband, dropped the jewellery in her bag, then returned to the kitchen.

"What you saw here, with my father, well . . ." Her skin crawled, her mouth went dry, and suddenly it was difficult to get the words out at all. "Please could you forget it happened? I want to leave this behind; it isn't—it's not who I am."

Ferain was still stretched out on the counter beside the window, her shadow cut into his profile. When he spoke, his voice was at once sincere and light. "I'm sorry, but who is your father again? My memory is terrible."

The force of her relief took Karys by surprise. After a second, she nodded, and managed a smile. Then she cast a final look around the kitchen, her eyes lingering on old familiar things. A small, mean place. It would have no hold on her again.

"Nobody," she said.

Outside, the sky remained clear and cloudless. Karys shut the kitchen door, and shouldered her bag. The sea breeze lifted her hair, carrying the smell of salt. She felt lighter. Back to Miresse—but from there she would move forward: forward across the border to Varesli, forward and nearer to her goals. In the bright cool morning, it all seemed more likely, more possible. At the fork in the road past the gate, Haeki was standing next to a wooden cart. She raised a hand and waved.

"So Haeki's Favoured," said Ferain. "Sea-blessed, you call it?"

Karys set off down the track. "I wouldn't consider Nuliere's attention a *blessing*, but yes."

"It's incredible that any Bhatuma survived the Slaughter." Abruptly, her shadow laughed. "Although I still can't believe you told your own herald to fuck herself. I thought you were going to die, then."

"It might have even been worth it."

"For you, maybe. I'd have had some objections."

"I wouldn't have heard them over her screeching, anyway." Karys glanced at him. "What she said last night? Don't give it too much weight. She wants something from you, and she'll spin a story to get it. Doesn't make it true."

"Hm." Ferain's humour faded. "Thanks, Karys."

Haeki crossed her arms when Karys approached the farm wagon, which juddered and droned with the power of a degraded Bhatuma-derived working. Her posture struck Karys as oddly defensive, almost combative: her feet planted squarely, and her chin raised. Like she was expecting an argument.

"Did Ané give you trouble?" asked Karys.

Haeki made a sweeping gesture to convey how little she cared about the priestess. "Nothing worth mentioning. Tion's taking the farm; he'll pay once he has the means, and I'll make sure the money reaches you. I figured that would suit everyone."

"Oh. I wasn't expecting—"

"It won't be much, and it won't be soon. But the place was yours by rights."

Karys frowned. "Does that matter now that I'm banished?"

"It does if I say so." A tiny glimmer of a smile appeared at the corners of Haeki's mouth. "Boäz doesn't have to like it, but they'll come to heel."

"Turning tyrant fast, huh?"

"You mean 'getting even.'" She flicked a lock of hair back over her shoulder. "Honestly, Ané and the rest can chew sand for all I care. I've got more important things to worry about."

"Such as?"

Haeki's chin jutted further forward.

"Nuliere has given me a task," she said. "My herald commands, and I obey. I am to accompany you and protect the Son of Night, ensuring that he is safely restored to his body in Eludia. In her infinite grace, the Lady of Brine and Urchins will also prevent the failed children of the usurpers from hunting you."

Karys adjusted the straps of her bag.

"Well?" said Haeki impatiently.

"Were you going to ask me, or—"

"Nuliere wills it."

"You shouldn't even be talking to me, Haeki. I'm an apostate."

"Oh, I know what you are."

"Then you also know the threat I pose to your herald."

"She has given me a task," repeated Haeki, jaw clenched. She looked so determined and so vulnerable. "My herald commands, and I obey. Are you going to break your promise to me a second time, Eska?"

Karys was silent a moment.

"Is this still what you want?" she asked, quieter. "Even now? You have a life here. Influence."

Haeki spat.

"Some life," she said.

"Now they know you're sea-blessed—"

"If I don't leave Boäz today, I never will," she said. "Karys, I've been staring at this road for fifteen years. Of course it's what I want. After you left, I lay awake every night and cursed you for breaking your word, because I didn't have it in me to follow you alone. Even though I *knew* why you ran, even though nothing stopped me from doing the same, I still blamed you. And I'm sick to death of feeling—" She broke off, and shook her head. "Me and Oboro, we got stuck here. And now it's just me."

The farm wagon rumbled in the quiet.

"I'm sorry," said Karys.

"Don't say that. Not to me."

Karys nodded slowly.

"Nuliere thinks she can stop New Favour from finding me?" she said. "Stop the Constructs?"

"That's what she told me."

Karys rubbed her forehead.

"Well, I suppose that will be useful," she said.

CHAPTER
21

Miresse had transformed; the grim, faded streets bustled with people. Liberation Day. The annual celebration commemorated the end of the occupation, and drew a slew of visitors from the surrounding villages and homesteads. The smells of meat and cooking oil hung over the town in the sweaty fog, and fat mosquitoes whined. Drunken toasts to the Vareslians' expulsion rang through the evening air.

"We choose our own gods here!" yelled a woman from atop a parade float, brandishing her cider. "This is Mercia! We choose our own gods."

Forty years since the signing of the Sovereignty Accord, and people were as zealous as ever. Karys elbowed her way through the throng. This close to the border, the occupation was keenly remembered—but the Ephirite were also more widely hated and feared. That tension lay thick in the air; despite the revelry, the atmosphere hummed with the threat of violence. Liberation Day: the end of the occupation, but at the cost of the Slaughter.

"Embrace-denying heretics," said Haeki darkly. She glared at the drunken woman. "As if the usurpers are *gods*."

Karys spied a gap in the foot traffic, and pushed her way toward it. They had reached Miresse in the late afternoon, and sent the farm wagon trundling back to Boäz at the outskirts of the South Quarter. By then, the festivities had already begun. Performers in homemade masks of clay and feathers aped the Bhatuma and Ephirite, enacting raucous confrontations for the crowds. Many had taken the role of Swask, and the streets were full of blue moon-round faces, innumerable phalluses bulging from arms and legs like water spouts. Haeki seemed torn between curiosity and disapproval at the spectacle.

"Treating it as a party," she muttered. "It's so . . . so *disrespectful*."

"I doubt Swask cares much now." Karys handed a tenth to a street vendor, and took two cups of watered wine from his stall. "Besides, it's sort of meant to honour the heralds. Here."

"Honour that they were all murdered?"

"People are just celebrating that the reekers are gone." Karys pressed the cup into Haeki's hand. "It's an excuse for drinking. Now toast like a good patriot."

Haeki did not toast.

"It feels like they're celebrating the usurpers," she said. "Like they're *happy* to have exchanged the heralds for the Ephirite."

"To liberation," said Karys, and tipped her cup back. The sweet wine seared her throat. "From one set of masters to the next."

A discordant swell of music and shouting marked the coming of another parade float: a great, wheeled, worked contrivance that lumbered along the road. It barely fit the street, almost as tall as the buildings, painted in garish yellow, green, and red. Carved animals reared out from the platforms; they barked and chattered, and their wooden bodies made small repetitive movements, raising their legs or shaking their heads. A crowd of children chased the vehicle, and the brightly dressed performers aboard tossed sugar-glazed shell biscuits to them. A group of dancers moved ahead of the float, clearing the way. They stamped out an old protest cressel: music that was half-humming, half-footbeat, conjoined by invented words.

"Impressive," remarked Ferain.

"And loud," replied Karys under her breath. Her shadow lay at her feet, perfectly unremarkable. She returned her cup to the vendor.

"It's festive. Although people's enthusiasm for 'breaking the reeker man's back' is slightly alarming to me personally."

Something small and hard flew into the side of Karys' head. She started and turned, and the wasp veered away. Then it came at her face again.

In a blink, Haeki's hand snaked out, and she plucked the insect from the air by its wings. Without expression or hesitation, she threw it onto the ground and stomped down. When Karys gaped at her, she shrugged and took a swallow of her wine.

"Nuliere was generous in her gifts," she said evenly.

"Turned you into a viper, more like." Karys looked down at the crushed smear of wasp on the road. *One of Rasko's?* The memory of the sting made her rub her neck reflexively. "Embrace. What else can you do?"

"A few things."

Aboard the float, one of the performers began beating out the rhythm of a popular song on their hand drum, and people cheered. The dancers peeled off, selecting onlookers from the crowd, pulling them toward the vehicle. One of them, a beardless man in a yellow and black costume, moved toward Karys. He bowed, and spread his hands in invitation.

"No thanks," she said.

"My apologies, cas, but your presence is required," he said pleasantly. "That is, if you are still looking to cross the border?"

She narrowed her eyes. The man smiled, entirely at ease, and beckoned.

"Bring your friend," he said.

The performers on the float hoisted the chosen members of the crowd up onto the first platform. The vehicle creaked and slowed, but continued rolling forward. A broad, laughing woman spun Karys around, then draped a bright red scarf over her shoulders. Haeki was handed a basket of the shell biscuits and ushered toward the rear of the float, where she was greeted by a flood of shouting children.

"Up this way, cas," called the man in black and yellow.

Karys followed him. Flowers and woven fabrics decked the second level of the float, piled over and around the worked mechanical animals. Up close, the contraptions appeared more crude; they thumped and shuddered heavily. Rasko stood at the railing of the platform, flanked by a lion on one side, and a buffalo on the other. He smirked when he saw Karys.

"How do you like my float, cas?" he asked.

She inclined her head. "Casin."

"I wonder how you must feel about Liberation Day." He gestured at the street, the dancers, the costumes—encompassing it all with one casual sweep of his arm. "As a deathspeaker, that is. A point of personal pride?"

Karys' stomach sank. *So he knows who I am.*

"It doesn't mean much to me," she replied.

"No? Not one for pageantry, then."

"No."

"What a shame." He motioned for her to come closer. "I've always supported the new order. Mercia has no reason to miss her heralds, those miserable bastards. Twenty years under Varesli's heel, and they never lifted a finger for us. Well, look what it got them."

Karys stopped beside him. From above, the crowd appeared smaller, their raised faces flushed with wine and exultation.

"Not that I like New Favour much either," said Rasko. "Too upright, too uptight. They're useful workings though, those Ephirite derivations. Don't you think?"

He was toying with her. Enjoying it. Karys shrugged. "I'm not a practitioner."

"Not at all?"

"I can do some very basic workings, mostly Bhatuma-derived. Simple bindings, nothing significant."

Rasko's smile did not shift. "I thought you were more ambitious than that, cas Eska."

Karys exhaled. *How much does he know?* Her real name, that she was a deathspeaker, but what else? She felt strangely unafraid, even though Rasko had the means to destroy her. The lion beside her opened its wooden mouth, and produced a worked rumbling sound.

"I'm curious," said Rasko. "Why *did* the Ephirite want to wipe out the heralds so badly?"

Down below, Haeki was throwing shell biscuits to the children. "I don't know. They hated them. Were jealous of them. It's difficult to understand the Ephirite's reasoning for anything."

"I suppose I expected you to have more insight. You don't know where they came from, then?"

She shook her head. "Only what everyone already knows—that the first saints of New Favour sought them out in order to free Mercia, and those compacts formed the Ephirite's gateway into the world. Their . . . anchor."

"And then," said Rasko, "the Slaughter."

The massacre of the old order, and the birth of the new. Varesli's martial supremacy had been founded on the benevolent support of their powerful heralds, and yet no Bhatuma had been prepared for the Ephirite's indiscriminate assault. The Embrace's emissaries proved fatally complacent—the weak were cut down like wheat under the scythe, the strong rallied far too late to save themselves.

"And then," Karys murmured, "the Slaughter."

Rasko chuckled. "So serious? You're an Ephirit's anchor too, I take it. Tell me, does that frighten you, cas Eska? The way you're bound to your master?"

"Yes."

Behind Karys, Ferain drew a surprised breath. Rasko's eyes gleamed.

"How much time do you have left?" he asked.

"The compacts aren't regular that way."

"You don't know."

"I don't like to think about it."

He barked a laugh. "No, I suppose not. Why did you leave Miresse a few days ago? Your departure was rather abrupt."

"I was saying goodbye to my family."

"Oh? Do they live in the region?"

"Not anymore."

Rasko arched one eyebrow. There was an acquisitive light in his expression, a certain kind of hunger.

"That bruise on your face is new," he remarked. "As is your red-haired friend. You collect distinctive company, cas Eska; first the Toraigian woman, now this stranger. Marishka Stallar is threatening to halt her trade with Miresse unless I help you, and I've just heard rumours that New Favour is looking for a death-speaker matching your description. Why is everyone so interested in you?"

She said nothing. Rasko made a sound of mild reproof.

"Come, now," he said. "Aren't we friends?"

He raised his left hand from the railing, and turned his palm upwards. A large wasp crawled out from the loose sleeve of his shirt, and climbed to the top of his index finger. Rasko twisted his wrist, admiring the insect like jewellery.

"I'm willing to help you," he said. "I'm even willing to ignore your friends, if they wanted to cross the border with you. But that requires some cooperation on your part."

Karys watched the wasp. Its wings had a hint of green iridescence. "What do you want from me?"

"Nothing too arduous. I'd like you to hand-deliver a package to a friend in Eludia. Discreetly."

"That's all?"

"I'm a generous man." He chortled. "And not eager to antagonise Marishka Stallar."

She did not trust him in the slightest. "What's in the package? Who am I delivering it to?"

"Questions, questions." He let the wasp wander over his broad knuckles. "A language teacher named Imolin Prete, who lives in the Sulluvin District on the south side of the city—you'll be provided with the address. The contents of the package are none of your concern."

At the mention of the teacher's name, Ferain had started—a very slight judder of Karys' shadow. *Someone he knows?* "What are they to you?"

"Also none of your concern. But you don't need to worry. What I'm sending won't harm them." He nudged the wasp with his right index finger, encouraging it back over his thumb. "You should count yourself lucky that it's an easy task. Although I will require insurance, of course. Come closer."

Karys stepped toward him. "Insurance?"

"A guarantee you'll fulfil your side of the bargain. You of all people should understand a compact, cas. Stay still now."

Rasko lifted his left hand, and cupped her chin. Karys stiffened. His skin was warm; she wanted to pull away, but her body felt rooted to the spot. The wasp crawled onto her neck.

"No, not again," said Ferain angrily. "Karys, stop it. We'll find another way."

The insect's feet prickled as it walked along her throat. Her voice came out tight. "You don't trust my word, casin?"

Rasko's breath smelled stale. "I believe in security. You'll have a week after crossing the border before things start getting uncomfortable. I'd suggest delivering the package before then."

The wasp drove its stinger into the flesh below her jawbone.

Karys gave a hoarse cry. Rasko clamped his other hand to her mouth, cutting off the sound. Whatever force had held her in place dissolved; she wrenched away from him, staggering backwards and reaching up to tear the wasp from her neck. Her fingers found nothing. The insect had vanished.

"There," said Rasko. "We have a deal."

On the street below, the festival continued undisturbed. Karys pressed her hand to the side of her throat. Her skin remained cool and smooth, but it felt like a knife had been shoved upwards through her jaw.

"An hour after midnight tomorrow, your guide will be waiting at the warehouse past the Norsom bridge. He'll give you the package." Rasko returned his attention to the crowd. "Once you're across the border, one of my contacts will escort you as far as Tuschait. A pleasure, cas Eska."

She was dismissed. Without a word, Karys turned and walked away. The man in black and yellow snickered as she passed, but she ignored him and climbed down to the lower level of the float. Although the burning sharpness of the sting was fading, the sensation still echoed through her body.

"I wish you hadn't done that," muttered Ferain.

Didn't feel like a choice. Haeki seemed to have given out most of her shell biscuits; when Karys called to her, she looked around. Karys nodded toward the street.

"Well, it's more that I wish I wasn't this useless." Her shadow sighed. "While you get repeatedly stung by wasps, I'm sitting around like . . . I don't know, a decorative vase."

Karys snorted, swinging her legs over the side rail of the float. The vehicle was moving slowly enough that she could easily hop off it.

"An *expensive* decorative vase," she mumbled. "You're going to pay me back, aren't you?"

"Yes. But still."

She waited for a gap to form in the crowd, then jumped down. "Not 'but still.'"

"I don't like seeing you in pain."

Haeki had not managed to get off the float yet; she seemed to be struggling to politely excuse herself. Karys shouldered through the dancing throng, making for a quiet, out-of-the-way alley. An orange tomcat hissed at her from the shadows, its eyes wide and shining.

"It's done now," she said. "And it will be worth it. Who is Imolin Prete? You recognised the name."

"Oh." Ferain paused. "Well, they're a language teacher who works for the Foreign Ministry. They helped me learn Toraigian. I have no idea what Rasko might want with them."

"Could they be a spy?"

"What, for Mercia? Unlikely, unless you're looking for intelligence on the intricacies of vowel displacement in transitive verbs."

Karys laughed.

Her shadow, careful and precise all evening, suddenly rippled over the ground. In response, the tomcat hissed again, the fur at the scruff of its neck standing straight up. Spine arched, it backed away a few steps, then yowled, turned tail, and fled down the back of the alley.

"What's wrong?" asked Karys.

"Nothing," said Ferain, although he sounded strangely flustered. "Sorry. It's nothing. It's . . . you know, I don't think I've ever heard you laugh before."

Her brow furrowed. "So?"

"It just struck me, that's all. You don't laugh much."

"Maybe you aren't very funny, reeker."

"Right," said Haeki, having finally broken through the crowd. "I'm not getting on one of those accursed things again. Where did you say we were staying?"

In spite of the half-hearted complaint, Haeki's cheeks were flushed and her eyes bright. She moved with a new lightness, as if buoyed along by the spirit of the festival, and the way she spoke sounded less guarded. For the first time since Karys' return to Boäz, Haeki looked open and easy and sure of herself, and the effect was transformative—she seemed almost to glow.

"Not far from here," said Karys. "This way."

The Orago was even busier than usual, and the square before the building played host to a troupe of acrobats and contortionists. They juggled and danced, and people stopped to watch them, gathering around burn barrels with mugs of sweet tea. The smoke from the fires smelled like charred sugar. Inside, a string band played old songs, and the elderly patrons at the bar nodded along to the music, smiling appreciatively.

When Karys knocked on Winola's door, there was a brief scuffle and a curse—it sounded like something had been knocked over. The scholar appeared in the entrance to the room.

"You're back!" she said. "I was beginning to wonder—oh, what happened to your face?"

Karys touched her jaw. The skin remained tender where she had been struck.

"I fell off a wagon," she said.

Winola winced sympathetically. "I know a working that might help with the bruising, if you like. How was the send-off? Were there any . . ."

She trailed off, noticing Haeki for the first time. A faint frown creased her forehead, and her lips parted slightly—for a brief moment, she stood silent in the doorway, questions forgotten. Then she seemed to gather herself again, and her expression cleared.

"Sorry," she said. "I didn't see you there. You're with Karys?"

Haeki studied the scholar warily before giving a single nod. "Haeki Maas."

"Winola Diasene. A pleasure to meet you. Are you also from Boäz? Karys never mentioned—"

"Maybe we can continue this conversation inside?" said Karys.

Winola appeared to have been in the midst of preparations for a working; a sheet of vellum had been stretched across the room's small desk, and precisely marked with ruled lines and fine metal pins. A stack of loose papers lay on the carpet beside the scholar's open notebook. She quickly crossed the room and moved a pile of her clothes off the second bed.

"Apologies for the mess," she said. "I've been a little busy."

"You didn't want to attend the festival?" Karys wandered over to the desk and examined the preparation. To her amateur eye, it seemed to be the explication for a very complex Bhatuma working. Something about it struck her as obscurely familiar. Haeki hung back near the door, her arms folded.

"I did," said Winola. "But I was making good progress, and then lost track of the time. How were your family?"

Karys gave an evasive shrug. She could feel Haeki's gaze on her back. "The same. But the send-off was good."

"I'm glad. I hope your brother has found his rest."

If he has, it's no thanks to me. Karys suppressed a shiver. Regret was pointless—besides, while Nuliere might be a hateful snake, the herald was still duty-bound to guide the souls of her adherents to the Embrace. Oboro had been faithful; he would find his salvation. She gestured to the preparation instead.

"What is this for?" she asked.

Winola's gaze travelled to Haeki. "It's . . . it's sort of an attempt at an accommodation. For your, uh, closest friend."

"I know about the Son of Night," said Haeki curtly.

"Son of Night?"

"She means Ferain," said Karys. "It's fine; she knows about him. It's why she followed me to Miresse."

Winola was now regarding Haeki with open curiosity. "Then do you plan to travel to Eludia as well?"

Under the scrutiny, Haeki's cheeks had coloured, and her manner had turned stiff and abrasive. When she spoke, her voice was low. "I'll go as far as is needed to safeguard the Son of Night."

"Why do you call him—"

"Yes, she plans to travel to Eludia," said Karys, trying to steer the conversation back to safer waters. "This 'accommodation' you're working on—you believe it might help Ferain?"

Winola did not miss the obvious diversion, and her expression strongly suggested that she was filing away several questions for later. Nevertheless, she crossed the room to join Karys at the desk.

"During one of our conversations, Ferain mentioned wanting to speak directly to other people," she said. "So I've been trying to formulate an adaption based on my limited exegesis of the Split Lapse that would slightly broaden the scope of the proximal overlay effect. Basically, make the original working less efficient."

"You could do that?"

"Maybe. As things stand, the Split Lapse is too complex for me to interfere with its primary functions—I can't really do anything that would directly interact with those workings. But my tests a few days ago suggested that the burden of Ferain's current manifestation falls to you. That's where the limitations of his projection reside." She grinned. "And you I *can* modify."

Karys hesitated.

"Don't worry, it's not dangerous," said the scholar, and then amended. "Not *that* dangerous."

"No, it's just . . . I can't have body modifications."

Winola's gaze softened. She tapped her forefinger to the outer frame of her glasses.

"I understand not wanting to alter yourself," she said.

"It's not that, it's—never mind. A deathspeaker thing."

"The modification would tie to your existing binding. Unbind the Split Lapse, and my adaption would be removed as well. For what it's worth, this would be no more permanent than the working you already applied."

And yet *that* binding was already proving impossible to dislodge. Karys' wrist itched. Bad enough to have the Split Lapse affixed to her. Still, she couldn't forget what Ferain had said on the beach, or how he had sounded: the cracked, hollow quality of his voice. *It just felt like being alive.* He had been so desperate for connection that he had chased down her brother's revenant.

"You shouldn't bother," her shadow murmured. "Once we're across the border, Eludia is only a few days away. It doesn't seem worth the trouble."

Liar. Karys knew Ferain wanted the modification. Even after they reached Eludia, there was no guarantee his father would have the answers they needed, or would be able to help them quickly. The truth was that neither of them had any idea how long the process would take. Maybe it would be days, or weeks, or never—but this was important to him now.

"You're sure it would tie to the existing binding?" she asked slowly.

Winola smiled.

"If it works at all," she said.

"Karys, you don't need to—"

"Quiet," she said to Ferain softly, then spoke louder to Winola. "How long would it take?"

"In theory, just a few minutes. I've mostly figured out all the authorisations, so I'd be ready to try the working by tomorrow."

Soon. But if Rasko's man was only meeting her in the early hours of the following morning, then perhaps it was a good window of opportunity. Karys opened her mouth to agree to the working, but stopped when she heard the door quietly close behind them. She turned. Haeki was gone.

"Oh." Winola's face fell. "Your friend, she . . . I did something wrong, didn't I?"

Karys shook her head.

"Give me a minute," she said. "I'll talk to her."

Haeki had not gone far. Beneath the shadow of the tattered awnings at the Orago's entrance, she stood and watched the acrobats tumble. All of her former energy had disappeared, all her vibrancy and fire. She stood—quiet, detached, and alone. When Karys leaned against the wall beside her, she grimaced faintly.

"I waited too long," she said.

Karys said nothing. Haeki's shoulders hunched.

"I'm not . . . anything," she said. "I don't belong here."

The acrobats tossed and spun coloured metal disks, filling the air with flashing streaks of bright blue and yellow. A few onlookers clapped. Above, the stars were dim through the smoke, and the moon had yet to rise.

"The way the two of you talked, I . . ." Haeki's throat moved, and her voice dropped. "I have nothing to say. What can I say? Embrace, I actually thought I'd be—"

She broke off with an angry jerk of her head, and pressed her lips together. Karys wanted to lean sideways, to touch Haeki's hand, but she resisted the impulse. It had been too long. She had no right to that closeness. Instead, she folded her arms and sighed.

"You're sea-blessed," she said. "Isn't that something? Give yourself time, Haeki; you only just got here."

"Exactly."

"But you *are* here now. You chose this, and that's something too."

Haeki was silent. Karys waited a moment, then straightened.

"Come back inside when you're ready," she said.

Haeki exhaled. Her eyes followed the flowing, effortless movements of the acrobats, and she did not reply.

As there were only two beds, Karys spent the night on the floor of their room at the Orago. The festivities carried on well into the early hours of the morning. From her place on the musty carpet, she listened to the shouting and singing, the irregular rumbling passage of parade floats, the music from the bar downstairs. Eventually, the celebrations drew to a close, and their clamour was replaced by silence and lilting birdsong. She watched the progression of the dawn light over the walls, and marked when Winola woke up by the change in the scholar's breathing.

Haeki remained asleep. After a few minutes, Winola got out of bed, and came to sit down beside Karys on the carpet.

"I know the two of you are hiding something," she whispered.

"Good morning to you too."

"Who is Haeki, really? What happened in Boäz?"

Karys considered. Then she gave Winola an abbreviated account of the Construct's appearance at the Penitence Pool, and explained what Ferain had told her about the creatures' origins and abilities. When she described how she had taken the Construct's workings apart, Winola's eyes widened.

"I didn't know that was possible," she said, hushed.

"Neither did I."

"Is it only Ephirite workings? Do you think you could take apart my derivations?"

The idea of opening the Veneer—of entering the seething, sickening rush once more—gave Karys a queasy feeling. "I don't know. Maybe."

Winola saw her reluctance, and did not press the issue. She drew her finger in a circle over the carpet, leaving a faint ring behind.

"So, how does Haeki fit into all of this?" she asked.

"I can't answer that."

"Can't or won't?"

Behind them, Haeki murmured restlessly and rolled over. Karys glanced at the bed.

"It amounts to the same," she said.

They left the Orago sometime after eight in the morning, heading to the cluster of abandoned caravanserais on the northern side of Miresse. The town was eerily quiet after Liberation Day, and coloured paper and shards of glass littered the streets. A broken-down float slumped against the ground at the crossroads past the canal, the vehicle's rear axle snapped in two. It had been Karys' suggestion to attempt Winola's modification working in the derelict warren of old travellers' inns—people avoided the area. If anything went wrong, they were unlikely to draw much attention.

"I've been thinking," said Ferain.

Karys walked a little ahead of Haeki and Winola. The scholar was asking questions about Boäz, attempting to draw Haeki out. "Is that unusual?"

Her shadow ignored the quip. "Rasko said his contact would take us as far as Tuschait. I have family living near the town who could help us."

"One of your countless cousins?"

"Second cousin, once removed, I think. My aunt runs a lodge in the area, sort of a retreat. When I was a teenager, my father sent me there for a few weeks to try and get my head straightened out." Ferain's tone went dry. "It didn't really work. But there's a Bhatuma relic at the lodge that my family uses to communicate with one another. If my aunt permits it, we could send word ahead to Eludia. Let my father know to expect you—I don't want to risk him turning you away."

"Couldn't we just send him a letter via Dispatch?"

Ferain snorted. "He's a professor. He never checks his mail."

They had reached the edge of the old commercial district. The streets here were rutted and forlorn, crowded with blocks of grimy, locked-up warehouses and dusty silos. Since the arrival of the trains and the Silkess, Miresse's old caravan traders had fallen by the wayside. Ahead, the ancient clay-brick hostels and roofless stables stood deserted and decayed, the roads giving way to weed-choked dirt paths.

I never expected to see this place again, Karys thought.

"And Boäz's priestess still holds her formal position?" Winola was asking. "That's uncommon. She must be very charismatic, maintaining that kind of influence so long after the Slaughter. Do you know if she was Favoured?"

Despite only having visited the gutted warren of the caravanserais once before, the collection of crumbling merchant inns and halls had remained fixed in Karys' memory. She walked down the path, and felt as though she were retracing steps taken in a dream. The fire-scorched brickwork, the coarse grey sand sloping up the walls. A few years ago, the sight of the hollowed-out buildings might have filled her with anger, but all she could summon now was a weary sadness. At the edges of her awareness, the fabric of the Veneer quivered like a wounded animal. She headed for the largest of the buildings; a thick-walled double-storey hostel with a wide central courtyard. A sea of grey grass and soft pink heather covered the ground within, and a broken fountain stood at the centre of the quadrant, filled with algae and sludge. The eastern side of the hostel had largely collapsed, letting in a bright arc of sunlight.

In her mind, she saw her younger self lying alone in the grass: cold, too exhausted to move, watching birds dart through the twilight air, feeling as though her body belonged to someone else. Feeling like something had ended, and nothing had yet taken its place.

"Karys?"

She shook herself, and turned. Winola was watching her from the entrance to the courtyard.

"Is something wrong?" she asked.

The scholar sounded tentative, unsure of herself. *Kind*. Karys smiled.

"No, just a memory," she said. "Will this place do for the working?"

Winola looked around. "Sure, I don't see why not. But are you certain you want to go ahead with it? If you're having second thoughts . . ."

"I'm not."

Winola wavered a moment longer, then gave a decisive nod. She shrugged off her bag and set it on the ground, digging through it for her notebook and workings materials—a flask of blood, a rattling metal tin. Haeki, frowning, moved to the fountain and studied the dark silt within. A vision flashed through Karys' mind: the water in the basin running red.

"Is it safe?" asked Haeki abruptly, and pivoted to face Winola. Her jaw had gone stubborn. "This working you're doing?"

Winola flipped through the pages of her notebook. "Quite safe. I'm a professional."

"But not a herald. Toraigus didn't even have heralds."

Winola didn't appear offended, exactly, although she sighed heavily.

"A derivation is a derivation," she said. "As long as it's performed correctly, the authorisations don't discriminate."

"But you're . . ." Haeki made an inarticulate, frustrated gesture. "How do you *know* what's correct? You're just making things up!"

"In part. That's the beauty of Ephirite derivations."

Haeki spluttered. The corner of Winola's mouth quirked upwards slightly. She unscrewed the top of her flask and tipped a small measure of blood into the lid.

"Heresy," muttered Haeki.

"You really are very conservative."

Haeki's scowl deepened. Winola, unperturbed, continued with her final preparations, scanning through her notes and mouthing phrases to herself. Haeki shoved her hands into her pockets, and kicked a pebble across the floor. After a few seconds, she mumbled something.

"Pardon?" said the scholar.

"I said, 'How does it work?'"

Winola was still and silent, and at first Karys wondered whether she might be angry. Then she realised the scholar was simply trying very hard not to laugh.

"Well," said Winola carefully. She coughed and cleared her throat. "Sorry, yes. Well, you know how Bhatuma workings derive their power by means of deferred authority? The Embrace granted the heralds the capacity to reshape the world at will?"

Haeki nodded.

"Practitioners like myself can, in some instances, emulate those workings through precise forms of mimicry and ritual—particularly if a herald once gifted their chosen adherents with certain kinds of guidance and permission."

"I know all of that."

"Of course, my apologies. But the problem with Bhatuma-derived workings is that they are effectively a fixed set. All you can do is apply the same workings in different contexts. Naturally, it can still go horribly wrong if you choose an unsuitable application, but otherwise they're very stable. Very predictable." Winola had warmed to the topic. "However, that's not how Ephirite workings function at all. The Bhatuma's power lay in authorisation, but the Ephirite produce workings—essentially—through *metaphor*. They cheat. They don't have divine sanction, so instead they try to force reality to bend by means of comparison, and in doing so they're able to confer the properties of a referent, the vehicle, onto a subject, the tenor. At least, that's how we're able to conceive of their power; for them it seems more intrinsic—what we might regard as poetry, they enact as engineering."

"Their workings are comparisons?" said Haeki slowly.

"I'm simplifying a little, but yes. By accessing a realm of extradimensional meaning-making beyond what's commonly called the Veneer, the Ephirite are able to unravel the equations of reality and rearrange those sums into new semantic configurations. Practitioners can then attempt to extrapolate and recreate those equations, but with a far larger scope for adaption and invention." Winola gave a quick laugh. "They're much more flexible derivations, but also much more likely to cause you to spontaneously combust if you include an unintended allusion."

"That happens?"

"Oh, mistakes in Ephirite derivations are almost always spectacular. Combustion is one of the better ways to go, all things considered." Winola waved aside the issue. "Ordinary practitioners are limited in the ways that we can interact with the Veneer; we need the fallible conduit of language. But someone like Karys, for example, can actually enter the extradimensional space—and, apparently, manipulate it."

Haeki looked at Karys, who shrugged.

"In the last forty years, research into Ephirite workings has barely scratched the surface of how this all functions," said Winola. "It's a fascinating field. Here, look."

The scholar turned back a few pages in her notebook, then rose and walked across the yard.

"I work most of my own derivations in Toraigian," she said. "But the original exegesis for this working was produced in Continental, and I copied out the text for reference. This is an example of a simple Ephirite construction, a metaphor that can be used for slowing the fall of objects in motion."

She held out the open book. Haeki did not take it. She seemed stuck in place; she gazed down at the tight scrawl of Winola's handwriting, and a strange expression crossed her face: a subtle tightening, a flicker almost like fear. Karys recognised the emotion, and swallowed the sudden ache that rose up inside her.

"Impressive," she said. "But even you can't expect to corrupt her *that* quickly, Winola."

The scholar blinked, startled. Then she laughed again, and lowered her notebook.

"Sorry," she said to Haeki. "Sometimes I get a little caught up when it comes to workings. I really didn't mean to lecture, or to make you uncomfortable."

"You didn't," said Haeki, but it came out a shade too forcefully. She dropped her gaze. "Thank you for explaining."

Winola smiled. "Anytime. Although I should probably focus on the modification we came here for. Karys, if you're ready?"

"What do you need me to do?"

Winola walked back to her bag, put away her notebook, and collected her measure of blood and the tin. "Come here and hold this for a moment."

Karys crossed the floor, and took the tin off the scholar. Winola dipped her ring finger into the lid of the flask, and applied a precise oval of fresh blood to her lower lip. She wiped the rest off on a handkerchief, and resealed the flask.

"You don't have to do this, you know," said Ferain.

Karys ignored him, and opened the tin. Inside lay a small collection of bronze filings. Winola scooped out a fingernail's worth, cupping the metal shavings within her palm.

"So that it ties to the existing binding," she said, by way of explanation. "Your left hand, please."

She was going to notice eventually, anyway. Karys grimaced, and proffered her arm.

"Before you say anything—" she began.

Winola drew breath sharply. She reached out and brushed her long, cool fingers over the Split Lapse scar resting on the slope of Karys' wrist. "It moved? When did that happen?"

"Before we left Psikamit. And again in Boäz. I don't know why."

"You should have said something."

"I was trying to avoid hearing about my chances of getting ripped in half."

Winola's voice turned pained. "Karys."

"Or turned into a corpse puppet. Do you think it will interfere with the modification?"

"It shouldn't, but that's hardly the point." She raised Karys' wrist to examine the scar more closely. "This must mean something."

"Something bad, probably. Although not immediately life-threatening."

Winola's eyes remained fixed on the mark. "I hope not."

"How reassuring," murmured Ferain.

The scholar's breath warmed Karys' skin, stirring the fine hairs along the side of her arm. Standing close, Winola smelled like lilacs and the Orago's herbal soap. Thin lines creased the space between her dark eyebrows. Karys shifted.

"The modification?" she suggested.

Winola lingered over the scar, absorbed in her thoughts.

"No, it won't change anything," she muttered.

"Winola?"

The scholar shook her head. A new briskness entered her movements—she straightened, transferred her grip to the back of Karys' hand, and tipped the glittering bronze filings from her palm onto the binding scar.

"The derivation will still work," she said firmly. "And again, this really is quite safe—but it might sting a little, so try not to move."

Can't be any worse than Rasko's wasps. "I'll do my best."

Winola nudged a stray metal shaving into place. Then she closed her eyes, exhaled, and went still. Her grip on Karys' hand tightened a fraction. For a few seconds the scholar did nothing; she stood motionless as if waiting for a cue, and a prickling quietness descended on the courtyard. When she finally spoke, it was in a smooth, unfamiliar tongue: the pronunciation clear and resonant and deliberate.

The bronze filings sank like melting butter into the Split Lapse scar.

Karys tensed, but there was no pain, only a dull red pulse of heat in her wrist. The blood on Winola's lip turned black. She released Karys' arm, and opened her eyes.

"Done," she said.

"Did it work?" asked Haeki.

Karys curled the fingers of her left hand into a fist, then shook them out. At her side, her shadow appeared stiff. Hesitant. *The one time he's actually supposed to talk, he doesn't.* Without meaning to, she found herself holding her breath. *Come on, reeker.*

Ferain made a rueful sound. "I have no idea what to say."

From the first syllable, Karys knew that the working had failed. It was evident in Winola's expression—the scholar continued to gaze at her shadow, impatient and expectant, without giving the barest flicker of a reaction. The edges of Karys' silhouette wavered; Ferain saw the truth as clearly as she did.

"No," said Karys heavily. "It didn't work."

Winola seemed to deflate. She made a small noise in the back of her throat.

"But it *should* have," she said. "I was sure . . ."

"Tell her it's fine," said Ferain quickly. "It doesn't matter. Please, Karys."

"He says it's fine. He's fine."

Winola's shoulders slumped. "I checked everything so thoroughly."

"Tell her I'm grateful. Tell her that I'm sorry for the trouble."

"He's grateful. He's sorry for the trouble." Karys forced a smile. "Is there anything you could alter in the derivation's construction? Maybe we could try again."

Winola wiped the blood off her mouth, smearing black over the back of her hand. "We could, but I'm not sure where to start. This should have *worked*."

"Tell her there's no need."

Karys sighed.

"She's done more than enough already," pressed Ferain. "Tell her."

Instead of answering him, Karys murmured an apology, then turned and walked over to the crumbled walls on the far side of the quadrant. Swallows' nests caked the wide cavities between the bricks, and silvery lichen grew on the shaded mortar. The sun threw her shadow long over the courtyard behind her.

"You're allowed to be disappointed," she said under her breath.

Ferain did not reply. Beyond the caravanserais, the old road snaked north between the thorn trees and brown scrub. Karys shielded her eyes against the light. In the far distance, a ridge of grey mountains hemmed the horizon in.

"If everything goes as planned, we'll reach Eludia in a few more days," she said.

Her shadow gave a soft huff. "Do you think you can suffer me alone until then?"

Haeki cursed.

Karys glanced over her shoulder. Beside the fountain, Haeki stood and stared at the long dark fall of her shadow over the grassy courtyard. Her face was inscrutable, her body tensed.

"I can hear him," she said.

A brief, uncontrolled shudder ran through Karys' shadow. Her heart lifted, beating quicker. "You can?"

Haeki nodded.

"He's got an accent," she said.

"Why is *that* the thing both of you focus on first?" Ferain broke into breathless laughter. "It isn't even that strong. Can you really hear me?"

"Count from ten."

"What?"

"Count from ten," repeated Haeki, although with a hint of a smile. Winola was watching her, wide-eyed. "I want to see something."

"Is that 'something' my accent?"

"Just count."

Ferain complied. As he spoke, Haeki took a few steps toward the entrance of the courtyard, then moved closer to the fountain again.

". . . six, five, four, three—"

Her smile widened. She pointed at the ground with an air of quiet satisfaction.

"It takes contact," she said.

The sunlight slanting through the ruined wall cast stretched shadows. Where Haeki stood, Karys' silhouette intersected her own. For a heartbeat, Ferain did not move. Then he veered across the ground to touch the shadow at Winola's feet.

"Can you hear me now?" he asked.

The scholar jumped.

"I—yes, I can." She beamed. "Hah, it worked. I *knew* it would work."

Ferain laughed again, warm and relieved, and a weight lifted from Karys' shoulders. His happiness was obvious; for once, he seemed entirely open and unrestrained, his carefulness laid aside. She felt glad for him.

"Looks like I won't be suffering alone, after all," she said. "And now Winola can interrogate you to her heart's—"

"Son of Night, I greet you once more," burbled the sludge in the old fountain.

Karys started. Winola gave a small shriek, and reeled backwards. Nuliere's voice had a different pitch and resonance away from her Sanctum; she sounded reedy and strained. The mud bubbled, forming a sucking whirlpool.

"The road ahead is long and perilous," continued the Bhatuma. "But with my aid, no harm shall befall you. I work to smooth your path."

"What is that?" whispered Winola.

Karys recovered. "When did he ask for your help, slug? Go back to your hole."

The whirlpool gurgled caustically. "Vile apostate, scourge of my territory—"

"You sound like a clogged drain."

"Faithless turncoat! Tool of the usurpers!"

"The fountain is talking," said Winola faintly. "Why is the fountain talking?"

The water sloshed in ineffectual wrath, churning the algae on the surface. Karys was not intimidated—although, beneath her anger, she felt the stirrings of disquiet. The herald had revealed herself to Winola. Forty years of silence and secrecy in Boäz, but now Nuliere spoke in the presence of an unknown outsider. Haeki looked appalled.

"I will see you liberated, kindred," said Nuliere, still seething. "I will free you from the coils of this shameless snake, whereupon she shall be *punished* for her impunity, she shall be made to know humility, be made to—"

"That won't be necessary," said Ferain hurriedly. "Is it true that you can prevent the Constructs from tracing us?"

Nuliere appeared to moderate her emotions somewhat. The sludge settled.

"It is true," she said. "So long as my sea-blessed remains by your side, the usurper's stillborn children will never find you. My Favoured's will is mine, and she will serve you."

"Haeki's not serving anyone," snapped Karys.

"Why do you call the Constructs 'children'?" Ferain drew a little closer to the fountain. "Haeki also referred to them as 'the failed children of the usurpers.' What does that mean?"

The herald made a coarse, wet sound. "They are the thwarted ambitions of the enemy's most ardent desire. Abandoned half-things, aborted monstrosities. It is the least of my powers to repel their attentions; you need fear them no longer, Son of—"

Burning pain lanced through Karys' skull, and her vision disappeared in a white flash. She clutched her head and swayed. Dimly, she heard Ferain's voice, sharp with anger and alarm, and Nuliere protesting in response. A jagged breath, and the world resolved once more. Her sight returned.

Sabaster.

The courtyard was bright, lurid in her vision. She could smell sweet decay, could taste it in her throat. Haeki had taken a few steps toward her.

"Karys, what's going on?" she asked.

The booming of her heart in her ears. Her tongue too thick inside her mouth. Karys swallowed. "Nothing."

Haeki's eyes flicked to Winola. The scholar stood with one hand pressed to her mouth, skin pallid. "That working, maybe—"

"I said it's nothing." Karys' voice came out harsh. "Nothing that concerns either of you. I'll meet you back at the Orago later."

"Karys," whispered Winola.

She ignored the scholar, striding across the courtyard and snatching the flask of blood out of the grass. Winola flinched. Karys kept walking, not daring to look back, not wanting to see Haeki. The sunlight pulsed in time with her breathing. Out of the hostel, out beneath the sky—the silos and the warehouses ahead of her, the air too warm and too still. The flask was slick with the sweat of her hand.

It's too soon.

She needed a quiet place, somewhere secure. She needed a gift, needed redness. Needed more time. Her steps were quick, her body wound tight. She reached the first of the warehouses, and its high walls swam in her vision. Nothing here, nothing she could use. Too soon.

"Tell me what's going on," said Ferain.

Karys stumbled a few feet further, turned down the side of the building, and vomited. Her chest heaved, and she bent forward, bracing herself against the wall. Her fist ground against the rough brickwork. She retched again.

"Too soon," she gasped.

Her shadow stretched up the wall in front of her. "What is too soon?"

She shook her head. Ferain made a frustrated sound.

"Talk to me," he said. "This is about Sabaster?"

Karys voice emerged in a rough, feverish whisper. "The callings are never this close. Never. It's too soon. This isn't how it works."

"You have to breathe, Karys."

She pressed harder against the wall, breaking her skin. A violent tremor ran through her body.

"No, listen to me." Ferain spoke with low insistence, controlled but fierce. "Take a breath, let it out, and then *listen*. You don't know what Sabaster wants, but you do know how to placate him. Correct?"

Karys gripped Winola's flask tighter.

"Correct?" he demanded.

She forced the word through gritted teeth. "Yes."

"You know how to please him, you know how he thinks," he continued. "Whatever he wants now, that stays the same. You're afraid—but you aren't helpless, and you aren't alone, and you've survived worse than this. I've seen how capable you are. You know how to handle your master."

The taste of bile was acrid in her mouth. She breathed in deeply, and the rushing inside her head slowed and grew less deafening.

"Yes," she repeated.

The air shivered.

Karys raised her head. Down the street, the windows of the warehouses were blown out. Flocks of shinglelarks nested in the cracked roof panels, but there was no one around, no noise, no movement. She pushed herself upright, wiping her mouth.

"What is it?" asked Ferain.

Karys held silent. At the end of the road, the dusty paving stones shimmered like a heat haze. Then they began to fold; stones snapping soundlessly inward.

Her heart clenched.

"Not a calling," she said, toneless. "It's a summons. He's pulling me into his domain."

The ground gave way smoothly as reality warped, clean as a blade through soft meat. Where the street met the junction, a flight of stairs descended into the earth. Each step sheened deep, glossy red: a scarlet polished to liquid brightness. Overhead, the sun dimmed in the cloudless sky.

Ferain's voice was equally blank. "You can't refuse it?"

She shook her head. "No."

The walls of the warehouses groaned on either side of her. The paint melted across the bricks as they stretched taller, reaching for the sky and bowing inward. The street behind her rolled up to meet the walls.

"Whatever happens"—Karys felt far from herself, far from the world—"whatever happens, whatever you see, whatever Sabaster does, don't move. Don't speak."

"Understood," murmured Ferain.

She shut her eyes. The blackness behind her lids was dizzying and unreal. Opened them again, and her shadow lay behind her.

Karys walked forward. Down the stairs, and into the dark.

CHAPTER

23

Each step she took down the stairs produced a faint chime, a high-pitched ring like thin glass splintering. The dimension folded closed after her, but Karys did not look back to see it. She fixed her gaze only on the next stair. The walls and the roof of the space were fathomless black. The light was low, sourceless.

She should not jump to conclusions. Her heart beat in her throat. She should not assume the worst. If Sabaster planned to call her compact, then he probably would not leave her with the chance to commit suicide. Other vassals did that, or tried, and even if the Ephirit thought highly of her, he could not be so naïve as to believe . . . no. He would not take the risk. This summons had some other purpose. If she kept her head, she could survive.

In the years that Karys had served him, Sabaster had summoned her only once, a few weeks after her twentieth birthday. A rare honour, a sign of his especial favour. Not long before, she had begun plying him with gifts, applying lessons learned during sleepless nights of research in the College's library, attempting to debase herself to best effect. It was a period of guesswork and fraught experimentation, scouring the limited accounts of earlier deathspeakers for advice, searching for any kind of guidance at all. When the initial summons came, it had seemed like it was intended as a reward—Sabaster gave her a strange tour of his domain, and Karys received the impression that he wanted her to approve of it.

Ting, ting, ting: her shoes rang on the stairs. In her peripheral vision, shapes bulged from the darkness. Karys refused to look at them directly, unwilling to acknowledge the malformed limbs as they grew more numerous. The impression of hands reaching toward her: slightly too large to be human, crooked joints, fingers clawing the air, some bent back upon themselves. There was hunger in their stiff, grasping movements, but they came no closer.

The stairs ended. The groundcover at its base was thick and fibrous, like grass but more slippery, and it moved with clear sensitivity. Thin strands probed at Karys' feet, hundreds of pliant, creeping cilia stirring to taste the intruder in their midst. Further ahead, impossibly tall tubes rose from the ground. They stood at precise intervals, emitting rings of crystalline white light that vanished into the cavernous space overhead. It was warm and very quiet; the air damp and heavy with the oily, sweet smell of Sabaster.

The ground trembled under her heels, the cilia rippling with alien feeling. Karys kept walking, following the crystal lights, one foot in front of the next. It was difficult to judge the size of the domain; it might have been infinite, but it felt inexplicably close. There were figures here too, standing just outside the circles of light. They appeared identical: naked, hairless, milky-fleshed men in the deep shadow. They did not move, and they stood with their backs to her, looking out at the blackness. The cilia had wound along their legs before pushing up and through the skin of their calves, then out again, like loose stitches in a tailor's mannequin. Rooting them in place.

I've seen how capable you are. Ferain's words repeated in her head. *You aren't helpless, and you aren't alone, and you've survived worse than this.* Not alone. Not alone, because she had dragged him down with her. She could detect her shadow even now, his presence at her back. It made her feel sick. It made her feel stronger. *Embrace, I'm sorry.*

Ahead was the palace—what she thought of as the palace. It was not exactly a building, but it seemed to be where Sabaster dwelled—a deliberate architecture, something made with purpose and intent. The structure reared up from the flat landscape, visible as a perfect snow-pale pyramid balanced on its peak. It glowed brighter than anything else in the environment, and stood at least fifty feet tall. Its outer appearance belied its true size and dimensions; Karys knew that from her last summons. What lay inside was far, far larger. As she drew up to its base, the light grew dazzling; she could not see through to the space within. She walked on into the whiteness, conscious of the ground sloping upwards, and then she was inside.

The antechamber was soaked in red. The colour suffused the air itself; it was illumination and haze, transparent and dense. The walls of the room branched in fractal formations, sharp, precise, and angular, and they moved ceaselessly like gears in a colossal machine. As they slid apart and re-formed, they spoke in a steady, monotonous chant. *Favour is ours, favour is ours, favour is ours.* Not human words, not a language Karys had ever heard, but she understood all the same. The floor was smooth red glass, and wet. She crossed the chamber and it reshaped around her, peeling back to admit her to Sabaster's trophy hall.

Why the Ephirite treasured the Bhatuma's corpses, Karys had never been certain. It struck her as some form of perversion. The way she had witnessed Sabaster croon over necrotic heralds was not strictly sexual, but reminiscent of that—an uncanny, tender state of arousal.

The beautiful Bhatuma—the largest and most prized of her master's collection—remained flayed out across the trophy hall, dripping slow yellow ichor. Swollen body parts hung in the air or were staked to the walls and floor, the entire gruesome display connected by stretched bands of shining sinew. The herald's face, the same face that had haunted Karys for almost a decade, looked serene in death. As large as she was tall, with moonlight eyes as wide across as her forearms.

Karys' nerve failed her; she stopped and a small sound escaped her mouth. It was the herald's eyes, always those silver eyes in that perfect face. Eyes that did not look dead, because they still *moved*. Their gaze roved the room, blankly absorbing the ruin of their body. Never blinking. They passed over Karys without recognition.

She dug her nails into her palms. It was dead. Whatever the Ephirite had done to preserve and animate the corpse, the soul within was gone. This was . . . puppetry. Karys breathed in. Kept moving, kept her eyes level and her head raised.

Sabaster waited on the far side of the room. The wings covering his body were fanned out, and they fluttered as she approached. The mouth of his lowest face hung open in a silent scream.

"Karys Eska," he breathed. "Vassal of my will."

He had company. Two other Ephirite hung behind him, smaller and more colourful, differently formed. Karys did not dare to look at them. She knelt and opened the flask of blood, spilling it over her hands and then her head. The cold dark liquid trickled down her face and back.

"My lord, I am undeserving," she said, bowed. "I was unprepared for this honour."

Her voice did not betray her; she spoke smoothly. She licked her lips. A small miracle—her throat felt dry as ashes.

"You are to be witnessed." Sabaster's rattling chorus of voices drew closer. Karys stayed stock still. "My will, my selection—it is to be measured."

She had never heard of the Ephirite observing each other's summons before. This was not regular, not normal, not a situation she knew how to navigate. She addressed the slick, shining floor. "How may I serve you?"

Sabaster circled around her once, unspeaking. Was this a test? She did not think so. Her master's behaviour seemed different; he fluttered and twitched, and a steady, rhythmic clicking sound filtered through his wing-shroud.

"Witness my will," he whispered. "Witness."

He was *nervous*, Karys realised, then flinched when something lightly tugged on her hair. Sabaster had arched over and picked up a bloodstained lock between his needle-pointed fingertips. She clenched her jaw, suppressing all sound. The Ephirit almost never touched her. His body's workings pulsed against her scalp; he rubbed the hair in his hand as if to test its texture. Or . . . or to reassure her? Karys' mind rebelled.

"She holds honour," he said. "Chief among my vassals, Karys Eska. My will is hers."

He pulled her hair sharply, jerking Karys' head up. A gasp of pain escaped her. Sabaster probably had no intention of hurting her; he seemed to have simply forgotten to let go. He moved toward the Bhatuma carcass, gliding across the floor.

His companions' attention remained fixed on Karys. The first Ephirit was a shorter, wider version of Sabaster, wing-covered and hook-spined, but with six smaller faces instead of three—they moved just as asynchronously, arranged in a perfect circle on its chest. Its fellow had no faces or feathers at all. It was the colour of spoiled meat, and its shroud continuously melted down its rake-thin frame like a mudslide, like skin sloughing off.

"It is small," said Six-Faces.

"Small," echoed Faceless.

"The scourge and the stain, it could not encompass them. The flesh is not suited."

"Not suited."

Karys stared back at the Ephirite, rigid and uncomprehending. *What is this? What do you want from me?* She could not navigate this conversation if she did not understand her master's intentions.

"This I will overcome," said Sabaster. "She can be re-formed and made fruitful, shaped to house my intention. This I will do. Witness."

With reluctance, the other Ephirite moved to join their host beside the corpse. Karys turned her head to watch them. Her master was swaying from side to side over the raw curve of a blistered Bhatuma organ. His mouths worked, and he spoke again.

"It grows still, I coax the receptacle to flowering. Where other means have failed, mine shall not."

The dead herald's flesh squirmed and swelled, as if something inside it strained to break free. Briefly, the tissue turned glasslike, revealing a large spherical object within—a translucent ball that pulsed with a muddy yellow light, something that had rotted without dying.

"It resists, but I tend it," said Sabaster. "Soon, it will unbend and be joined to my vassal. She will substitute the Disfavoured, and I will wed her."

Karys did not mean to rise, was not even conscious of her body moving before she was on her feet. "My lord, I do not—"

"The vassal is small," said Six-Faces with stubborn insistence. "The receptacle is broken."

"I would have no other." Sabaster's shroud flared, wings pinioning outward so that he seemed even larger and more terrible. The air around his body rippled with workings. "The receptacle will mend. This is our Favour, this is our reproduction. Am I not Prince?"

"You are Prince."

"She shall be the culmination of our will wrought in flesh. I choose her to bear that first honour." Sabaster settled, the air calmed. "I will sire our Favour."

"No!"

Karys' shout rang through the trophy hall. She shook violently, she clutched the empty flask and dripped with blood, she did not think. The Ephirite had gone still. Her head pounded.

"This wasn't in my compact." The words tumbled from her mouth. "No. I *never*—I cannot accept this. It was *not in my compact*."

A brief silence. Then Sabaster made a warbling, crooning sound. His companions repeated it.

"You have honour enough, Karys Eska," he whispered. "First of my vassals, you will be reshaped to bear the blessing."

Incapable of speaking through her horror, she shook her head—but the Ephirite would not understand that human gesture. They would not even understand the concept of a vassal refusing them.

"I measure. She is witnessed," said Six-Faces.

"Witnessed."

"No." Karys' tongue felt paralysed. "No, my lord—"

"You will be summoned once the receptacle blooms." Sabaster's faces grinned and wept and howled. "I will honour you beyond understanding, Karys Eska."

The floor melted under her feet before she could speak again. It collapsed like a wave, and she fell into nothingness as the domain disappeared above her. The summons was over.

CHAPTER

24

When Haeki and Winola found her, it was dark. The moon gleamed yellow-orange in the south, and the etherbulb lamps along the canal's edge sputtered as palm-sized moths battered their glass. Karys sat with her legs hanging over the side of the Lavidas Bridge, her arms threaded through the rails of the parapet. Concealed between the bridge's columns, she was easy to overlook. Few locals had noticed her even before night fell, and those who did gave her a wide berth.

Ferain reached out to touch Winola's shadow as she passed.

"She's here," he said quietly.

Dried blood was caked into Karys' hair. It flaked off her skin, itching. She had been sitting in the same place for hours, the useless empty flask still in her lap. Water trickled along the thick mud under the bridge, and the surface swarmed with midges.

"Karys?" said Winola.

She did not look around. Footsteps drew closer, but stopped a little distance before reaching her.

"You never came back to the Orago," said Haeki. Not an accusation or a complaint, just a statement.

There was a hollow space in the wall underneath the bridge, a sheltered alcove wide enough for a body between the support struts. Someone had built a small shrine to Swask there, and filled it with blue ribbons and bowls of clam shells. Ready to be washed away with the flood, carrying prayers down to the sea.

"Have you ever been hungry?" Karys' voice was low. "Really, really hungry?"

Neither of them answered her. Ferain had returned to her side; her shadow a darker smear on the moonlit stones. She had not spoken to him since the domain spat her out between the warehouses at the edge of town. He kept close and quiet; she hardly felt him there.

"I don't think I really understood what hunger was before Miresse. Or cold." She pointed down at the support strut on the eastern bank of the channel. Her hands were scored with blood, dark ridges around the bed of her fingernails. "I found a dead riverfowl here once, after the floodwaters passed."

There were worms in its feathers. Its eyes had gone white.

"Swask's gift, I thought. It wasn't a small bird; it seemed like I should be able to salvage something."

She tasted its wrongness from the moment it entered her mouth. A sour rankness. She kept eating anyway.

"I was so hungry. There was nothing that year. Too prosperous—people are always more charitable during hard times, and the crops had run strong the previous summer. They called it the Golden Year, for the harvest and the money. Miresse had never been richer, but I had nothing, and no one would help me."

She crawled into the alcove under the bridge, and the fever took her. Shuddering, burning, wretched. The poison was inside her, and she could not retch it out. She dreamed her mouth was full of feathers, woke half-crazed with thirst and drank from the river like a dog. In her delirium, she could not tell how much time passed; it was day and then night, and the shadows under the bridge bloomed with sickening colour. She slept, dreamed, woke. In the midst of it, she retained a single clear, lucid thought: *This will kill me.*

"I couldn't get rid of the taste," she said, staring down at the riverbed. "I still remember it now. All the water couldn't wash it away."

But she survived.

"I'm so sorry," said Winola in a hushed undertone.

"There was never any work back then." Karys did not turn. "Not for me. I scraped by for a year and a half, until that winter. I knew I wasn't going to make it. No one was coming to save me." Her hands tightened around the rails, her knuckles white. "And I wanted to *live.*"

It had been a conscious choice. She had dragged herself out from under the bridge and decided: No more. No more of this.

Even friendless in the town, she had heard about the child-killer. It was a scandal; the Vareslian man accused of murdering his own eight-year-old. When the authorities apprehended him, he had requested the services of a deathspeaker in exchange for a reward. Without a Haven in Miresse, the magistrate's court had requisitioned the services of a saint from Psikamit, only to have their application denied. Miresse was out of the way, obscure, and too close to the border. Not worth the trouble when New Favour had far greater goals to pursue.

So Karys had shambled down to the Silkess station, found New Favour's office, and demanded her own proselytisation. The manager refused to summon a representative to accommodate the rites, so she returned again the next day. The day after that. The passengers grimaced at the starved, half-dead vagrant girl, and held their luggage closer. They muttered but did not look at her directly. On the fourth day, a functionary arrived to facilitate the Audience.

The working to call the attention of the Ephirite was simple and ceremonial. Karys was taken to the abandoned caravanserai at the border of the town, where the functionary—not a deathspeaker himself—explained what she needed to do and provided her with the materials. He never once tried to caution or dissuade her from going ahead with the task. Later she hated him for that—for his bored, perfunctory disinterest. At the time, however, she simply repeated the metaphors he gave her, and laid out the metals and the powders as he prescribed. He did not stay to oversee the rest; he only told her to report to New Favour if her compact was successful.

Four Ephirite responded to her call, but three departed as soon as they perceived Sabaster. He bled into the room and Karys' blood ran cold at the sight of him. She almost ended things there; she felt the full weight of the choice she was making, had the first real sense of its depravity. Sabaster spoke the terms of their agreement, offered the compact, and she hesitated. Then she accepted it. The Ephirit reshaped her, and she became a deathspeaker.

The child-killer, it turned out, was innocent. The girl's aunt had been the culprit—a Mercian woman, her motives inscrutable. When Karys revealed the crime, she had stood unrepentant and proud, and denied nothing. Miresse hanged her, and the little girl's father was freed to grieve and gather the pieces of his life.

He was kind to Karys, in his way. She remembered how he had looked when she performed the speaking, the expression on his face as she repeated the words of his dead child. He gave her more money than promised. He pressed the cret into her hands and closed her fingers over the notes. It had been the first real gentleness she experienced since arriving in Miresse.

"I sold my soul for food and shelter. Not for anything important." Karys gazed down at the wavering lights and shadows below her feet. "I became a deathspeaker because I was hungry and cold, and I needed the money."

That night, she had paid for a room at the Orago, and ate until she was sick. Her stomach rejected the abundance, and, seventeen and alone and feeling safe for the first time in her memory, she had wept.

Haeki laid a hand on Karys' shoulder, bringing her back to the present. Her palm was warm and steady; she did not say anything. The water trickled on under the bridge and the wind carried the smell of woodsmoke.

"I just wanted to live," said Karys softly.

Below, a moth flew too close to the false lights of the river. Its wings dipped into the water, and it floundered, thrashing. Still unspeaking, Haeki sat down next to Karys. She put her arms through the parapet too, like they were the bars of a cage. She did not look sideways, didn't make eye contact. She was just there, quiet as the ocean depths.

"If you were wondering, that's why I never sent letters." Karys watched the moth drift away. "Once I could afford to, I figured you wouldn't want them anymore."

Haeki's mouth did a strange thing. She drummed her fingers against the metal rails, just once.

"You're covered in blood," she said.

"It happens."

Another silence.

"I suppose I also wanted you to imagine I had made something of myself," said Karys. "Like we used to talk about."

"Why should that have mattered?"

"I don't know. It just felt like it did."

Behind them, Winola gave a small cough, then cleared her throat. "About the blood. I could . . . I could fix that, if you like. You must be cold, I could—there are workings. They might help."

Karys glanced over her shoulder. The scholar stood a little way back. Her face was very pale in the darkness; she seemed strangely frightened.

"You're kind." Karys returned her gaze to the canal. She had a vision of the flood that would rip away Swask's shrine and wipe the banks clean. A violent cleansing. It was awful; it felt like she had never left this place. She got up—her hands and feet had gone stiff; she had not noticed the cold until then—and held out the empty flask to Winola. "This is yours."

The scholar wavered, then stepped closer. "May I?"

Winola's workings were quick and elegant; a series of Bhatuma constructions that felt warm and liquid, like getting doused in soapy water. The blood leeched from Karys' clothes and skin, and calmness settled over her, an unnatural but not unpleasant sense of peace. *An even better practitioner than I realised, if she's capable of that.* Karys sighed, and let the chill fade from her limbs.

"Thanks," she said.

Winola nodded, wiped the blood off her bottom lip, and lowered her hands. "It's not much, but you're welcome."

"I'm leaving for Varesli later tonight."

"It can't wait?"

"The errand I agreed to run has a deadline." Karys shook her head. "Winola, after everything you've done for me, there's no obligation—"

The scholar made a soft disapproving sound.

"Nothing's changed," she said. "I knew where you were headed when we left Psikamit, and Eludia's libraries will have answers—I can solve this."

"The crossing is going to be dangerous."

"That's fine." Her mouth turned wry, and faintly bemused. "Besides, Haeki has, well . . . she told me about Nuliere. It's difficult to believe, but a living herald, a survivor of the Slaughter? How could I ever let you go on without me?"

Karys rubbed a hand over her face, hiding her expression. Beside her, Ferain shifted to cross Winola's shadow.

"My father's position at the university means that he can access resources unavailable to the public," he said, his tone difficult to decipher. "If you want those books, you'll have them."

"I might. I'll need to see what I can find on coalescence." Winola's voice grew gentler. "And how to remove the Construct's effect. Separating the two of you is the last hurdle, not the first."

He's right, though. Wanting to get away before my time runs out. Karys exhaled. But that moment had not yet arrived. She would not go to pieces. She would keep moving, keep adapting. Until Sabaster called her compact, she could still fight.

Nothing's changed. Nothing's really changed at all.

"All right," she said. "Let's go meet our guide."

CHAPTER
25

The man waiting for them outside the dilapidated workshop had a strange look. He was of average height and build, but his limbs seemed a little too long; especially his arms, which hung like leaded weights at his sides. He wore dark glasses with round lenses even in the dead of night, and a coat made of some kind of coarse, bristling fur. He introduced himself only as Pavian.

"It's the wrong phase of the moon for a crossing," he said with a scowl. "I won't be held accountable for what happens. And I didn't know there would be three of you."

"I'm sure you've been compensated for the trouble," said Karys coolly. Although she was weary, Pavian's hostility had a curiously steadying effect on her—this was familiar, this she knew how to navigate. "Rasko gave you this job, so you can take up your complaints with him. Do you have the parcel for me?"

He did. It was smaller than Karys had anticipated: a sharp-edged cube the size of a snuff box. The exterior was a smooth, unadorned grey, and it had a complex metal catch on the one side. When she took it from Pavian, the box proved unexpectedly light—it felt empty. She turned it over in her hand. No rattle or movement that she could detect.

"Thank you," she said, shoving it into the side of her bag. "How long will the crossing take?"

"Depends."

"On?"

"How quick you walk. How well you follow my orders."

Haeki snorted.

"Where exactly are we crossing?" asked Winola mildly. "Not at the border post, I take it."

Pavian's eyes narrowed behind his glasses; he regarded the scholar with open suspicion and dislike. She was wearing her guise once again, her Toraigian features concealed, but something about her still seemed to bother him. "What do you mean 'where'? The pinch-point at the bridge is watched and guarded, and you wanted to get in quiet—that's why you needed me to begin with."

"So, through the Riddled Gorge?"

"Unless you want to float over to Varesli on a cloud, then yes. Through the Gorge, about three miles south of the post. If that suits you?"

"It suits us fine," said Karys. "And we'll walk fast."

"Your friend's new pack and clean shoes say otherwise, but I'm not going to be held accountable here." He scratched his thinning hair irritably. "All of you, understand this now. If you don't follow instructions, I'll leave you behind. And none of you will last an hour down there on your own. The Gorge doesn't like strangers."

"You do your job, and we'll follow," said Karys.

Pavian mumbled darkly to himself, then jerked his head in the direction of the road leading out of town.

"Oxcart's half a mile down the track," he said. "We'll get to the edge before sunrise, and make the most of the daylight."

The vehicle was waiting as promised, the black oxen hitched to a sturdy farm gate. Pavian checked the animals' halters before taking up the reins. He muttered, too low to understand, and watched Winola out the corner of his eye.

The road past the gate was badly degraded; the cart bounced and creaked as they rolled over the hard earth. In the starlight, the pale track ran like the shed skin of an old reptile, and the oxen's snorting breath joined the sound of cicadas and night birds as they drew further from Miresse. It was warm and quiet otherwise. The moon lapsed back toward the horizon by slow degrees. At the gate of another nameless small holding, Pavian stopped the cart and grunted for them to get off. They left the animals lowing in the field, and followed him on foot.

There was little indication that anyone still lived out here. The land was uncultivated scrub; a flat, rocky plateau of sandstone, grown over with beardgrass and ancient quiver trees. No lights in the farmhouse when they passed it, no smoke from a kitchen. In the distance, a jackal yipped.

"Watch for snakes," said Pavian. He moved easily through the dark, his long arms swinging. "The adders won't warn before they bite."

Karys picked her way after him. There were old sheep droppings on the ground, pellets scattered over the dry soil. The animals themselves were nowhere to be seen.

"How often do you make this trip?" asked Winola.

"About twice a month."

"Oh, so quite regular. Do you have many takers?"

"Why do you want to know?"

"Curious, that's all."

"I'm not in the business of curious. You should be grateful I'm taking you at all."

Winola shrugged and let it drop. A few feet to her left, Haeki stopped walking and squinted at the scrub.

"What's that?" she asked, and pointed.

A lump lay in their path, an object unlike the rough, thorny underbrush. Softer. It took Karys a moment to recognise it in the dimness, but it was a sheep. Part of a sheep. Its grubby fleece was blackened with blood, its rear legs and half its head missing. The gore glistened.

"Oh, poor thing," murmured Winola. "What happened to it? A leopard? Or wild dogs—"

"That's not their work, they don't waste." Pavian kept walking. "That was sport."

"Excuse me?"

"Fun. A game. A plaything. It must have gotten separated from the flock." Unexpectedly, he chuckled. "Don't worry, I'll introduce you to old clever fingers. Nothing to worry about, so long as I'm around."

Karys' misgivings deepened, and Haeki muttered something. Winola, however, only smiled at Pavian.

"That's comforting," she said.

The canyon appeared like a worked trick; the plateau gave way to the air with unnerving suddenness. One moment, ground, the next, the great, swallowing gulf of the gorge. The sight brought Karys up short. The opposite wall was miles away, little more than a suggestion of light above the dark pit, a sheer rockface riddled with caves and cracks. The base of the ravine was near-invisible, the last of the moonlight could not pierce its misted depths. Only the very highest peaks of the maze of walls below were visible, glints of blue like ice floes on water.

This was always here. For all the years Karys had spent in Miresse, this vast abyss had existed right beside her, and yet she had never seen it, and she felt so small, standing before it now. The sky in the east held the faintest violet cast, dawn approaching. Air swirled up from below, chilled and smelling of old dust and stone.

Pavian walked a few paces further right, stooped, and picked up something from the ground: a coiled rope. One end was tightly knotted around the shaft of a metal stake hammered into the rock.

"The elevator is below," he said. "After me."

In the half-dark, the rope provided a small measure of security. Karys followed Pavian and Winola down the steep trail, and Haeki brought up the rear. Their movements sent stones rolling over the cliff edge; the clatter echoed across the canyon, causing roosting birds to erupt from cracks in the walls. They reached a small wooden platform, sheltered by the bluff of the plateau, where a metal cage hung from a rickety winch bolted into the promontory. A rudimentary crank stood inside the elevator, blackened with grease and rust.

"A fast death, at least," Haeki mumbled.

It was not a smooth ride. The chains clanged as they juddered through the mechanism, and the cage sank in slow, painful starts while Pavian worked the crank. Overhead, the sky paled with the sunrise. The light bloomed gold on the sandstone walls, and picked up other colours in the rock: streaks of ochre and russet, deep greens in the fissures where moisture collected to sustain hardy, clinging moss. A flock of fan-winged birds wafted on the thermals, moving like white sails through the dissipating mist. They reminded Karys of manta rays, their flight weightless as the air.

"We'll reach the other side by sunset." Despite the morning chill, sweat beaded Pavian's forehead. "No stopping. You don't want to get caught here after dark."

"Why not?" asked Winola.

He acted like she had not spoken.

The canyon floor was colder than the air up on the plateau. Ahead, twenty-foot sandstone walls cast stretched, hazy shadows over the ground. The work of some long-forgotten herald, they were holed through at irregular intervals by tunnels and clefts, like a score of giant worms had eaten their winding way through the rock. Desiccated trees grew where tributaries of the river had once flowed, crooked and white with age. Karys could hear water nearby—beyond the first of the warren's walls—but the ground at her feet was dry and sandy, the colour of old hay.

"No stopping," repeated Pavian, and then loped off like he wanted nothing more than to leave them behind. His movements had an animal intensity: his gait ugly but efficient. *At least he seems to know where he's going.* Karys lengthened her stride to keep up, following as he ducked under the low shelf of an overhanging rock.

They found the stream soon enough, the water nothing but a meandering brown trickle. Pavian's course seemed needlessly twisting; he took them up narrow passages and then cut back in the direction they had come, squeezing through apertures between the walls. After his initial surge of speed, he slowed to a more reasonable pace. The gorge seemed to have a calming effect on him. Winola, following behind him, occasionally asked questions, and he largely ignored her.

"Karys, can we talk?"

Her shadow had been silent so long that Karys started at the sound of Ferain's voice. His tone was calm, impenetrable. Careful, once again. She dropped back slightly, letting Haeki pull ahead.

"Since when do you feel the need to ask?" she muttered.

In truth, his new quietness had begun to grate on her nerves. She had the sense that he might be judging her, like the scales between them had shifted too far. She had revealed herself, and now he held her at a guarded distance, tiptoeing around like she was some terrible, breakable, already-mangled thing.

"How are you feeling?" he asked.

"Fine."

A pause. "Are you sure?"

Karys breathed out through her teeth. "I don't need your pity, Ferain. Stop being so irritating."

"I'm not pitying you. And I resent 'irritating,' by the way."

"Oh? You learned that I used to live under a bridge, and now you're doing that stupid thing with your voice."

He sputtered. "'Stupid thing with my voice?'"

"Where you go all soft and whispery."

"First of all—"

"Talk like a normal person."

"*First* of all, I don't do any stupid things with my voice." Ferain took a moment to gather himself. "And secondly, I'm just worried about you. That's not the same as pitying you."

Karys was quiet. The canyon was warming; Pavian led them southward through the maze, and fork-tailed flycatchers swooped overhead, snatching insects from the air. Distracted, Ferain had slipped out of her silhouette, and her shadow did not fit her.

"I don't care that you used to live under a bridge," he said. "It doesn't matter. Or it does, but not like that. I know how you got there, and I hate the thought of—I'm trying to say that you're still the same to me. Does that make sense?"

She shrugged.

"Don't shrug at me."

"You really don't pity me?"

"No."

"Hm." She crossed the stream, stepping from one rock to the next. Ahead, she could hear Winola quizzing Pavian about seasonal changes in the gorge, the difficulties of flooding. Haeki studied the walls around them as she walked.

"I'm on your side, Karys," said Ferain. "You know that."

"It's not like you have anywhere else to go."

"Very funny." Her shadow rolled over the sand. "For what it's worth, I understand. I know you don't want to talk about what happened yesterday, and that's fine."

Karys' mouth tasted bitter. "Do you?"

"Do I want to talk about it?"

"No. Understand."

He considered, then gave a tiny shake of his head. "No, probably not. But I was there. I saw. I heard what Sabaster said. I know you're afraid."

She scoffed.

"Am I wrong?"

"You're right that I don't want to talk about it."

"Then we won't talk about it."

"Good."

"But I won't let you face this alone either."

Karys made a small angry movement with her head. "You have no—you have no *idea*. Do you honestly think—" She broke off, temporarily unable to speak. Her blood pounded in her ears. She drew a quick, unsteady breath. "Do you honestly think that makes a single *shred* of difference to me? Are you planning to hold my hand, Ferain? While Sabaster binds a rotting corpse to me, and then tries to breed new fucking Ephirite in it?"

Silence.

"It isn't your concern," she said, voice hoarse. "I'll get you to Eludia, I'll get you unbound, and then you'll pay me. That's it. Do you hear me?"

"I hear you," he said softly.

She needed to hit something. Or scream. She needed to drive Sabaster out of her head, because every time her concentration slipped, the Ephirit was there. *I will honour you beyond understanding.* Karys pressed her fist to her mouth, hard. Embrace, she was going to be sick. Reproduction. The Ephirite had failed with the Constructs, and now her master planned to try another method with the . . . the receptacle, he'd called it. The yellowed, decaying organ. Fuse it to her body, and then . . . then . . .

A stone clattered down the wall behind her. It struck the pebbled bank of the stream, and the sound rang loud and hollow, not quite echoing, but producing a deeper, more ominous resonance. Karys jumped, and looked around in time to catch a flash of dark movement at the top of the wall.

What was that?

Ferain fell back into the ordinary shape of her shadow. While they had been talking, the others had pulled further ahead. No one else appeared to have heard the noise or noticed anything out of the ordinary.

"Maybe it's nothing," said Ferain. "But don't get left behind."

Karys nodded stiffly, and broke into a jog to catch up. The passage ahead was long and curving. The stream hushed down its centre, but it was otherwise quiet. The birds were gone. As she drew up to the others, more gravel slid down the wall; this time to her left. Haeki looked around and frowned. She slipped one hand into her pocket.

"An animal?" said Karys.

Haeki scanned the top of the wall. "It sounded large."

Pavian slowed, and grew still. Then he crowed.

"Clever fingers!" he called. "My beauties!"

A rumbling repetitive bray answered him, an inhuman voice. Sound moved strangely between the walls of the gorge, through its tunnels and bends—it was difficult to trace. Snorting. A brief screech.

"Over here," said Pavian. "Come on, come on, it's only me. What has upset you, my sweets?"

"I don't like this," murmured Haeki.

Winola edged toward her, moving away from Pavian. Their guide swept his arms out wide, threw back his head, and produced a braying call of his own. The hooting increased, coming from every direction. The wild assault of noise was intimidating, but there was something more insidious in Pavian's behaviour, something greasy and fevered.

"Was it the reekers again?" he simpered. "Did those nasty patrols set their horrid workings on you?"

Twenty feet ahead of him, a hulking figure sidled out of a concealed fissure in the curve of the wall. The baboon was far larger than any Karys had seen; nothing like the shy, salted-grey creatures that roamed the coast around Psikamit. This animal was brown-furred and horse-faced and heavy. Close-set red eyes gleamed beneath the ridge of its brow bone. Its wide shoulders seemed disproportioned; too large for its wiry arms and leathery hands— hands that looked both human and not, the joints in slightly the wrong places, the fingernails entirely black. *Like Sabaster's hands,* Karys thought, and took a reflexive step backwards. The baboon moved like it could not settle between walking on two legs or four. When it reared up, it was nearly as tall as Winola.

It approached Pavian, making a low, repeating sound in its throat. In response,

Pavian rounded his own shoulders and grunted. The baboon showed its teeth; canines long and yellow, lips and snout creasing back.

"What is this?" muttered Ferain.

"That's it, my clever boy," said Pavian, wheedling. "It's only me and a few friends. A few lady friends for old Pavian."

Haeki's mouth twisted. Pavian lumbered toward the animal—Karys saw now that he moved like the apes, the same swinging upright gait—and reached out his hand. Instead of biting it off, the baboon permitted Pavian to stroke its head. Its eyes closed and it snuffled. Pavian clucked his tongue, then began to groom the animal's fur.

"They don't let anyone through but me," he said, in a more normal tone. "They'd tear you apart if I wasn't here."

"How did you win their trust?" asked Winola.

"They've always liked me. That's all there is to it."

More baboons were appearing, clambering down from the walls. Karys had an unpleasant vision of the dead sheep up on the plateau. A plaything, Pavian had said. The animals did not appear aggressive now, only a little jumpy. They skirted around the stream, hooting softly; they cracked their jaws and bared their teeth.

"Why are they upset?" asked Winola, turning on the spot to study the troop.

"Can't say. They're badly spooked, though." Pavian pinched an insect out the baboon's fur, and flicked it into the stream. "The reekers at the border post go after them sometimes; they call it 'population control.' I'd like to control *their* population."

One of the baboons started screeching, and the others flinched. The male Pavian was grooming abruptly pulled away, slinking backwards over the sand. The animals looked around, but it wasn't clear what had disturbed them. Pavian gnashed his teeth.

"What is it?" he asked. "What's the matter, my sweets?"

"Karys, above you!"

A heartbeat after Ferain's shout, the baboons scattered like streaks of mud-coloured lightning. Karys' head jerked up. Dazzled by sunlight, she was briefly struck by the conviction that enormous birds were swooping down on them. Then the shapes resolved into three men in billowing grey coats.

Oh shit, she thought, as the New Favour saints dropped from the sky.

She had time to yell a warning, and then the first of the men reached the ground. He was slim, grey-eyed, and dark-skinned; he stepped smoothly from the air onto the sand beside Pavian. In his left hand, he held an odd sort of flail. The leather tails ignored gravity, as if they were only feathers. With a flick of his wrist, the saint snapped the weapon outward and the tails flew with magnetic precision to coil around Pavian's neck.

Pavian made a single choked sound. In an instant, his skin turned bloodless; his flesh withered and shrank in on itself. The saint pulled the weapon back, and he collapsed.

Winola screamed.

Pavian? Karys felt dazed. *What is—how are they here? How did they find me? I thought—*

Haeki pulled something from her pocket and threw it: a handful of white powder. It landed harmlessly in the stream, nowhere near the saints. All three had reached the canyon floor now, and they moved with unfeeling purpose.

"Karys, get back," said Ferain urgently.

Winola was caught with a saint on either side of her. The scholar lifted both hands, terrified and stammering, but the men advanced without hesitation. They held identical worked flails.

"Stop!" Karys snatched a stone off the ground. She threw, and hit the back of the first saint's head, causing him to stumble. "Winola!"

The second saint raised his weapon to strike the scholar.

Somehow, Haeki came between them. Her eyes were glazed; she shoved Winola roughly out of the way, then pivoted, ducking left and under the hungry tails of the whip. Her limbs were loose, her body impossibly quick. She flowed like water—with a thoughtless economy of motion, she shifted her weight forward, closed the distance to the saint, and brought the flat edge of her hand down on his outstretched wrist.

Bone shattered. The man screamed and dropped the flail. Swift and sure as a coin flip, Haeki followed up with the fist of her other hand, punching him in the chest. His ribs stove inward.

"Karys, *move!*" cried Ferain.

She had been too caught up in Haeki's fight to notice the third saint closing in on her. Karys scrambled backwards. The man had a hard, sharp face—attractive features, all angles and cheekbones, but on him they appeared inhuman and cold. No trace of mercy in those brown eyes, nothing but intent focus. He drew back his weapon, and the tails of the whip wafted lazily upwards. She was too close, still far too close. The wall of the passage was behind her; she had nowhere to go and no means to defend herself. The flail unfurled before her face—

A heavy force collided with her torso, driving her clear of the saint's reach. Karys stumbled, and her back hit the wall. An instant later, a violent weakness swept through her body. Her shadow loomed in front of her; a formless black column between her and the saint.

"Oh," whispered Ferain.

Karys pressed a hand to her chest, heart racing, breathing ragged. Beyond Ferain, the saint's eyes had gone wide. His hand clenched around the handle of his weapon, and he stared at the shadow hovering in the air before him.

He pushed me, thought Karys, dazed. *Ferain pushed me out of the way.*

Her shadow shivered, rippling like a mirage. Then Ferain changed shape, adopting his own silhouette. He rolled away from her, light and liquid, and tilted to cross the saint's shadow on the sand. He spoke so that the man would hear him.

"That was a mistake," he said.

The saint swore and struck at the darkness with his flail, but the weapon went straight through, touching nothing. In response, Ferain gave a breathless little laugh—an oddly menacing sound to Karys' ears. Then he punched the man under the jaw. The saint's handsome face snapped back, his eyes rolled, and he dropped.

A heartbeat later, the world exploded into black. Karys' limbs turned boneless, and she sagged. It felt as though something vital was being wrenched out of her; her blood turned to ice and her ears filled with roaring. She tried to speak, tried to warn Ferain, but all that left her mouth was a thin gasp.

Somewhere to her right, Winola cried out in pain. Haeki cursed viciously. Karys' vision returned, blurry, and she could make out the scholar collapsed on the sand, pale face covered in blood. Her glasses were broken in her hands, and her guise had fallen away. Haeki shielded her from the first saint: the one who had killed Pavian. His half-shaven scalp shone in the sun, and his companion lay prone and unmoving on the canyon floor.

The ground trembled.

Karys pushed herself away from the wall. *Haeki.* The pebbles along the edge of the stream rattled again, clicking together. Haeki panted, her gaze fixed on the saint. He was more cautious now; keeping his distance, but he still held his flail. One strike that found its mark, one mistake . . . Karys stooped and grabbed another stone.

With a low growl, the water in the stream drew together. It defied natural order, changing course so that it pulled into a single churning pool—and then, seething, it rose into the air. Blue fire swirled through its muddied heart, staining the canyon walls. The saint turned, startled.

"Nuliere," breathed Karys.

A jet of water scythed outward, precise and thin as a blade, and cut open the saint's throat. Blood sprayed. The man lifted his hand to the wound, blinking rapidly. The water sliced again. More blood. He dropped his flail. His mouth worked without a sound.

"Stop," said Karys, unthinking. "Stop it."

Nuliere slashed again, carving a red line from the saint's shoulder to hip. He fell, and the water rained upon his back, slicing through his worked coat like it was damp paper. With each strike, the torrent hissed out a word.

Apostate! Apostate! Apostate! Apostate!

Haeki, standing behind the saint, was painted crimson. She flinched with every blow, but otherwise did not move. Her eyes shone blue with hallowfire; she watched her mistress strip the flesh from the man's back.

"Stop!" said Karys. "He's dead, stop!"

The saint Ferain had punched was trying to rise; the one Haeki had dropped remained unconscious. Without pausing from her bloody task, Nuliere impaled them both with spears of water. Karys felt the men's deaths bloom against the Veneer.

Apostate! Apostate! Apostate!

"Enough!" barked Ferain.

Nuliere paused. The sound of dripping was loud in the quiet that followed. After a second, the mass of water and mud sank back to the riverbed.

"As you wish," said the Bhatuma silkily.

Karys was shaking. She found Haeki's gaze. Nuliere's voice echoed between them, whispering over the mutilated corpse at their feet. *Apostate. Apostate. Apostate.* The stream sighed, resuming its course. Blood diffused through the water. Behind Haeki, Winola was crying.

"You're sick, Nuliere." Karys' voice dropped. "You're fucking depraved."

The water, serene, did not reply.

26

Pavian could not help them.

Karys spoke to his apparition first. She was shaken and sick and fumbling. With his body still warm under her hands, it should have been the easiest speaking she had ever performed. Instead, she could barely bring herself to open the Veneer. Peeling back the fabric, a nauseous, primal wave of fear rose up in her; she could taste the lurid colours, smell the acid chaos of the other side. It was Boäz all over again—she had not touched the Veneer since falling into the Penitence Pool, and now, with her hand resting on a corpse's shoulder, the copper smell of blood in the air, she felt paralysed.

Pavian's flesh was ashen and pale. His dark spectacles sat askew; his eyes were glassy behind them, fixed upon the blue sky. He smelled like sweat.

I'm sorry, Karys thought, and steeled herself.

In death, he proved inexpressive, answering her questions with dull indifference, and never growing agitated. His resentful aggression was stripped away, and he appeared as a wan, flat spectre. Usually, some trace of personality lingered in the memories of the dead—with Pavian, there was a void.

Had he seen New Favour saints in the Riddled Gorge before?

No.

Had anything seemed especially unusual about this border crossing?

No, only the timing.

Nothing strange about Rasko, nothing that struck him as suspicious?

No and no.

Before leaving Miresse, had he talked to anyone about the job?

No, he never did. He seldom talked to anyone, unless it was necessary for work.

Winola sat by the river with her body angled away from the gristly scene, while Haeki carefully cleaned the blood from her face. The gash to her eyebrow was shallow; the saint's flail had only caught the rim of her glasses. Whatever workings powered his weapon had sheared through the guise, causing it to explode in the scholar's face. Half an inch lower, and she would have lost her eye. With light, deft fingers, Haeki placed a small strip of gauze over the cut. She said something to Winola, quiet and serious. The scholar did not respond.

"Can you give me directions out of the canyon?" Karys asked Pavian.

There was a pause. An expression of mild consternation crossed the apparition's face.

"I only know the way when I see it," he said slowly.

Karys' stomach tightened.

"What do you mean?" she asked. "There must be landmarks. How do you know the right path?"

"It feels right."

"No, tell me about features. Where do we go from here?"

"I don't know where I am."

Haeki looked over at Karys. Her face was almost as blank as Pavian's. "What is he saying?"

Karys waved for her to be quiet. She kept her tone neutral.

"I need you to describe your usual path through the Gorge," she said.

No matter how she rephrased the question and coaxed, the apparition could tell her nothing. The ghost's expression was placid, uncurious; he was maddeningly apathetic. Karys knew it wasn't his fault, but she found herself growing increasingly frustrated with every dull-voiced reply. The sun was moving across the sky, and she was getting nowhere.

After half an hour, she broke off the speaking. The apparition vanished. Haeki and Winola were both watching her now, and they knew; Karys could see it on their faces.

"I'll try again." She looked down at the river. At the shadow of the canyon walls. "Give me more time. I'll get the answer."

Haeki did not betray even a flicker of feeling. "Is it safe for you to carry on?"

An irrational anger flared inside Karys. She tamped it down.

"Safe enough," she said. "And necessary—unless you've got a better source for directions?"

Winola said nothing; she just walked over to the passage wall and crouched there like she wanted to be sick.

The saints' bodies lay where Nuliere had killed them. In the midday heat, the flies had followed the smell of their blood, and buzzed over their wounds. No vultures yet, but they would come. The sand had turned black around the corpses. Karys knelt beside the man with the handsome face.

"You're tougher than me," muttered Ferain.

She did not look at the raw hole in the saint's chest. "I've had practice."

The apparition appeared larger than the man had been in life, and his angular features were calm and composed. His attention settled on Karys, and he frowned slightly, as if she were something he could not quite put a name to. His gaze gave her an eerie feeling. She had never done this to a fellow deathspeaker before.

"I don't like it," he said, unprompted, his voice liquid-smooth and deep.

Karys waited to see if he would continue. He did not, so she asked, "What don't you like?"

"The other one, she screamed. They were afraid. I never thought I would be asked to hunt women. To hurt them."

"The Supremes gave you this task?"

"They gave us all this task." The apparition nodded his head in vague agreement. "The deathspeaker, Karys Eska. We must find her, and erase her. Only then, the Supremes say, will we be safe. The Ephirite cannot know."

Karys' mouth was dry. "What can't the Ephirite know?"

"The Supremes won't say more than that, not to us. Our masters must remain ignorant and calm, and that means Karys Eska must be disposed of. That is what we have been told—that you don't start a wildfire just to torch a spider's nest."

Her heartbeat quickened. "So the Supremes, they are . . . lying to their masters? About Karys Eska?"

"Not lying, only silent. The Constructs stopped seeking her, and we hoped that meant she was already dead, but the Supremes said we needed to be certain. They believed she might try to cross the border to Varesli."

"And they sent you here to keep watch?" New Favour had not tracked her; they had just anticipated her movements. "How many more are stationed along the border?"

"Another two teams between Geoi and Hasare. There are saints at every post, but we are overstretched."

Desperate. What had the Supremes so terrified? Ferain kept still and silent at her back, but Karys sensed that he was listening intently. "Why is Eska such a threat? What about her is worth all of this?"

"I don't know."

"But the Supremes believe that she might upset the Ephirite. Is that right?"

The man was silent a few seconds. Then: "My master frightens me. I don't want her to call my compact."

The smell of his blood burned in the back of Karys' throat. At the edges of the apparition's form, the Veneer pulled taut. "Is that what you've been told? That if Karys Eska survives, your master might call your compact?"

"My service will be needed."

What did that mean? She could not afford to push too hard; the saint's form was already unstable. It sounded as though the Supremes were keeping the lesser saints in the dark, holding back information. Concealing secrets even from their own. *They're trying to cover something up.* "What do you know about Ferain Taliade?"

"I don't know that name."

"How about Varesli? Why was that ship attacked in Psikamit's waters?"

The apparition gazed at her, still with the same expression of faint perturbation on his face. "I've never been to Psikamit; I don't know what danger my leaders saw there. They only told us that our compacts will be called if we fail in this. My master frightens me. I don't want her to call my compact."

Karys briefly pressed her free palm against her forehead. It didn't feel like she would get anything more from this conversation, and she could not afford to continue going in circles—too much time had already passed. She felt woozy with exhaustion. But the truth was so *close*. There had to be a way to draw it out, if she could just find the right question—

"Karys," said Winola.

She flinched, and turned. Winola was standing at the border of the stream, her face grave and yet strangely resolute. She made a small motion, gesturing for Karys to finish the speaking. In her hand was a bundle of sticks. Karys hesitated, then nodded. She turned back to the saint.

The apparition was losing focus, growing ever more restless and agitated. His incorporeal skin rippled with rainbows, and his edges blurred into the fabric of the Veneer. Less than an hour ago, this man had been breathing and vital and alive. His corpse was cold now.

"You don't need to be afraid anymore." Karys lowered her voice. Tried to make it gentle. "She won't call your compact. You can . . . you don't need to be afraid. It's over."

She removed her hand from his face before he could say anything else, and let the Veneer fall closed. The apparition vanished, but the coolness of his skin lingered on her fingertips. It felt unclean. She sank back on her heels.

"You got all you could from him," murmured Ferain.

I achieved nothing. "This is taking too long. I should've—"

"Don't be so hard on yourself."

Karys flexed her fingers, then curled them inward to form fists. Behind her, she could hear footsteps on the sand.

"I'll try Pavian again," she said, louder, not turning around. "I'm sorry. I just wanted answers. I'll get the directions, the saints might—"

"No need," said Winola.

Karys looked back. Winola still held her bundle of sticks, which, on closer inspection, were all coloured white on one side, like they had been dipped in a pot of paint. The scholar squinted slightly, struggling to see without her glasses.

"I'll be the first to admit that this sort of practical, outdoors working isn't my strength," she said. "So it took me a while, but I think I've figured it out. Look."

She spread the sticks out like a fan, and then carefully let them go. Instead of falling, they hovered in midair. After a moment, they began to shuffle over one another.

"It's a similar principle to deathspeaking," said Winola. "Not a fraction as sophisticated obviously, but it should do the trick. Haeki is helping with the calibration."

Karys stood up, brushing the sand from her trousers. "What is it?"

"A furrow print. All it does is detect extremely low-level, non-specific psychic residue through the Veneer. I've heard that more complex versions are used on ships to track existing trade routes, but it only works in places where there are very few people. Oceans, deserts, that sort of thing. There's too much interference otherwise." Winola watched the sticks revolve. "So where your powers allow you to interpret death impressions, this basically just points to past human traffic of any kind. If Pavian made this journey regularly, the furrow print should trace his footsteps out of here."

"That's remarkable," said Ferain.

Winola started, surprised by his voice. "Well, if it works. I read about the principles a few years ago, but I never thought I'd need them. And after I was so useless when New Favour—when Pavian—" She shook her head. "I hope it will work."

A piercing whistle echoed down the stone corridor, and a second later the sticks pivoted sharply toward the sound. All the white sides faced forward.

"Is that good?" asked Karys.

Winola nodded. "Yes, I think so."

A moment later, Haeki reappeared at the end of the corridor, and jogged back to join them. Winola must have performed a working to draw out the saint's blood from her hair and clothing, because she appeared much cleaner than before. She was also holding a marker; this one stained dark red.

"Well?" she asked.

"Promising," said Winola. The ghost of a smile touched her lips. "A useful piece of heresy, don't you think?"

Unexpectedly, Haeki offered a quick, tired smile of her own. "At least nothing caught on fire. It'll lead us to Varesli?"

"That's the idea. Whether it actually works . . ." Winola sighed. She glanced over her shoulder at the corpses and the stained sand. "We can only try. What should we do with the bodies?"

The sheep on the plateau: soft fleece and glistening black wounds. A plaything, Pavian had said. A gristly game. Karys knew that Haeki and Winola's thoughts ran in the same direction, even though the idea was too terrible to voice aloud. If the troop returned, the corpses here could make for much larger sport.

"We leave them," she said. It came out steadier than she had expected. "There's nothing else we can do now. If we're lucky, New Favour won't immediately notice their saints' absence. Maybe . . . maybe they won't find them at all."

Winola nodded, swift and unhappy, but Haeki's face had gone stiff. She wouldn't meet Karys' eyes.

"Give me one minute," she said.

"Haeki, this isn't—"

She brushed past, gaze still on the ground. "One minute."

Winola did not understand at first—her confusion was obvious when Haeki pulled the coin purse from her waistband and crouched beside Pavian's body. She removed his dark glasses with quiet solemnity, setting them down on his chest. Then she sorted through her meagre stash of cret to find two matching coins, a pair of polished copper halves, and laid them on top of his eyelids. Her cheeks were flushed; she touched Pavian's lips very gently and murmured a few words before moving to the first of the saints to repeat the rites.

Karys turned away. Haeki's reverence filled her with an ugly, angry feeling; something she could not quite articulate. It wasn't about the money, although she knew Haeki had no resources and could not afford to throw cret away. No, it was something else, something bound up in Haeki's stillness while Nuliere had whipped the saint to death—the sudden, certain knowledge that too much separated them now to ever go back. The girls who had dived for pearls were dead. Haeki offered the saints' souls to the care of the same herald who had slaughtered them, and didn't seem to see any irony in it, didn't perceive the awful joke at the heart of it all.

Don't you ever dare lay coins on my eyes, Karys thought, but when Haeki finally rose, finished, she did not say a word.

Winola led the way, following the minute, twitching movements of her furrow print. The sun was hot; the winding stone corridors branched and divided in a serpentine maze. It all looked alike to Karys. Sometimes they followed the river, sometimes not, but little else differentiated the route. She traced the progression of the light over the canyon walls, watched the band of yellow shrink up the rockface. It was hard to know how much further they needed to travel. Her head felt thick and her legs heavy. The scar on her arm now rested just below her elbow joint—when Ferain had pushed her, she had distinctly felt her flesh rearranging, crawling like a nest of insects under the surface of her skin. Not painful, but disconcerting. She was too tired to worry about what it might mean.

"What are they like? The dead?"

Haeki's voice pulled Karys out of her thoughts. Although she spoke quietly, there was a new hardness there, a rough demand. Winola was a little way ahead, stumbling after her markers. Ferain kept tight to Karys' heels.

"Why?" asked Karys.

"You don't like the question?"

Not the way you're asking it. "They're just echoes—they usually look like the person who died. Why do you want to know?"

Haeki did not immediately reply. She seemed to be grappling with something.

"Doesn't it bother you?" she asked at last.

"No, not really. It isn't like speaking to a person, only an imprint of their memories. What they thought about themselves, what they remember."

"You talk to them like they're real."

Karys shrugged.

"Well? Why do that?"

"How else should I talk? It works better that way."

"But if they're not people—"

"It just works better." She could not keep the brittle, defensive edge out of her own voice. "If you agitate the dead too much, they can become dangerous. Should you be asking me about this? Nuliere won't like it."

Haeki scowled.

"I suppose not," she said. "I only wanted to know if you got the chance to say goodbye to Oboro."

Karys' step faltered. They had not spoken about her brother since the send-off. Haeki's mouth tightened, her eyes flinty. She shook her head, and moved to catch up with Winola.

"He was faded," Karys said abruptly. "But I—yes. I spoke to him."

Haeki did not look back, although she slowed. Then she shook her head again, and kept walking.

First Ferain, now her. Karys dropped her gaze to the ground, and trudged onward. Her feet sank into the loose sand, steps dragging. She felt so tired. None of it really mattered. She just needed to get Ferain out of her shadow before Sabaster called her compact. Needed her money. Needed to get out of this cursed gorge. She could not afford to be distracted, not with the cost of failure so high. One foot in front of the other. The rest didn't matter.

A sudden shiver ran through her shadow. Karys frowned.

"What is it now?" she asked.

Ferain waved one hand. "Nothing. Don't worry about it."

Karys looked back down the passage. She could not see anything unusual; it was quiet and still. The sun had sunk below the western wall of the canyon, and the dusk was settling in. High above, a flock of white winged birds drifted on the thermals.

"Did you see something?" she asked.

"Nothing important." Her shadow swept out in front of her. "Come on, keep up with the others."

She didn't trust his nonchalance, but tried to move faster anyway. Winola and Haeki were walking more quickly, side by side, their heads bowed together as they spoke in low, terse murmurs. They had left the river behind again, and the air tasted of dust.

A clatter of stone. Karys turned. Pebbles skittered down the passage wall, rolling to a stop in the sand. Silence again.

"Shit," she muttered.

"Keep going," said Ferain. "I'm watching your back, but don't slow down."

The baboons kept their distance as the daylight faded, padding quietly over the walls, not hooting or calling. Karys did not know for how long the animals had been stalking them. Out of the corner of her eye, she caught the quick movements of long shadows. Soft snuffling. The rattle of falling stones. When she flagged, the sounds grew louder. Ferain was tense at her feet; her shadow kept shifting around her as he watched the walls.

"Karys . . ." he began.

"Shut up." Her legs were too heavy. "I know. I'm trying."

"Then tell the others to wait."

She pressed her lips together.

"Karys, stop being so—"

"There," said Winola.

The scholar pointed to the end of the passage, where the sandstone walls reluctantly gave way to a semicircle of open space. Beyond, the canyon's cliffs reared skyward. Through the encroaching gloom, Karys could make out the metal cage and heavy chains of the elevator. She sagged, and her knees almost buckled before she forced them straight. The sticks of Winola's furrow print slowly sank to the ground.

A loud bark reverberated across the gorge.

"Come on," said Ferain. "Don't stop."

Karys' muscles trembled with fatigue, but she drove her body forward. Haeki strode over the sand and dragged the cage door open. The metal hinges produced a rusted scream, painfully loud in the gathering dusk. Winola flinched at the sound. The scholar's skin was alabaster pale, and blood had soaked through the gauze over her eyebrow.

"Hurry up," said Haeki.

Karys closed the last distance to reach the cage, staggering into the elevator after Winola. The scholar looked at her with surprised concern.

"She's fine," said Ferain, crossing Winola's shadow. "I'll explain later."

Karys slumped against the bars with a grimace. *Easy for him to say.* Her exhaustion went beyond anything natural, anything normal, but she closed her eyes and nodded. *Fine. I'm fine enough.* She started at the brush of warm fingers against her forehead as Winola straightened her sweat-damp hair.

"You should have said something," said the scholar softly.

Karys jerked away. Nearby, a baboon grunted, and Haeki pulled the cage door shut with another metallic screech. Ferain stretched across the floor to her.

"Can you operate this thing?" he asked.

"What do you take me for, reeker?" Haeki moved to the crank, grasped it, and pushed downwards sharply. The cage left the ground with a strained creak. "Of course I can."

The elevator rose, slow and swaying, and the evening shadows grew dense as they ascended. Stars appeared, scattered like tiny shards of broken glass across the sky. Karys gripped the bars of the cage. There was movement in the gorge below: strange loping figures running through the alleys of stone, snatched impressions of long, dour faces. Even as the baboons began to shriek and bark, Haeki never paused. Her lean, corded arms moved smoothly. She appeared focussed and unafraid, neither tired nor flustered. A cold wind swept up the cliffs and rattled the elevator's chains.

It was entirely dark when they finally reached the upper platform. Winola pushed open the cage door, and they all stepped out onto the narrow deck. A short trail led up through the rocks to the top of the gorge.

Varesli, Karys thought. It was the first time she had ever left Mercian soil. The dust tasted the same.

A pale, white-haired man waited at the end of the track. He was seated beside a lantern, alone in the veldt. A large awrig hovered a few feet behind him. He smiled to see them. When he spoke, it was with a heavy Vareslian accent.

"One of you is Rasko's woman, I presume?" he said. "Welcome. I've been expecting you."

CHAPTER

27

Rasko's contact introduced himself as Vuhas Gota. Karys wasn't sure what to make of him. He wore a green velvet travelling coat with silver clasps, and brimmed with a frothy exuberance that seemed too unremitting to be genuine; he talked slowly, but with a theatrical flair that demanded that they hang on his every word. His spry expressiveness—hands waving, fingers dancing, eyebrows waggling—gave the impression of a man thoroughly convinced of his own charms.

"So good to meet you," he drawled, stringing out the vowels. "You were beginning to worry me, arriving this late."

He did not ask about Pavian, or the bloodstains on Karys' clothing. Although his smooth-skinned appearance suggested that he could not be many years past forty, he behaved like a much older man. *Something about his mannerisms,* Karys thought. They felt affected. She climbed into his awrig, and was immediately assailed by a fog of perfume. She wrinkled her nose. *True to form, reeker.*

The vehicle was comfortable, generously sized, and low-lit. Vuhas explained travel arrangements: they would be staying at his house for the night, and depart for Tuschait in the morning. From there, it was a day's journey to Eludia via train. Karys found it difficult to concentrate on what he was saying. Winola, seated on the bench beside her, was warm, and the Bhatuma-derived workings powering the awrig emitted a soothing hum like a purring cat. Little orange etherbulbs dotted the roof of the vehicle. Outside, the landscape stretched dark and featureless, the moon yet to rise. She should not be this tired, she should—

The vehicle rolled to a smooth stop. Karys opened her eyes with a guilty start.

"Welcome to my humble abode," said Vuhas cheerfully.

The manor sat in the bowl of a small valley, surrounded by vineyards. Light shone behind the windows. The building seemed bewilderingly large and out of place; it stood two storeys high and sprawled decadently, lower-floor extensions locked like puzzle pieces to the main structure. The exterior was painted a rich orange brown, and glassy ceramic tiles decorated the window frames and ran in neat lines below the roof soffits.

A young woman waited outside the front door, her hands clasped at her waist. She offered a shallow bow as they got out of the awrig.

"We're staying here?" asked Haeki, looking up at the rows of long, shining windows.

"Correct." Vuhas straightened his coat, and then dismissed the awrig with a smooth gesture. The vehicle coasted down the road. "My home is yours. It's all been organised, don't worry. Now, Winola, was it? Yes, please come with me—we'll see to that scratch on your face. Yviline, will you show our other guests to their rooms for the night?"

The woman, unsmiling and silent, nodded.

Inside, the house was pristine. High-ceilinged passages dripped with glass chandeliers, and their footsteps echoed on the polished granite tiles. Paintings decorated the walls, mostly portraits of Vareslian Bhatuma in their common aspects; Karys recognised the great two-headed ape as Eliskus, the woman with metal scales over her eyes as Tirrio. It was extremely quiet. Yviline stopped outside a polished wooden door on the first floor. She pressed a fingertip to the lock to open it, and then bowed again, motioning for them to enter.

"Thank you," said Haeki.

Yviline nodded again, but her mouth remained severe. She kept her gaze lowered.

"What's her problem?" Ferain muttered.

Standard Vareslian hospitality toward Mercians. Karys gave the smallest of shrugs and walked through the door. Vuhas' servant obviously wasn't thrilled about their arrival. And yet, in some minor, obscure way, Ferain's obliviousness pleased her—although she did not have the energy to interrogate why.

The guest quarters comprised two adjoining bedrooms, a small washroom, and a parlour. Warm, quiet, clean, and well-lit as the rest of the manor. The dusty imprints of their shoes vanished as they walked across the cream-coloured carpets, absorbed by a subtle working. Four brown leather couches surrounded a teak coffee table beneath an ornate Toraigian tapestry, and a vase of fresh flowers sat on the mantel over the fireplace.

Behind them, the door closed with a click. The sound of Yviline's footsteps receded down the corridor, and a deep silence descended on the room. Haeki shivered and brushed her fingertips over the back of one of the couches, as if she was not quite convinced it was real. She glanced at Karys.

"Do you think Winola will be all right?" she asked. "On her own?"

"She can handle herself."

"I know, it's just . . ."

"Just?"

Haeki gestured to the luxuriously furnished room like that was an answer in itself.

"You're worried about her?"

A hard scoff. "I met her two days ago."

"So?"

"These people are strangers. I don't know." She sank down onto the couch. "I'll wait up for her here. Go to bed, Eska."

Through the windows of the first bedroom, the vineyards formed uniform lines to the edge of the estate. Beyond, only dusty scrubland. No movement, no sound. Karys drew the curtains. Her shadow lay long across the floor, stretched to the entrance of the room. She shrugged off her pack, struggled out of her soiled shirt, and fell onto the bed in her underclothes.

Not what I was expecting, she thought. Through the wall, she could hear the ticking of a clock, the muted rustle of Haeki shifting on the couch. *Why would Vuhas be involved with the likes of Rasko? It can't be about cret.* Her eyes closed. *Makes no sense. I should ask Ferain.* She dimly heard Haeki cough, and then sleep claimed her.

The morning brought strong winds gusting through the valley; Karys woke to the sound of the windowpanes rattling. She lay quiet a while, listening. There was no other movement, nothing she could hear from the rest of the house. On the other side of the bed, Haeki remained asleep, her breathing slow and even, her long red hair spilled over her pillow like a banner. When Karys slipped out of the bed, she did not stir.

The door to the second bedroom stood ajar; through the gap, Karys could see Winola curled up on a four-poster. She carefully leaned the door closed, then padded over to the bathroom. Painted in pale green and white, it was as immaculately clean as the rest of the guest quarters. Karys drank straight from the tap. Her haze of fatigue had lifted; she still felt tired, but no longer drained. Through the small window set at the top of the wall, the sky appeared cloudless, a blue like spilled ink.

"You feel better?" asked Ferain from the doorway.

"Mm-hm." She splashed water onto her face.

"You definitely look it."

"Thank you?"

"I wouldn't. Your condition seemed to be my fault." He paused. "Did it hurt? When I, you know . . ."

Karys dried her face on a towel. "Dropped a saint by punching him in the face?"

"That."

She shook her head, and replaced the towel on the rail. "Just made me feel tired. How did you do it?"

"I'm not sure. It was sort of instinctual. Like . . . like finding gravity? I anchored myself against you, and used that purchase to push outward. Does that make sense?"

"Not at all. Can you do it again?"

"What, now?"

Karys nodded. "I want to make sure it still works in case there's an emergency."

Her shadow hesitated, then flowed into the bathroom. "An 'emergency,' like you wanting me to punch someone else in the face?"

"Possibly. You might have other uses, but that's a start." She lifted her arm to watch the Split Lapse scar in the crook of her left elbow. "Don't do anything too drastic, I only want to see—"

Cool fingertips of shadow brushed the skin of her upturned wrist. Her stomach lurched, the scar rippled, and Karys jerked her arm backwards.

"What's wrong?" asked Ferain quickly. "Did that hurt?"

Her skin crawled. "No, no, it's fine. You just surprised—"

There was a curt knock on the parlour door. Karys fell silent instantly.

"Casin Gota requests the pleasure of your company for breakfast," came a muffled female voice.

Karys glanced up at the window again. It seemed that Vuhas was an early riser. From Winola's room, she heard a distinct thump. When she walked out of the bathroom, the scholar was blearily peering out into the parlour. The gash to her eyebrow had vanished, and she was wearing a new pair of glasses with delicate copper frames.

"Why is it so . . . morning?" she mumbled.

"Not much sleep?"

"It can't even be five o'clock yet."

Karys smiled. "I'll hold him off for you."

Yviline was still waiting outside when she opened the door. The servant's expression remained grim as Karys explained that the others would need a little longer to get ready for breakfast.

"Of course, cas," she said. "This way, please."

Now awake and alert, Karys studied the manor with interest. Yviline led her down a long passage gleaming in the early sunlight. There was no trace of dirt or disorder, and still no sign that anyone lived here apart from Vuhas and his solitary servant. And if that was the case, then the place must be absolutely crawling with workings—expensive, complicated ones. Karys had grown up on a far smaller farm, and even her father's wind-wracked fruit trees and hardy goats had demanded constant labour. Between Vuhas' immaculate house and his expanse of tidy vineyards, there was no way he could manage out here without significant worked assistance.

Part of her felt tempted to peel open the Veneer to determine just how many derivations surrounded her, but she held back. The fear that had overcome her in the canyon was much fainter now, more discomfort than dread—but even so, it lingered. She didn't want to touch the other side. Didn't want it to touch her. Absentminded, she rubbed the skin of her left wrist.

The dining room was as opulent as the rest of the property, all polished hardwood and cut crystal and brass. Vuhas was already eating when she entered. When he saw her, he pushed back his chair and stood up. "Good morning. Karys, wasn't it? You look well-rested."

The table was laden with food—cut fruits, pastries, steamed vegetables, and oil-soaked fritters. A small feast. "You didn't need to do so much for us."

"Nonsense." He pulled out the seat to his left, and motioned for her to join him. "I do hope you're hungry."

Gilded porcelain plates and silver cutlery set the table, flasks of ice water slowly beaded with condensation. Karys crossed the room and sat. Behind Vuhas, a massive painting of a Vareslian Bhatuma hung on the wall.

Out of the corner of her eye, she saw her shadow flinch. It was only a tiny movement, but something had startled Ferain. She looked around the room again, trying not to be too obvious. Vuhas offered her a sugared fruit pastry from one of the platters.

"You like art?" he asked.

"Excuse me?"

"You were admiring my painting." He gestured to the portrait genially. "It's an original Liresti. His depictions of Ambavar are amongst my favourites."

Ambavar. So that explained Ferain's reaction. The Lord of Night's aspect was mostly human in the painting; he appeared as a tall, austere man with deep brown skin. His eyes were transfixing; the artist had painted a golden crescent in each iris, as if the Bhatuma held twin waning moons within himself. His dreadlocks glittered with yellow stars; his cloak was black and edged with grey velvet. In his raised left hand, he held up an inverted chalice, smoke falling from the cup.

"Ambavar himself has always drawn me in," said Vuhas. "Amongst our greatest, and such a romantic figure too. There's something tragic about him—the broken-hearted herald presiding over the darkness. It's a mercy that he was gone long before the Slaughter arrived."

"It's a very impressive painting." Karys lowered her gaze to meet Vuhas'. *An unsettling coincidence. Of all the Bhatuma . . .* "You have a lot of artworks."

"I'm something of a collector." Vuhas seemed perfectly at ease. He picked up his cutlery again. "I worry about running out of walls for them all, but somehow there's always room for at least one more."

Karys had scarcely finished her pastry before Winola and Haeki entered the room, causing Vuhas to spring to his feet once again. Haeki frowned as he ushered her to a chair, uncomfortable and unsure of herself. Winola eyed the food with obvious interest.

"Sit, sit," Vuhas encouraged. "Please help yourselves. Yviline, could you bring the oatmeal?"

"It must get lonely out here," murmured Ferain. "He's very eager to please."

To please or to impress? The ostentatious chivalry still felt like a performance to Karys; something about it struck her as overly calculated. Of course, she was being unfairly judgemental—she had no real foundation for her dislike of the man. Vuhas had been nothing but generous, and Ferain was probably right: he was likely just happy to receive guests. Vareslians were known for being expressive; there was nothing *wrong* with that. Just a different set of cultural expectations. Karys poured herself a glass of water. Besides, what did it matter? They would be leaving soon enough anyway.

"How did you meet Rasko?" she asked.

Vuhas resumed his seat.

"Through the arts, funnily enough," he said. "A lot of valuable work was lost during the Slaughter's upheaval, and he's helped me to recover several paintings in Mercia. In exchange, I provide the occasional favour."

"Like helping us?"

"That's right. Speaking of which . . ." He spread his hands apologetically. "I'm afraid there's been a bit of a hitch. My long-distance awrig is an antique vehicle. I haven't used her in a while, and unfortunately the propulsion working has degraded. I'm so sorry to hold you up, but the issue should be resolved by tomorrow morning."

Karys' stomach sank. "That's—"

"May I take a look at it?" asked Winola, setting down her spoon. "It's not my speciality, but I know a reasonable amount about mechanical workings."

"Oh!" Vuhas laughed. "Oh no, please don't trouble yourself. She's a finicky old girl, but I've fixed her up in the past. It won't be a problem."

"You are a mechanical workings practitioner?"

"More a generalist—I dabble in a bit of everything. It keeps me busy, although I used to take the craft more seriously when I was younger. I take it you're a fellow hobbyist?"

"I'm a practitioner, yes." There was a definite primness to Winola's tone now. "I've noticed some interesting domestic workings around your house, not to mention your kind assistance with my injury last night. That all seems fairly accomplished for a hobbyist."

The world's most polite pissing contest. Karys tried to conceal her frustration. "I'm sorry that your awrig is broken, but we have urgent business—"

"Yes, of course. In Eludia," said Vuhas. "My dear, I understand your anxiety, but once I've repaired my vehicle, you'll be able to make up the lost time. Even at her advanced age, she's a quick one."

What could she say? It would take days to reach Tuschait without an awrig. Repressing her sense of foreboding, Karys nodded reluctantly. "Of course. I— of course. Thank you."

"My pleasure. The application of the working depends on the angle of the sun, so I'll only be able to attend to it this afternoon. In the meantime"—he removed the cloth napkin from his lap, dabbed the corner of his mouth, and set it down on the table—"could I interest you ladies in a tour of my home?"

"We could hardly refuse," said Winola, perhaps a shade too brightly.

Vuhas started on the second floor of the manor. He had inherited the property from his uncle twenty years ago, and spent much of the following two decades refitting and renovating. Where once the house could have comfortably slept thirty, he had since converted many of the bedrooms to working spaces for his "little projects." Putting aside his self-deprecation, Karys judged that their host was, if nothing else, absurdly well-resourced. He kept stores of workings materials that she had only read passing references to: ambergris from the river whales of Ruthaen, spiderspun platinum from the far north. As he rattled off the contents of his supply cabinets, Winola's expression grew increasingly strained—the scholar was clearly half-mutinous with envy.

"Maybe Rasko is supplying more than stolen art," suggested Ferain, as Vuhas showed them around his third workings studio.

That would make sense. Karys trailed her gaze over the wall-mounted shelves, the neatly labelled flasks and phials and jars. How much money in this room alone? It would be unconscionable to rob a man who had offered them his hospitality, but she could not say she wasn't tempted. A few cret might soften the blow if her gamble with Ferain didn't pay off. Then again, Vuhas doubtless had security workings throughout the house, which would probably be triggered if she tried to lift anything—but maybe she could unwork those defences. Pull them apart, like how she had unbound the Construct. There was sure to be a buyer for this stuff in Eludia, and Vuhas could not possibly *need* it all . . .

"Fingers itching?" inquired Ferain.

"Mind your own business," she muttered.

Vuhas turned to look at her. "Sorry, I didn't quite catch that."

"Oh." She stepped back from the shelves. "Nothing."

There was a strange keenness in Vuhas' eyes. He smiled at her, as if he could guess the trajectory of her thoughts. Karys' skin prickled.

"I might have gotten carried away," he said. "This sort of thing probably doesn't hold much interest for the layperson. Come, let me show you my gallery of curiosities."

The artefact repository stood adjacent the guest quarters: a large, windowless room filled with freestanding oak pedestals. There must have been over sixty; each bearing a single object. These ranged from the unremarkable—a tarnished amulet, a stained drawstring bag, an ordinary glass phial with a fluted stopper—to the disquieting—a headless rat's corpse with a twitching tail, a cracked stylus lying in a pool of strangely glistening ink—to the beautiful—a tiny tree blooming with metal fruits like apricots, a conch shell engraved with pulsing beads of ice-blue light.

"My Bhatuma collection," said Vuhas, spreading his arms in welcome. "Class A relics of the heralds of Mercia, Varesli, and the wider western Sunite region. The likes of which are only found in the best museums of the old capital."

Haeki regarded a broken spinning top with such blatant scepticism that Karys almost choked. Winola, in contrast, appeared entranced.

"They're genuine?" she said, then seemed to realise the question might be rude. "That is—how did you acquire so many?"

Vuhas gave an enigmatic shrug, and winked. "I can't go revealing my sources. But unless I have been terribly deceived, yes, they're genuine."

He went around the room, introducing each item with obvious pleasure. The stylus had been used by Iros to transcribe the names of his Favoured prior to their consumption; the tree had been a lover's gift from Babelire to her human mistress, each fruit delivering ecstasy when touched to the tongue. The rat was one of Tirrio's victims, worn by the herald as jewellery; the conch shell had briefly served as Kortisath's Sanctum. The amulet was Noaj's; it prevented the wearer from performing workings. The phial had imprisoned Dimisci for sixty years; she had irritated Yarinu by altering the weather at the border of the far more powerful herald's domain, a poor choice. The bag . . .

"My father would love this," muttered Ferain. "Although it's probably all fake anyway."

Karys leaned closer to Babelire's tree, examining the fruit. She spoke under her breath. "Why is it that all the nice things belonged to the Vareslian Bhatuma? Our heralds just ate us."

"I'm pretty sure Babelire was eating her Favoured too."

Karys parsed that, coughed, and hurriedly straightened. Ferain laughed. Although Vuhas was busy answering Winola's questions, Karys caught him watching her.

Don't worry, she thought. *I won't steal your toys.* She moved to the next pedestal, peering down at Dimisci's Prison—which was near indistinguishable from the empty phials in Vuhas' workings stores. *Although, if I did, they probably wouldn't fetch very much anyway.*

"Shall we carry on?" Vuhas suggested. "There are still the grounds to see. Perhaps there will be time for you to sample some of my wines, if we—"

"Excuse me."

Haeki spoke in a reserved undertone. Vuhas blinked, like he had forgotten she was even there.

"Uh, yes?" he said.

"Please could I have a bowl of sugar?"

The request seemed to temporarily confound him, but, to Vuhas' credit, he recovered quickly. "Of course! Would you like anything with that?"

Haeki shook her head. "Just the sugar. Thank you."

Winola tilted her head a little to one side, like she did whenever she saw something that interested her. Vuhas cleared his throat, then clapped his hands together.

"I'll let Yviline know, and she'll sort that out," he said. "Right. Let me show you the grounds."

Invisible from the front of the manor were two large greenhouses: one for tropical flowers, the other for uglier plants used in particularly obscure workings. The sun had reached its zenith, and the air outside was dry and parching. Nothing edible grew on the estate except for the grapes, which were currently out of season. The vineyards rustled in the hot wind; the sky was a cloudless empty blue.

Why do you live out here? As Vuhas explained his irrigation systems and weekly food deliveries, Karys studied the bare dusty landscape. It was beautiful, in its way, but even if Vuhas had inherited the estate, the way he lived seemed wildly impractical. And he didn't behave like any recluse she had ever met.

"You're frowning again," remarked Ferain.

She smoothed her face. None of her business anyway, the strange choices of reekers with more money than sense. Maybe he liked the solitude. And he had been a generous host. Gracious.

"Where do you keep your awrigs?" she asked.

Vuhas paused in the middle of an anecdote about orchid sellers in Cosaris.

"I have a small storehouse beyond the winery," he said, and pointed to a barn at the end of the gravel track between the vineyards. "Over there. Why do you ask?"

"I've always been interested in transport workings, that's all."

He smiled warmly. "Mercians tend to be a little more novel in that area, I'm afraid. No, I have two vehicles: one for short journeys, the other for serious travel. I'll be happy to show you both before you leave tomorrow, although they're nothing revolutionary."

"I'd like that."

"On the subject, however . . ." He consulted his pocket watch. "I should probably get to work on my old girl. If you're hungry, Yviline can arrange a late lunch? I hate to cut this short when there's still so much to show you."

"It's no trouble," said Winola. "Thank you for the tour."

Vuhas nodded. "My absolute pleasure. I won't be too long."

Karys followed Winola and Haeki back up the stony orange track to the house, dragging her heels and thinking. She glanced around. Vuhas, walking in the opposite direction, had nearly reached the barn. Silhouetted against the sun, his hair haloed his head in pale fire. There was a cheerful bounce in his step.

She shook her head, and hurried to catch up with Haeki.

"I want to check something," she said. "You two go ahead without me."

Haeki's brows drew together.

"Okay," she replied slowly.

"If you run into Yviline, just say I had a question for Vuhas."

"Are you going to tell me what stupid thing you've got planned?"

"It'll be fine."

Haeki rolled her eyes, not quite concealing her unease. "Sure. Whatever you want."

When Karys looked around again, Vuhas was gone. She broke into a quick jog, gravel crunching under her shoes. Haeki wasn't wrong, this was probably stupid, but she couldn't shake her sense that they were being lied to. The sun was painfully bright, and she felt exposed. She moved onto the grassy verge, well-watered by the vineyard's irrigation system, where her footfalls made less noise.

"Is this a good idea?" asked Ferain.

"Probably not."

"Well, if it's any consolation, I don't trust him either."

Karys slowed as she approached the barn, moving more quietly. Cicadas hissed from the shade, and the smell of sawdust and sour wine hung thick in the air. The main doors stood slightly ajar, but she could not hear anything from inside. The hair on the back of her neck stood on end.

"Can you try to see what he's doing?" she whispered.

Her shadow stretched over to the entrance, paused a moment, then returned to her.

"Reading a book," he said. "He could be consulting it for the working."

She pursed her lips. "And the awrigs?"

"Two of them, like he said. He's facing the other way; you can get closer."

She nodded, and padded over the long, yellowing grass. White paint had peeled off the barn wall in strips, and nails stuck out from the wood. The building did not look as well-maintained as the house. Karys took a steadying breath, then felt for the edges of the Veneer. It was thin here, light and unresisting in her senses. Unthreatening. She drew it aside.

Through the barn wall, she could detect the glow of workings, but not their precise shape. Ahead, an ephemeral mesh of elegantly constructed silver wire draped across the door, some kind of Bhatuma-derived security working. She was not sure what might happen if she touched it. She sidled closer. Didn't need to go inside, just needed to *see* inside.

"He's still reading," said Ferain softly. "Careful."

Karys peered through the narrow gap, holding her breath. A freestanding lamp shed a ring of orange over the workbench where Vuhas consulted his book. To his right, the two awrigs stood side by side. Their propulsion engines gleamed a misty green, humming gently in her senses. The vehicle they had travelled in yesterday was the smaller of the pair—the long-distance awrig was boxier and more rugged, with large, dark windows.

Karys squinted, studying the workings. From her distance, they looked almost identical. She could see nothing wrong with either, no sign of degradation at all. If anything, the larger awrig looked in better condition. She didn't know enough about mechanical workings to be certain, she could easily be wrong, but—

Vuhas sneezed. Karys flinched, taking a small step backwards. A stone rolled under her heel with an audible crunch. She froze, her heart leaping to her throat. *Not good, not good, not good . . .*

He kept reading.

Karys cautiously let out her breath. She took another step back. Her pulse thrummed, her blood beat loud in her ears, but he had not heard her. She took a few more steps, and the rush of adrenaline faded. *Lucky.* She let the Veneer fall closed once more.

"I could go inside alone," said Ferain.

She shook her head, continuing to back away from the barn. She spoke in an undertone. "I don't think there's anything else to see here. Did you notice the awrig's working?"

"While you had the Veneer open?" Her shadow made a noncommittal sound. "I saw a lot of lights, but they don't mean anything to me; I can't interpret workings like you do. Why, what was wrong with it?"

Karys reached the edge of the vineyard. "Nothing. As far as I could tell, there was nothing wrong with *either* awrig."

Her shadow sighed. "I had a feeling you were going to say that."

"I could be wrong, but I don't think I am." She wiped sweat off her forehead. "So he *is* lying to us, then."

"Could he be working with New Favour?"

Karys grimaced, then turned and hurried back up the track toward the manor. "No, then we'd be long dead—you heard the saint in the canyon. I don't know, Ferain. What is this all for? He didn't have to give us that tour; there was never any reason to impress us."

"That we know about."

"What?"

Her shadow gave a small shrug at her side. "Maybe he does want to impress you. It's not impossible."

"But *why?*"

"Maybe the man enjoys a challenge." Ferain blithely ignored her withering glare. "Or it's leverage, possibly. He might want something from you—a favour, future goodwill, a word in the right ear. It's soft diplomacy: creating the best conditions in which to befriend you."

"Sounds like Vareslian logic." A thought crossed her mind. "Is this what you did as a diplomat?"

"Are you asking if I was nice to other people?"

"No, I'm asking if you ever stranded anyone in the desert to bribe them more effectively."

"Never came up." He fell back into her silhouette as they approached the side entrance to the manor, mirroring her movements perfectly. "We don't know what Vuhas wants, but he's given no indication that he means to harm you. You need that awrig to reach Tuschait."

"I know." She glanced over her shoulder at the barn. "It's just . . . this doesn't feel right. It doesn't make sense."

"I don't like it either. But I'll watch him. And, you know, in an emergency, I *can* punch him for you."

She snorted and pushed open the door, walking into a wave of cool air and the silence of the house. The dust vanished from her shoes as she crossed the clean tiles of the antechamber. "As a last resort."

"That is how diplomacy goes, yes. First you offer them food, then—"

Karys came to a sharp stop. After the brightness outside, her eyes had been slow to adjust to the relative dimness of the interior, and she had failed to notice Yviline standing in the entrance of the first-floor corridor. The woman looked uncomfortable; her cheeks were pale and her shoulders stiff. She stared at Karys.

"I was just . . ." Karys' mouth had gone dry. "A question for Vuhas."

Yviline's expression was difficult to read. A muscle jumped in her jaw. "Yes, cas. Of course."

Did she hear me talking to Ferain? "Well, that's . . . thank you. And you can just call me by my name, there's no need—you've both been very gracious. We appreciate it."

Yviline shivered suddenly, as if touched by a cold wind.

"Leave," she said.

"What?"

The woman winced. She turned and quickly walked away; her footfalls ringing loud and swift over the tiles. The whole exchange had been so abrupt that Karys could do nothing but stare after her in confusion. The sound of her footsteps faded, swallowed by the walls.

"What was *that* about?" asked Ferain.

Karys shook her head. For a brief moment, there had been something in Yviline's eyes. Something like fear.

"I don't know," she said softly.

CHAPTER

28

"Have you considered that he might just be lonely?" asked Winola.

The guest parlour was pleasantly cool; the late afternoon sunlight filtered through the gauzy curtains and tinted the cream-coloured walls orange. New flowers filled the vase on the mantel, smelling sweet and faintly of citrus. The wind had abated; the afternoon had a glazed quality. Karys sat cross-legged on one of the leather chairs, watching Winola play a complicated-looking board game against herself.

"That's what Ferain said this morning," she admitted. "But if he's so miserable, why would he stay here? He clearly has the resources to leave."

"Oh, Karys."

"What?"

Winola shifted one of the game's tokens three places to the left and then rotated the board ninety degrees. "You're entirely too practical."

"Explain?"

The scholar studied the spread of the tokens. "Sometimes the places that you love grow teeth. Sometimes, home can swallow you. And even if that hurts, losing it still seems worse—because what if you let go and never find a better place? What if there's nothing else? Vuhas has built a life here; I don't think he would easily abandon it."

Karys snorted. "And that gives him the right to—what? Kidnap friends?"

"I never said that. He seems happy to have company, that's all."

"You feel sorry for him."

"Oh, I'm *far* too envious for that." Winola tapped one token against another of the opposing colour, then removed both from play. "I would kill for his workings materials alone, never mind the relics. It's hard to pity a man who uses spiderspun platinum in pursuit of his *hobby*."

She pronounced the word with such venom that Karys had to smile. Outside the window, the sun had descended over the veldt and soaked the hills in amber. A solitary crow was sitting on one of the vineyard stakes, cawing intermittently. Ferain rolled over the floor and up onto the coffee table to study the game.

"What's the saying?" he said. "'An artist is not their tools?'"

"They certainly help." Winola rubbed her temples. "I'm just being bitter—he is clearly an accomplished practitioner. Which would be fine, if he wasn't so damn nonchalant about it. 'Little projects,' *hah*. Yesterday, he bound closed my injury immaculately and worked a new pair of glasses in under an hour. And whatever derivations he has around this house, they're potent."

"But could he have produced a furrow print out of a handful of sticks and some paste?" Ferain pointed a shadowy finger to three blue tokens at the corner of the board. "You've lost this game already, by the way. Or won it, depending on your perspective."

Winola pushed her glasses up the bridge of her nose and leaned closer. "Have I?"

"I'm afraid so." He slid one of the tokens over the board in an L-shaped pattern, then moved another to the right two places. Karys felt a sharp tug in her chest. "Or congratulations."

Winola whipped her hand back from the table. "How did you do that?"

"Surprise," said Karys, and Ferain laughed.

It took a little while to explain. Winola listened, unspeaking but intently focussed, as Ferain tried to find an accurate way of describing how he could touch the world—*like gravity? it's pushing and pulling at the same time, but outward*. Karys showed the scholar her scar, tucked into the crease of her elbow.

"It doesn't hurt you?" asked Winola. "When he draws on you?"

"Drawing" seemed like a surprisingly good way of describing the sensation. "No, it's just tiring—if he does something forceful, it's worse. But it doesn't feel bad, only . . . strenuous, I suppose. Do you have any idea why it would cause the scar to move?"

The scholar shook her head. "Not a clue."

"But you don't think I'm harming her?" Karys' shadow wavered on the table. "Even if she can't feel any pain?"

"Honestly, it doesn't sound like it." Winola picked up one of the discarded tokens from the game, and mindlessly turned it between her fingers. Her forehead creased. "I'm making an educated guess here, but I suspect you're leeching your power off her normal metabolic reactions. I've seen that in other contexts, generally in experimental animal modification. Provided you don't overtax her, she should be able to sustain your new physicality without suffering any permanent harm. Have you been feeling hungrier than usual, Karys?"

"Not that I noticed."

"Hm. Well, still make sure you eat and sleep enough. Oh, and if Ferain *does* draw too much of your energy all at once, your body will probably shut down and die."

"Fantastic."

"It's very interesting, though." Winola stopped flipping the token, and dropped it back on the table. "Look, I could be wrong about how this works, and there might be hidden side effects. But the two of you have survived this long together, and that wouldn't have been possible if the nature of your relationship wasn't largely symbiotic. This could be a good thing. I mean, it's already proven useful, hasn't it?"

Karys shivered. "Yeah. Useful. Thanks, Winola."

"Anytime." The scholar looked down at the game board and sighed. "Although I wish I knew more. You should ask our host; he probably has all the answers."

"Absolutely not."

"Hah. I wonder when he will be done pretending to repair his awrig."

"Whenever it suits him, I guess."

Winola's eyes flicked to the closed parlour door. Her lips thinned. "Yes, well . . . I do understand your reservations about him. The awrig is . . ." She made a face. "It doesn't look good, but maybe it's not as bad as it seems. I hope he's harmless."

"Me too."

"We know to be more cautious, if nothing else." She reset the game board, neatly lining up the tokens for another round. "If he tries to delay us again tomorrow, we'll need to press the issue. Or walk; we might be able to hitch a ride with other travellers once we're nearer civilisation. But I don't think it will come to that. We aren't entirely without options, or, frankly, protection. I don't suppose you know why Haeki wanted sugar from Vuhas?"

Karys uncrossed her legs and stretched. "I do."

"But you aren't going to tell me."

"It's a personal matter. Nothing important, but—"

Winola waved a hand. "I don't want to intrude on her privacy. She has been in that bedroom a long time, that's all. I was concerned."

Karys imagined Haeki's reaction to discovering herself the object of Winola's concern, and found the idea faintly amusing. "You don't need to worry. I'll check on her."

The bedroom was half-lit; the curtains drawn so that only a slender bar of light fell across the floor. Haeki, kneeling on the carpet below the window, did not move when Karys walked in. Her neck was bent; she gazed down at a shallow dish of water held between her hands. In the soft gloom, her parted lips glittered with a crust of fine sugar. Karys closed the door behind her.

"For Pavian?" she asked quietly.

Haeki's voice was scarcely audible.

"For all of them." Then, after a pause: "I don't care what you think."

Funeral rites for strangers. Delivering heretics to Nuliere's care. Karys sat down on the edge of the bed.

"Haeki, she killed them," she said.

"She did what she needed to." Tiny white crystals flaked from Haeki's mouth. "It's not our place to question her. Especially not yours."

"Is she here?"

A single shake of Haeki's head, a marginal movement. "She exhausted herself in the canyon. I don't know how long it will take her to recover."

"I see."

"I don't think you do."

"All right."

Another pause. Haeki lowered the dish. Her eyes sheened with the faintest hint of blue.

"You know, she'd forgive you," she said. "If you showed her respect, she would be your herald again."

It was a lie, and Karys suspected they both knew it. For whose benefit, she was less sure. She nodded toward the dish. "Salt in the water, same as you threw in the river? A clever trick. What else do you have up your sleeve?"

Haeki shrugged, and looked down again. "Nothing much."

"Looked like something yesterday. So, do you think the Embrace will accept deathspeakers?"

"Karys," murmured Ferain.

Haeki's fingers tightened around the dish, ridged knuckles pressing up against her skin. Her voice, however, remained even.

"I do," she said. "Whatever heretical pact those men made, they died human. If it falls to me to lay coins on their eyes and wear sweetness on my mouth for them, I will. Even if they don't deserve mercy, I'll ask for it. Don't you dare tell me I shouldn't."

"I'm not telling you anything. You wouldn't listen even if I did."

Haeki wiped the sugar from her lips with the back of her hand, and set down the dish. "Well, what about your false heralds? Do you think *they'll* shepherd you to the Embrace?"

"No. I don't think that holds any interest for them."

"They probably couldn't either."

"Probably."

"And that's not worrying you? Not at all?"

"Not right at this moment."

"Because you think Nuliere will take pity on you in the end? When you die, and your usurper master leaves your soul to rot, you'll wait for her to guide you home."

From the parlour, Karys heard voices: Vuhas and Winola's. She spoke carefully. "I would trust the Ephirite's mercy before ever placing my faith in Nuliere again."

A shadow crossed Haeki's face. "You're that proud?"

Karys smiled slightly, and got up.

"Come," she said. "I'm sure our host is expecting us."

Winola was discussing the awrig's working when Karys re-entered the room. Vuhas stood beside the mantel, unflustered and cheerful, his white hair combed back and his clothing pristine.

"The old girl is as good as new. You'll be on your way by nine o'clock tomorrow morning," he said. "Ah, Karys, Haeki, there you are. I was just telling Winola that the issue with the awrig has been resolved. Everything is in order."

He seemed as sunny as ever, no sign that he might harbour a guilty conscience. Karys felt no less wary. Vuhas did not intimidate her, exactly, even with all his casual displays of wealth and power, but something about him still set her teeth on edge. Here he stood, so earnest, so eager to please, and yet . . . what was it about him? At odd moments, she thought she had caught glimpses of a hungry light behind his eyes—but standing there now: nothing. Beneath the skin of his bubbly, bumbling geniality, he remained a complete enigma to her.

Leave, whispered Yviline.

She tamped down her paranoia. "We're in your debt."

"Oh, it's no trouble." He laughed, warm and paternal. "You've been very generous, letting me ramble on about my little projects. It's only too easy for me to get carried away, I'm afraid."

"You don't say," muttered Ferain.

"Anyway, you're probably all hungry by now, yes?" Vuhas continued without waiting for an answer. "I was rather hoping you would join me for dinner. It's nothing too ostentatious, but I would love your company. And it won't take long to get there, I promise."

Karys frowned. She glanced at Winola, but the scholar appeared no less confused. "Get to where, exactly?"

"Oh!" Vuhas' face brightened. "Of course, yes, I haven't explained; forgive me. To the clubhouse of the Grateful Society."

CHAPTER
29

The sun had set; the evening was warm and dry, the air clear, the sky a bruised shade of lilac pricked with stars. The awrig coasted along smoothly. It was the same vehicle they had travelled in previously; Vuhas had assured them that reaching the club would take less than thirty minutes. He sat opposite Karys now, dressed in a tailored blue coat despite the heat, his smart black shoes polished to shining.

The Grateful Society, he had explained, was a collective of local property owners who worked together on various philanthropic projects—supplying water and other resources to struggling communities in the region, performing surveys of rare fauna and flora, fundraising research into life-sustaining workings further afield. Membership totalled near a hundred individuals, and a contingent of them met regularly at the society's official premises.

"I wasn't aware that so many people lived in the area," Winola had remarked.

There were farms and estates all along the Vareslian length of the border, home to families that went back generations. The properties were merely spread out in such a way that the land appeared deserted. Despite the distances, they were a very close-knit group—while members enjoyed their space, from time to time everyone needed a little conversation. It got too quiet otherwise.

"Why 'grateful'?" Haeki had asked, which caused Vuhas to blink as if he was surprised, once again, to find her both present and capable of speech.

"I beg your pardon?"

"If you're the ones helping people, why are you 'grateful'? Shouldn't it be the other way around?"

He had laughed at that. "Grateful for our advantages, I suppose. For our kinship and good fortune. I'm not certain of the precise origin of the name, but gratitude seems like a good foundational principle, don't you think?"

Surrounded by the awrig's plush kid-leather seats and gilded window frames, Karys reflected that Vuhas certainly didn't lack advantages. If he had access to this society, perhaps he wasn't a lonely recluse either. None of this made her feel especially comfortable. She had the sense that control of the situation was sliding further and further out of reach—but she did not want to risk doing anything to offend him either. Keep Vuhas amiable, keep him happy, and they could leave for Tuschait in the morning. If they didn't have an awrig, it would take days to reach the town. More time than she could afford.

Don't think about Sabaster. She looked out the window at the rolling dark. *Just get through this.*

The clubhouse's lights burned like beacons in the flatlands. As they approached, the shadowy mass of the building resolved into an elegant double-storey complex, ringed by tall, incongruous date palms and blooming frangipani. The walls, like those of Vuhas' home, were a rich ochre colour. Balconies ringed the upper floor, draped with hanging creepers and baskets of lush ferns. Twin rows of awrigs lined the road leading up to the building.

"Here we are," said Vuhas, as his vehicle slowed to a whisper-smooth stop before the entrance. The tall double doors stood wide open, and a few people milled around the steps and foyer. "It looks like a busy night."

"He's nervous," muttered Ferain.

Karys couldn't see it; Vuhas appeared as relaxed as ever to her. She followed him out of the awrig. The smell of the flowers perfumed the evening, and it was curiously humid close to the building, likely due to an atmospheric working intended to sustain the tropical plants. The people outside were less formally dressed than Vuhas. A few waved to him, but none approached.

"We seldom have any new faces at the club," said Vuhas breezily. "Let me show you around."

The décor inside was baroque and shining, casually lavish. People lounged in sumptuous sitting rooms, draped themselves over oiled leather armchairs and claw-footed divans. From what Karys could tell, most of the patrons were men between the ages of thirty and fifty. They glowed with the robust health of the well-moneyed, and their dress varied widely: some styled in the opaque robes of the hedonistic priests of far-off Emiea, others in lynx furs and knee-high riding boots. While the majority dressed more plainly, adopting fine linens and supple weaves, none of them, on first inspection, looked anything like farmers. Vuhas strolled from room to room, pointing out artworks and amenities, and Karys felt the club's eyes upon them. The attention struck her as unfriendly.

As they entered the bar on the upper floor—quieter, intimate, the walls hung with blue satin, low tables and cushioned mats arrayed across the floor, white roses set in slender vases—a woman on the adjoining balcony called out to Vuhas. The stranger was short and rake thin, perhaps in her early forties, wearing half-moon spectacles set with amber studs. Her expression acidic, she cut across the room to meet him.

"What is the meaning of this?" she demanded.

If Vuhas was surprised by her aggression, he did not show it.

"Ah, Ciene," he said. "You're looking lovely as usual."

She thrust a finger toward him, coming just short of poking him in the chest. "You'd better have a very good explanation, Vuhas. If this is another of your—"

"May I have a private word?" he asked.

Ciene scowled. Her eyes skipped across Karys, and she nodded once toward the corner of the room, where the tables were unoccupied. "Fine. Make it quick."

Vuhas smiled. "The very soul of brevity. Ladies, please excuse me for just one moment. Why don't you get yourselves a drink?"

Karys exchanged a look with Winola, and the scholar gave her a tiny shrug. Haeki was already walking, eager to get away from their host. The bar on the far side of the room was recessed into the wall, discrete and elegant and out of the way, lined with unlabelled bottles of dark liquor. Karys reluctantly moved toward it. She wanted to eavesdrop on Vuhas' conversation, but the room was too well-lit for Ferain to stretch over and listen. The blandly attractive man behind the counter sighed as they approached.

"Seems that Vuhas isn't too popular here," said Ferain. "Interesting."

"Can't imagine why," murmured Karys.

"Our presence definitely isn't helping. I get the impression strangers aren't meant to see this place. I'll bet that whatever is going on at this club is both illegal *and* exclusive." Her shadow snorted. "Maybe Vuhas thought he had the authority to bend the rules a little. A miscalculation, judging by that woman's face."

Karys glanced over her shoulder. Vuhas had his back to her, but Ferain was right: Ciene looked livid. Splotches of dark pink coloured her pale cheekbones, her lip was curled. Karys turned around again. Illegal and exclusive seemed about right too.

"I'm trying to read her lips. I think she said: 'your responsibility,'" said Ferain. "She seems pissed. Oh, she's storming off now. No, don't look; Vuhas is coming."

Karys heard brisk footfalls behind her, signalling the man's return.

"Sorry about that, friends—just a small misunderstanding," said Vuhas. "Where were we? No drinks yet?"

He clapped Karys on the shoulder as she was turning to reply. It was a completely harmless, friendly gesture: over-familiar and thoughtless, but unremarkable. In response, her shadow rippled, slipping out of her silhouette for a fraction of a second.

Haeki's eyes widened, and Karys' throat went tight. In the brightly lit room, the distortion had been far too obvious. Karys forced a laugh, and slid her shoulder out from under Vuhas' hand.

"A little overwhelmed by choice," she said. "Your friend seemed upset. I hope there isn't a problem."

Vuhas smiled in a way that Karys did not like. Sharp, satisfied. "All resolved. We'll be sharing a private room with her for dinner, actually. May I recommend the house wine? It happens to be one of mine." He gestured to the barman for four glasses.

"Sorry," whispered Ferain. "I—he surprised me."

How? You saw him coming! Karys swallowed her irritation. Well, even if Vuhas *had* seen the movement, he wouldn't know what it meant. Just a trick of the light. She accepted a blush-pink wine in a glass veined with swirls of soft copper. It was unusual for Ferain to slip like that in public. He was always so careful, so meticulous. She took it for granted by now. Even in Sabaster's domain, he had matched her perfectly, even when . . .

"Something the matter?" enquired Vuhas.

Karys looked up from her glass.

"Just admiring your wine," she said. "It's such a pretty colour."

Vuhas took this as an invitation to talk about viticulture yet again. The club was only growing busier as the evening progressed, patrons circling through the rooms, greeting each other with the ease of long familiarity. There was a prickling itch under Karys' skin; she felt increasingly frayed and paranoid: mired in the oozing wealth of this place and the constant surveillance of strangers—and overcome with a sudden, renewed, and acute awareness of time passing. Wasted time, so much wasted time; the hours of her life ticking down while Vuhas gushed and blustered about nothing at all.

Although she tried to block it out, her thoughts kept straying to Sabaster. The Ephirit had said he planned to summon her when the receptacle bloomed—how long would that take? As Vuhas paused to describe the famed origins of yet another priceless painting, Karys felt the walls pressing tighter around her. *Don't think about this, not now.* Dwelling on the situation didn't help, was worse than useless; it was all outside of her control. *Stop. Let it go.* Her breathing had quickened. She could almost hear them, those inhuman voices chanting within the shifting red corridors of the palace; could feel the tiled floor growing soft and fibrous with cilia beneath her feet. Could smell *him,* sweet and rank. How long? Why was she still snared here? It was obscene; she didn't have time for this. She wanted, irrationally, to scream, smash something, hurt someone; anything but to continue standing there listening to Vuhas speak.

"I need some air," she said, cutting him off mid-anecdote.

Vuhas frowned. "My dear?"

Don't call me that. "It's too hot in here."

"If you aren't feeling well—"

"Five minutes." She was being too short; she knew it, but she could barely contain her frustration. "I'm a little lightheaded. I'll be back in five minutes."

Maybe it was her expression, but Vuhas did not argue. Winola looked concerned, and Haeki . . . Haeki recognised something in her face, saw what was written there all too clearly. Karys turned away from the scrutiny. The door to the balcony stood ajar. She walked toward it stiffly, pushed it open, and stepped through.

There was no one else outside. A cool breeze lifted her hair, and she breathed in unsteadily. A small mercy, to be alone. It was quieter here. The silent rows of awrigs framed the road, snaking away in the thin moonlight. She moved over to the railing and leaned against it, wrapping her fingers around the smooth metal bar one by one.

"Do you want to talk?" asked Ferain.

Did she? Not as much as she wanted to scream, or to pitch forward over the edge, let her body drop, let—Karys breathed in again. No. The flatlands were dark and grey beyond the ring of the club's lights.

"It's nothing," she muttered. "Just time. It feels like so much time, wasted."

"Yeah. I know."

Inside the club, a man laughed uproariously. Karys flinched at the sound. She tightened her grip on the railing. "I wish I knew how long I had. It's the not knowing that—I can't prepare. I can't guess when he's going to summon me. We might not even reach Eludia."

"Don't worry about Eludia. We'll make up the time."

Have to believe that. Somehow. She forced herself to loosen her hold on the bar, then scrubbed a hand over her face. "Just being stupid."

Ferain made a low sound of disagreement. "I don't think so."

"No, I am. I don't know why it came over me so suddenly." She exhaled, slow and heavy. "What I said to you in the canyon? About it not making a difference if you were with me when Sabaster calls my compact?"

"You don't have to—"

"It would," she said. "Make a difference. I was—I'm not handling any of this well. I don't want you to be dragged down with me, that's all. For it to be my fault."

Ferain was quiet a moment. Karys' shadow spilled over the balcony and onto the terrace below, falling amongst the palms and the flowers. However, when he spoke, it sounded like he was standing right in front of her.

"Don't sell yourself short, Karys," he said. "You're handling this better than I could ever hope to."

His tone pulled at something inside her chest. Too serious, it didn't suit him. Still, she had wanted him to know . . . Karys shook her head, and produced a weak smile. "I was trying to apologise, actually."

"That's new. I don't think you've quite mastered the technique."

She made a small, rude gesture with one hand.

"That's not it either."

"It's all you're getting now."

"You know, contrition doesn't really suit you." His lightness faded, replaced once more by the same gentle sincerity. "Besides, there was never anything to apologise for."

Behind Karys, the door creaked. She glanced back, and found Haeki standing in the entrance, expression wary.

"Are you ready to come back, or should I make an excuse?" she asked. "The reeker says it's time for dinner."

Karys tucked her hair behind her ears, and straightened.

"No, I'm fine now," she said. "I'm coming."

The private dining room was small, host to a single rectangular table set for five. White pebbles covered the rear wall; water trickled gently over them and into a recessed tank in the floor. Lethargic orange jellyfish ballooned through the water, frills trailing behind them like lace. When Karys and Haeki entered the room, Vuhas, Winola, and Ciene were already seated. Ciene looked calmer, although far from happy.

"Ah, you're back," said Vuhas, pleased. "Feeling better?"

Karys sat down beside Haeki. "Much."

A silent attendant glided into the room with a new bottle of wine, followed by trays of tiny, artfully prepared delicacies. He set each down without saying a word or making any eye contact, and withdrew through the door, bowing.

Karys could not immediately identify most of the food: it was prettily arranged and colourful, but not wildly appetising in appearance. Much of it comprised crisped vegetables flecked with bright sauces; slivers of charred leaves and unidentifiable cuts of meat arranged to resemble flowers. She speared a mysterious gelatinous ball wrapped in a miniature cabbage leaf with her fork. Vuhas was making introductions, gregarious as ever. He and Ciene had been friends for decades; she was a great historian and fellow workings practitioner, one of the Grateful Society's shining lights, a pioneer of Bhatuma-derived innovations, and the author of multiple seminal papers. Ciene accepted the flattery with tight-lipped forbearance, and sipped her wine.

"Are you affiliated with a particular university?" Winola asked politely, as Vuhas' ramblings dried up. She was seated next to Ciene, and Karys couldn't help but notice the similarities between the two women. Winola was paler and not as thin, but they both wore glasses and had a certain ascetic, scholarly look. It suited Winola better, Karys thought. Seemed more natural on her.

"I've been independent for the last few years," said Ciene. "Formerly, I studied at Basamat University of the Arts, and most recently at Joisen College."

"Oh, Basamat. I've heard their History Department is excellent."

Ciene shrugged once, and returned to her wine. Winola looked somewhat daunted, but persisted.

"Who did you study under?" she asked. "Psikamit College recently hosted a colloquium, and there were several—"

"No one you will have heard of."

"And your specialisation?"

"Ciene contributed to the identification of physical isolation and extraction workings, drawing on Jervadi's miracles," Vuhas jumped in. "Enormously useful stuff for mining, animal mending and modification, even the culinary arts. She explicated the Bhatuma's working to draw out a specified element from a body without materially damaging it."

Winola nodded in appreciation, although she looked a little uncertain. "I thought that Jervadi's miracles had all been extrapolated two centuries ago. I suppose it goes to show that there will always be further applications for Bhatuma workings."

Ciene swirled her wine within the glass. "Nuances, mostly. After all, there won't be any *new* Bhatuma miracles to emulate. I must say, it's strange for a Toraigian to profess an interest in workings. Seems sacrilegious."

Winola's smile tightened. "Yes, well, I left home when I was twenty-two. Ten years ago. And I wouldn't say it's a religious consideration especially—my nation's antipathy for workings, that is."

"What sort of consideration is it, then?"

"A practical one."

"Oh?" Ciene raised an eyebrow. "You know, it strikes me as rather *impractical* to shun all the world's advancements in favour of tradition. 'No workings shall trespass the Wall, no herald born, naught built but by the hands of men.' Do I have that right?"

Winola was briefly silent. She studied the vase of silver-stem orchids and violets in the middle of the table, seeming to give her response careful consideration. When she spoke, it was without inflection.

"The price of those advancements—workings—would be independence," she said. "The Unbroken Wall, for better or worse, kept Toraigus sovereign."

"That's a rather cynical outlook. Care to expand on it?"

Winola shrugged. "Every other country in the region had heralds. None of them escaped occupation and war; not Mercia, not Varesli. Once you start peeling off the paintwork, no state on the continent has more than four hundred years of history. Except for Toraigus. Our size should have made us an easy target, and yet we've never been conquered. I don't think I'm a cynic, but you're the historian, so you tell me—was Varesli never tempted by the strategic value of our ports?"

"This is certainly a lot of politics before the main course," said Vuhas, and laughed. "Perhaps, a lighter topic might—"

"Oh, come now. Varesli could have taken Toraigus at any time," said Ciene. "I imagine, even now, we possess the resources for it. We simply chose not to."

"How comforting. Strange that my country didn't found its security on the presumption of an empire's goodwill." Winola picked up her cutlery and sliced a small pastry neatly in two. She seemed to be warming to the topic. "But no, it would not have been easy to invade Toraigus. The thing about workings is that you grow to rely on their power. Strip away your weapons, your disguises, your means of navigation, your intelligence gathering capabilities—ship only ordinary soldiers out to sea, and let them throw rocks at us. All the world's *advancements* mean nothing where the Wall is concerned. Toraigians know exactly how to live, fight, and survive without workings, and an invading force does not."

"It seems simple enough to learn."

"One would think. And yet, no one has breached our defences thus far. What the heralds' power cannot touch, they cannot claim."

Ciene smiled for the first time. "Or perhaps seizing a thorny little convent in the middle of the ocean wasn't considered worth the trouble."

"Doesn't it amount to the same? If Toraigus endures by virtue of being too inconvenient to destroy or too small to matter, so be it. Whatever keeps the wolves at bay."

"Do you regard Varesli as a wolf?"

"Half a century ago? Yes. But now?" Winola gestured vaguely. "Maybe an old dog. Hungry but impotent."

Ciene barked a laugh. She seemed, increasingly, to be enjoying herself. "Is that so? Perhaps we should bare our teeth more often. I'll note that, for all its history and sufficiency, *you* did not stay in Toraigus. Why forsake such a paradise?"

"Come, Ciene, you're being belligerent," said Vuhas.

Winola appeared unperturbed. "I wanted to learn how to perform workings."

"And how have you fared?"

"Well enough, I suppose."

"That would be 'well enough in Mercia,' no?"

"Your point?"

Ciene's eyes glinted. "Oh, simply that excellence is graded on a curve. You would only have to exceed the intellect of your immediate contemporaries."

"Ciene!" snapped Vuhas. For a moment, his affectedness fell away, and beneath the mask was the hint of something else entirely; the undercurrent of a sharp, brutal force of will. Karys was not sure anyone else saw it—Winola and Ciene were focussed on each other, and Haeki was glaring daggers at the latter. The tension ran thick. Water dripped down the rear wall, and the sounds from the rest of the club formed a low, wavering hum. Winola set down her cutlery.

"You clearly haven't met many Mercians," she said.

Ciene made a wry, pitying sound. She reached across the table and refilled her wine glass from the bottle. "Enough, I think."

She was looking for a rise, apparently for personal amusement—or perhaps to spite Vuhas for bringing outsiders to the club in the first place. *A petty little vengeance.* Unfortunate, that Winola had taken the bait; the scholar was visibly upset. Too sensitive, too sincere, too protective; she was outmatched by Ciene. That was the problem with caring about other people. It meant getting hurt.

Karys pushed a strip of dense red meat onto her fork, and resumed eating. No one else touched their food. The meat was covered in some kind of syrup, tasting both oily and sweet and raw. She swallowed it without grimacing. Ciene's gaze settled on her.

"Hungry?" she asked.

Karys used an artfully burned vegetable to soak up the sauce on her plate. "I never reject free food."

"You've been very quiet this evening."

"I was surrounded by towering intellects. Maybe I didn't have much to say."

Ciene tapped her forefinger to her lips. "No, don't deprive us. Surely you have opinions? There's no need to be shy; share the Mercian perspective that your friend finds so valuable. What do you think: is Varesli still a wolf?"

The vegetable tasted of charcoal and cumin. Karys chewed mechanically, and forced it down.

"I don't care," she said.

"Excuse me?"

"I don't care." She made a crude, dismissive motion with her fork. "Mercia, Varesli, the sea could swallow them both. It's nothing to me."

A flash of irritation crossed Ciene's face. "Really, no national pride? I hardly think—"

"National pride? What, banners and flags?" Karys laughed loudly. "National pride, is that it? Listen, you're more than welcome to believe I'm stupid because I was born in Mercia. How you maintain your daydreams is none of my concern; if that's what helps you sleep at night, go ahead. I have no pride—I'll pledge allegiance to whoever pays me. I'm as faithless as they come."

Ciene's lips curved, although her eyes were stone cold.

"So you can speak, after all," she said.

"Ciene, a word outside?" Vuhas stood up. "*Now?*"

Expression unchanging, Ciene rose. She was unhurried; she set her chair back in place and dropped her napkin on the table.

"Illuminating. I'm unconvinced, Vuhas, but willing to be proven wrong. At least you were correct in judging my tastes." Passing the back of Winola's chair, she reached out and caressed the loose hair at the nape of the scholar's neck, curling it through her fingers. She leaned in to speak. "I'd like to have you."

Haeki's chair scraped; she was on her feet in an instant. Winola's eyes widened. She tried to push away Ciene's hand.

"No," she said. "No, Haeki, just—"

"Get your hands off her." Haeki's voice emerged in a rasp. "You fucking reeker creep."

It was like a switch had been thrown. The hairs on the back of Karys' arms stood on end; the air rippled with unnatural electricity. Nuliere might be absent, but the Bhatuma's Favour remained—Haeki was still sea-blessed. More than human. She seemed to stand on the precipice of violence, her body taut with anger.

"Well." Ciene withdrew her fingers from Winola's hair. She showed no sign of discomfort or unease; her low voice was an edge smothered in velvet.

"Those are strong words. Mercian poetry, almost. Forgive me, I'd taken you for an illiterate mute."

Haeki drew breath like she had been slapped. Karys found herself standing. She did not know whether she meant to attack Ciene or hold Haeki back, but the small gasp cut her like broken glass.

"All of you, stop," said Winola.

Haeki had paled. Ciene looked smug, like she knew that she had scored a point. In that moment, Karys had never wanted to hurt anyone more. She needed to wipe the smirk off that thin, haughty face. Make her sorry, make her hurt, make her—

"Easy, Karys," muttered Ferain. "Don't give her the satisfaction. We're out-numbered."

His voice jolted her. He had been quiet since the balcony, and her shadow lay flat and formless at her feet.

Karys realised her fists were clenched. She uncurled her fingers. She had been so ready, so eager to attack. Hungry for it. *My father's child, after all.* She swallowed the bitter taste in the back of her throat.

With a contemptuous snort, Ciene turned and crossed the room to the door. Vuhas followed her, his shoulders tense. At the entrance, he paused.

"Please forgive me," he said. "I will be back in just a moment."

Then he was gone, and it was quiet but for the trickling of water.

CHAPTER

30

They left the club soon after, returning to Vuhas' house. The ride home was uncomfortable.

"I should have warned you that Ciene can be contrarian," said Vuhas. "She likes to provoke, but doesn't mean anything by it. I really do apologise. This is very embarrassing."

Crickets chirped from the low grey shrubs of the wilderness. Haeki stared out the window of the awrig, her face drawn.

"No need to apologise." Winola sounded tired. She sat with her hands folded in her lap and her legs crossed. "It was an interesting evening. You've been extremely courteous."

Karys gazed down at her own hands, resting slack upon her knees, palms turned upwards. The memory of her father's face hovered before her eyes. She pressed her lips together. The awrig felt crowded; too warm and airless.

Yviline was not present to greet them when they reached the house, although all the lights remained on, orange and gleaming in the dark. They disembarked, and the awrig slid off in the direction of the barn. The vineyards rustled in the breeze. It was a little before midnight, and the moon shone directly overhead, dimming the stars. As they climbed the stairs to the front door, Vuhas touched Karys' shoulder.

"May I have a quick word?" he asked quietly.

She nodded, and slowed to let Winola and Haeki draw ahead. Winola noticed, and gave her a questioning look, but Karys motioned for her to keep walking. Haeki stalked down the passage toward the guest quarters.

"What is it?" asked Karys as she turned to Vuhas.

He ushered her through the door, then closed it behind him, murmuring a word to lock it. When he faced her, his expression was grave.

"There's a private matter I'd like to discuss with you," he said. "I know it's late, but would you be willing to come up to my study to talk?"

What is this about? "Maybe in the morning? I don't think—"

"It's important. I promise the conversation won't take long, but there's something you need to know."

The last thing Karys wanted to do was spend any more time in Vuhas' company. She swallowed her annoyance. "Fine."

"Meet me there in fifteen minutes? Second floor, last door on the right."

She assented. Vuhas smiled reassuringly, and patted her shoulder for the third time that night. Ferain did not react.

Part of her *was* curious. Karys followed the corridor to the guest quarters. Mostly vexed, but she couldn't help wondering what could be so urgent that Vuhas refused to wait until morning. Strange. Something to do with Rasko, presumably, given that he wanted the conversation private. The Bhatuma portraits loomed from the walls, and the house remained eerily silent. Alone in the pristine, shining hallways, she felt oppressed and unnerved. *This place is like a mausoleum.*

"I'm not sure about this," said Ferain.

"Didn't want to seem rude," she replied under her breath.

"After what happened at his precious club, you're entitled to be. Embrace, I wish he would stop touching you. There is something . . . off about him. About all those people."

"Not your crowd, then?"

He made an indignant noise. "Why would you ask that?"

"You're rich, they're rich. You're Vareslian, they're Vareslian."

"Please don't tell me you think I'm anything like *Vuhas*."

She refused to smile. "I don't know. Are you?"

"Why not stab me in the heart? No. No, they are not 'my crowd.'"

I know. Her impression of Ferain's life might be limited, but Karys found it impossible to imagine him fitting in with the likes of Ciene. She remembered the way he had once spoken about his father wanting to get closer to history— the scathing contempt in his voice. *Nothing like Vuhas, with all his relics and his artworks.* She kept the thought to herself. Reaching the door to the guest quarters, she stepped inside.

"—a fraud anyway," Winola was saying. "Jervadi's extraction workings have been mined to death. The best she can probably claim is refinements in olive pit removals or something. She was a *hack*, Haeki."

Haeki's door was closed. Winola was standing outside it, raising her voice to be heard.

"None of what she said matters. Don't you see? She needs nationalism to cover up her frankly *obvious* mediocrity. If her supremacy isn't inherent, what does she have? It all turns to smoke, it all falls apart. You never need to try when you're brilliant by birthright, and that's all she can hold on to. But she wasn't brilliant. She really wasn't."

No response.

"Haeki?" Winola folded her arms. "Will you please talk to me?"

"Leave her," said Karys.

The scholar winced. "But—"

"Trust me, you aren't helping."

A tangle of emotions passed over Winola's face: surprise, hurt, displeasure. She lifted her chin. "And you will?"

"Probably not, but you're the one who said you didn't want to invade her privacy. If you meant it, then leave her be."

Winola held her gaze a second longer, defiant. Then she shook her head and walked toward the second bedroom. She paused in the doorway.

"We're not all as practical as you, Karys," she said. "Try to remember that."

"Meaning?"

"Work it out for yourself." The door closed with a loud snap.

Karys grimaced. *What is that supposed to mean?* The night seemed to only be getting worse; now Winola was mad too, and Karys wasn't even sure why. She sighed and knocked on the door to her shared room with Haeki. When there was no reply, she walked in.

Haeki was seated on the bed, her back against the headboard, her knees pulled up to her chest. The only light came through the window; she had extinguished the lamps, and the room was silvery and dim. She glared at Karys. Her cheeks were dry.

"Go away," she said.

Karys leaned against the wall. "Where do you propose I sleep?"

"I don't care."

"You're not helping yourself, you know." She nodded toward Winola's room. "Blowing it out of proportion. It was just a stupid comment."

"Shut up." Haeki drew her knees in even closer. "What do you know?"

"That you're embarrassed and acting like a child about it?"

"I'm not *embarrassed*." She almost spat the word.

"No? Then what?"

"Nothing. Nothing at all. And you're a liar. Leave me alone."

"A liar?"

Haeki raised the pitch of her voice in mockery. "'I have no pride, I'm as faithless as they come.' Hah. You wouldn't bend your neck for a low doorway."

Karys shifted her weight to her other leg. "Do you want a list of the ways I've degraded myself?"

"Lies and more lies."

"Gave up my herald, abandoned my family, begged from strangers, sold my soul to—"

"Is it really all the same to you, Mercia and Varesli?"

Karys rubbed the back of her neck. Her jaw ached.

"I don't know," she said. "Maybe not entirely. But I don't think home ever gave me much, and the hills never demanded my loyalty. One place is the same as the next to me."

Haeki scoffed. "And you're telling me that opinion's got nothing to do with your reeker?"

"What, Ferain? No. No, it's mostly that I've been spat on everywhere I've lived. Look, if you're already homesick for Boäz—"

"Just get out."

Karys raised both her hands in surrender. Haeki's skin was still flushed and her muscles bunched, but she looked less sad than before. Not much of an improvement, but something. "Suit yourself."

The line of light below Winola's door had already disappeared, and the parlour's silence felt heavy. Elsewhere in the house, a clock struck the hour. Its peals drifted faintly through the thick walls. Karys was already going to be late and suspected that if she didn't turn up at his study soon, Vuhas might come looking for her. *Oh, I was getting worried, my dear. What kept you?* She could hear his drawl already.

"You all right?" asked Ferain.

Karys shook herself. "Fine. Just thinking."

"You didn't do anything wrong."

"What?"

"Winola and Haeki. They aren't really angry with you."

He had misread the source of her consternation. She smiled. "I was wondering about Vuhas."

"Oh. Right."

Karys stepped out into the corridor and quietly shut the door behind her. She might as well get this over with. Her shadow slipped alongside her, silhouette diverging from her movements.

"I have a theory, actually," he said. "Hear me out. Cannibalism."

"You . . . what?"

"No, listen. Remember how I said that club must be involved with something illegal and exclusive?"

"Ferain, he doesn't *eat* people."

"It adds up," he insisted. "Why would people this rich live out in the middle of nowhere? Do you know how difficult it must be, running that club? The nearest town is almost a day's ride away; arranging the food alone must be a feat of logistics. It makes *far* more sense to found your society near a city, near culture and other people, and the inconvenience isn't justified unless you have some other motive for settling down in the wilderness. Like not wanting to be noticed."

"Noticed by who?"

"I don't know, the Ministry of Internal Security?"

"He's not a cannibal."

"You don't know that. Come on, look at Ciene. Vuhas was 'correct in judging her tastes'?"

"I'm sure Winola is delicious, but no."

"You don't think some of the things on your plate tonight—"

"Ferain!"

He laughed, and fell back into step with her movements. They had reached the stairs to the second floor. Karys took them two at a time. *Absurd.*

The study sat in the southernmost corner of the manor, at the end of the only corridor not fully illuminated by scores of chandeliers. They had not come down this way during the tour. The walls were lined with portraits, but, unlike the rest of the house, these were of ordinary human men. There seemed to be an underlying resemblance in all their faces, or perhaps in their expressions— clearly Vuhas had inherited the supercilious cast of his forefathers' eyes. One of the older portraits had suffered significant damage; the canvas had been sliced like someone had gone at it with a knife. The study door stood a little ajar, spilling a triangle of yellow onto the thick pile of the carpet runner outside. From within, Karys could hear a fire crackling.

She stopped a few feet from the door, listened, then reached out with her senses and caught the edge of the Veneer. It felt curiously sticky, but opened readily enough. She shrank as the skein of hidden colours and sounds bloomed around her.

As expected, Vuhas' mansion breathed workings—etherbulbs, water systems, locks on the doors, fortifications in the walls, dust absorbers in the floor. All dizzyingly complex, but orderly and banal in function. Security workings too, silver-edged threads draping the portraits and glistening over the carpets, running along the skirting boards like tangled metal wires.

With the door in her way, Karys couldn't detect much in the study. It struck her as quiet—although, against the chatter of the rest of the house, any subtler workings would be drowned out. She could tell that *something* was moving around, and that was a little unusual. It could be a worked biological entity like Psikamit's hounds or Rasko's wasps, but she would have expected to then feel its presence more keenly. This seemed veiled, familiar. A binding of some kind? She ventured a little deeper into the Veneer, trying to see more clearly. A Bhatuma-derived working, probably.

"Don't be shy, my dear," called Vuhas. "Come in, come in."

Oh, she thought with a rush of embarrassment. *It's a body modification.* Vuhas was altering his appearance or physical attributes, most likely for very personal reasons that were none of her business. She pulled the Veneer closed and stepped into the room.

The study was huge and full of books. Shelves lined the walls and rose to the ceiling, and every single one was crammed with leather-bound manuscripts. Two large red armchairs occupied the floor in front of the fireplace, and the mounted head of a snarling leopard hung above the mantel. More books clustered on top of the coffee table; a massive thesaurus, an Ephirite logic guide, several volumes of poetry—*not a complete Bhatuma-workings purist, then*—beside a silver tray with a flask, two ceramic mugs, and a bowl of rolled date sweets. Vuhas was standing beside one of the chairs. He smiled at her.

"I was growing concerned," he said. "Please, sit, be comfortable."

"You said it was urgent?"

He beckoned, lowering himself down with a little sigh. "I won't keep you long."

Karys walked over to the other chair and sat. The fire crackled to her left, too warm for autumn. Vuhas leaned over and picked up the flask. He poured into both mugs and set them down on the table.

"Spiced chocolate," he said. "I like to add a little nutmeg and pepper."

"Is this about Rasko?"

He appeared momentarily perplexed. "Rasko? Oh! Oh, no, nothing to do with that. Sweet?"

He proffered the bowl to her, and Karys grudgingly took a date ball. It wasn't like she wanted any more Vareslian food, and, for all his insistence on urgency, Vuhas didn't seem eager to get to the point. He settled back onto his chair, self-satisfied as a cat in sunshine.

"Good, good." He picked up his mug and took a quick sip of the chocolate. "No, this is just a private concern of mine. Tell me, have you ever read Diarcicardi on the subject of extradimensional manipulations? Specifically his treatise on spiritual displacement and reintegration?"

"You should have gone to bed," groaned her shadow.

Karys kept her expression neutral. "I haven't."

Gratified by her ignorance, Vuhas started to say something else, but she continued over him.

"Unfortunately, I'm not a trained workings practitioner," she said. "Which means my reading has been mostly recreational, and my knowledge of extradimensional manipulation is limited to Osarg and Lefiont on the Bhatuma side. To be honest, I've always found Ephirite workings theory more compelling; Nossark's ideas about Veneer spatial exclusion for example. I liked her comparison of the Embrace's domain with the Toraigian workings exclusion zone. Have you read it?"

There was a brief silence.

"So you really did use that library," murmured Ferain.

Vuhas seemed surprised and more than a little annoyed, as if he had just discovered that the animal he had taken for a house pet was a wolverine. Karys popped the date ball neatly into her mouth.

"I can't say I have." He collected himself. "My interest mostly skewed in the opposite direction, toward Bhatuma derivations. Nossark, you say? I imagine she's Mercian."

The sweet proved bizarrely salty. Karys tried to swallow it without chewing too much. "She was. Her Ephirite master called her compact before she finished her treatise, but she left the incomplete manuscript to Psikamit College."

"Very interesting," said Vuhas, although Karys could tell he did not think so. He seemed on edge. "Unfortunate for her, yes. But you've never studied Diarcicardi?"

Where is he going with this? Karys picked up her drink and swallowed some of the chocolate, hoping to wash away the salty fruit taste. Instead, she was assailed by nutmeg. "I've never heard of him. Why do you ask?"

"The book *Beyond Mortal Bounds* is unfamiliar to you?"

"Yes." She was running out of patience. "Forgive me, but I don't see how this is urgent."

"Bear with me, you'll understand in a minute." Vuhas glanced at his pocket watch. "Let's see, how to summarise . . . Diarcicardi published only one book in his lifetime, a seminal and transgressive work for which he was later executed. That was, oh, six hundred years ago? Varesli was still part of the Osiran Empire. As you can imagine, the original editions are vanishingly rare; there might be two or three left in the world. Copies are also extremely hard to come by, most having been destroyed or lost over the years. In fact, to the best of my knowledge, fewer than thirty now exist. I wondered whether you might have stumbled across one."

"Why would you think that?" An idea occurred to her. "Is Rasko trying to acquire this book for you?"

"No, no, I already told you this has nothing to do with the man. Besides, I have my own copy; I don't require another." He gestured at his bookshelves. "Would you like to see it?"

Why was he toying with her? "No, thank you. I don't understand what this has to do with me."

Vuhas sipped his drink. He smacked his lips in satisfaction. "If you *haven't* read Diarcicardi, then you're an interesting anomaly. Or, more likely, someone else's mistake."

"I don't follow," she said coldly.

Vuhas' eyes glinted in the shifting firelight.

"*Beyond Mortal Bounds* is the only reputable guide to human binding," he said.

Karys' grip tightened reflexively around her mug. She was still for a heart-beat too long, then leaned forward and set the drink down on the coffee table. "I can see why that would be transgressive. What exactly are you accusing me of?"

"My intention is not to make an accusation but an offer. Care to hear it?"

"Not really." At her back, Ferain was tense but silent. "I suspect there has been a misunderstanding."

"Do you?" Vuhas reclined in his armchair. His expression was no longer genial. "I couldn't help but notice: you talk to yourself rather a lot. Strange, that."

"I'm good conversation." Karys rose. "And I think I'll be leaving now."

"No, stay, indulge me. I won't bite."

She folded her arms. Vuhas remained seated, at ease.

"What's your offer?" she asked.

"Let's see." He raised his eyes to the ceiling as if considering the matter. "How about membership to the Grateful Society in perpetuity? It's been a long time since we had a new initiate."

"Thanks, but I'll pass." Karys turned and walked to the door. "Goodnight, casin."

"Oh, but the offer wasn't for you."

The door was shut, although she could not remember having closed it. When she tried the handle, she found it locked. Her heart beat loudly in her ears. She felt sick.

"Would you care to guess," said Vuhas, "how old I am?"

The offer wasn't for her. What did that mean? The door handle was slick beneath her sweating palm. What did Vuhas want from her? "I've never liked riddles."

"Two hundred and four."

"What?"

"As of three weeks ago, I am two hundred and four years old," said Vuhas.

Karys looked back. Her white-haired host smiled from his armchair, blithely unconcerned. He tapped his index finger to his lips.

"Deathspeaker Karys Eska," he said. "Born in a nameless little village, lived as a vagrant in Miresse, formed a compact with the Ephirit Sabaster at around the age of seventeen. Moved to Psikamit, irregularly employed by a local rack-eteer named Marishka Stallar, who, I imagine, assisted you in slipping out of town before New Favour could close their net around you. Something of a loner otherwise, no family, no friends, no lovers. No one to come looking if you were to vanish."

Silence. Karys did not move.

Vuhas raised an eyebrow. "And no comment either?"

Her voice emerged low and harsh. "How did you know?"

"About your history? I did a little research." He gestured toward his vast collection of books. "As a rule, I like to be well-informed. Having heard a ru-mour through my contact with New Favour, I thought it might be worth my time. Tell me, does the name Ferain Taliade ring any bells?"

Karys instinctively took a step backwards, and her heel hit the door. Vuhas laughed, this time with genuine amusement.

"I'll take that as a yes," he said.

"What did you hear from New Favour?" she demanded. "What do you want with him?"

"So it *is* Taliade who's bound to you?"

"Answer the question."

"I already did—I'm offering him membership to the Grateful Society. Salvation, in effect."

"I'll pass," muttered Ferain. "Karys, I'm going to try to get the door open. Keep him talking."

Be quick, she thought fervently. "Salvation?"

"From his imprisonment. However you have repressed or contained him, it must be unspeakably painful. I want to help him."

She scoffed. "He's not in pain. Whatever you think—"

"It's akin to withdrawal. 'To be outside one's body, even for a short space of time, is to crave reunification with the flesh.' That's Diarcicardi, by the way. If my understanding of the situation is correct, Ferain Taliade has been in such a condition for almost two weeks. A terrible fate."

She could feel Ferain drawing on her; her shadow trying to force open the lock behind her back. "And you want—you want to help him? How?"

"Well, by freeing him, of course. I imagine he was the one who established the binding? It's a very delicate process, easy to fumble. I am giving him the ability to reassert control over his vessel."

"He didn't . . ." She leaned back against the door. Her skin was damp, too hot. "His vessel?"

"You, my dear."

Karys' heart hammered. She had known something was wrong; she should never have come here. "So that's it. The Grateful Society—you're skin thieves."

Vuhas leaned forward and picked up his mug again. "Don't be ridiculous. Superstitions have their sources, I suppose, but I'm hardly some kind of monster hiding beneath a child's bed. No, the Grateful represent the greatest aspiration of mankind. Together, we have defeated death itself."

She did not know what expression crossed her face. "You're a murderer. *Worse* than a murderer."

"Less histrionics, please."

"How many 'vessels' have you stolen, then?"

"Eleven. Some fit better than others." Vuhas consulted his watch. "If Taliade finds your body does not suit him, the Society can acquire a replacement. We would be able to provide anything he needs."

Whatever her shadow was doing, it didn't seem to be working. Karys clenched her jaw, keeping her head raised. "And what would happen to me?"

"Oh, you'll be long gone by then. There's no way to claim a vessel without displacing its existing inhabitant."

Behind her, Ferain swore.

"I can't get the door open," he said. "We need a new plan."

"I have shown Taliade only a fraction of what the Grateful Society has to offer," said Vuhas. "He is welcome to our fraternity, guidance, and aid; our resources go far beyond what he witnessed this evening. The choice is his."

Karys spoke through gritted teeth. "And if he refuses? If *I* refuse?"

Vuhas' gaze was pitying. He shook his head. "A little late for that, I think."

"Karys?" Ferain's attention was back on her. His alarm increased. "Karys, what's wrong?"

She refused to allow her knees to bend. "The chocolate, right?"

Vuhas inclined his head in acknowledgement. "In part. The compound reacts to a reagent in the fruit sweet. The salt was to make you thirsty."

"Hah." She pushed damp strands of her hair back from her forehead. "I assumed horseshit was just a flavour you reekers enjoyed. You never had anything to do with Rasko, did you?"

"Your Miresse man? No, I'm afraid not. I merely intercepted his contact on this side of the border."

Of course he had. From the start, Vuhas' connection to Rasko had made no sense. She had *known* that, she had known the story didn't line up. Her limbs trembled, feverish, and her thoughts came slow. The tour of the house and the Bhatuma relics, the visit to the club and the dinner: none of it was intended to impress her, Winola, or Haeki—it had all been for Ferain. She had been pulled along like a puppet on strings.

"He drugged you." Ferain's voice held a strange flatness. He did not move; her shadow stayed the same size and shape, but to Karys' eyes it seemed to grow darker. Her vision swam. She needed to act, and soon. Needed to do something.

"What have you poisoned me with?" The words were heavy, difficult to pronounce.

Vuhas checked the time again. "Just a little safety measure for Taliade, something to render you incapable of contesting his claim. The Grateful Society developed it a century ago; we use it for all our revivals now. The activated compound is also going to stop your heart in another three minutes or so."

She tried to take a step toward Vuhas, but her body no longer cooperated as it should; she fell to one knee. Sharp pressure spiked at the base of her skull. With effort, she lifted her head.

"Fuck you," she panted.

"If Taliade claims your body, I'll neutralise the poison. No permanent damage."

"Feels . . . damaging right now."

"Think of it as a mercy, a gift," said Vuhas. "You'll be spared the fear and grief that await you. Your Ephirite master will never call your compact. In exchange, an innocent man is given a second life. Isn't that worth something?"

Tendrils of cold inched across her torso. "I had a . . . fucking plan, you . . . fucking skin-stealing prick."

"Don't be so vulgar."

Doubled over, she made a wordless noise of rage. She had come too far for things to end like this. *Get up!* There had to be something she could do, some way out of this. If she could just *think,* she would be able to find the answer.

"Do you trust me?"

Ferain asked the question softly, and with the same absence of emotion in his voice. Karys dug her fingers into the carpet, and the rich weave of the rug blurred before her eyes. It was getting harder and harder to speak.

"Why?" she managed.

"You know too much now," said Vuhas, mistaking her. "I couldn't allow you to live."

At least on the surface, Ferain was composed. He spoke like they were alone, like Vuhas did not matter or exist. "If you don't want me to take over, I won't. I'll die before stealing your body, Karys. But if you trust me, if you are willing to trust me now—I'll fix this. I swear. Say my name, and I'll make him pay."

Her tongue felt thick in her mouth. She was so heavy, so tired, so slow. *I don't want to disappear.* Even if it meant facing Sabaster and the consequences of her choices, even if there was no hope. *I wanted to live.* Ferain sensed her reluctance.

"I understand," he said. "I'm sorry we didn't have more time."

Her arms trembled and she slumped. Concealed from Vuhas, her shadow touched her cheek, light as air. He spoke so quietly that she almost did not hear him.

"Thank you for carrying me out of the dark," he whispered.

Karys squeezed her eyes closed. White stars blossomed across the lids. Her heart beat erratically; her thoughts tangled like nets in a wind-tossed sea. Trust him? When was the last time . . . when had she ever . . . ? Her body was cold. But she did. Trust him.

Some final, desperate gasp of self-preservation seized her—her lips parted and she choked out her shadow's name.

For an instant: nothing. Then Ferain sank into her skin.

CHAPTER

31

Icy coldness. Disorientation overwhelmed her; her perception of the outside world vanished, and she was lost in a frigid white vortex. Turning, turning, turning; the storm whipped around her and she had no control, no power, nothing to ground her. Through the suffocating cold, she sensed a foreign presence, something hungry and formless and intelligent. It could see her.

Without quite knowing what she was doing, Karys tried to flee deeper into the storm.

Stop! I'm not going to hurt you.

It was Ferain's voice, but different: the tones richer and much, much closer. It seemed to come from every direction at once. Karys slowed, shrinking like cornered prey.

You have to stop panicking already.

Easy for you to say, she snapped. *Nuliere alive, why did I agree to this?*

Because you trust me.

The words were accompanied by a heady rush of feeling—something like pride or exhilaration, but more determined. The emotion swept through Karys and out into the swallowing white, startling in its intensity, its foreignness, its nearness. For a brief moment, the storm retreated.

Ferain, was that . . . you?

Exactly who else would it be? A touch of exasperation, faint amusement. *Are you keeping anyone else prisoner in your shadow?*

Then the realisation hit her like a blow. They weren't speaking. They weren't making any noise at all. *He can hear my thoughts. Oh shit, he can hear that as well. And that. And—*

Yes, correct, but try to—

He can hear me thinking.

And you can hear me too, so let's call it even.

Embrace, he's inside my head. This can't be happening, this can't be happening, this can't be—

I'm afraid it is, in fact, happening.

She wanted to curl into herself. There was nowhere to hide; Ferain's mind pressed up against her own, so near that they almost melded into one. Every feeling and secret shame lay upon an altar before him, every unspeakable desire, every terrible part of her—all of it only a thought away. It was the most terrible intimacy, and there was no way out; no defence, no shelter, no respite. He was everywhere, and so was she.

I'm not looking, Karys.

But he would see anyway.

There's a difference.

Her shadow stretched out of shape across the bathroom floor. His promise that she never needed to talk about her father, his stillness in Sabaster's domain. Always, in his way, excruciatingly careful. She knew. Even now, she could sense him straining to hold himself back, trying not to touch her despite their proximity.

I'm afraid, she thought. *It's so cold here. Ferain, I'm afraid.*

I know. I am too.

He was. His fear had a different taste to her own, less . . . acidic. It was shame and concern, laced with something else, something leashed so tight it might have strangled him. Through the white, Karys caught sight of moving shapes, misted figures. She tried to gather her mind, distance herself from her awareness of him.

Haeki and Winola, we have to warn them, she thought. *I brought them here. If they—if Vuhas—*

I won't let that happen.

It will be my fault. Haeki. Please, not her. If anything—

Karys.

Embrace, I was so stupid and careless.

No, none of that. Anger, not directed toward her. The storm grew wilder, and then subsided again. *None of this was your fault.*

Am I dead?

A rush of guilt. Fear. *No.*

Dying, then?

Not if I have anything to do with it.

He said two people couldn't exist in one body. That I would disappear.

You won't.

He said you were in unspeakable pain.

What Vuhas said doesn't matter. We're not bound like he is to his victims. It's different. We're . . . partners.

He was avoiding the question. While he couldn't lie, Ferain could still dodge. Think around the truth, refocus his attention to conceal his thoughts. That was worse, somehow, than just having him admit it.

Karys, no. It's not like that.

She felt very tired. *I wanted to help you.*

You have. Deep pain, a twisting ache not unlike grief. Burning resolve. *We are* not *like him, and you aren't to blame for any of this.*

The storm turned, growing louder, denser. *I'm sorry.*

Acute wordless denial from Ferain. The cold was closing in around them; it was getting harder for Karys to concentrate. Far away, she could make out Vuhas' voice, although the words were garbled. He was speaking, offering congratulations.

I'm going to take care of this. Ferain's thoughts reached her through the tumult. *Hold on, okay?*

". . . there much resistance?" Vuhas was saying. "I wasn't sure you could hear me."

Ferain spoke through her mouth. It was the strangest feeling, but Karys lost what he said as the white swallowed her up completely. She drifted into some deeper, windswept nothingness. It was not so cold anymore, or maybe she had grown numb to the chill. She could not form thoughts; she was only aware of sensation. A sound like rushing water.

Then the world tilted back into focus. They were now inside a bright corridor. Ferain walked beside Vuhas, and they were talking.

". . . source of New Favour's aggression?"

"Not exactly," said Vuhas. "They are looking for something called the 'last harbour.' A potential threat to the Ephirite's interests, from what I could gather."

A nauseous feeling in Ferain. "But what does that mean?"

"I'm not sure. They were fixated on that ambassadorial mission to Toraigus, but they don't seem aware that *you* escaped, specifically. That's my impression anyway—I myself was only able to identify you as the survivor after I caught wind of your dispatch to the Foreign Ministry. Connecting the dots, you know? The Ministry is keeping the affair as quiet as they can, but I've got a man on the inside."

Ferain?

"Whatever the case, we can mitigate the threat," continued Vuhas. "New Favour is looking for Eska—once we find a new vessel, that link will be severed and they won't have any means of tracing you."

Haeki and Winola are both safe for now, Ferain thought to her. *Are you all right?*

I think so.

"I still don't understand how she worked that binding in the first place," said Vuhas. "Or *why.* You say she was completely estranged from New Favour?"

Ferain's tone was pleasant, at odds with his feelings. "It seemed that way. I think she meant to extort me. She appeared to believe that the binding would be reversible."

"Oh, so she would release you in exchange for a fee? How very Mercian." Vuhas shook his head. "Short-sighted on her part, although I have no idea how she managed to repress you so effectively."

Karys did not feel entirely lucid; her senses were alien, her limbs moved without her intention. When Ferain spoke, she heard her own voice, but with his accent and inflections; when he walked, his stride was longer and his gait more relaxed. She had no recollection of this section of the house, no sense of how much time might have passed. The dislocation filled her with an inarticulate fear.

If you can, go back to sleep. Ferain continued to smile at Vuhas with her face. *It will make this easier for me.*

She could not make sense of the emotions that accompanied that instruction, but her mind was slipping and she obeyed, sinking back down through the cold and into a dream.

It was late afternoon, and rose-coloured light diffused through the bay windows. Furniture covered in white sheets surrounded her, and there was a potent, breathless stillness to the air. A bedroom. It held a flowery smell, a lingering fragrance like magnolia. Blood streaked the drapes, dark and dried against the cream velour. Beyond the glass, the trees stood in their silent dignity—leaves like plum skins peeled off ripe fruit.

Karys' feet moved; she walked toward the window. In the intervening distance, the sheets folded back from the furniture, revealing a woman seated on a chair below the falling dusk light. She wore a pale gown, no shoes; she might always have been there. Her hair formed a pure white bun at the nape of her neck, not a strand misplaced, and her skin was light brown. Her pallor had a wintery, indoor quality; that of a person long deprived of the sun. She might have been sixty, perhaps older, and she sat still as a stone.

Karys stopped at the woman's side. When she looked down, she discovered flowers in her right hand. Peonies and carnations, bundled together with a beaded lace cord.

"I bought you flowers," she said.

The woman stared at the trees, expression vacant. Her wrists were bound to the arms of the chair with thick leather restraints. Karys set the bouquet in her lap. When she turned to leave, she found the whole room full of flowers; bunches stacked to the ceiling, blooms in every shade of red.

The dream receded; she rose from the winter haze and back to her body.

Elsewhere again. The guest quarters. Winola stood in front of her, dressed only in her shirt and underwear, her raven-hair sticking in all directions. She looked horrified, her face colourless in the dimness.

"What have you done?" she whispered.

"I had no choice," said Ferain.

Winola lifted her hand to her mouth. Her fingers trembled. "Have you . . . is she . . . ?"

"Karys agreed to it." The tension bled into his voice. "There isn't much time. I need your help, Winola. Please."

Where did Vuhas go? Karys wondered sleepily.

The world dissolved once more.

Another bedroom, much smaller, drenched in morning sunshine. Karys was on her back on a four-poster. A slender woman with honey-yellow hair was on top of her, naked and laughing, making love to her.

Even immersed in the soft logics of the dream, Karys was startled—a jolt of recognition, at the back of her mind, that this was not her, that this moment had not been meant for her to witness. She—the part of her that was *herself*—had not been touched like this. And yet her hands were at the woman's waist; she felt desire thrilling through her, and deep affection for the stranger. Tresses of the woman's hair brushed her chest, light as feathers.

"Ilesha," Karys gasped.

The woman grinned, wickedness glittering in her dark eyes. She adjusted her position, moved much slower. "Say please?"

Quick and sure, Karys reached out and caught the woman by the back of the neck, then drew her down into a kiss. Ilesha's body was warm and familiar; her hair had the heady, earthy smell of the oils she used.

She laughed into Karys' mouth, trying to squirm away. "Cheating!"

"Forgive me." Karys tangled her fingers up in Ilesha's amber curls, her other hand reaching down the slope of her hip. "How should I make it up to you?"

Ilesha made a low sound in the back of her throat, a little breathless now as Karys' hand continued to tease downwards. "That's a start."

I should not be here, Karys thought through the heat and the sweetness. The yearning, the lust, it could have been her own, but that was not her lying on the bed. She tried to move away, and the world shifted in response.

Ilesha sat on the cushioned window seat, wrapped in her sheet and smoking osk through a thin reed pipe.

"Why not stay?" she asked. "You could get a better post in a year. Less, probably."

Karys stood by the wardrobe, dressing. "Are you saying you'll miss me?"

Ilesha huffed. "No. But Toraigus?"

"My Toraigian is very good."

"It's a dead end. You know that. The offer is practically an insult; no one actually expects you to take the first job the Ministry puts on the table." She frowned, struck by a thought. "Wait, is that why you're doing it?"

Karys pulled on her trousers. "I've heard they have great food. Very nice weather."

"If you were closer by, Rain, I'd smack you." She blew a stream of smoke through her lips. "Come on, what are you doing? Toraigus, of all places. Stuck out on a raft in the ocean—you won't even be allowed to make land. Someone must have pulled strings to get an appointment that low assigned to you."

Karys snorted. "I'm not headed into a war, you know. There's nothing wrong with Toraigus."

"Exactly—the role asks nothing of you. You're being wasted."

"The preliminary mission will only take a few months. It might even fail."

"And if it doesn't? If you get stationed there permanently, then what? I just want to know who you're trying to impress."

Karys had her back to Ilesha, which was a mercy. A hollow loneliness had wrapped around her chest, and she felt in that moment untouchable and alien—because how could she explain? She did not understand it herself, not entirely, but she was not trying to impress anyone. She was running away. She pulled her shirt on, closed the wardrobe door, fixed her smile, and turned around.

"Would it be gauche to say 'you'?" she asked.

Ilesha returned her gaze evenly, eyes gentle and soft and sad. Not fooled.

"I think we both know that this isn't going to work," she said.

The clear daylight of the bedroom dissolved into white.

Karys slid back to awareness like ice melting, only without any warmth. Less lucid, less awake; she seemed stretched thinner each time she surfaced. Within her body, she felt small and eroded.

They were back in the study. One of the ceramic mugs had smashed on the ground, and chocolate stained the carpet. Vuhas was tied to his desk chair. His white fringe of hair flopped over his forehead, and a bloody bruise dominated the side of his face. One eye had swollen shut, the other was wide open and furious.

"You bastard!" His lip was thick, his usual drawl distorted. "You ungrateful, treasonous bastard. I'll flay you alive."

Ferain flexed and relaxed the fingers of Karys' right hand, shaking them out. "Terrified."

Winola was by the fireplace, clutching a book to her chest. She looked like she might start crying. A circle of red on her bottom lip marked where she had applied blood for a working. "Ferain, I don't—I don't know if I can do this."

"And *you*." Vuhas turned his attention to the scholar, and she flinched back a step. "With your pretty little guises and cosmetics. Oh, you think you're so clever, don't you? You think you can make a fool of me?"

"She already has," said Ferain.

Vuhas replied with filthy invective. Despite his predicament, he did not seem afraid or even pained, only seethingly angry—he glared at Ferain, producing a wet wheeze with each breath.

"I wanted to save you," he growled. "I was trying to help."

Ferain made a contemptuous sound. "You were trying to salvage your own social standing."

Vuhas strained against the bindings on the chair. His face was red and shining. "So, what, you choose to throw your lot in with a gutter-raised Mercian instead? The Ephirite whore isn't coming back now. You've destroyed her."

"Stop talking."

Although it was not loud, Ferain's voice caused Vuhas to fall silent immediately. In the quiet that followed, his laboured breathing sounded much louder than before. The embers in the grate shifted and settled.

Ferain gave a low sigh. He briefly pressed one hand to his forehead, as though in pain. When he spoke again, the words sounded different—he had switched to Toraigian.

"We both know this isn't a question of ability, but ethics," he said, lowering his hand. He looked at Winola. "I'll understand if you won't do it."

Winola's eyes were large behind her spectacles. She hesitated, then replied in Toraigian. "If I make a mistake—Ferain, these workings are no better than human binding. I could make a chimera of him, or worse."

"I know what I'm asking."

She laughed: a cracked, hoarse sound. "No, you don't. You really don't. Even if I get it *right*, it would be a transgression of the highest order."

"I can guess what you're talking about," said Vuhas loudly.

"I'm asking for her sake," said Ferain, still in Toraigian. "I take all responsibility; the transgression would be mine. If anything goes wrong—"

"You'll only obliterate yourself, you know." Vuhas shook his head in disgust. "Keep to your juvenile workings, girl. This is out of your reach."

A muscle in Ferain's jaw twitched. He returned his gaze to Vuhas. Something in his eyes caused the older man to shrink; when he spoke, his voice was dangerously smooth.

"I don't think you've grasped the situation," he said. "You had better *hope* she agrees to this—because if she doesn't, I'm going to kill you myself."

Winola flinched. The edges of the room were turning pale and translucent in Karys' vision; the dreams reached to claim her again. Before she was swallowed up, she saw the scholar give a shaky nod. Then Karys' mind crumbled like sand into water; she washed away once more.

A party: a shining room flickering with candlelight, heavy tapestries glimmering with hundreds of bright colours, whisper-thin screens woven from silver silk. A crowd of men raised their glasses in toast; they seemed in high spirits. Karys stood at the wall, wine glass dangling from her fingers. A white-skinned, elderly woman wearing a magnificent orange and blue shawl sat in a wheelchair at her side.

"Did you receive the blessing on arrival?" the woman asked.

"The full retinue did." Karys enjoyed the way the words slid off her tongue, the foreign syllables worn smooth and easy with practice. She had worked hard for this; she could show off. "Which was generous—we believed Ambassador Corbain would be the only one to merit the honour."

"You were pleased?" The woman's eyes twinkled. "The ceremony can be very long, I know. We like our traditions here."

"I enjoyed it. The Amity Bead was unexpectedly crunchy."

"Wicked man!" The woman laughed. "Where is your respect?"

"Lost at sea, possibly."

"You *are* terrible. If I were younger, I might have smuggled you through the Wall and kept you."

"I wouldn't have been opposed to that."

"Terrible, terrible man." She fanned herself with one hand, still smiling. "You'll cause a diplomatic incident; your ambassador should be keeping a closer eye on you. Where is she?"

"I'm not sure." Karys allowed her gaze to travel the hall; there was some commotion outside the door. Two people were trying to cross the threshold, but had been barred by the gilded pikes of the ceremonial bastireu guards.

The newcomers looked old, frail, and furious, but as well-dressed as any of the other dignitaries at the party. They were arguing, pointing at the Vareslian delegation. Curious, Karys took a step toward the door . . .

. . . and found herself soaking wet and surrounded by screaming.

Waves crashed against stone in the darkness; she could hear the terrified cries of her colleagues, sailors shouting. Something had gone horribly wrong. Corbain was trying to rally everyone; her voice boomed even over the raging tumult. Then, abruptly, she fell silent. Blue lights burst to life, dashed like electric fire over the rolling water, and Karys caught glimpses of something else amidst the chaos, mercurial in speed, yellow glimmers of trapped lightning, and then screams cut off. She drew her sword . . .

. . . complete darkness. Her arm buzzed with a sick, vibrating heat. She leaned against the side of a sarcophagus—although the hallowfire had faded after she had established the Lapse, she had seen the room, and knew she was surrounded by the dead. How long had it been now? In an earlier desperate moment, she had used up the last of her worked metal to conjure a tiny ether—just enough to see her timepiece before the light flared out. Two days at least; that was all she could say with certainty. Within the Lapse, she felt neither hunger nor thirst, and she could not sleep—time dropped like grains of sand in an hourglass.

It would not be so terrible, if only it wasn't so dark. In the absence of light, her mind remained trapped between the water and rocks, hearing them all scream and then stop, scream and then stop. In a panic, her body had fallen into automatic movement, the sword drills of her youth taking over her limbs. She thrust and slashed at the Construct with pure, unthinking, cornered aggression, and drove it back just far enough that she could slip past.

Then it lashed out with a yellow whip of an arm, and grazed her left bicep. A molten stripe of agony blistered her flesh, but momentum carried her. She lost her sword and ran.

Now, however, she knew it would have been better to die down there with the others. Better than this lingering, hopeless state; better than being alone. She could go no further, and she wanted to howl, to curse, to break down and beat at the walls. If she turned off the Lapse, it would end. But she could not bring herself to do it.

If only it wasn't so dark.

A sound. At first, she thought it was a trick of her mind. Karys lifted her head from her chest. It seemed like . . . beating. A drum, or footsteps. No, definitely running footsteps, and they were getting louder, getting closer. Through the arch of the doorway, she saw the gleam of hallowfire, a faint blue cast to the stones. She staggered to her feet too quickly—fuck, it hurt—and struggled over to the entrance. The light was growing brighter. It was real. She heard someone gasp, and almost called out to them—*here, I'm here!* They sounded afraid, breathing loud and harsh, and Embrace, there was light, there was so much light, and she saw the woman running down the stairs, and she stepped out and caught the stranger in an explosion of agony and relief. Hard contact, a lurch, and whiteness swallowed her up for the final time.

Karys inhaled. Warm air filled her lungs, and she made a sound like a sob. She was alone in her body. Ferain spoke from her shadow, sounding wretched.

"It's done," he said, and then nothing more.

CHAPTER

32

Karys did not see Vuhas again. In the morning, Yviline passed on his apology. He had fallen ill, and was convalescing in his room, unable to see them off. It was nothing to be concerned about; he often suffered terrible migraines at this time of year. He hoped that they had enjoyed their brief stay, and wished them well on their journey.

Yviline was white-faced. She would not make eye contact, and spoke in a low monotone. It was unclear what exactly she had expected, arriving at the mansion that morning—what she might have guessed of her master's intentions, what she knew of the Grateful Society. Perhaps not everything. But enough. She withered under Karys' stare.

"I'll summon the awrig," she whispered.

One garbled warning meant nothing. Ambivalent or not, Yviline had been complicit in this. Unspeaking, Karys followed her through the back door. A coward, a timid little mouse of a woman, content to serve Vuhas his breakfast and bring him his slippers. Pathetic. She had done next to nothing, and now . . . now . . .

Now, Ferain would not answer.

Karys had not slept at all—her shadow had only returned her body an hour before dawn. She had sat alone in the guest parlour as the sun rose, listening to Winola retch in the bathroom. When the scholar finally emerged, the vineyards were touched with pale gold. Karys tore her eyes from the long rectangle of light cast through the window, from the juncture where her shadow merged with the armchair's, where the darkness lay bunched and inert.

"Tell me what happened," she said.

Winola took one look at her face, and recoiled as if struck. "Embrace, Karys . . ."

"Tell me."

The scholar slumped onto the opposite couch. She wet her lips and shut her eyes for a moment, gathering herself. Then she spoke.

Ferain had woken her a little before three in the morning. He had not explained much then; only that Vuhas had poisoned Karys in order to recruit him to the Grateful Society, and that he needed her to perform a working. From his pocket, he had produced a handful of date sweets. He asked her to extract the salt from them, and then to wrap them in a guise. Make them look and taste like bread. When she was done, slip down to the kitchen. The house's security workings were inactive; she would not be noticed or harmed. Leave the bread in the pantry, and hide in the broom cupboard. Wait for him. Do not wake Haeki.

He had taken Rasko's parcel from Karys' bag, and disappeared again.

Removing the salt was trivial; any first-year workings student could accomplish that. Shaping the sweets into something that resembled bread was also reasonably straightforward. But making the taste and texture convincing? That was not a guise; it was material, structural working. And it had felt like such a stupid task. While struggling to persuade dates and sugar to taste like wheat, Winola had known they were in terrible danger. She had suspected that Karys was already lost.

She managed to produce a single roll. Small, dark and dense, but close enough to bread to pass as the real thing. Afraid and alone, she crept down to the kitchen, placed her creation in the pantry, and shut herself in the closet.

When Ferain and Vuhas arrived, it was clear they had been drinking. Winola watched them through the keyhole. They spoke loudly, in high spirits; Ferain praising Vuhas' collection of artefacts, thanking him for the private tour, promising favours, information, resources. He had been loquacious and at ease, all traces of his former tension gone. Seeing Karys possessed had already been uncanny, but for Ferain to fit so naturally into her skin? If not for their earlier conversation, Winola would have believed him genuinely happy. Genuinely grateful.

Vuhas sat down on one of the kitchen stools, turning over Rasko's box in his hands. He had not opened it; he was speculating that the contents were worked and organic, possibly dangerous. Ferain asked whether it might be a relic. Vuhas said that was a possibility. He could perform a few tests on it tomorrow. Very curious. He was clearly intrigued; he held up the box against the light, studying it from different angles. Ferain interrupted to apologise. It had been weeks since he had tasted food and—Vuhas quickly assured him that he completely understood; Ferain was welcome to whatever he could find. Ferain asked, jokingly, if Vuhas would break bread with him.

"He made it seem so effortless," whispered Winola. "Karys, you don't understand. Ferain was—*I* believed him. Vuhas never suspected a thing."

It took less than a minute. Ferain, with the neutralising agent still in Karys' bloodstream, ate unaffected: still talking, still laughing, disarming, flattering.

But Vuhas had drunk a full mug of spiced chocolate earlier in the evening—and now unwittingly swallowed the other half of his own poison. Inebriated and distracted, he didn't notice the heaviness of his limbs until he was almost falling off his chair. Even then, faced with Ferain's wide-eyed concern, he seemed unable to put two and two together. He joked about the years catching up with him, about being unable to hold his liquor. Ferain swung a supportive arm around his shoulder.

Vuhas seemed on the verge of blacking out before the truth finally sank in. Too weak, too slow, he fumbled for an ampoule in his pocket. Ferain knocked it away, then clamped a hand over Vuhas' mouth to prevent him from triggering any worked defences. Vuhas thrashed, Ferain held fast. After a few seconds, the struggles subsided. Ferain lowered him to the ground.

"He called to me, and I came out," said Winola. "And when he looked at me . . . I knew what came next would be worse. I don't know how much he had planned, how much he was improvising. He said that there wasn't much time; he could feel you fading. He looked scared."

They had dragged Vuhas back to his study. While Winola tied him to his chair and fed him the contents of the ampoule, Ferain ran down to the artefact repository and retrieved Noaj's amulet. By the time he returned, Vuhas was already stirring, mumbling unhappily. Ferain tied the amulet around his neck. Then he turned to Winola and told her what was needed.

The problem was not Vuhas, but his friends. If it wasn't for the Grateful Society, Ferain could have killed Vuhas on his own. It would have been ugly, but far simpler. He had the will for it. Although he had never killed anyone before, he would have done it.

No, the problem lay in the fact that Vuhas had talked. Ciene, and probably others, knew of his suspicions regarding Karys. Knew who she was, knew something of his plans. If Vuhas showed up dead in the morning, all eyes would turn to her. All the Society's resources, all their power—if Ferain killed Vuhas, she would never be free. The Grateful would hunt her down.

What was needed, therefore, was for Vuhas *himself* to call off his friends. If he told the Grateful that Karys was nobody, they would believe him. The situation would make for an amusing anecdote: the time that the Society almost inducted a hapless Mercian into their ranks. Of course, admitting to his mistake would make Vuhas a laughingstock, and further degrade his social position. He would never agree to that kind of humiliation.

Which left only one option.

"The four great sins in working." Winola's eyes were red-rimmed, her voice hoarse. "Human binding, apotheosis, soul retention or obliteration, and mind manipulation. Earlier this morning, I performed the last. I broke into Vuhas' head, and changed his memories. I cracked him apart and rearranged him, so that his thoughts bent to my will. I forced—"

Her lower lip trembled, and she touched her mouth. Karys kept quiet.

"I forced myself on him," she said. "Not physically, but it amounts to the same."

In the end, the choice had been hers. Establishing the working was difficult—she had needed to refer to Vuhas' own manuscripts for guidance on its intricacies—but once it was in place, the rest was sickeningly intuitive. Vuhas sat and listened to her, eyes glazed, and she told him what to think.

All along, New Favour had been mistaken or misled: Ferain Taliade was dead with the rest of his retinue, the letter to the Foreign Ministry had been a ruse, and Karys Eska had only ever been an unlucky, unremarkable victim of circumstance. Under the drug's influence, she revealed nothing that suggested familiarity with human binding. Instead, she had seemed sweetly eager to please. She was forthcoming and grateful for the safety he had provided.

Vuhas had found himself unexpectedly affected by her trust. In spite of her sordid history, the deathspeaker remained a rare innocent. And so, while she was distracted, he had slipped the neutralising agent into her drink. The impulse surprised him; it was not like him to be so sentimental. Still, it felt right. When Eska left, it was with a kind smile on her face.

Was he disappointed? Of course. It was going to be embarrassing to admit to his error. In fact, if he could, he should avoid talking about the affair altogether. Let the Society make their own assumptions, let them even believe he had disposed of the woman. It would be difficult, but he would endure. He always did.

In any case, that was a problem for the morning. His troubles would wait, because he was not feeling well. Not well at all—cursed migraines, always this time of year. In a sudden spell of dizziness, he had fallen and knocked his face against his desk. Nothing seemed broken, thankfully, but he would stay away from company for a while. Ridiculous, really. It almost looked like he had been punched.

Winola's voice faded toward the end; it dropped to a murmur and then to nothing. Without it, the silence of the parlour was suffocating. No wind today, no birds, only a queasy stillness outside, and emptiness within. Pressure bore down on Karys' chest. She could not feel her shadow. Its subtle coolness, its familiar weight . . . gone. She could not feel anything.

Ferain?

Behind her, a floorboard creaked. Karys started, and Winola jumped up from her chair. But it was only Haeki, tousle-haired and barefoot, leaving her bedroom. She stopped when she saw them.

"Karys?" Her voice went tight. "Karys, what—what's going on?"

They left the mansion under the same airless silence. Early though it was, the sunlight burned and the scrublands shimmered; in a few hours, the heat would scorch the barren waste. In the canyon, what remained of the dead would wither—Pavian and the saints covered in flies, decaying, the baboons picking across the soft sand.

"You had no right," said Haeki.

The interior of Vuhas' awrig was cool; the windows tinted to diffuse the glare. Karys watched the house as the vehicle pulled away down the vineyard-lined track. The building appeared grossly out of place, like one image cut out and stuck on top of another. The long windows threw back the light, and hid all that lay within.

"I was right there." Haeki's voice was rough. "Why? Why didn't you wake me?"

Winola would not look up. She sat on the opposite bench, her hands bunched in her lap. "Ferain told me not to."

"I don't care what the reeker told you, I was *there*. I'm Favoured; I could have—" She broke off, too angry to speak. She breathed in, unsteady. "Why?"

Winola looked small, the lineaments of her face sunken and sharp in the daylight. "Because if you had learned what Vuhas did to Karys, we would not have been able to stop you from killing him."

"Bullshit."

"The situation was too delicate."

"Is that what you think of me?" Her voice rose. "That I can't be trusted to—"

Karys laid her hand on Haeki's knee. She didn't say anything—she felt too tired, too empty—but Haeki fell quiet nonetheless. Beneath Karys' palm, her leg was shaking.

"I'm sorry," said Winola.

So tired. Karys tilted her head back and closed her eyes. The darkness was a welcome relief. She didn't want to think anymore, didn't want to hear the silence. She let her hand slide from Haeki's knee. They should never have come here.

She did not fall asleep exactly; it was deeper and more vacant than that. Her mind went blank, and she descended into a dreamless, unfeeling void. No sense of time passing or her own body—when she woke, she was lying sideways across the bench, her head cushioned on Haeki's thigh.

Karys sat up quickly, muttering an apology. Haeki never moved; she continued to stare out the window to her left, fist against her mouth. The landscape had changed; they passed through rolling hills covered in faded green and purple, low grasses and heather. It looked to be mid-afternoon, and bulbous clouds crowded the sky, blinding in their whiteness. Winola was curled up on the other bench, turned away from them. The scholar's breath rose and fell in slow waves.

"She said you needed sleep," murmured Haeki.

At Karys' shoulder, there was a fading heat, as though a hand had been resting there until recently. She straightened her hair, fingertips brushing the warmed skin. "How long has it been?"

"Hours. She dozed off not long after you did. Seemed . . ." A small movement of her hand. "Like she was barely even here."

"And you?"

"And me, what? I didn't need any more sleep."

"Haeki."

"I never wanted to be a burden. I thought—Karys, all she had to do was knock on the door."

Haeki's hair glinted like loose coils of copper, and she seemed, in that moment, achingly fragile. All of her strength and fierceness lost, all her anger faded.

"You're no burden," said Karys quietly.

Winola's shoulders hitched in her sleep. Haeki lowered her hand from her mouth, although she did not turn away from the window.

"What happened to him?" she asked. "Your reeker? He hasn't moved in all the time you were sleeping. Hasn't said anything to me."

The pressure on Karys' chest grew heavier.

"He . . ." She took a breath. "He's just tired."

There was a long pause. Haeki finally looked at her.

"He'll be all right," she said.

Karys nodded. The awrig altered course slightly, curving its path around the slope of a hill. Winola mumbled something inaudible, and Haeki glanced at the scholar. An odd, uncertain expression crossed her face.

"What is it?" asked Karys.

Haeki shook her head slightly.

"There's something I've been wanting to ask you," she said. "It isn't important."

"I'm listening."

Haeki sighed. She rubbed her thumb back and forth across the knuckles of her left hand.

"That letter I sent you about Oboro?" she said. "I got the man at the counter to write it for me."

"I figured."

A small grimace. "Right. So, that's . . . I can't read."

Karys knew that the admission hurt, and so she kept her voice light. "You and the rest of Boäz. What of it?"

"*You* can."

"I paid a tutor when I moved to Psikamit." It hadn't been cheap. "He forged a library card for me to use at the College."

Haeki shifted on the bench. "Was it difficult?"

"Yes."

"Will you teach me?"

"To read and write?"

A quick nod.

Karys looked down at her hands. There wouldn't be enough time; Sabaster would call her compact before Haeki even mastered the basics. Delusional to think otherwise. Just one more regret to weigh her down before the end.

"I can," she said. "If that's something you want."

Haeki breathed out. She leaned back on the bench, offering a small smile when Karys glanced at her.

"Thanks," she said simply.

"It won't be easy."

"I know. But . . . thanks."

Karys turned her gaze out the window, watched the rugged hills slide by.

What was one more delusion? At least for the moment, this one felt like it mattered.

CHAPTER

33

Tuschait nestled into a fold between the hills. From a distance, the town looked small and picturesque, neat houses surrounded by dark green canola fields. It seemed more of a village to Karys; it appeared to comprise fewer than fifty buildings in all. On the outskirts, an enormous bronze sculpture stood in the long grass—an elephant and calf, trunks intertwined in perfect spirals.

Haeki leaned closer to the awrig's window. She squinted against the late afternoon sun.

"Where do you suppose the train station is?" she asked. "I don't see any tracks."

"It's probably on the far side of town." Since waking, Winola had been subdued and withdrawn. Her pale skin looked sickly, and she kept worrying the broken skin around her fingernails. "There must be tunnels running through the hills."

As they drew up to the tree-lined streets, the awrig slowed. It came to a final stop at the end of the main boulevard, and the faint hum of its propulsion working faded. In the quiet that followed, the sound of insects rang loud: the hissing of cicadas, the low, irregular rasp of bush crickets. There were no people around. A flock of green birds pecked at the soil along the edge of the road.

"What now?" asked Haeki.

Karys shouldered her pack, and pushed open the door. The air outside was hot and dry. She climbed down from the vehicle.

"We find Ferain's relatives," she said.

Neither Winola nor Haeki questioned this, although Karys caught them exchanging a meaningful look. Didn't matter. Her plan might have flaws, but she would deal with each problem as it arose. One step and then the next. She needed to make contact with Ferain's father before they reached Eludia. For that, she needed to use his family's communication relic. For that, she needed to find his relatives. If she kept things simple, momentum would carry her. Thinking any further ahead was . . . She dug her nails into her palms. Unnecessary.

"He mentioned that his aunt ran a lodge near Tuschait," she said. "There can't be that many around here. We'll just have to ask."

Emptied of its passengers, Vuhas' awrig produced a small sigh. It glided away slowly, back in the direction they had come.

Many of the buildings along the main boulevard were shuttered; old shops and cafés locked up and empty, the paint peeling from signs hung above their doors. The town looked more lived-in as they walked south; a few people sat on benches, or else swept well-kept yards filled with rows of potted plants. At every junction, large stone elephants held up signs bearing the streets' names—Serenity, Peace, Joy. Smaller elephants guarded private doorsteps, trunks raised in greeting. Some wore homemade sunhats or scarves.

The door to a cramped curio shop on Peace Street stood open. It seemed a good place to ask for directions, so Winola went in and rang the bell on the counter. From the rear of the building, a man shouted something unintelligible. A moment later, he appeared through the fringed curtain between two stacking cabinets, looking flustered.

"Hello," he said. "How can I help you?"

Karys and Haeki pretended to browse the dusty wares while Winola did the talking. Her ordinary Mercian accent was conspicuously absent; she spoke with a slight Toraigian lilt, introducing them as travellers. The man listened to her intently. He was middle-aged, short, and had large brown eyes. He nodded a lot.

"It's wonderful to see visitors during the off-season," he said. "These days, Tuschait usually only expects guests during early spring—for the canola flowers, you know? How long do you suppose you'll stay?"

His tone suggested that he hoped the answer would be "forever." Karys wandered over to the window display, where a velvet case of tarnished silver jewellery was turning grey with dust. Impatience gnawed at her, but it was better that Winola handle this. She suspected the man's enthusiasm might evaporate if he realised they were Mercian. She leaned closer to the display, feigning interest in a swallow-shaped pendant. To her left, Haeki riffled through a crate of moth-eaten scarves.

"Not too long," said Winola vaguely. "We were hoping to stay at a lodge nearby. We heard that it's run by the Taliade family?"

The man hesitated. "The only lodge still open belongs to Malika and Frere Agonasis. The others, well . . ." He gave a little shrug. "They couldn't really operate without the Auric. Now that sightings are so rare, demand has dried up. It's been a hard blow for all of Tuschait."

Winola made a sympathetic noise. "I can imagine."

That must be the place. Presumably a branch of Ferain's family with a different last name. Karys felt a grim satisfaction—fortunate, for there to be only one lodge; it would save them some time. Progress. Now she just had to find these people and convince them to help her.

"Very sad," the man affirmed. "Business has suffered. A lot of people left, those that could afford to, but the rest of us persevere. It's a good town."

"Oh, I can see that. It's very peaceful here."

The man smiled. "Tusch's lingering influence, we like to say. Do you need help reaching the lodge?"

"If you could point us in the right direction . . ."

"No, no, I'd be happy to take you myself. Let me just go ask my brother. We've got an old wagon, and he's probably not using it right now. I won't be long."

"We couldn't—"

He waved his hand, already walking toward the door. "No trouble at all. Just one moment."

As he left, Winola glanced at Karys. She made an enquiring gesture.

"Must be the right place," said Karys.

Winola moved closer to the window. "Ferain didn't mention the name 'Agonasis' to you?"

"Not that I can remember. But if it's the only lodge, then it has to be them."

"Hm." A pause. "He hasn't . . . ?"

"Not yet."

Winola studied a display of carved figurines. She brushed the dust from the back of a tiny yellowwood elephant, and lowered her voice. "This is—Karys, I know you're taking this hard, but you've got to be realistic."

Karys kept her face blank. "How so?"

"We should find the station and head to Eludia directly. These Agonasis people won't listen to you, especially not without proof that Ferain is alive."

There was a heavy weight in the pit of her stomach. She turned away.

"Karys . . ."

"They'll listen," she said shortly. "I'm going to wait outside."

The shopkeeper returned a few minutes later, leading two old mules hitched to an ancient wagon. He whistled cheerfully, and smiled at Karys as he drew up to the store.

"I'll just lock up, and then we'll be on our way," he said. "Your name was . . ."

She spoke carefully, stretching the vowels a little. "Marishka. And yours?"

"Hetan. It's a pleasure to meet you."

She nodded. "Likewise."

Less than a mile from Tuschait, the orderly patchwork of fields gave way to the wilderness once more. Burbling streams crisscrossed the road, the larger ones spanned by creaking wooden bridges. Thickets of fleshy-leaved purslane trees grew in abundance, and the clouds hung over the sky like lambs' wool. Although it was growing later, the air remained the same: warm and breathless.

As they rolled along the track, Hetan talked easily. He seemed to have overcome his earlier nerves, and spoke with a natural warmth and charm, detailing local history and customs, telling jokes. It was simple enough to let him carry the conversation. Winola asked a question from time to time, and Haeki nodded without saying much. Karys watched the shadows of the hills grow longer.

She wasn't being unrealistic. In fact, under the circumstances, her position was the only rational one. The only option that made any sense. Because if she followed Winola's logic to its inevitable conclusion, then she wouldn't even bother going to Eludia. She would just give up. Just . . . stop.

"The family tried a breeding program about a decade ago," said Hetan. "They brought in Eludia's most renowned animal workings practitioners; it must have cost an absolute fortune. It was never going to work, but for a while we got our hopes up. Sad, very sad."

To come all this way, to drag Haeki and Winola all this way, for nothing? A trail of dead bodies in her wake, her savings drained, her life uprooted, indebted to Rasko, haunted by skin thieves—for nothing? She could not accept that. She could hardly bear thinking about it.

Or about him.

"There are still sightings, but the animals lost something when Tusch died. Or maybe they're just old and tired now. I've seen them, of course, but they keep their distance and almost never show up for the guests." Hetan pointed at the road ahead. "There you go. Sanctuary Lodge."

Karys looked around. The mules were labouring over the ridge; the road beyond dipped into a sheltered valley, and there, hugging the slope of the hill, was the lodge. The main building sat between two rows of timber chalets, all perched on stilts and overlooking a dark lake. From a distance, the water appeared black, except where the late sunshine caught its wind-rippled surface and unspooled in ribbons of gold. Thickets of acacia and fever trees grew along the water's edge, and the slopes of the hillside waved with grass like yellow hair.

"Pretty, isn't it?" said Hetan. "And the Agonasis family was Favoured, you know. Back in the day. Ah, look, Old Panlo's coming out to welcome us."

A thin man with pale skin was walking up the road toward them, accompanied by a large grey dog with drooping jowls. When Hetan waved, the man nodded in acknowledgement. He looked to be in his late eighties, but moved with great poise and dignity.

"I brought you company," called Hetan, as he drew up to the stable yard. There was only one other vehicle standing there, an ancient green awrig painted with yellow elephants.

Panlo nodded once more, surveying Hetan's passengers. "I see so. Welcome to Sanctuary Lodge, dear guests. My name is Panlo Imest, and I am the house steward here. How may I serve you today?"

"It's a pleasure to meet you," said Winola. She climbed down from the wagon, and dusted off her clothes. The dog wandered over to her, tail wagging slowly. She scratched behind his ears. "We were hoping to speak to Malika and Frere Agonasis? I believe we're friends with a member of their family."

Panlo's expression did not change, but his voice grew more guarded.

"I'm afraid that won't be possible," he said.

Karys' stomach sank. She swung down from the wagon. "Why not?"

Panlo's eyes settled on her, and he frowned a little. "Cas and casin Agonasis are away on business for the next month. As it is the off-season, I'm serving as the lodge's caretaker during their absence."

"A month?" Karys felt the ground crumbling beneath her feet. "That can't—a *month?*"

"Indeed." Panlo's frown deepened. "Cas, may I ask where you are from? Did you travel far to reach us?"

"Quite far," said Winola quickly. "From Basamat, actually; we're making a tour of the countryside. Is there any way we might contact the Agonasises? Our business with them is urgent."

Panlo was suspicious now, and even Hetan was beginning to look uncomfortable. "If you would like to leave a message with me, I could write them a letter, but I can't guarantee a response. May I ask which family member you are friends with?"

"Ferain Taliade," supplied Winola. "From Eludia?"

He shook his head. "I can't say I'm familiar with the name."

Is this the wrong lodge? Karys felt sick. She needed forward momentum, she needed to keep moving; the thought of remaining too long in one place filled her with dread. Maybe Hetan had been mistaken, maybe there was another resort nearby. Or maybe Panlo did not know the family that well. Her skin was cold, even standing in the sun. Why hadn't she asked Ferain about any of this?

"Panlo?"

A girl—tall, brown-skinned, doe-eyed—poked her head out of the door to the main building. She was probably around sixteen, with a round face and expressive mouth. She smiled brightly at the sight of the small crowd gathered in the yard.

"Oh, guests!" she said. "Hello!"

Panlo's jaw tightened, and his eyebrows drew together. He inclined his head politely toward Winola.

"Would you excuse me one moment?" he asked. "I must speak with—"

"No one *ever* turns up during the off-season." The girl practically bounced as she walked toward them. "Don't look so sour, Panlo. I won't forgive you if you scare these nice people off. Hi, Hetan."

Hetan gave her a weak smile. "Hello, cas."

"Lindlee." Panlo's voice was strained. "A word?"

She ignored him, sunny and unbothered. "Welcome, honoured guests, to Sanctuary Lodge—where rooms are always available. What brings you to the middle of nowhere? I'm Lindlee Agonasis, by the way. My parents own the place, so I'm trapped here until term starts."

Karys' stomach fluttered. If this girl was the owners' daughter, if there was still a chance that the Agonasises were related to Ferain . . .

"Please can we use your family's communication relic?" she asked abruptly.

The girl blinked.

"Uh . . . why?" she asked. "How do you know about that?"

Where to even start? "I need to . . . I have to contact the Taliade household. It's important. Ferain Taliade told me to come here. He said his family would help us."

"This is preposterous," said Panlo.

Karys kept her eyes on Lindlee. "I'll pay whatever you want. Please."

"Ferain?" Lindlee pursed her lips. "I think I had a second or third cousin who . . . What are his parents' names?"

Shit. "I—"

"No, this has gone far enough." Panlo quivered with suppressed outrage. "You will not harass my charge any further. We cannot help you, cas, and I must ask you to leave now."

Lindlee scoffed, and cast the old man a remonstrative glance. "Don't be such a prig, Panlo. It's late, and Hetan brought them all the way here. Do you want them to sleep in the bush?"

He held his head high. "That is not our concern. Frankly, we don't know who these people are, where they have come from—"

"Isn't that part of running a lodge?"

"—and your parents left me responsible for your safety."

"And they left *me* responsible for taking care of guests." Lindlee folded her arms. "Or maybe that was just talk? Come on, we're supposed to be hospitable. Think of Sanctuary's reputation."

The way she pronounced the word suggested that it was an ongoing point of contention. Panlo's nostrils flared and displeasure radiated from him in waves, but he said nothing. The dog gave a small, unhappy whine. Lindlee turned her attention back to Karys.

"You wanted to use the relic?" she said.

Karys nodded. "Yes, to reach Ferain's father."

"Come inside, then. I'll show you around the lodge, and see what I can do. I haven't used the relic very much, but I'm sure I can figure it out."

"Thank you," said Karys.

Panlo grumbled, and turned away. He snapped his fingers, and the dog obediently trailed after him. Hetan muttered a sheepish goodbye.

"We appreciate your help," said Winola.

He winced, and clucked his tongue at the mules.

It was dark and quiet inside the lodge. The black eyes of taxidermied buffalo glinted from high up the rough-plastered walls, and the pungent smells of varnish, leather, and thatch hung in the air. Stacks of wood were piled beside an enormous fireplace, but the grating was clean, as if it had not been used in some time. Bare tables stood below the windows, leading out onto a viewing deck for the lake. Everything was swept and tidy, if a little austere. Woven reed tapestries hung from the walls, and worn animal skins dressed the floor.

Panlo marched straight down the hall, his shoulders rigid and his steps loud. Lindlee watched him go, and doubt briefly flickered across her young face—she looked like she wanted to call after him. Then she shook her head, and rallied.

"Don't mind him," she said, turning to Karys. "He'll come around."

In truth, Karys did not care. It was clear what Panlo thought of her, but so long as Lindlee was willing to help, the caretaker did not matter. "I—sorry for the trouble. Ferain said his father wouldn't meet us in Eludia unless—"

"No, no, don't worry." Lindlee waved both hands. "This is the most interesting thing that's happened in weeks; I've been wasting away out here on my own. Well, not really on my *own;* there's Panlo and Ree, and Cook Marvis, and Oma of course, but *almost* on my own."

"Your parents left you in charge?" asked Winola.

"Sort of." Lindlee let out a long-suffering sigh. "They want me to take over the lodge one day. This is supposed to be practice."

A sudden bolt of hot pain ran through Karys' jaw. She automatically brought her hand up to the soft triangle of skin below her left ear.

"Karys?" said Haeki.

There was nothing there. As quickly as the sensation appeared, it was gone again. She lowered her fingers. Rasko had told her she had a week in Varesli to make the delivery. This was probably his idea of encouragement. *Bastard.*

"Something wrong?" asked Lindlee.

"No, it's nothing. I just—" Karys broke off, struck by an awful thought.

The parcel. Winola had said that Ferain took it, that he gave it to Vuhas as a distraction. Karys had been so exhausted that morning, it had never even occurred to her to check, but . . . *Did we leave it behind?*

"Actually, is there a washroom I could use?" she asked.

"Of course," said Lindlee. "Just to the left of the kitchen, over there. Are you all right?"

"Fine." A great yawning feeling opened up inside Karys. Her heart thumped. She could not go back. Whatever happened, she could not go back. She wanted to rip off her pack and tear through it right there on the floor. "You all go ahead. I'll catch up."

The washroom was warm and spacious. High windows flooded the space with light, and dust motes swirled through the air. Four white basins and a dressing table stood against the far wall, everything painted in contrasting shades of pale blue and orange. It smelled of soap.

Karys shut the door, strode across the room, and dumped her pack on the table. She fumbled with the clasps. Embrace, how could she have been so careless? If the parcel wasn't here, how would she ever get it back? Stupid, so stupid. It would have cost *nothing* to check that morning. She threw open the flap, and shoved aside her clothing. *Please. Please let it be here. I can't—*

The box lay on top of her spare shirt.

Karys' muscles went weak with relief. She braced herself against the table, breathing heavily. Safe. Whatever else happened, she did not need to go back to that place. She could keep moving forward. The thought was dizzying; her heartbeat resounded in her ears. No need to go back to Vuhas. If she ever saw the man again, she did not know what she would do to him.

Down the side of the bag, against the canvas lining, was something else. Something new. Shaking, she picked it up.

The clear glass phial was roughly the length of her hand from index finger to wrist. It had an unusual weight, much lighter than it appeared. The neck spiralled as it tapered, the stopper was delicately fluted. There was nothing remarkable about it otherwise. A scrap of paper had been shoved inside, the torn-out page of an old book.

Karys unscrewed the seal, and pulled out the paper. A short message was written in black ink on the one side. The words were almost illegible.

Not 15000, but something.

Karys stared at the page. That was all that was written there. The final 'g' slanted violently, as if the hand writing it had slipped. The other letters were shaky, uncertain.

It's done, Ferain whispered in her memory, his voice desolate.

She turned, and hurled the phial against the wall.

It hit the tiles with a sharp crack, and fell to the ground. Despite the force of the blow, the glass did not shatter. The phial bounced and rolled, coming to a rattling stop at the foot of the basin nearest the door. Not so much as scratched.

Beneath Karys' fingers, the yellowed paper crumpled. She did not make a sound. The silence was all around, growing louder, ringing inside of her, inescapable, impossible to ignore, cold and empty and final. She could feel the ridges of the balled page inside her fist. He was gone. Her shadow was a dead thing at her feet.

It's done.

She felt so angry, so unspeakably angry. The feeling lit her up from the inside, burning through her body like dry tinder. She could not move, could not speak. If the fire went out, she sensed that there would be nothing left of her, nothing but grief clawing through her chest like a blind animal.

It's done.

She did not know how to bring him back.

The washroom door swung open.

"Hey," said Lindlee. "So, I thought I'd check if you need a drink . . ."

She stopped at the threshold, and her smile faded as she took in the room. Her gaze flicked to the open pack on the dresser, then back to Karys' face. In one hand, she held a glass of water with a slice of lemon in it.

"Should I . . . call someone?" she asked.

Karys pressed the back of her hand to her mouth, hard. She shook her head. "It's nothing," she muttered.

Lindlee's expression was dubious. "Well, you said that before, but you've gone really pale. Maybe you should sit down."

"I'm fine." Karys turned around. She closed her pack, began fixing the clasps. "Thank you for the water. You're very kind."

"Hold on, I think you dropped this."

Karys glanced back, and found Lindlee crouching to pick up the phial.

"It must have fallen out of your bag." Straightening, she offered it to Karys. "I'm surprised it didn't smash. Lucky."

Karys hesitated a second, then took the phial. "Thanks."

The sound of wind chimes drifted through the open door. The noise was not loud, but it had a pure, piercing quality, a clarity like water. Lindlee started. A strange puzzlement crossed her face, and she turned quickly toward the foyer. Then she looked back at Karys.

"Oh," she said, and her voice held an odd mix of curiosity and pity. "Oh, you're the one who called them, aren't you?"

"Called who?"

Lindlee didn't seem to hear the question. She walked toward the door.

"Come with me," she said.

The sun was setting over the hills beyond the deck, dazzlingly bright. Side by side and silhouetted in yellow, Haeki and Winola gazed down at the lake. Lindlee led Karys out to join them. The air had cooled; a breeze whispered through the trees and the tall grass. The chimes tinkled gently from the eaves.

From a distance, the animals seemed to be shaped from liquid gold—from trunk to tail, their skins were a numinous shade of platinum. Their shadows appeared black as night beside that glow; they came along the shore of the lake, leaving round prints in the mud. They walked slowly, quietly; there were nine of them, each around ten feet tall.

"The main herd," murmured Lindlee. "It's the first time I've seen them this year."

The elephants were so graceful and lovely, so otherworldly in the twilight with the banks of bronzed cloud overhead and the shifting water at their feet, the trees rustling in the wind. They gradually made their way toward the lodge, then stopped and gathered closer to one another. Even from a distance, Karys sensed the animals' attention. They were waiting.

"The last of their kind," said Lindlee. Her voice was low and dreamy. "Tusch's gift: our golden empaths. People used to come from everywhere to see them, to get close to them. When I was a kid, my parents tried to work ordinary elephants into Auric. They could make the animals gold, but the empathy? Never that. It was cruel, all those poor gilded fakes. It was never the same."

Down below, the elephants fanned their ears, but were otherwise quite still.

"They're beautiful," whispered Winola.

"Yes." Lindlee turned from the scene, and smiled. "They come when needed. This way."

A small footpath wound around the side of the building, through the scrub and down the slope of the hill. Swallows wove through the air, quick and sure, swooping for insects that flew up from the grass. Frogs croaked in the water ahead.

Lindlee's steps were light as she led the way. Karys followed Haeki and Winola. She felt strange, outside of herself. The world seemed vast and fragile around her: the touch of the air on her skin, the fall of the light on the grass. And ahead, the elephants. Their shining bodies moved with the breath of their great lungs. They waited. It did not occur to Karys to fear them; it would be like fearing the lake or the trees or the sky. Their eyes were large and sensitive, framed by long black lashes. When Lindlee reached the base of the hill, one of them—a female—stepped away from the herd and moved slowly toward her.

"Hello," said Lindlee.

The elephant huffed. Her skin was wrinkled and creased, and the subtle light she exuded moved in barely perceptible waves, as if she existed underwater. She extended her trunk, and, with extreme care, tapped the girl on the head. Lindlee laughed. The rest of the herd approached, unhurried. They smelled like sun-soaked leather and dry grass and mud.

The female took another step, moving past Lindlee. Her dark eyes settled on Winola, and she cautiously stretched out her trunk in greeting.

Winola abruptly shook her head. She backed away.

"No," she said. "No, I don't deserve this. Not now. Not anymore."

Her voice was raw. The elephant made a rumbling sound, and lowered her trunk. Winola continued to shake her head, stumbling backwards through the grass. She knocked into Haeki and flinched, but her gaze remained fixed on the animal.

Haeki's face was calm. She looked down at Winola with an expression Karys had not seen before: clear-eyed, her features both soft and focussed. She reached out and took hold of the scholar's wrist.

Winola breathed in sharply. Before she could protest, Haeki lifted her hand, raising it toward the elephant. The movement was smooth and quick, but not forceful—although Winola tensed, she did not pull away. Her arm trembled, a single shiver that travelled from her wrist to the ends of her outstretched fingertips. For a moment they simply stood like that, close and quiet. A lock of Haeki's hair blew across her shoulder, brushing Winola's cheek.

More tentative now, the Auric reached out again. Winola shut her eyes briefly. When the elephant's trunk met her palm, she made a choked noise, and, all at once, something inside her seemed to give way. Her body eased like a sigh, the muscles in her shoulders unwinding. When Haeki released her wrist, she did not drop her hand.

Small and pale, Winola gazed up at the Auric. The elephant breathed slow, and she exhaled in time. She was crying. She did not make a sound as the tears ran down her face.

"Sorry," she said. "I'm sorry."

The rest of the herd drew closer, and their glow suffused the air. A large male approached Haeki; without fear or hesitation, she reached up and patted the curve of his tusk. Cool air shivered through the trees further along the water's edge. The lake pooled orange with the last of the sunlight, and the sky through the clouds was an insubstantial blue, almost grey.

A smaller female turned her head toward Karys. The elephant's midnight eyes were ancient and penetrating, drawing in the world, laying its beauty bare. The hair lifted off the back of Karys' arms. With the Auric's concentrated attention upon her, everything else fell away. Her mind had gone still, and she was conscious only of a heavy, aching longing.

Shaking slightly, she lifted her hand.

The Auric blinked. Meeting her gaze felt like staring into the depths of the ocean—fathomless, those eyes. She regarded Karys in silence, and something changed in the air: a current shifting. For a second, the great ageless creature appeared unsure.

Then she turned away.

The other elephants moved slowly around one another, a few breaking toward the water to drink. Karys let her hand fall back to her side. She did not move; she stood untouched among the quiet giants. No one else had seen the denial.

The Auric were a herald's gift, the Embrace's creatures. She was Ephirite-touched; she could expect no grace. She knew that. And she would never have taken this moment away from Haeki or Winola. The Auric, the sky, the water. The breeze in the fever trees, the whisper of the grass, the intimacy they now shared.

In her left fist, Karys still held Ferain's crumpled note. She gripped it tighter. She had never felt more alone.

Karys woke, aware that something had changed.

With the curtains drawn, the room was dim. Winola and Haeki were sleeping in the main lodge, but there had not been enough rooms readily available, so Lindlee had suggested Karys take one of the freestanding cottages at a discount. She had an enormous bed to herself, piled with blankets too warm for the climate, and a small deck overlooking the lake. Birds twittered outside the window. Judging by the light, the sun was up. On the wall above her head hung yet another taxidermied trophy—a waterbuck—which gazed morosely down at her tangled sheets.

"It gets very boring," said Ferain. "The sleeping."

Karys' breath caught. She sat up quickly.

"You have no idea the number of hours I spend staring at wallpaper." Her shadow was seated on top of the headboard. "And you don't even do anything amusing. Snore or talk, I don't know—"

"Ferain," she interrupted, and then found she could say nothing more. Her chest felt painfully tight. He sounded normal, the same as he had before they ever met Vuhas.

"Oh, what's that face?" He slipped down from his perch onto the bed next to her. His voice turned a little sly. "Did you miss me?"

He really was back. A storm raged inside Karys—the violent internal pressure crushing her lungs was spreading, filling up her whole body. Too much, she was overcome. Instead of answering him, she rolled over and snatched the crumpled note off her bedside table. She thrust it toward her shadow.

"What," she asked huskily, "is this?"

"Not the reaction I was hoping for."

"You—" Karys stopped, closed her eyes, and took a breath to steady herself. She tried again. "What were you thinking?"

"It wasn't clear?" He sounded surprised. "I thought you could sell the relic in Eludia, make back some of the cret I—"

"No, you stupid fucking idiot, I understood *that*. I'm asking how you could . . ." Karys had to pause again, her throat locking up. She had the awful sense that she might start to cry. "How could you worry about something so *stupid*?"

Ferain's tone was mildly affronted. "It's not stupid; it was meant to be insurance. Why are you mad at me?"

Because I didn't want insurance! She bunched the sheet beneath her hands. Insurance meant Ferain had *known* he might not come back. He had planned for it. She was so relieved to hear his voice again, but at the same time she wanted to strangle him. "You think all that matters to me is your money."

"Do I?"

"You saw inside my head, and you still—"

"The money *is* important to you," he said. "Which is why it mattered to me. I didn't want to leave you with nothing."

Karys made a sound of frustration, and buried her face in her hands. The room felt too hot. He was back—that was the important part. Why was she feeling all of this now? She spoke into her palms. "I was worried out of my mind."

There was a faint pull inside her chest, and her shadow nudged her arm.

"I'm here now," he said.

Outside, the birds continued to sing. A dog barked from the direction of the main lodge. Ferain's nearness, the cool weight of his presence, seemed more pronounced after his absence.

"I thought you might be dead," Karys muttered.

He did not reply. After a moment, she lowered her hands. Her shadow was still lying on the bed beside her, soft-edged in the low light.

"Winola told me what you did," she said.

He gave a small shrug.

"Embrace, Ferain. How did you pull that off?"

"To be fair, it was mostly Winola."

"That's not how she made it sound." She shook her head. "Vuhas' security workings? How did you convince him to disable them?"

Ferain stretched as if stiff. Her silhouette spread long and distorted. "I asked nicely."

"What?"

Her shadow returned to its usual shape. When he spoke, it was with a certain reluctance. "I know men like Vuhas. He wanted me to be grateful, so I gave him gratitude. He wanted to be my saviour, so I was saved. Really, all it took was flattery."

"I don't understand."

"That's because there isn't much *to* understand. I asked how his house was protected, and he showed me." A pause. "Well, I suppose I did also get him a little drunk first. But it turned out that his worked defences were interlinked, so if he commanded one derivation to stand down, the others followed. He gave a demonstration."

"Just like that?"

Her shadow shrugged again. "The easiest person to manipulate is the one who wants to use you."

Karys frowned. She remembered the look on Winola's face when the scholar had described Ferain that night. *He made it seem so effortless.* "Use you for what?"

"Social influence. Vuhas is a climber, but he's fallen out of favour with his friends, so he needs new, loyal allies. Who better than a man who owes him everything?" Ferain sighed heavily. "And he also has a . . . well, a certain fascination regarding Ambavar. I imagine that he saw me as a curiosity worth collecting."

"I still can't believe he would be that careless."

"He felt safe. Anyway, I fawned over him, was so *honoured* by his trust, asked to see his relic collection . . ." Her shadow waved one hand to encompass everything else. "And here we are."

He acted like it had been simple—easy—to manipulate a paranoid, centuries-old skin thief. Karys had always known that Ferain was a good liar, but this went way beyond smooth-talking. He kept it hidden most of the time, but the man in her shadow could be just as sharp and calculating as any in the Grateful Society, and far more subtle. Far more dangerous than he allowed other people to perceive. *Here we are.*

"What's worrying you?" he asked.

Karys picked up his note again and smoothed it against her leg. The ink was smudged, the thin paper creased to leathery softness. "You don't think Vuhas will object to us robbing him?"

"Winola encouraged him not to notice anything out of the ordinary."

She snorted. "'Encouraged.'"

"She did what she could. Unless someone specifically draws his attention to that relic, he'll never suspect anything is amiss. He'll just look right past the phial I left in its place. See what he expects to see."

Karys carefully folded the paper in two, then into four. She set it back on the bedside table. There was more she wanted to say, but she was not sure how. "I should tell the others you're back."

"Where are they?"

"At the main lodge." She smiled slightly. "Probably wondering why I'm taking so long to get out of bed."

"A question that's very often on my mind."

She swatted her shadow, and he laughed.

The lake gleamed like a mirror to the morning sky. Winola and Haeki were sitting at one of the tables out on the deck, eating breakfast and talking. Haeki's hair hung long and damp down her back, newly washed, and she appeared relaxed, almost lazy—she lounged in a chair with her legs outstretched to catch the sun. Winola seemed better rested too; the circles under her eyes had faded, and her face had regained some of its former animation.

"So she *didn't* show herself to the rest of the village?" she asked.

"No. Just to me."

"And you didn't tell anyone?"

"Never."

"Weren't you tempted?"

Haeki chewed her lip. "Maybe once or twice—Ané was very irritating. Mostly, I wanted to tell Oboro."

"Karys' brother?"

"Yes, her older brother. We were close. In the end, he was the only one that I still . . ." Haeki saw Karys approaching, and stopped. She straightened in her chair, then muttered something to Winola. The scholar's head swivelled around.

"I didn't want to interrupt—" began Karys.

Winola spoke over her. "Is it true? Ferain's back?"

Karys came to a startled halt. "How did you know?"

The trace of a smirk crossed Haeki's face. She leaned back and folded her arms. "You were smiling."

That didn't seem like much of an answer, but Karys had no opportunity to question it—Ferain shifted a few degrees out of her shadow's correct alignment, intersecting with the mingled shade beneath the table and chairs.

"Hello again, Winola," he said. "Haeki."

Winola's grin lit up her face. She dropped her half-eaten toast onto her plate. "Ferain! Oh, that's such a relief. You really scared us."

Haeki gave a single guarded nod. "Reeker."

"Are you all right? We weren't sure when you might come back."

"I'm fine." Ferain's tone was oddly formal. Stiff. His discomfort set Karys on edge; she had seldom known him to be nervous, let alone awkward. "I regret that I worried you. And that I . . . that I ever put you in that position."

Winola's cheer faded; her expression grew tired, and a little sad. She exhaled and shook her head, turning toward the lake. A few slender antelope drank at the water's edge. Sleek brown ibises waded in the shallows.

"It's done now," she said. "It can't be taken back. And you got what you wanted, didn't you?"

"Not in the way that I wanted it. I'm sorry, Winola."

She watched the animals. "Any lingering effects?"

"Not as far as I can tell."

"Good. Let me know if that changes." She adjusted her glasses, then glanced at Karys sidelong. Unexpectedly, the corners of her mouth curved upwards. It was not clear what had amused her, but when she spoke again, it was in Toraigian. Without Ferain inside her head, Karys could not understand the scholar.

"Of course," said Ferain, surprised. "Whatever you like. What is it?"

Winola tilted her head to the side, resting her chin against her palm. She asked a short question.

Karys' shadow flinched.

"What's wrong?" asked Karys quickly.

Winola made a quelling gesture. Her gaze remained on the floorboards of the deck, observing Ferain. She asked the question again, tone light. She might have been making a joke, except that Ferain's reaction made no sense; he had gone dead still. Winola did not press further. She only waited.

There was a long silence.

"Yes," he whispered at last.

The scholar's expression softened. She gave a small, satisfied nod.

"Suspected as much," she said.

"What are you talking about?" asked Karys.

"Oh, nothing important. Indulging my curiosity, that's all." Winola picked up her toast again. "Do you want something to eat? There's food in the kitchen, and Lindlee said we should help ourselves."

The evasion was blatant and shameless. Karys fixed the scholar with a hard look. In response, Winola took a bite of her toast, nonchalant, and raised an eyebrow.

"Aren't you hungry?" she asked.

Karys grunted irritably, and moved to investigate the kitchen.

There was a loaf of bread, a bowl of fruit, and a selection of chutneys and jams. The pan on the stove was still warm; Karys cut three slices of bread and arranged them on the hot, greased surface. While they browned, she peeled a large orange and divided it into segments, lining up each piece in a curve along the edge of her plate. Her stomach growled; melted butter spat and fizzled in the pan. After a while, she found she was humming tunelessly to herself. She stopped, embarrassed, but Ferain didn't comment on it. He seemed distracted.

She had transferred her toast onto her plate, and was slathering each piece with additional butter and a smooth apple jam, when Lindlee breezed into the kitchen. The teenager wore a flowing yellow and grey skirt, a fitted white blouse, and a ridiculous blue sunhat that flopped down over half her face.

"Good morning!" she said, and hopped up onto the countertop. "You're looking so much better!"

Karys was unsure if anyone had ever greeted her as enthusiastically, and found the experience slightly unnerving. Lindlee swished her skirt from side to side, kicking her feet. She smiled.

"You're welcome, by the way," she said.

Karys looked down at her plate. *Was three too many?* "Winola said we could use the food in the kitchen?"

"Oh." The girl waved a dismissive hand. "Sure, no problem. Cook will be in later, but take whatever you want."

"Who is this?" whispered Ferain.

"Thank you," said Karys.

Lindlee rocked back on the counter. "Well, someone has to be hospitable around here, and Panlo is still sulking. But I wasn't talking about *that*."

Karys knew she was supposed to ask, so she did. "What were you talking about?"

"Eludia."

"What about it?"

Lindlee's smugness was unmistakable. She adjusted her hat, eyes glittering. "The train arrives later this morning, and I'm going with you. It's all taken care of; I got permission from my parents, and my uncle's going to reimburse us for the tickets. Panlo will have to take care of the lodge on his own."

Karys felt baffled. "Why?"

"Why what?"

"Why are you coming with us to Eludia?"

"So I can escape Tuschait until term starts, of course." She laughed. "It's perfect. Uncle Rhevin asked me to escort you to the city."

"That's my father," said Ferain.

Several things clicked into place. "Wait, so you figured out how to use the communication relic? Ferain's father is willing to talk to us?"

"Yes, very willing—he was really worried about his son, actually. Something about a ship late to arrive in Cosaris. Anyway, he'll be expecting us at the station."

Relief washed over Karys. Based on Ferain's descriptions, she had expected his father to be suspicious and reclusive; she had anticipated arguing with the man, or at least being forced to provide proof that she knew his son personally. This was almost too simple.

Outside the kitchen, someone spoke in a quavering voice. "Linus?"

Lindlee's smile disappeared, and her legs stopped swinging.

"Who are these people, Linus?" demanded the voice, drawing closer to the kitchen. "Are they guests? Where are all the guests?"

Lindlee slipped down from the counter. She seemed to deflate before Karys' eyes, her brightness and confidence seeping away. A diminutive woman appeared in the doorway. The newcomer looked old and frail; she had coils of stark white hair and dark wrinkled skin. Her gaze was unfocussed, her expression distressed.

"Yes, Oma," said Lindlee. "They are guests."

"You must show them the Auric, Linus."

"It's Lindlee now, Oma. Remember?"

The woman seemed not to hear. She squinted at Karys. "The kitchen is not for guests. You don't belong here."

"Sorry, I didn't mean to intrude." Karys moved toward the door, but the woman's body blocked the way. She shrank from Karys with a whimper, and her misted eyes grew larger.

"I don't know you," she whispered. "I don't know you."

"Oma," said Lindlee, pained. She brushed past Karys, and took the old woman by the arm. "She's a guest. A friend of the family."

"Where are the elephants?" The woman pointed a trembling finger at Karys. "Oh, they won't have you. You shouldn't be here."

Lindlee steered the woman firmly out of the doorway. "A *guest*, Oma."

"Everyone comes for the elephants." Her voice rose, thin and frightened, even as Lindlee drew her away. "Where are all the guests?"

Lindlee's reassurances, pitched low and soothing, faded. Alone in the kitchen again, Karys looked down at her plate of orange segments and toast, now stone cold. *Three slices of bread was excessive.* She had not intended to trespass, or to intrude on Lindlee's privacy. The girl clearly hadn't wanted Karys to see any of that, and the old woman probably believed there was a foreign thief raiding her kitchen.

And . . . and Karys could have sworn that no one had witnessed the Auric reject her. But it was as if the woman *knew*, as if she could sense a moral deficiency in Karys, as if that spiritual deformity was evident even to ordinary—

Her shadow flowed up from the floor and tapped her shoulder.

"You should eat," said Ferain, his voice surprisingly gentle.

"Right." Karys shook herself. "Yes. Just thinking."

"Less thinking, more toast."

She swatted him away again.

In any case, it didn't matter. Karys carried her plate out onto the deck and sat down next to Haeki. She had her priorities. Ferain was safe, and they were headed to Eludia. The obstacles in her path had melted away—for once, things were going *right*. If everything continued to fall into place, then, maybe, they could be unbound in a matter of days.

The thought made her feel as though she were standing on a high ledge with the wind whistling around her, the drop yawning at her feet. Strange. She should be eager. They had come so far, and the money was itchingly close, and, despite everything, they were both still alive. And yet she didn't really know what she felt. Uneasy, maybe. Maybe the situation just seemed too good to be true, and maybe their separation would take longer than expected. There was no guarantee that Ferain's father would have an immediate solution to the problem of the locked Split Lapse, and besides, they had to find a way to cure Ferain first. It would be complicated, all of it. It would take time.

"Problem?" asked Haeki.

Karys started on her breakfast. Even cold, it tasted good.

"No," she said. "Everything is fine."

35

As Winola had guessed, Tuschait Station stood on the far side of town. The terminus was overgrown and deserted; when they arrived, the only other person present was the station manager. The woman sat alone inside her musty office, and sniffed disapprovingly when Lindlee wafted through the door to buy tickets. Panlo hovered like a thundercloud behind his young charge, teeth grinding audibly. Lindlee seemed too happy to notice.

They had all travelled down from the lodge in the old green awrig painted with elephants. Panlo insisted on accompanying them, and spent the full duration of the trip watching Karys with undisguised mistrust. She ignored him. Her jaw had started to ache again, less sharply but more persistently than before, and she did not want anyone to know about it. Lindlee chattered away about Eludia.

They stopped briefly in the town so that Panlo could send a letter, most likely a complaint addressed to Lindlee's parents. Haeki wandered off alone, claiming that she wanted to stretch her legs. Still prickly, she had been distant ever since Ferain's return. Karys waited with Winola and Lindlee under a tree in the town square.

"Most of my friends live in Eludia," said Lindlee. "During term time, we all board in Notea, of course, but over the holidays that's where they go. There's Esa, the twins, Moore, Quinn, Treshi . . ."

If the teenager was still bothered by what had happened in the kitchen earlier, she did not show it. She kept adjusting her ridiculous hat, apparently finding it impossible to sit still, her excitement bright and irrepressible. While Karys had never met anyone who talked as much, she also couldn't help finding Lindlee's expressiveness rather endearing. There was something sensitive and unguarded about the girl, an open desire to please.

Haeki returned a few minutes before Panlo, and they all rode the awrig the rest of the way to the station. The building wasn't much to look at from a distance. As they drew closer, Karys realised she still could not see any tracks.

"Do the trains run under the hills?" she asked.

Panlo scoffed as if the question were ludicrous.

"It's not that sort of train," said Lindlee, more patiently. "It's worked. One of the famous northern heralds made it. Narcalis? That was before, you know . . ."

Winola leaned forward. "A prismatic train? I didn't realise they still ran in this region."

"Just between some of the smaller towns and Eludia." The awrig coasted up to the station, and Lindlee pointed. "Over there is the light catcher. I don't really understand how it works. I've only made the trip twice."

The light catcher was a diamond-shaped metal cage that surrounded a floating black orb. It stood just past the end of the platform; Karys had initially taken it for some kind of emergency stopping mechanism. A single set of tracks lay half-buried in the grass, ending fifty feet beyond the station.

Lindlee went off with Panlo to organise the tickets. The morning had warmed, and flies buzzed around the dusty wooden benches along the platform. A line of ancient bulletin boards still featured yellowed posters and advertisements, now scarcely legible—lodges, tours, musical and theatrical shows. Handwritten letters had been pasted over the older notices; most seemed to be requests for employment. The whole place was empty, eerily quiet. Winola wandered to the edge of the platform, and leaned out over the tracks to study the light catcher. Then she craned her neck upwards, squinting against the sun.

"It was busier when I was fifteen," said Ferain. "Lindlee was born later that year, I think."

Karys scuffed her shoes on the weathered floor tiles. Weeds were growing through the grouting. Behind her, she could hear Lindlee asking whether any food was included in the fare. "Did you see the Auric?"

"I did. Sightings were more common back then." He hesitated. "Is Haeki all right?"

Karys gave a minute roll of her shoulders. Haeki was slouched on the bench outside the office, methodically cleaning her fingernails with a metal file. "I don't know. Better than yesterday morning, but it might take her a while to forgive you."

"Because I told Winola not to wake her."

Karys moved her head slightly in acknowledgement. Ferain sighed.

"It was the right choice," he said.

"She feels like a burden now."

"She told you that?"

Another tiny nod. Inside the office, Lindlee was counting out cret, cheerful as ever. A dry wind rattled through the station, tugging at Karys' hair. She tucked it back behind her ears. Her shadow shifted slightly at her feet.

"Ciene wanted Winola for a vessel," he said, voice low. "I'm sure you worked that out. You would have been mine, Winola would have been hers—but Haeki wasn't accounted for. She meant less than nothing to Vuhas; he would have killed her without a second's hesitation. So yes, I kept her out of harm's way. You would never have forgiven me if I hadn't."

Karys fixed her gaze ahead. "True. But my forgiveness isn't the problem."

"Tickets!" Lindlee emerged from the office, waving a small stack of papers. "We're all set. Oh, Winola, you shouldn't stand there; the train is going to arrive at any minute. I heard about a man who got decapitated leaning over the tracks like that."

The scholar stepped back smartly.

Lindlee's warning proved unnecessary: the train did not appear for another quarter of an hour. While they waited, she passed out stale sandwiches from a brown paper bag. Panlo continued to glower at everyone, and, after a few awkward minutes, Haeki got up and walked along the line of bulletin boards, pretending to read the posters.

Winola, who had been periodically glancing at the light catcher, was the first to notice the change. At her exclamation, Karys turned and saw the orb inside the cage shift from black to a deep, molten red. Then the air *creaked*. A line appeared across the blue sky: a searingly white band that grew brighter as it extended downwards to meet the light catcher. The orb turned pink, then tan, then yellow, while the band expanded until it formed a fifteen-foot wide tunnel through the air.

The train melted into existence. Gaining substance as it descended, it glided to the ground, and its wheels met the tracks with a ghostly whisper. It was not much like an ordinary train, more of a grey stone tube. Its sides tapered smoothly, windows shining black in the sunlight, and a lush sprawl of green vines sprouted from the network of hairline cracks covering its exterior surface. It slowed, slowed, and came to a quiet stop alongside the platform. With a rumble, a door near the front of the vehicle opened.

Winola gave an appreciative sigh.

"Wonderful," she said.

Curious, Karys followed Haeki to the door. The vehicle's interior resembled a cave. Pale lichen dressed the walls, while seaferns and saltmoss grew along the narrow channels of water scoured into the floor. It smelled earthy and briny and damp. Irregular stone formations formed sheltered alcoves, dividing up the space into a series of smaller chambers.

"I really thought all prismatic vehicles would have been decommissioned by now," said Winola, climbing aboard. "Even minor damage to light catchers has been known to cause itinerant material to fall out of interstitial suspension."

Karys eyed her. "You're saying the train could drop out of the air while we're in it?"

"Well, yes. But that probably won't happen."

Lindlee still stood on the platform. Panlo was talking to her, his expression strained and serious. As Karys watched, he leaned forward, kissed the girl's forehead, and then straightened her hat. Lindlee looked embarrassed, but nodded in agreement with whatever he was saying. She picked up her suitcase, gave him a quick hug, and then hurried over to join them.

"All ready?" she asked.

A deep vibration thrummed through the floor, and the door juddered closed. From the platform, Panlo gave a dignified wave. Karys suspected that he could not see them through the dark windows, but Lindlee waved back. Her gaze flicked toward Karys and Haeki.

"You know," she said, "I've heard that people in Mercia ride around inside giant spiders worked by their false heralds."

"Sounds heretical," said Haeki.

The train rolled sedately sideways along the rails. The floor tilted and then, without a hint of resistance, the vehicle slid into the air. Karys steadied herself against the wall. Panlo and the station vanished as the view outside the window dissolved into a white haze. Winola drew closer to the glass, captivated.

"I've always wanted to travel in one of these," she said. "I wonder where the navigation working is situated."

"Please don't upset the train," said Karys.

"Probably near the front of the vehicle. That would make sense."

"Winola."

"Oh, don't be so grim." Winola turned from the window. "We're almost at Eludia. Shouldn't you be happier?"

"I would actually like to *reach* Eludia."

"If you're interested, I think there's a historical exhibit near the back of the train," said Lindlee. "Old papers about Narcalis and some other heralds who gifted us transport workings. I remember reading the plaques."

"Oh?" said Winola.

"I can show you, if you want. It isn't very exciting, though."

"No, I'd like to see. Karys, Haeki?"

Haeki shrugged. "I don't mind."

Karys' jaw was throbbing in time with her heartbeat, hot and insistent. "I'll pass for now. Try not to break anything important."

"Why would I break a historical exhibit? How would I break a historical exhibit?"

Karys moved toward the alcove nearest the train door. "Just stay away from whatever is keeping this thing in the air."

"Baseless mistrust," Winola called after her.

The alcove formed a sheltered nook; the stone extruded to serve as a comfortable bench beside the window, and a soft bed of greyish-green saltmoss carpeted the floor. Karys reclined against the slope of the wall, the surface pleasantly cool against her shoulders. At her feet, water trickled along the channels scored into the rock. It smelled clean and damp, faintly minty. Through the window, the pale light of the tunnel spun in rainbows, and the spectrum played across her skin. She absentmindedly kneaded the muscles of her neck with her fingertips.

"Stiff?" asked Ferain.

"Hm." Karys let her hand fall. "Slept wrong, I guess."

Her shadow stretched out across the opposite end of the bench, extending up the wall so that he appeared to face her.

"Strange to think we're almost there, isn't it?" he said.

"Mm-hm." She studied the lichen on the wall beside her head. It looked as delicate as folded paper.

"What is it?"

"Nothing." She made an effort to relax her shoulders. "Yes, it's strange. Are you sure you're all right?"

"I could ask the same of you."

The pain in her jaw was settling, fading once more. Before they left the lodge, she had made doubly sure that Rasko's parcel was still in her bag—whatever that box contained, she needed to deliver it as soon as possible. She had also stowed Ferain's stolen relic, although she was uncertain what to do with the old phial. Selling priceless artefacts in an unfamiliar city seemed complicated.

"Can't really complain." She touched the lichen with one fingertip. Felt like feathers. "I'm about to get a lot richer, assuming you haven't conned me."

"You don't believe that."

"No. But I've been wrong before."

By his voice, Karys could tell that Ferain was smiling.

"Oh?" he said. "You have?"

"Shut up." She tried to suppress her own smile, not entirely successfully. "What did Winola ask you this morning?"

"You do realise that she spoke in Toraigian for a reason?"

"Yes, so that I wouldn't understand her."

"Very astute. I'm glad you picked that up."

"You seemed upset."

He shook his head. "I wasn't, not exactly. Just surprised."

"Ferain, come on. Tell me."

"I've been formally trained to resist interrogation. You aren't going to draw it out of me."

"What if I reduce the interest on my travel expenses?"

"It's intriguing that your next angle is bribery. Still no."

She huffed and crossed her arms, although she wasn't really upset. Her shadow sat across from her, unmoved and at ease. *He really is all right.* It was difficult to forget what Vuhas had said, but Ferain seemed so comfortable, so normal. The tension inside Karys unwound. *If he was in pain, I'd know. I'd be able to tell.*

"Can I ask a question?" she asked.

"Another one, you mean. Go ahead."

"While we were—while you were in my head?" She wavered, then pressed on. "I could see things. I think they were memories. Your memories. I wasn't trying to pry, but—but I couldn't really control it. Did that happen to you too?"

Her shadow's head cocked to one side.

"A little," he said.

"What did you see?"

"Haeki when she was younger. A boy I assume was Oboro. Your father. Miresse. I wasn't going to bring it up."

Disquieting. Karys shivered. "Right."

"It was only fragments."

"No, I . . ." She unfolded her arms. *Doesn't matter, he already knew anyway.* "I just wondered. Who is Ilesha?"

Ferain flickered, startled. "That's who you saw?"

"Amongst other people. She stood out."

For some reason, that answer amused him. "You liked her?"

"What?"

"Ilesha was my fiancée."

It was Karys' turn for surprise. "You had a fiancée?"

"Why is that so shocking? Yes, I had a fiancée, and I hope you'll get to meet her. What was the memory?"

The scene remained all too vivid in Karys' mind. She could feel her face warming, and strove to keep her voice casual. "Oh, just the two of you talking about Toraigus. I could feel . . . I could tell you liked her a lot."

"Figures. We were engaged for five years before she broke it off." Ferain's tone turned fond. "The circumstances were impossible, although I refused to admit that at the time. She wanted to stay in Eludia, I needed to leave it, and marriage is a slightly hollow promise when you're living hundreds of miles apart. In the end, neither of us wanted to hold the other back. So we separated."

"That's sad."

"It is, and it isn't. I'd still go to war for Ilesha if she asked. We're best friends."

The last statement gave Karys an unexpected pang. Somehow, she had not imagined Ferain having a best friend either—she had foolishly assumed that his life mirrored her own. *A recluse diplomat—very likely.* "So, what is she like?"

Her shadow considered the question for a moment, deliberating.

"Formidable," he said. "Clever. Very perceptive; you can't slip much past her. Decisive, quick, tougher and more principled than people assume. Keeps her true opinions close to her chest. Good at making people feel comfortable, even when they shouldn't. Generous to a fault, very little patience for fools. Terrible cook."

Karys absorbed that, trying to square his description with her brief impression of the woman. "She seemed protective of you."

"I suppose she can be. Not that I deserve it. You mentioned other people; who else did you see?"

She raised her gaze to the ceiling of the train. Her recollections of the night had grown jumbled: some memories crystallised, others blurred. There was the Sanctum and the dark, the party in Toraigus. Vuhas in his study, Winola with blood on her lips.

"A woman with white hair," she said slowly. "She was tied to a chair, looking out a window. I—you brought her flowers, I think. Red flowers. Something was wrong with her."

"My mother."

Karys looked down, hearing the change in his voice. Ferain sounded calm and open; possessed of the same rare and unflinching sincerity that she had come to trust.

"She died two years ago," he said. "Her caretaker made a mistake, and she got away. Jumped from the roof."

The statement was simple and matter-of-fact. Karys felt at a loss.

"I'm sorry," she said.

Her shadow made a small gesture, as if to brush away her concern. "Thank you, but it's all right. I knew it would happen eventually. She made the first attempt when I was eight, and after that it was . . . well, inevitable. That's the family inheritance, courtesy of Ambavar—an irrepressible tendency for suicide."

There was no trace of self-pity or anger in his words, only a touch of irony. He sounded older, and tired. Karys remembered his claustrophobic loneliness— Ilesha in the sunlit bedroom asking who he was trying to impress.

"You miss her," she said.

Although her shadow did not react visibly, Karys immediately knew that she had misspoken. There was no way to take back the inane, inadequate comment once it had left her mouth, but Ferain replied without a hint of reproof.

"It's senseless," he said. "Grieving an empty shell. There was never any chance of recovery. She hadn't recognised me in twenty years, didn't speak, didn't hunger, never reacted to anything around her. I hated her, and I miss her constantly."

The water trickled along the moss. The light through the window remained bright and constant.

"It mostly manifests in the women of my family," he said, after a moment. "Not all of them, obviously, and it's much less common now. My mother was the first in three generations. The worst part is that there's never any warning—one day, they're fine: planting flowers in the garden. The next, they crack and try to cut their throat with a letter opener. And once that first break happens, there's no return. Everything else empties out, except for death."

Karys touched the stone bench where her shadow lay. Ferain made a rueful sound.

"Sorry," he said. "Morbid. It's part of the reason why I dislike my heritage. Not that I actually believe I'm related to Ambavar, but he did Favour one of my ancestors, and that came at a cost. Please stop looking at me like that, Karys."

She spoke softly. "I'm sorry I saw something so personal."

"Don't be stupid. Besides, I don't mind if it's you."

A strong feeling rose up within her. She could not identify the emotion, but her head felt lighter than it should, and her body seemed too warm, and the world had narrowed down to the curving slope of the wall opposite her.

Then the floor of the train tilted, and the feeling was swallowed by a rush of alarm. Karys pushed herself up from the bench.

"I *told* Winola not to go near the train's workings," she snarled. "If she drops us out of the sky, I swear—"

At the sudden lurch, her shadow had gone dark and tight, but now he relaxed. "It's fine."

"It is *not* fine."

"Karys"—Ferain was clearly trying not to laugh—"we're descending to the next station."

It took a second for his words to sink in. She subsided back onto the bench. "Oh."

The train flowed down through the air, and the light of the tunnel dimmed, growing translucent as they slowed. The landscape here was greener, more pastoral than the hills around Tuschait. Orchards of citrus trees appeared from the haze, and then the station came into view: a square, redbrick building surrounded by neat grass lawns. With a barely perceptible clink, the train met the rails alongside the platform. The floor levelled, and they drew to a gentle halt. The door rumbled open.

"I think there were five or six stops along the route," said Ferain. "But I slept through most of the ride last time, so I don't really remember."

A few people were boarding the vehicle. Karys could not see them from inside the alcove, but she heard their footsteps. One of them coughed. A few seconds later, the door rolled closed once more, and the train began to move. Her shadow fell into the correct shape at her side.

"Ferain, I've been thinking," Karys said in an undertone. "Once we reach Eludia, when you get your body back—"

A young woman appeared in the mouth of the alcove, and Karys stopped talking immediately. The stranger smiled at her.

"Sorry," she said. "I hope I'm not bothering you. The station manager said that there was some sort of exhibit aboard? Do you know where that might be?"

Karys straightened up. "I think it's down the—"

The woman moved like lightning. The knife came down hard—the blade black, edged with pondscum green—but Ferain was faster. He caught the woman's wrist inches from Karys' face. Without a second of hesitation, he snapped it.

Bone cracked, and the woman shrieked in pain, dropping her weapon. The drawing hit Karys like a body blow; a gasp left her mouth, but she was already scrambling for the knife, snatching it up from the ground. Ferain shoved the woman out of the alcove to give Karys space. The drawing hit again, and she staggered.

"Stop," she choked.

Ferain snarled and fell back to her side. Karys used the bench to rise. Her head was spinning, but she held the knife in front of her. *Shit.* The woman clutched her arm and whimpered, her right hand hanging limp. A tall man appeared in the corridor behind her; he thrust the woman out of the way, and stepped into the alcove. There was another knife in his hand.

"Karys," said Ferain tightly.

She shook her head, breathing hard. *Not yet.* If Ferain burned through all her energy, she would be left helpless to defend herself.

"Her shadow," moaned the woman. "Unnatural . . ."

"Shut it," said the man.

Karys pulled open the Veneer, and the strangers lit up with workings. Body modifications and worked tools, all Ephirite-derived. *New Favour. They've found me.*

The man lunged. Instinct moved her; Karys raised the stolen knife to shield her face. Simultaneously, her shadow pushed away the man's weapon, causing him to stumble. Her blade nicked his cheek.

The man jolted as if shocked by an electric current. A heartbeat later, Karys' vision went dark, and she slumped sideways into the wall. Couldn't keep this up, not with Ferain drawing constantly. Someone was screaming. Her vision cleared, and she found the man reeling away from her—cursing, scrubbing at his face. His blood glowed through the Veneer; between his fingers, the tiny cut on his cheek grew rapidly, his flesh splitting open and peeling back. With a dull pop, his left eye burst. He howled.

"Fuck," Karys whispered.

Ferain threw himself in front of her, blocking her view, but she could still hear the man as his screams turned to wet gurgling and then a clicking, crunching noise.

"It's the Construct's effect." Her shadow cursed. "The knife, they've done something to it."

Karys looked down at the blade in her hand. The edge was barely red; she had scarcely touched the man. A gossamer-like web of light glinted where the metal was slicked by the bright green liquid. Her voice came out high and strangled. "Ferain, move. I need to *see*."

"Not this," he said.

She could hear the woman's rapid, panicked breathing outside the alcove; nothing now from the man. *That would have been me. That would have been me if either of them cut me.* Karys bit the inside of her cheek, tasting blood. Needed to keep her head.

"How did you find me, saint?" she called hoarsely.

The woman did not answer.

"I don't want to hurt you." Karys stepped through the black wall of her shadow, out into the passage. "Talk."

The woman stood with her back pressed to the train wall, her face grey. No trace of the man remained except for his dropped knife. Karys kicked it out of reach. The woman flinched and shrank, crushing the lichen behind her. She could not have been much older than twenty.

"I didn't know it would look like that," she whispered. "Oh. Oh, Embrace."

"*Talk.*" Karys lifted her knife. "How did you find me?"

"The Constructs woke." The woman's words emerged garbled, her accent Mercian. "They had lost your trail, but then they roused for half a day, and led us to the Riddled Gorge. We found the bodies there and spoke to them. We learned you were headed for Tuschait, and from there to Eludia—we knew there was a chance we could intercept you, so we paid the station manager to alert us when unfamiliar women boarded the train."

"How many more saints are waiting?"

"It was just us, I swear. If we'd held out for reinforcements, we would have lost you. There wasn't enough time."

"But New Favour will send more. What are the Supremes so afraid of?"

The woman swallowed, eyes wide. "The last harbour, the reeker you bound. If they survive, everything that New Favour sacrificed will be for nothing. War—it means a war of vengeance with Varesli."

"New Favour assassinated an ambassador and blew up the embassy. If the Supremes want peace—"

"Only because Mercia holds the advantage." The woman's voice was imploring, frightened. "Varesli won't attack from a position of weakness. We had to stop them from regaining power, disarm them while we still could."

"What power?" Karys stepped closer. "Why was the retinue attacked?"

"It's not about them, it's about what they—"

Something cold wrapped around Karys' hand, and jerked her arm forward. The knife pierced the woman's stomach, sliding smoothly into her flesh.

Karys stopped breathing. The woman blinked, shocked. Her eyes were a deep brown flecked with amber, and up close she smelled of sweat and something floral, sweet. She gazed at Karys without accusation; she looked lost and scared and small.

"Kill me," she said.

There was a roar in Karys' ears. She still held the knife, and she could not move. *I didn't . . .*

Her shadow swept forward, curled around the saint's throat, and snapped her neck. The woman crumpled, body folding inward even as she fell.

The world went black. Karys dropped, her body giving way completely as the roar turned to a terrible ringing. Her knees hit the floor of the train, and the knife clattered. *I didn't . . . I didn't . . .* Everything spun around her, echoes deafening.

"Karys? Karys?"

Ferain's voice. The train swam back into focus. She was on all fours, shaking uncontrollably, her shadow draped over her shoulders. Her body felt freezing cold.

"I didn't!" she gasped. "I wasn't going to hurt her."

The woman was gone, leaving only crushed lichen and broken ferns behind. Karys could feel the knife sliding in: the gentle resistance, the moment of give. She lifted her trembling hand. Her skin was wet. Not with blood. Water.

"Karys!"

She flinched at the sound of Haeki's voice, and pushed back onto her heels. The world tilted in her vision, light flaring like white fire across the walls. The resistance, and the give. She tasted bile in her mouth. Haeki, out of breath, dropped to a crouch beside her.

"Nuliere said apostates were trying to kill the Son of Night." She spoke in a rush. "She said—"

"Saltmoss," whispered Karys.

All along the channels in the floor, dull and grey and familiar. It grew in seawater; it had been everywhere in Boäz, common to the coast around Psikamit. The Bhatuma's words resounded in Karys' head: *Where there is salt in the water, so am I.* The floor and the walls of the train ran with brine—Karys had smelled it, but given it no further thought.

"Oh, you monster," she said, voice low. "You craven, cowardly piece of shit."

The water in the channel made a sound like waves lapping sand.

"Am I not to expect gratitude, then?" asked Nuliere.

Karys struck the channel, grazing her palm. Her body would not stop shaking; she gritted her teeth to keep them from chattering.

"She was *scared*," she hissed.

Nuliere made a derisive noise. "The apostate attempted to kill you and the Son of Night. I acted to protect—"

"She was too frightened to move! You . . . you *used* me."

The Bhatuma was unperturbed. "You are a daughter of Boäz and fall within the sphere of my influence."

"*Now* I'm yours again? You turn me into a murderer, and *now* you claim me back?"

"I do not claim you, apostate. I do what is necessary to safeguard my kin with the tools that are available to me. If I must guide your unworthy hands, so be it."

Karys let her head fall. She did not know what to do with her fury, with her horror, with her despairing hatred of the herald. Her entire body felt numb and weak; she had no reserves left. Two people dead by her own hand, one after the other. She knew they had meant to kill her, but for it to happen so quickly, for it to be so brutal and so close—

"Convenient timing," said Ferain.

He spoke without expression, distant and polite—but there was a sharp edge to the angles of Karys' shadow. The water in the channels stilled to mirror flatness.

"Son of Night?" enquired Nuliere.

He did not answer her, instead shifting to cross Haeki's shadow.

"Can you help her?" he asked, softer. "I took too much. She needs warmth, and if Lindlee has any more food, that would probably—"

Before Haeki could touch her, Karys forced her legs to work. She stood up on her own.

"Don't treat me like a child," she said harshly.

"Then learn to ask for help," Ferain snapped back. "And by the way, I think you'll find that *I* killed that woman, not you."

"She was already dead."

"Funny, it didn't feel that way when I broke her neck."

"Son of Night, have I given offence?" asked Nuliere.

Silence. After a moment, Karys' shadow loosened, dark angles giving way.

"No," he said. "No, but in future I would prefer if you didn't . . . guide her hands."

Karys made a sound of disgust. She shambled back into the alcove, and bent to pick up her bag. The effort almost unbalanced her.

"Of course," said Nuliere. "My apologies, kindred. My exertions in repelling the last apostates resulted in a momentary weakness, and during that time I was unable to shield you from the enemy's sight. I regret this, and in future will keep them at bay."

Karys found the thin coat Marishka had given her, and tugged it on. Out of the corner of her eye, she saw Haeki stooping to retrieve the dead man's knife.

"Don't touch that," she said sharply. "If it cuts you, you're dead."

Haeki hesitated, before taking the knife by the handle and lifting it up to the light. "Then I won't let it cut me. Is this Ephirite-worked?"

"Ephirite-derived, I think. There's a second one by the door."

"I saw it." Haeki lowered the knife again. "You should sit down. I'm going to talk to Winola, and we'll tell Lindlee you got sick. Are you hurt?"

Karys scoffed. "Not at all. Your herald made sure of that."

"Then you should be thanking her."

"Oh, my gratitude is boundless—I get to watch as she culls apostates one by one. When do you suppose it will be my turn?"

Haeki's forehead creased.

"Stay here," she said. "I won't be long."

Even exhausted, Karys wanted to lash out. She needed Haeki to react, to get mad, to admit the truth, to acknowledge the lines drawn between them. To hurt her. Not to walk away, steps light and swift, as if nothing had happened. Karys sank down onto the bench, and hugged her arms close to her chest. Although her relentless shivering had eased, the bone-deep chill remained. Ferain pooled at her feet, watchful and unspeaking. Angry. She shut her eyes.

"Thank you," she muttered. "For what you did. Sparing her."

A long silence. The water in the channel moved soundlessly.

"I don't think I deserve thanks," he said. "It felt like the only choice."

His voice was controlled and calm. Karys did not like it.

"At least we learned something," she said bitterly. "It seems like your heritage had nothing to do with—"

"Not now," he interrupted.

She was spent. The sliding sensation of metal parting flesh lingered in her hand. "I'd have thought you'd be happy."

Her shadow did not reply. The train was quiet, and the echoes of the man's screams reverberated inside Karys—the awful noises of his body rupturing and folding, tearing itself inside out. *Ferain said that was the Construct's effect.* She had seen how Coren Oselaw died, but that violence had been swift. Gruesome but total. Slower was so much worse, slower was near unspeakable, and the idea that the same end awaited Ferain was beyond her. And for *him* to see it up close, intimately, for him to recognise that horror . . .

"We'll stop it," she said. "That won't be you."

"Enough, Karys."

His sharpness stung, but she could not stay silent. "Whatever it takes. Not this, not you. I've broken promises before, but this one I'll keep. Not this, and not you."

He made a frustrated sound. "You aren't *listening* to me."

Something about the way he pronounced the words, a slight shift in his cadences, penetrated the fog of her exhaustion, and she finally understood. *Nuliere.* Although the herald had gone silent, she would still be present, still able to eavesdrop on their conversation. No doubt she had been listening all along.

And, for whatever reason, Ferain did not want the Bhatuma to hear them talking.

"Right," said Karys softly. "Not now."

CHAPTER

36

Karys slept through most of the day. Her rest was plagued by visions of the dead woman's face, the echoes of screaming, the smell of brine and the sound of water. Confused dreams, in which she repeatedly drove the knife into her own stomach. Instead of blood, the wound ran with dense shadow, and the dead woman said, over and over: *I didn't know it would look like that. Oh, I didn't know it would look like that.*

She woke up stiff and groggy, and discovered the floor of the train listing downwards. Through the window, the hazy impression of great dark trees closed around the vehicle. Karys rubbed her eyes. Winola was seated on the floor of the alcove, writing in her battered notebook. The scholar finished a sentence, blew gently on the ink, and snapped the book shut.

"How are you feeling?" she asked.

Karys twisted her head to the side, cracking her neck.

"Hungover." After a second of thought, she added: "And hungry."

Winola tucked the book into the front pouch of her bag. "Well, I believe we'll be disembarking now. We should be able to find something to eat in the city."

Startled, Karys looked out the window again.

"We've reached Eludia?" she asked.

The trees crowded out the sunlight, sweeping up to the sky. The train slowed, the floor levelled, and they came to a clean, smooth stop.

"Yes," said Winola simply.

A few more passengers had boarded along the route, and they gathered at the door now—men and women carrying heavy cases, murmuring to one another. Haeki and Lindlee stood behind them, and the teenager shot Karys a concerned look when she emerged from the alcove with Winola. The train door rolled open, and the small crowd filed out onto the platform.

Dusk. The air was cold and bright. On every side, unfamiliar trees spread their branches, their leaves a deep, vibrant green, and birdsong rang between the boughs. Although it was not yet dark, orange etherbulbs illuminated the station, each drawing a powdery cloud of moths.

This is . . . Eludia? Karys had expected a city like Psikamit, not a forest grove. The earthy scent of the trees felt gentle and clean, the wind held the early bite of winter. She breathed deeply.

"So he actually came," said Ferain.

A handful of people milled around the benches along the platform, rising to meet the trickle of passengers. A man caught Karys' eye—pale-skinned, slender, his thick dark hair liberally streaked with grey, his jaw dusted with stubble. He might have been sixty, dressed in muted greys and browns, with a stiff-shouldered formal jacket. Something about his appearance struck her as obscurely familiar.

"I'm surprised that he was worried. He doesn't normally pay that much attention." Ferain sounded wary and puzzled. "Maybe the Foreign Ministry sent word about the retinue. They must have."

"Oh, wonderful, I think that's Uncle Rhevin over there." Lindlee dragged her large suitcase off the train. "He said he would be waiting to meet us."

She waved. The man noticed, acknowledged her with a brief wave of his own, and strolled across the platform to meet them. He extended his hand to Lindlee. She shook it, then realised he was trying to help with her suitcase, and flushed.

"Pleased to meet you," said Rhevin, amused. "Lindlee, wasn't it?"

Huh, thought Karys. *Sounds like Ferain.* Not quite the same; Rhevin's voice was deeper, his accent more pronounced, his intonations flatter—but she would have guessed they were related just from hearing him speak.

"That's right." Lindlee ducked her head. "Thank you for inviting us to stay."

"My home is yours." His eyes were an unusual reddish brown and deep-set. They passed over Winola and Karys, settling briefly on Haeki. "These are the people you mentioned? Welcome to Eludia. I am Rhevin Taliade."

Lindlee quickly made the rest of the introductions. Karys studied Rhevin. She could not remember much of Ferain's appearance from the Sanctum. She thought he might have been taller than his father, his complexion darker. The rest was murky.

"A pleasure," said Rhevin briskly. "I hope your journey was uneventful. This way, please."

They followed him through the quiet station, out to a flagstone road cut between the trees. Fireflies glinted in the air between the trunks, swift yellow glimmers. As they walked, Lindlee answered her uncle's polite enquiries about her parents, the care of the lodge, the Auric. The path climbed, and the forest ahead opened up to the lilac sky. The peak of a mountain rose into view, tall and alone, midnight blue in the twilight. A little further and they crested the hillside.

Eludia dwarfed Psikamit. The city grew in every direction—lights winding all the way to the mountain, architecture rearing up to the sky—and the land beneath it lay stark and sweeping. Nothing existed on a level plain; promontories gave way to deep ravines, valleys curved up into sheer bluffs. Clusters of houses gathered between corridors of forest and stone; they stood along the precarious ridges of windswept cliffs, and crowded the shaded banks of low hills. Slender bridges connected the buildings, arching over the roofs and the high trees and the clefts in the land, their weathered support pillars whorled with veins of indigo stone.

"Home again," murmured Ferain.

A bird of prey hovered overhead, riding a warmer current of air. The view was impossible to absorb at once: all of it so foreign, so unlike any place Karys had ever known. She had lived by the sea, she had lived in the arid heat of Miresse, but neither had felt like this. Eludia's atmosphere held a vast calm quiet, a peace deeper than sound.

"I don't imagine you've been here before," said Rhevin.

Karys turned from the vista. Ferain's father was watching her, his expression difficult to read.

"I believe there's a lot we need to discuss," he said.

She nodded. "There is."

"Is my son alive?"

"Yes."

Rhevin did not appear surprised or relieved. His face did not change at all. "Good," he said.

They took an awrig down a zigzagging path to reach the floor of the valley. Haeki, beside the window, sat entranced and silent, her warm breath misting the glass as her eyes drank in the city. The sky's colour had deepened, and the lamps at the roadside glowed steady and bright. Karys rubbed her thumb back and forth along her aching jaw. Eludia, at last. The old capital. Ferain's home.

War—it means a war of vengeance with Varesli.

She grimaced, and dropped her hand to her lap. New Favour might have known where she was headed—but in a city this huge, they would struggle to find her now. Desperation could only carry the saints so far; without Constructs to guide them, without knowledge of Ferain's identity, they would be left scrambling in the dark. That thought should have comforted her, but instead Karys' mind spiralled around scores of unanswered questions.

Why had New Favour attacked the retinue? Why were they so desperate to see Ferain dead? How could he possibly start a war with Mercia?

And what was Nuliere up to?

There was no real evidence that New Favour held any interest in Ferain's ties to Ambavar. As far as Karys could tell, the saints did not even know which survivor they were hunting. So why would Nuliere claim otherwise? It was possible that the herald was deluded, so alone in the world that she sought kinship where none existed. She certainly had been kind to Ferain, and taken enormous personal risks on his behalf. Yet her generosity was precisely what Karys mistrusted—her childhood had been shadowed by a cold lurking presence; from her earliest years, she had been instructed in the demands of the sea: penitence and punishment and secrecy. Nuliere's moods might be fickle, but the herald had never been sentimental. Not until now.

Still, they could not afford to openly question her motives. For the moment, they needed Nuliere, and Ferain clearly intended to maintain the charade.

The awrig passed below the arch of one of the towering bridges, and slipped onto a narrower road. Green beds ran along the verges of the street, flush with hundreds of white flowers. The buildings here were large, ornate, and old; most plastered the same shade of light ochre brown, and decorated with coloured tiles around their windows, doors, and eaves. Trellises of climbing roses and wisteria draped the walls. People wandered the neighbourhood, enjoying the cool evening; couples strolled arm in arm, groups of children ran and called out to one another.

The vehicle slowed at the end of the street, and stopped at the steps of a double-storey house covered in ivy. Trees surrounded the building, screening all but the façade from view. Rhevin opened the awrig door, and picked up Lindlee's suitcase.

"There are two bedrooms you may share, both on the second floor," he said. "You're also welcome to any food in the kitchen—you'll find dinner on the stove. I want you to be comfortable here. Cas Eska, once you've put down your bag, could I speak with you privately?"

"Of course," said Karys.

"My study is down the hallway from the bedrooms." He touched his hand to the front door, unlocking it, and gave a shallow bow. "Please come inside. Make yourselves at home."

The interior was airy, spacious—the floorboards solid walnut, the walls a warm cornsilk colour, the long windows hung with white gauze curtains and pale velvet drapes. Dustless and sparse, the furniture seemed too small for the size of the rooms; wooden tables and straight-backed chairs marooned on woven carpets, adrift and untouched. As Karys climbed the stairs to the second floor, she received the curious impression of the place being impermanent, arranged like the children's dollhouses she had sometimes seen while working for wealthy clients in Psikamit. No art on the walls, no clutter, no sign of personal attachment at all.

"Is this where you grew up?" she murmured to Ferain.

Her shadow had been meticulous in matching her ever since they had arrived at the station. He trailed her up the stairs now. "For a few years. Before my mother's first attempt, I lived with her in a house outside the city, just below the mountain. My father owned a few different properties back then, and we moved between them until he settled on this one. It was closest to the university." After a second, he added, with a hint of acidity: "And furthest from my mother."

The rooms that Rhevin had offered them each contained two narrow cots and an empty wardrobe. One faced the street, the other had a balcony overlooking the garden. Karys took the former with Winola, and left Haeki to share the larger room with Lindlee.

Through the window, the evening sky had darkened, the trees turned to black silhouettes. Lights shone in the houses across the road. Karys set down her bag at the foot of the bed nearest the door.

"I was expecting more questions, to be honest." Winola walked over to the window, and peered out. "He's very hospitable."

"Worried?"

"No, no. Pleasantly surprised, that's all. Once you've explained things, I'll need to discuss my observations with him, but the situation seems promising." She flashed a quick smile. "One step closer to freedom for you and Ferain."

Again, the discomforting sense of vertigo. "If Rhevin can get into the Lapse."

"True, but if he's able to counter even one of the relic's authorisations, I think we'll be able to reach the binding and dissolve it. Go on, talk to him."

The door stood ajar at the end of the corridor. Karys tried to relax the tension in her neck as she approached the study, rolling out her shoulders. They had come so far—they had crossed half the continent in the hopes that Rhevin might be able to help. It suddenly felt like an insane gamble.

"Winola wasn't the only one expecting questions," mumbled Ferain. "This is so unlike him."

"He must have been very worried about you," Karys replied under her breath.

Her shadow gave an uncomfortable shrug. "You're a complete stranger who he has no reason to trust. Even if he was worried, it's just . . . it's not like him."

Similar thoughts had crossed her mind—*why doesn't he suspect a ruse?*—but, under the circumstances, Karys was not about to question Rhevin's generosity. She knocked on the door, then stepped inside.

In marked contrast to the rest of the house, the large study appeared cluttered and cramped. The room held a desk below the window, a workbench against the wall, an armchair, and a number of glass cabinets housing small, broken ornaments. Bhatuma relics, Karys guessed. Ferain had said that his father was a historian at the university. The usual working accoutrements were also stacked under the bench: phials of blood, bone, and metal shavings, chalk, knives, and clamps. Unremarkable for an average practitioner, nothing to rival Vuhas' stores.

Rhevin was leaning against the edge of his desk, reading a file. He put it down when Karys walked in.

"I believe you've made a long journey." He gestured for her to shut the door. "I assume from Psikamit? The Foreign Ministry contacted me in private, told me there had been a political incident and the situation was still under investigation. Take a seat."

Karys moved over to the armchair. "So they explained what happened?"

"Not in any real detail; they want the affair kept quiet. But they did indicate there was a slim chance my son might have survived the massacre." He folded his arms. "Then my niece contacted me out of the blue, claiming a Mercian woman had arrived in Tuschait, and was insisting on talking to me about Ferain. At any other time, I would have called the girl foolish. But . . ." He made an offhand gesture. "Hope makes a hypocrite of us all. So, Karys Eska: you have come a long way to deliver a message—which can only mean you expect to be paid for the trouble. What is your offer?"

She met Rhevin's gaze levelly. "More than a message."

"You know where he is?"

She nodded. "I found Ferain up the coast from Psikamit, near the wreckage of a Vareslian ship. He was badly hurt, preserving himself within a stasis dimension generated by the Split Lapse relic."

Rhevin's face gave nothing away. "You spoke to him."

"He told me he couldn't leave the Lapse. The situation was dangerous, and I didn't think I could bring help to him." Karys took a breath. "So instead I brought him to help. To you."

A pause.

"And yet, I don't see my son," said Rhevin.

Ferain sighed. He stretched across the floor to lie in his father's shadow.

"Were you really that worried about me?" he asked.

Even having explained the situation, Karys had expected Rhevin to be shocked or appalled, or perhaps to accuse her of fraud and then throw her out the house. Instead, his eyes only widened fractionally. Nothing else—he did not move from his desk, cry out, flinch. Just a small flicker of his eyelids, as if none of this really came as a surprise to him.

"That idea pleased you, didn't it?" he said. "Me, grief-stricken at the loss of you."

Ferain made an annoyed sound. "Why do you have to be like that?"

"Anything that puts you in the centre of attention." Rhevin uncrossed his arms. "Well, it seems the Foreign Ministry's intelligence was credible after all, although I'd still appreciate a full explanation. What happened?"

Karys kept quiet while her shadow talked. Ferain was to the point; he sketched out what had happened to the retinue, how he had been injured, the effectiveness of the Lapse, the Constructs' connection to New Favour. Rhevin listened and nodded occasionally, but none of what his son described seemed to upset or alarm him. It was only when Ferain came to describe Karys binding the Split Lapse to her body that his expression soured.

"That relic was irreplaceable," he said.

"Funny, so am I," said Ferain.

Rhevin did not deign to reply to that. He turned his attention to Karys. "The binding would have left an impression, correct? May I see it?"

Karys hesitated. After New Favour's attack on the train, the scar now rested on the inner slope of her armpit. She would have to undress to show it to him, and that seemed— *Oh, don't be stupid.* She lifted her arms to take off her shirt.

"It can wait," said Ferain hastily. "There's the matter of payment to settle first. Karys risked her life to save me, and I vouched that she would be compensated for her efforts."

Rhevin raised an eyebrow. "I'm sure we can arrange a commensurate fee—"

"Fifteen thousand cret. And expenses."

His father frowned. "Commensurate and *reasonable*, to be paid once you have been restored to your body."

"I gave Karys my word, and I won't go back on it. If anything, fifteen thousand is too low. The money was my inheritance, and it's within my power—"

"You would struggle to sign for it presently," said Rhevin.

"Well, when you put it that way, we should probably also discuss the matter of compound interest—"

"Fifteen thousand," said Karys. "Once he's healed."

Her shadow retreated to her side, out of Rhevin's hearing.

"Karys, stop ceding ground," he snapped. "I'm not going to let my father cheat you. He can pay now."

She brushed him off, keeping her gaze on Rhevin. "Those were the original terms of our agreement. His life in exchange for fifteen thousand cret. I spoke to a mender, and she claimed that the binding I worked is locked inside the Lapse, and that opening it requires countering the relic's authorisations. Ferain said you were an expert on the Split Lapse. If we can find a way to heal his injury, would you be able to open it?"

Rhevin appraised her, his rust-coloured eyes thoughtful.

"Probably," he said. "I would need to do some research."

The knot of tension inside Karys loosened. Not a dead end. So long as Rhevin believed he might be able to help, there was hope. Until that moment, she had not realised how heavily the prospect of failing Ferain had weighed on her.

"Please do," she said.

Her shadow continued fuming even after they left the study, mumbling darkly and veering out of her silhouette. *Unusual for him to get so heated.* Winola wasn't in the bedroom when Karys returned to it. The scholar's spare clothing hung neatly in the wardrobe, and her notes and workings materials were arranged at the foot of her bed.

"I should have known that he would be like this," muttered Ferain. "I don't know why I expected anything else."

"He thinks he can help you."

"How generous of him. Surprising that he would bother."

"Ferain."

"Although I suppose I should be happy that he believes I'm more valuable alive than dead. Reasonably more valuable. Not quite commensurate at the price."

"He was clearly worried about you."

"'Clearly'? I didn't think so." Her shadow rippled irritably, and then settled. He sighed. "Your neck is bothering you."

"What?"

"Yes, very convincing. You keep touching it." He slipped up her side and brushed her jaw, feather-light and cool. "There."

Karys' breath caught in her throat. A chill broke out across her skin, the drawing pulled inside her chest, and she clamped her hand down on her neck. Her voice came out higher than she meant it to. "Haven't you drained me enough for one day?"

"Either something happened on the train, or it's Rasko's wasp," he said. "Based on the location, I'm guessing it's the latter. Didn't he say you had a week?"

"He's a third-rate Mercian fixer. Precision probably isn't his strong suit."

"How bad is it?"

She scowled. "A headache. I was going to take care of it tomorrow."

"Are you sure? We could go now."

"Your teacher isn't going to welcome a courier in the middle of the night. Leave me be, Ferain. It's nothing." Karys tramped back into the corridor. "And I'm hungry."

She found Winola and Haeki downstairs in the kitchen. A pot and pan rested on the stove, steaming gently, and the fragrance of onion and ginger hung in the air. Haeki washed dishes in the sink under the window, while Winola sat at the table with New Favour's knives laid out in front of her. The scholar was carefully applying a thin line of salt to the edge of each blade.

"Embrace, do you have to do that here?" asked Karys.

Winola's eyes remained fixed on her task. "How did your conversation go?"

"He said he needs to do some research, but thinks he'll be able to open the Lapse."

"So fairly well, then."

"I think so. Where's Lindlee?"

"Out visiting friends. She wanted to surprise them." Winola finished with the salt, and leaned over to pick up her blood flask. "She said that she hopes you feel better soon."

Karys crossed over to the stove. The pot contained a broth, the pan held fried pork and vegetables. "Is it safe for her to be wandering around on her own like that?"

"Haeki asked the same thing. Apparently the neighbourhood where her friend lives isn't dangerous."

Karys ladled a large portion of vegetables and meat into her bowl, and poured broth on top. Kernels of sweetcorn floated to the surface. Over at the table, Winola used a teaspoon to drop a small measure of blood onto one of the knives. The instant the liquid touched the metal, it hissed and evaporated. She repeated the test with a greater quantity of blood, and louder hissing ensued.

"You know that if one of those cuts you . . ." Karys began.

"Yes, yes. Rapid personal disintegration, violent excruciating death."

"You haven't seen what it looks like."

Winola glanced up.

"Sorry," she said. "Insensitive of me. I'm trying to establish how New Favour applied the Construct's effect to these weapons. What the working responds to, and the scale of that response. I'm hoping that might give me a sense of how to counteract it. I'll be careful, I promise."

Karys shook her head. "No, of course. Is there anything I can do to help?"

"Not at this stage." Winola returned her attention to the knife. She tapped the back of the spoon to the blade, and it gave an ordinary metal ting. "I mostly just need to think."

Haeki hung her dishtowel over the drying rack. "Which means: 'leave me alone.'"

The scholar's lips quirked. "I wouldn't say that."

"But you might think it."

"Maybe."

Karys raised a hand in surrender and backed out of the kitchen, taking her bowl to the dining room across the hallway.

The broth was salty, slightly sour, and hot, and eating it eased the pain in her jaw. The house was quiet and warm. It felt safe. Karys finished her food, then sat at the long, bare table for a while, thoughtlessly twirling her spoon around the empty bowl.

"Ferain?" she said.

"Mm?"

"Do you know if your father keeps any scrap paper? Reports or general forms from the university, that sort of thing."

"He used to store uncollected student essays in the basement for administrative purposes. Why?"

"Do you think he would mind if I used those?"

"No, not at all." Her shadow sounded curious. "He burns them every few years anyway; storing them is just an administrative formality. What do you need paper for?"

Karys smiled. She turned in her chair, and raised her voice.

"Haeki," she called. "Can you come here?"

CHAPTER

37

Karys' jaw hurt like someone was boring into the bone with a burning drill. The skin remained cool and unblemished.

There must have been a better way of getting across the border. She stepped down from the worked tram, out into the morning sun. *If I ever see Rasko again, I'm going to shove one of those hideous wasps down his throat.*

A brisk wind winnowed through the city's valleys; locals wore light jackets and coats, long skirts and heeled boots. Imolin Prete's address had taken Karys to the southern side of Eludia. The blue mountain loomed close, its summit crowned with wisps of cloud. It was fortunate that Ferain knew the area; without directions, she would have gotten hopelessly lost.

"Nearly there," said her shadow encouragingly.

"You already told me that," she replied under her breath, "half an hour ago."

"You looked like you needed the motivation."

"Ferain, please understand that the one thing I don't lack right now is sufficient *motivation*."

The Sulluvin District rested at the edge of one of the city's many escarpments, the land dropping away steeply on its western flank. The view was probably quite beautiful, but Karys didn't care to look at anything beyond the road directly in front of her feet. Rasko's parcel nestled in her coat pocket, safe and snug.

She had departed the house shortly after sunrise, taking care not to disturb Winola. The scholar had only gone to bed in the early hours of the morning, staying up late to discuss her ideas with Rhevin. In the pre-dawn dark, she had slipped quietly into their room without turning on the lamp. A sweet gesture, but an unnecessary one: Karys had still been wide awake. Between intrusive memories of the saints' deaths, and the increasing discomfort of her jaw, sleep had proven elusive.

"What did Rhevin think?" she whispered as Winola lay down.

The scholar did not answer immediately. She rolled over and faced Karys.

"I'm not sure," she murmured. "Seemed . . . impatient. He'll grant me access to all research materials at the university library, but I'm not sure he trusts my abilities. Whenever I speak, he acts like he already knows everything I'm telling him."

"Frustrating."

"A little. But at least he's willing to help."

Karys nodded.

"I appreciate it, you know," she said. "I'll never be able to repay you for everything you've done, but I'm thankful. And sorry."

"For?"

"Vuhas, mostly."

The scholar sighed. She turned over again.

"Go to sleep," she said.

Karys did not. She waited until the sun touched the gables of the dark roofs along the street, then crept out of the house.

The journey took longer than expected, and Karys' mood grew steadily worse as the morning progressed—after an hour and a half spent traversing the city, she saw white stars every time she turned her head to the left. If they had arrived in Eludia even a day later, she doubted she would have been able to reach Prete's address, and it was only her fifth morning since crossing into Varesli. How Rasko believed anyone would survive the full week was beyond her.

Underhanded little rat bastard, she thought savagely.

"Karys," began Ferain.

"If you say 'nearly there' one more time—"

"It's the next building on your right."

Karys lifted her head. *Praise the Embrace.*

The residence was much smaller than Rhevin's: a tidy and unremarkable townhouse with a pair of lemon trees growing in ceramic pots before the entrance. Pale brown walls, as with most of the buildings on the street, and a wreath of fresh flowers hanging from a nail in the door. A tabby cat snoozed on the window ledge in the sun.

Karys climbed the front steps and pulled on the bell cord. *Please let them be home.* The thought of having to return later made her feel nauseous; she just wanted to be done with this. From inside, she heard footsteps. The door opened, and a nervous, brown-eyed woman peered out at her.

"I'm looking for Imolin Prete," said Karys.

The woman opened the door fractionally wider. "I'm their wife."

Karys was not sure why, but, based on Ferain's description, she had envisioned Prete as a sort of dusty ascetic linguist living at the Foreign Ministry. It had never occurred to her that they might be married. "Are they available? I have a parcel I'm supposed to deliver to them."

The woman's eyebrows drew together.

"A parcel?" she said uncertainly.

"It's somewhat urgent."

"Could I take it for them?"

Karys shook her head—a mistake, it sent a bolt of pain lancing through her jaw. "Unfortunately, I was told to deliver it to them directly."

"I see." The woman wavered, then steeled herself and opened the door completely. She was middle-aged, with a heart-shaped face and tight black curls. "They're probably working in the conservatory, but I can fetch them for you. Would you like to come in?"

The unexpected offer left Karys cornered. "That's, uh . . . that's nice of you."

The woman perked up a little. "No, it's nothing. Really, please come in."

Prete's living room contained more uncomfortable hints as to their personality and family life. Children's drawings hung on the wall above a sagging couch decorated with hand-embroidered cushions. A heavily clawed cat's toy in the shape of a monkey lay next to the fireplace; stacks of dog-eared dictionaries were piled up on the floor by an old rocking chair.

"I'll tell them you're here," said the woman. "They get so involved in their work; they barely hear anything going on around the house. Just a minute."

Karys found herself standing alone in the middle of the living room, wishing very much that she had opted to stay outside. She didn't know what Rasko wanted with Prete, but she doubted it would be anything innocent. Proudly displayed above the children's pictures was a certificate from the Foreign Ministry, thanking them for thirty years of faithful service. Looking at it made her feel dirty.

Doesn't mean anything. Even people with wives and cats and pretty cushions could hide secret lives. *Maybe Prete's had dealings with Rasko for years.* Besides, she was committed. She had made her decision in Miresse, and had no choice but to see this through now.

Prete's wife returned, smoothing her hands over her skirt.

"Lin will be here in a minute," she said.

"Thank you."

"You're very welcome." The woman continued to fuss with her clothing. "So you're a courier? How interesting. You must have been to so many different places. Where are you from originally?"

"A village in eastern Mercia."

"Right, yes. I had wondered, hearing you speak . . ." A tiny wince of embarrassment. "It's a lovely accent, of course. Short and sharp. We must sound so drawn out in comparison."

Karys forced a smile. It resulted in a swift, stabbing pain below her left ear. "No, I've gotten used to the Vareslian accent. I like it."

"You do? That's very kind."

A brief silence yawned between them.

"The Mercian expansion was a terrible business," said the woman suddenly. "I always thought so, even as a little girl. It wasn't right."

Karys could not fathom how she had ended up in this conversation. It felt surreal, standing in a stranger's house with her jaw on fire, clutching a box of unknown contraband while being told that her own country's occupation had been terrible. She was stumped on how to respond.

"I . . . wasn't born yet?" she ventured.

The woman's cheeks darkened with shame. She looked like she might cry.

"The place where I grew up was very remote," added Karys hastily. "Out of the way. Even during the occupation, nobody really bothered with us."

They were both spared further mortification by the arrival of a short person in a green tunic—Imolin Prete strolled into the living room. They had grey hair and mobile eyebrows, and a curious expression on their face.

"Hello," they said. "Sorry, I was caught up in a translation. How may I help you?"

"Imolin Prete?"

"That would be me, yes."

Karys' stomach clenched. *Just get this over with.*

"I have a parcel for you from Miresse," she said.

Prete's eyebrows travelled further upwards. "Miresse?"

"From a man named Rasko. He gave me this address."

Prete hesitated, and glanced at their wife. "I don't understand. I don't know anyone from Mercia."

Karys' foreboding increased. "Are you sure?"

"Yes. I'm afraid there must have been some kind of mistake; I can't imagine anyone going to the trouble of couriering a parcel across the border to me. That must be awfully expensive. Is there any chance you might have the wrong address?"

Her jaw throbbed, caustic and raw.

"I . . . I don't think so," she said.

Prete quickly raised their hands. "Oh, please don't look so worried, dear. I'll still accept delivery if you need me to. I'm only concerned that I might be stealing someone else's mail."

She didn't want to give them the parcel. She only wanted her jaw to stop hurting. She wished that she had never accepted Rasko's deal.

Karys held out the grey box.

There was an instant, as they reached to take it, when she nearly pulled away. Prete's fingertips were stained with splotches of blue ink; their skin felt dry when it brushed against hers. *No, don't,* Karys thought, too late, and then the parcel had left her hand.

"Thank you," they said kindly.

She could only nod. Prete smiled, and turned their attention to the box, examining it with interest. They shook it gently, then pressed their thumb to the complex metal catch on its side. The mechanism appeared to be jammed. They moved over to the window to see better, lifting it closer to the light.

The lid of the box popped open with a puff of grey smoke. Karys jumped, but nothing else happened. Prete wrinkled their nose, and wafted the smoke away. Their face fell.

"Oh no," they said. "It's broken."

The incessant burning heat in Karys' jaw vanished like a snuffed candle flame, and a small sound left her mouth. Prete turned, interpreting the noise as dismay.

"Oh, I'm so sorry, dear," they said. "Look. It must have shattered on the road."

Inside the box was a little bronze figurine on a stone pedestal. A wasp, crudely sculpted, in flight. It had originally been encased in a globe, but the glass had smashed, and the creature's right wing was bent out of shape.

"What a shame," said Prete. They showed it to their wife, who mumbled something inaudible. "It was probably quite pretty. Maybe we could have it repaired—"

"No," said Karys hoarsely. "Get rid of it."

Prete's wife flinched, taking an involuntary step backwards and knocking into the side table. Prete's forehead creased.

"Why?" they asked.

Nothing had happened. Rasko had sent an ugly little statue to a stranger. If the wasp was meant to be some kind of message, no one here understood it. And yet Karys couldn't shake her unease. She reached for the fabric of the Veneer, and pulled it back. Nothing. The box and its contents showed no trace of workings. The room was entirely silent.

"Because you don't know who sent it, or their intentions," she said, and let the Veneer slide closed once more. "I have a bad feeling, that's all."

Prete pressed their lips together. Their eyes flicked toward the wasp, and they flipped the lid of the box shut.

"Well, there's no harm in caution," they said. "You're right; it is a strange situation. Thank you, dear, and I'm sorry you went to all the trouble of finding me. You're very kind to be concerned."

If she was kind, she would not have given them the parcel at all. But it was done now. Her side of the bargain fulfilled, her ties with Rasko severed. Done. Karys mumbled goodbye, unable to meet either Prete or their wife's eyes, and left as quickly as she could. No workings, not that she had seen, but the broken statue's appearance stayed with her. *What did Rasko stand to gain here?* Whatever the fixer had intended, his plan didn't seem to have quite come together.

The district outside remained quiet and blustery; the wind chased yellow leaves down the street. Karys glanced back at the house once, then hurried away.

"The pain is gone?" asked Ferain.

"As soon as the box opened."

"I'm glad."

She grimaced. "I don't understand what Rasko was trying to do. What was that thing?"

Ferain was quiet. Karys kept walking. The road curved; the mountain filled the sky.

"I don't know," he said at last. "But I think we're fortunate that it broke. You didn't have a choice, Karys."

"They hung their certificate on the wall."

"What?"

She made an angry movement with her head. "Never mind. I just wish I hadn't been invited inside. Which way should I go? I wasn't paying much attention earlier."

Ferain directed her to a set of stairs leading down the escarpment and into the valley. Not the way they had come, but Karys didn't question him. At the foot of the cliffs below, she could see the gleam of water through a screen of trees: a lake or dam. Sleek black birds swooped above the woods, wheeling in figures of eight. As she descended, a few people passed her, smiling and nodding in polite greeting. Making the careless assumption that she was one of them.

But she wasn't. In all her life, Karys had never felt more Mercian, or more like an imposter. And it wasn't that she resented the people here, not really. She just couldn't imagine living their lives. Couldn't imagine herself as Prete, taking that parcel without suspicion, more worried about inconveniencing a courier than any threat the delivery might pose. Or their wife, wide-eyed and anxious, trying so hard not to give offence—like it mattered, like Karys' opinion of her was the most important thing in the world. They were so far away from it all. Everything Karys had ever known was reduced to words on a page, lines shifting on a map, uncomfortable pauses in conversation.

And she could not get it out of her mind that, since arriving in Varesli, she had not seen a single beggar.

"Left at the end of the stairs," said Ferain.

Who would she have been if she had grown up in Eludia instead of Boäz, if she had been born in Varesli instead of Mercia? All her scars and damage smoothed off, all the grime and salt washed away. Never a deathspeaker, never hungry, never on the run. It was difficult to imagine—her alter-self formed only the vaguest outline in her mind. Someone naïve, softer, less afraid. Some-one happier. At the shaded base of the stairs, old women stood behind rows of wooden stands filled with flowers: carnations, cornflowers, marigolds, others that Karys lacked names for. Passersby stopped to chat and buy the flowers; the sellers carefully selected individual blooms to make up each bouquet.

"I used to walk this route often," said Ferain. "The Eludian branch of the Foreign Ministry is a district over, and I liked to cut through the Greens to get to my old apartment. It helped me think. Take the smaller footpath over there; it'll come out by the water."

Karys followed his direction. The trees rustled in the wind; they were tall and broad, their canopies dense, their bark the colour of old parchment. The path sloped upwards, curving back and forth like the tide. "Think about what?"

"Whatever was on my mind, I suppose. I found it calming, the solitude." Her shadow was difficult to discern in the deep green shade. "Karys, what do you need the money for?"

Between the trees ahead, a soft silver light kindled, then faded. Karys could not see its source.

"Why, are you thinking of reducing my pay?" she asked lightly.

"No. I've just been wondering for a long time."

"A life of debauchery, what else? Expensive clothing and parties."

"You don't have to tell me if you don't want to."

She continued walking. Another silver glimmer where the path curved, the brief impression of water glinting on fur. Gone again. She drew a slow breath.

"I don't tell people," she said. "Marishka knew, Busin knew. Even that was . . . I could never stand people pitying me. Haeki calls it pride, and maybe she's right, but that's not all of it. I'd mostly hate to be told I'm wrong."

Her shadow moved silently alongside her. Karys could not bring herself to look in his direction.

"It always sounds stupid when I say it aloud." She shook her head. "But since you asked—Toraigian citizenship."

A long pause.

"Oh," said Ferain.

"I've been saving for years. Busin could get some of the documents forged, but the bribes necessary are . . . well, I wasn't even close to making what I needed. Not until you came along." Karys smiled, humourless. "The lie about the parties was more fun, wasn't it?"

"Why?" he asked simply.

At the top of the slope, the same silvery gleam lingered—starlight suspended in smoke, the suggestion of slender limbs. Pale fire through deep water. Karys stopped, and watched as the figure dimmed and disappeared once more.

"What is that?" she asked.

"A sheen. It won't hurt you. They protect people walking alone along the forest paths."

"I haven't heard of them before."

"One of Ambavar's creations."

She nodded. The breeze rose and fell, muted through the branches. She resumed walking. Up ahead, the forest thinned; she could see patches of blue sky.

"There was another deathspeaker," she said. "Marei Nossark. An independent pledged to Sabaster, like me. She lived and worked in Psikamit about twenty-five years ago—before my time, so I never met her. Nossark collaborated extensively with the College, providing firsthand accounts of her experiences, trying to map out how the Ephirite function, how their power works, what they want. New Favour hated her, of course. She gave ordinary practitioners insight into higher Ephirite workings, laying the foundations for outsiders to derive and reproduce powers that deathspeakers had bartered away their souls for. That was dangerous. It threatened New Favour's control."

She reached the top of the ridge, and the land veered downwards once more, the trees ending where the water began. The lake shone bright in the sun. Small, stony islands punctuated its smooth surface; egrets sunned their white wings.

"Nossark was really interested in spatial exclusion," she said. "Physical places or effects from outside of our plane of reality, or superimposed on top of it, or cut away from it. Like the Embrace's domain, the Veneer, the Ephirite's realms— she would have loved the Split Lapse, I think, although her research didn't really touch on temporal workings. Anyway, she became obsessed with Toraigus."

The path joined up with a raised wooden walkway that ran alongside the water. There was no one else around. Karys paused, gathering her thoughts. *This is where I lose him.*

"You'll have heard that a deathspeaker's compact is an anchor," she said. "It binds us to the Ephirite; we're spiritually conjoined by the agreement. In the same way that I don't need to see my hands to use them, Sabaster can find me without a thought."

"Yes," said Ferain softly.

"And you'll also have heard that this anchor grants the Ephirite a footing in the world. Where I go, I open the way for my master. That was the Slaughter, after all—the point at which we threw open the gates for the herald-killers." Karys shrugged. "So Toraigus should offer no safety. Neither the Bhatuma nor the Ephirite can cross the Wall, but it wouldn't matter: I am Sabaster's private gate. If I were inside, he would be too. Ready to drag me back home. You know all of this."

Her shadow nodded.

Until now, the explanation had come easily. She had not risked anything yet. Karys closed her eyes for a second, her throat dry. *Tell him.*

"Nossark, she . . . she had an alternate theory," she said. "New Favour refuted it outright, and the College, well . . . they were sympathetic, but it had been twelve years since she had formed her compact. Easy to dismiss her as desperate or delusional under the circumstances; everyone knew her time had run out. She was on her own, still writing up her notes, still pushing through with this treatise that no one else would touch, everyone acting like she was a lost cause or tragic or mad—"

"Karys," murmured Ferain.

"Nossark believed that the Unbroken Wall isn't a spatial exclusion, but the border of one." She spoke in a breathless rush. "She believed that Toraigus *itself* is the workings exclusion zone. And that means that no Ephirit can ever touch it."

Silence, but for the wind. Karys' heart pounded like she had been running. Her head felt light, unstable.

Ferain's voice was low. "You would be safe?"

"I read everything Nossark left behind, and everything I could find about exclusions: all the theory, every reference, every footnote. She wasn't just desperate; her ideas made sense. Of course, Toraigus would never knowingly let a deathspeaker inside the Wall. They're scarcely willing to admit anyone, never mind—"

"When you told Vuhas you had a plan, this is what you meant?" Ferain interrupted.

"I don't remember saying that."

Her shadow was agitated, its shape unfixed. "You have to talk to Winola about this. She might know—"

Karys shook her head, hard. "No. Not her. No one else."

"Karys—"

"This is all I've ever found," she said. "My one way out. It's all I've got to hold on to."

She heard herself in that moment, how pathetic the words sounded leaving her mouth, how stupid and irrational and deluded. *It's real,* she wanted to insist, but that would only make things worse. Make her look even more weak. This was why she could never talk about Nossark; she would always sound like a child grasping after a fantasy, and she couldn't stand Ferain thinking less of her, couldn't bear his pity. Out of everyone, losing his respect would hurt the most.

"Well, you still could have told *me* sooner," said her shadow, annoyed. "How long will it take to get the forgeries once you have the money?"

The sunlight reflected off the water. The black-winged birds wheeled above, their movements mirrored on the lake.

"You don't think I'm deluding myself?" she whispered.

Ferain scoffed. "No, of course not. You're much too proud for that, right?"

He could be lying. Karys didn't think he was. It shouldn't have mattered as much as it did, but, standing there beneath the trees, she felt achingly grateful. Not just because he believed her, but because he was there at all. Because when he spoke, she felt less afraid and less alone, and because he had always acted like she had a future.

An urgent, formless desire came over her: to thank Ferain, to explain herself— she wasn't sure what she wanted to say, only that it was important. From nowhere, the memory of her shadow touching her jaw returned to her. The cool, careless brush of his fingers over her skin, at once gentle and unbearable. Unthinking, Karys moved her hand upwards as if to imitate the gesture. Then she caught herself.

What am I doing?

She quickly let her hand fall. That had been—what had that been? *What is wrong with me?* The hair lifted off the back of her neck.

"Something wrong?" her shadow asked.

Gratitude. She was grateful to Ferain. That was all. He represented her best chance of escaping Sabaster, and he had been a friend to her. That was all. Embrace, that had to be all.

Wordless, Karys started down the boardwalk, heading back north to Rhevin's house. The wooden planks creaked under her feet, silver smoke glinted between the trees. She buried the thought that, for a moment, she had wanted Ferain to touch her again.

CHAPTER

38

Haeki glared at the page, her pen awkwardly pinched between her fingers. Lines of large, wobbling black letters ran from left to right, covering a student's essay on the proper care and maintenance of Class C medium-scale Bhatuma relics.

"There must be an easier way," she grumbled. "I'm never going to remember this."

They were up in the garden-facing bedroom. The sun streamed in through the wide bay windows; a tray bearing an untouched carafe of water and a little bowl of sweets stood in the corner. Outside, Lindlee was hosting a small party. Irregular bursts of drunken teenage laughter wafted up from the tree-shaded yard.

Karys reclined on Haeki's bed, a dusty book about workings coalescence and interdependence propped open against her knees. Despite her best efforts to concentrate, she had now read the same paragraph four times over. Two days had passed since she had delivered Rasko's parcel—two days, and nothing to show for it. Haeki sat cross-legged on the wooden floorboards, surrounded by a ring of loose pages covered in more stumbling letters. Ferain hovered at her side, correcting her penmanship.

"Do you want to take a break?" he asked.

Haeki's scowl deepened. Although she had been working all morning, she set her pen to the paper again.

"No," she said.

When Karys first tried to teach her letters, Haeki had frozen up any time Ferain moved or spoke. Admitting her illiteracy to Karys had been difficult enough; having it paraded in front of a stranger was near intolerable. There was no helping the situation—as much as Karys might have wanted to, she couldn't conceal their lessons from her shadow. And, after a while, it had gotten easier. The initial sting of shame wore away, and Haeki's self-consciousness diminished as she grew accustomed to Ferain's company.

It also rapidly became apparent that he was a much better teacher. He even seemed to enjoy it.

"That line curves the other way," he said.

Haeki swore at him.

At least she seems to have forgiven him for Vuhas, Karys thought, then realised her eyes had wandered from the paragraph for the fifth time. She sighed, irritated. All day, she had been restless and distracted; too aware of the hours sliding by while she accomplished nothing. Rhevin scarcely returned home from the university, Winola spent every spare hour at the library, and still—nothing. It didn't help that Karys' only contribution was combing through the mouldering old books Winola brought back home, an activity which had grown to feel increasingly pointless. The authors had never heard of Constructs, and possessed no specialised knowledge on the Split Lapse. Karys had the sneaking suspicion Winola had only given her the task to keep her occupied.

Ferain slid up the side of the bed, out of Haeki's hearing.

"What's bothering you?" he asked.

Then, of course, there was the matter of Ferain himself.

"What do you think?" she mumbled.

"The waiting?"

"Yes, the waiting."

"Go for a walk, clear your head. Haeki needs a break anyway." He nudged the book's cover. "You haven't turned a page in the last twenty minutes."

She made an annoyed noise, waved him away, and started on the paragraph for the sixth time. *The conditions under which interdependent workings arise organically are varied; such melds may be affected by phases of the lunar cycle, the ambient temperature of the surrounding environment at the point of either working's instigation, the volume at which key spoken formulations of the derivation are produced by the—*

"Karys?" Winola called up the stairs.

At the sound of the scholar's voice, Haeki went rigid. Then she scrambled to collect the pages spread out across the floor. Karys dropped her book and jumped up from the bed to help, but Ferain got there first. Her shadow swept out in front of her, snatched the papers and the pen out of Haeki's hands, shoved them and the remaining essays under Lindlee's cot, and pulled down the blanket to conceal everything from sight. Karys' body protested the unexpected drawing, and she sat back down sharply.

"Thanks, reeker," whispered Haeki.

"Anytime."

Winola appeared in the doorway a second later, holding yet another stack of books. Her cheeks were flushed from exertion, and sweat dampened her forehead. It looked like she might have run from the library.

"I know how to remove the Construct's effect," she said without preamble.

Karys sucked in breath, and sat up straight. "You've worked it out?"

"In theory. Putting it into practice . . . not entirely. And there's another problem." Winola looked around the room distractedly, taking in Haeki, Karys' dropped book, the rumpled bedclothes. She shifted the weight of the books to her other arm. "Or there *might* be a problem, I don't know. The movement of your scar could be evidence of accelerated workings degradation. Possibly."

Karys' stomach knotted. "What does that mean?"

"It means the binding could fuse permanently, so we need to separate the two of you now, if we want to have any hope of separating you at all." Winola wiped her forehead. "Assuming that it isn't already too late. I need to talk to Rhevin. By now, he *must* know which authorisation—"

"But the Construct's effect," said Karys, "you can fix it?"

"Maybe. I understand the principles, but I haven't entirely worked out how to . . ." The scholar grasped for a word. "Displace the effect? Basically, it's like a boulder rolling down a mountain—now that it's in motion, I can't stop it, but I might be able to alter its course. I think the effect could be fully redirected into non-harmful expression, it's just that forcing that displacement requires a huge amount of power applied extremely precisely."

"And if it goes wrong?"

"I'm sure you can guess. The effect runs its course; we lose Ferain. With more time, I could probably find safeguards, but if the scar's movement really is an indicator of workings degradation, then that's time we don't have. I should have considered all of this sooner."

Karys' shadow spread, reaching over the floor to cross Winola's.

"Maybe that means we need to reconsider our priorities," he said.

Winola frowned. "Those being?"

Ferain spoke in Toraigian—and although Karys did not understand him; she could guess the drift of his answer by the scholar's shocked expression. She rose from the bed.

"No," she snapped. "I know what you're saying, Ferain, and no."

With a sigh, her shadow returned to her, drifting out of the others' hearing.

"Be practical," he said. "You need the time."

She balled her fists. "I also need the money. Your father's not going to pay me for a corpse."

"He will if I force the issue." Ferain remained infuriatingly calm. "My point is that we can't afford to wait for guarantees or safeguards—never mind workings degradation; the longer this goes on, the greater the risk to you. Too long, and payment becomes irrelevant."

"What's that supposed to mean?"

"Karys, you know exactly what it means. Money can't save you if Sabaster—"

"Go fuck yourself," she snarled.

Haeki and Winola both flinched.

"You've thought about it," said Ferain, undeterred. "I know you have."

"We did not come all this way just so you could pull off a noble *suicide*." She spat out the word. "Your life for fifteen thousand cret, Ferain. I gave you my promise. If you wanted to die, you could have done it in the fucking Sanctum."

"This is not suicide. It's calculated risk."

"Your calculations are shit."

"Sabaster could call your compact tomorrow."

He said it without feeling, simple and direct. Karys felt like he had punched her in the gut. She opened her mouth to speak, but nothing came out.

"Twelve years, right? Since you formed your compact?" He continued in the same blank, cool tone. "Sabaster said he would summon you when the receptacle blooms. Maybe that's tomorrow, maybe next month, maybe years from now—but every day the odds increase. We both know what you gamble by waiting. We both know what he intends. When the time comes, you need to be beyond your master's reach, and that means Toraigus."

He knew exactly where her weaknesses lay. She had shown him just where to slide the knife.

"I wish I'd never told you," whispered Karys.

Her shadow rippled, her silhouette splintering and then re-forming. When he spoke again, Ferain's voice was quieter, but steady.

"Once Winola has worked out the mechanics, let me take the risk," he said. "Before it's too late. Please, Karys."

No, she thought. *You won't frighten me into this. You think you're so clever, but I know what you are trying to do.* The tension in the room ran high and tight; Haeki looked frozen, Winola alarmed. They could only hear her side of the conversation, and it must have sounded ridiculous, but neither of them was laughing.

Before Karys could continue the argument, however, the water carafe in the corner of the room spoke.

"Let me be of service, Son of Night," said Nuliere.

Winola dropped her books with an exclamation. The heavy volumes thumped loudly to the ground, covers splaying open, spines cracking.

"Oh, sorry," she said, hastily stooping to collect them. "Sorry about that."

Without a word, Haeki crouched down to help the scholar. She carefully smoothed the pages where they had folded, her head bowed. Even when she rose, handing the books back to Winola, she did not look up. There was no need to guess who had salted the water.

"What do you want, slug?" asked Karys harshly.

A sustained hissing emanated from the carafe, as though the water inside were under immense pressure. Karys considered overturning the vessel, or throwing it out the window. She wanted to do something vicious and senseless. She wanted to storm out of the room. She wanted everyone else to go away.

Nuliere, however, seemed better able to get a handle on her temper.

"In spite of your boundless ingratitude," she said, her whistling voice taut with effort, "I have diverted the enemy's attention."

"How? Did you kill them all?"

The herald did not take the bait.

"Their trail now leads further east, toward the capital," she said. "While their resources are stretched thinner across Varesli, this ruse will not last forever. Time is short, apostate."

"So everyone tells me. What do you want, Nuliere?"

"What I have always wanted." The water subsided, the hissing faded. "To help the Son of Night. It might be within the scope of my power to heal his affliction."

Karys jerked. "What?"

"He is touched by the enemy's power. I believe I can draw out their poison."

Could she . . . ? Karys' head spun. "Why—why didn't you say anything before now?"

Nuliere hummed, producing a high clear sound like a finger traced around the rim of a glass.

"The faithless woman spoke of turning aside falling boulders," she said. "Under the right circumstances, water may move mountains. It is possible."

Winola's eyes had gone round and large behind her glasses. "Are you saying you could provide the power to displace the effect?"

The same pealing ring. It set Karys' teeth on edge.

"Under the right circumstances," repeated the herald. "I would need to be made manifest. The binding to the apostate must be cracked open but not sundered, not until the Son of Night is restored."

Karys felt overwhelmed and confused, and yet, even in the midst of her disorientation, there was something in Nuliere's voice that gave her pause. A kind of practised smoothness. From the faint tightening of her shadow, Ferain had detected it too.

"You heard everything Winola said?" he asked.

"Of course, kindred—I have heard all, and I understand what is required."

"And it would be safe?"

"So long as the binding is maintained until your affliction is healed."

What isn't *she saying?* Despite everything, Karys wanted to believe the herald, but Nuliere was making this sound too easy. And if she failed to displace the Construct's effect, if something went wrong or her power wasn't sufficient . . .

The doorbell rang downstairs, jarring Karys out of her thoughts. Winola and Haeki's heads turned toward the hallway in unison.

"Seems someone's looking for my father," muttered Ferain. He addressed Nuliere again. "Herald, thank you. This has given me a lot to think about—although my father doesn't know how to open the Lapse yet."

"I strive to help you," said Nuliere. She paused before adding: "Remember that, Ferain. I am your ally."

The bell rang a second time. Karys shook her head, and brushed past Winola out into the corridor.

She did not know how to feel. It was true that Nuliere held a measure of the Embrace's authority—impotent by the standards of other Bhatuma, but not entirely powerless. She might truly be able to heal Ferain. The curtains in the passage rippled in the breeze; outside, one of Lindlee's friends cracked a joke, and the others jeered and laughed. And yet . . . *Surely she would have known it was possible before now?* In all the time they had travelled, not one word about her power to mend him—but after an abbreviated explanation from Winola, suddenly Nuliere held the answers? Karys descended the stairs two at a time. Waiting, lurking, listening in. Embrace only knew what else she had overheard, or how many innocuous glasses and vases around the house were rimmed with salt.

"I think," said Ferain in an undertone, "that we need to be more careful around Haeki."

Karys did not bother replying. What was there to say? She reached the base of the stairs as the bell rang out yet again.

"Didn't hear you the first time," she said. She crossed the entranceway, unlatched the door, and pulled it open.

Standing at the top of the front steps was a woman with amber-coloured hair and sharp dark eyes. She stood very straight, a few inches taller than Karys, and wore a draping blue vest and narrow trousers cinched at the waist. One hand was planted on her hip, the other held the bell cord.

"I'm looking for Karys Eska," said Ilesha.

Oh no, thought Karys distinctly.

The woman standing in front of her was beautiful. Not pretty; she seemed too sharp for that; her features held a peregrine edge despite the smooth lustre of her skin, her eyes strikingly dark against her complexion, her brows sleek and predatory. Not pretty, but beautiful. And Karys knew the smell of her hair, knew how her body moved, knew the warmth of those slim, fine-boned fingers—and worse, wanted them.

Oh no, she thought again.

"Ilesha," whispered Ferain.

The woman arched her eyebrow at Karys' silence. She had a thin pale scar below her left temple, and her long hair was bound in an elegant twist that spilled over her right shoulder.

"Is that going to be a problem?" she asked.

Karys shook herself. "No. No, that's—I'm Karys."

Ilesha's lips thinned.

"Good," she said. "We need to talk."

Karys' mind was in turmoil; she felt an inexplicable affection for this stranger, a sense of security and familiarity and, yes, desire—but those feelings should not belong to her. It was bewildering, it was wrong. *I know you, but you don't know me at all.* Judging by Ilesha's expression, the attraction was far from mutual.

"This won't take long," she said. "I only need to clarify a few things."

Karys nodded, tongue-tied. "Sure."

Ilesha drew back her shoulders. She breathed in deeply, and when she spoke her voice was flat, rehearsed, and clipped.

"First," she said, "although you have duped Rhevin, you are not going to fool me. While I really don't care if you bleed the old man dry, I take issue with using Ferain's name to accomplish that."

"That's not—"

Ilesha continued, unassailable. "Second, you should be aware that I have done my research. I know you're a deathspeaker, cas Eska. My understanding is that communion with the dead involves direct contact with their remains. If you know enough to reel in Rhevin, then you have spoken with Ferain's ghost, and you know the location of his body. You are going to tell me where to find him, and you are going to tell me who was responsible for killing him. Then you are going to leave Eludia and never return. If you do that, I will pay you. If you do not, I will render your life not worth living. Does that make sense?"

Formidable, thought Karys.

"Cas Eska?"

"He's not dead." She loosened the tension in her jaw. "Ferain, that is. He isn't dead."

If possible, Ilesha's face grew even colder.

"Don't try that with me," she said, dangerously low. "I already told you, I won't be—"

Karys' shadow moved swiftly, snaking out the door and into the light. Ferain rose and touched Ilesha's cheek. The drawing pulled gently inside Karys' chest.

"I'm not dead," he said.

Ilesha's skin went white. She stumbled back, clasping her face where he had touched her. Karys automatically reached out to stop her from falling down the steps, but Ilesha jerked away.

"What was that?" she demanded.

Karys lowered her arm. "Him."

Ilesha's mouth twisted; a brief, suppressed flash of anguish crossed her face. She dropped her hand from her cheek. "Is this a trick? One of your perverse deathspeaker powers? You'll have to do better, I won't be—"

Ferain reached out for her again, and Ilesha staggered away from him, down onto the street. She made an angry, pained sound. Karys' chest tightened with concern, but she pushed away the feeling. Emotional detritus, nothing more; just Ferain's presence still echoing inside her head. She folded her arms.

"Not a trick," she said. "Perverse, maybe, but not a trick. Is there anything else you wanted to tell me? You can keep your money, by the way; I have no intention of leaving Eludia yet. Go ahead—try and make me."

Ilesha glared up at her, contempt and fear warring on her face. Two houses down the street, small children shrieked, oblivious. To Karys' surprise, she stepped forward again.

"Prove it, then," she said. "If it isn't a trick, show me."

Karys shrugged. She made a peremptory gesture toward her shadow, a flick of her fingers.

"This wasn't how I envisioned the two of you meeting," muttered Ferain.

Far more slowly, he advanced down the steps. Ilesha watched, her body tense, but she held her ground this time. Ferain touched the shadow at her feet.

"Hello," he said. "It's me. I don't need avenging just yet."

She started, and her hands rose again slightly as if she wanted to ward off the sound of his voice.

"Mimicry," she said. "Cruel, but well-worked; I'll give you that. I didn't know something like this was possible."

Ferain sighed. "Really?"

"Preserved sounds, a few repeating phrases—"

"I've missed you. I'm sorry that I scared you."

"*Scared* me?" Ilesha repeated, strangled. "Scared me? You were buried without a grave, you were gone. I first heard the whispers two weeks ago, and the Foreign Ministry's silence all but confirmed them. *Scared?* I didn't get the chance to be scared; I was already grieving. What is this? What have you done?"

"It wasn't his fault," said Karys.

Ilesha laughed, hard and mirthless. "Is that right? Was it yours, then?"

"Ilesha." Ferain's voice was pained. "Come on."

She pressed her palm to her forehead, closing her eyes for a second. Karys could almost have pitied her, except that the comment about perversity had struck a little close to home, and she had thought Ferain would come to her defence. Which was stupid; he wouldn't take her side over his former fiancée's, but . . .

"All right," said Ilesha, more controlled. She exhaled heavily, and dropped her hand. "Fine. Explain it to me."

Karys ground her teeth together. "Maybe you should try *asking*, instead of—"

"Karys?" said Haeki.

Karys glanced back through the front door. Haeki stood at the base of the stairs, holding the banister. Her expression was guarded, but there was an entreaty in it. Anxiety in the lines of her shoulders.

"Is something wrong?" she asked.

A bitter taste welled up in the back of Karys' mouth. *Now you're worried.* All those hours spent together: the sense that maybe they could recover, maybe there was still a way back, maybe the distance between them could be bridged, and an apostate and an adherent could come to common ground—a lie. For all that time, Nuliere had been present. And Haeki had known.

"No," said Karys shortly.

Haeki held firm. "Are you sure? If you need me—"

"Certain." She turned around again. "Having a conversation with a friend of Ferain's, that's all. We were just leaving."

"Oh. I see."

From her tone, Haeki wanted to say something more. Karys didn't give her the chance. She pulled the door closed with a loud snap.

"Lover's quarrel?" asked Ilesha.

Karys gave her a withering stare. "No."

"It sounded like one."

"If you're going to talk, then talk to Ferain." Karys started down the street toward the wooded path beyond the houses. "I don't need to be a part of this."

"Touchy."

"Will both of you stop it?" said Ferain, which Karys thought was unfair—she was under no obligation to be nice to his erstwhile future wife, especially considering the woman had all but spat at her. Which, granted, she should be accustomed to, but it had been a difficult morning, and if she was a little more sensitive than usual, well, no one could claim she didn't have cause. She stalked down the road, not bothering to check if Ilesha was keeping up. The flagstones gave way to gravel, the verges on either side of the path bloomed with pink and white wildflowers. *Have your reunion, I don't care. It's not like I have any bigger problems to worry about.* The shadows of the trees thickened. At the base of an old oak stood a rickety bench; Karys marched over to it, dropped down on the seat, and spread her legs out insolently wide.

Ilesha remained standing. The dappled light caught on her hair. She studied the long irregular shape of Karys' shadow where it spilled over the grass at her feet.

"Well?" said Karys. "Go on, then. Talk."

Ilesha lifted her gaze.

"We haven't had the best introduction," she said.

"And?"

"I think we should start over. My name is—"

"I know who you are," said Karys, cutting her off. She heard the edge in her own voice, brittle resentment threatening to crack. She looked away, and tried to moderate her tone. "Ferain told me about you. And you already know all about me, apparently."

"I wouldn't say that."

"No?"

"Very little, actually. Name and occupation, and that you worked in Psikamit. That you arrived in Eludia with two other women, and Lindlee Agonasis. That Rhevin has found you persuasive." A lithe, rolling shrug. "He told me that you had information about Ferain. I wanted to look into your background, but I'm not very well connected in Mercia."

"And you assumed I was here to scam Rhevin."

"I was surprised that you seemed to be succeeding." Ilesha held out her hand. "My apologies."

Karys wavered. Then she leaned forward and shook it. Ilesha's skin was smooth and firm, her nails short, perfectly shaped half-moons.

"To be fair," said Karys, "I *am* charging the man fifteen thousand cret for his son's return."

"Pre-negotiated," said Ferain.

Ilesha jumped again at the sound of his voice. She released Karys' hand.

"This isn't a trick?" she asked.

Karys leaned back on the bench. "If you want to speak to Ferain privately, he's able to move about twenty feet away from me. I can wait here."

"Maybe in a moment. I'm still . . . this is a lot to take in." Ilesha gave an ironic, self-deprecating smile. "'Doesn't need avenging just yet.'"

"Or ever," said Ferain. "Although I was flattered."

"You would be." She curled the end of her hair around one finger. Her humour faded. "Everything I heard indicated that you were dead. Is it permanent? What you've done?"

Ferain's voice turned deceptively light. "There have been a few complications. My father believes that he can separate us."

She wasn't taken in. "You don't know."

"Well, the alternative was dying. Under the circumstances, I think—"

"Rain, what really happened in Psikamit?"

He fell quiet. Ilesha looked down at him, her face drawn, and waited.

"Has the Ministry revealed the murder of the retinue?" he asked.

"No, they're keeping it quiet. Stuck in a corner."

"But they've spoken to my father. What's the official line?"

"That the retinue is 'late to arrive in Cosaris.'" Ilesha wrinkled her nose. "They're stalling. The embassy bombing was impossible to conceal, although they've gotten some news-sellers to float that it was a workings accident."

"Did anyone buy that?"

"Not as far as I can tell. The usual crowd have already started salivating about repercussions. Throw in another public incident, and it's open provocation, it's an insult. More people are going to start listening to the glory days brigade, and the Ministry knows it."

"That's what I feared."

"You can kind of see their point, though; it does make Varesli look weak. The whole retinue is gone?"

"Everyone but me."

"Embrace, what a mess. I'm sorry. And if the truth comes out, I don't see how the Ministry de-escalates this. Assassination demands a response, and Varesli's in no position to make one."

"I know."

"Your father's in with the patriots. Near the front of their ranks, actually."

"Of course he is."

"But that's the odd thing, isn't it?" Ilesha jerked her head in the direction of Rhevin's house. "You say the Ministry told him what happened. They know his affiliations—so why would they risk informing him? And why *hasn't* he shared the news with his friends?"

Ferain was silent a moment. He seemed disquieted. Listening to him and Ilesha talk, Karys felt the strangest sense of dislocation. He wasn't behaving differently, exactly; it was more like the two of them spoke in their own personal dialect, quick and sure and layered with meaning. And although they were both right in front of her, she felt cut away from him.

"I don't know," he said at last. "I don't know, but I don't think he's sharing everything. He hasn't been himself."

"Sounds like an improvement."

"Hah." Ferain shook his head. "Did he tell you about any of this?"

"Why would he? There's no longer a formal obligation, and he never liked me to begin with. No, I found out about the retinue on my own. Only whispers, for now. The truth hasn't spread far yet." Ilesha rubbed her neck. "It was devastating, by the way. Learning you were dead. You couldn't have sent a letter?"

"I was hoping you wouldn't find out about the incident."

"Well, that was stupid of you."

"I didn't want you to worry. I'm sorry."

"So you said earlier."

"And I meant it. Both times."

Ilesha seemed to reach some silent conclusion. She nodded to herself and crossed her arms. Her manner turned efficient and businesslike.

"Later," she said. "I have much more to ask, but later. What can I do to help?"

Ferain thought for a moment.

"A few things, actually," he said. "Some more dangerous than others."

"Interesting."

"Does the phrase 'the last harbour' mean anything to you?"

"Should it?"

"Thought I'd check, that's all. Nothing?"

"Nothing."

"Pity. Never mind, forget that."

"What else, then?"

Again, Ferain paused. Karys received the impression he was undecided on something; her shadow shifted back and forth on the ground. Then he spoke quickly.

"Toraigian citizenship," he said. "Watertight, no questions asked, no background enquiries, immediately available. How much would that cost?"

Karys stiffened. Ilesha issued a low whistle.

"A *very* large bribe," she said. "Buying into Toraigus is hard enough when it's done legitimately. Getting in on false papers . . . I don't know if that's even possible, but I can find out."

"Please. The sooner, the better."

Private, that was private. Heat rose in Karys' face. Ferain knew her plans for Toraigus were a secret; she had told him as much. She had explained why. Her voice came out harsh. "I don't recall asking for help."

Ilesha looked at her curiously. Karys wanted to sink through the bench and into the ground. *No one else was supposed to know.* She felt suffocated; she could not explain this again. Ferain drew closer to her, slipping out of Ilesha's shadow.

"That's the problem—you never do," he said. "Karys, it'll likely be faster than returning to Psikamit. Ilesha knows people, and she's good at this. Let her at least ask the questions."

And if the answer to those questions is "no"?

"The citizenship is for you?" asked Ilesha.

With effort, Karys met the other woman's dark eyes. "Yes. For me. Is that a problem?"

Despite Karys' tone, Ilesha appeared more intrigued than offended. Somehow, that seemed worse.

"I guess we'll see," she said. "Forgive me for asking, but is there any physical indicator that marks you as a deathspeaker? Some kind of body modification . . ."

Karys shook her head. "No."

"And nothing else the Toraigian authorities could identify or test for?"

"No. I'm human."

The corner of Ilesha's mouth twitched upwards. "Doubtless. In any case, give me a few days, and I'll see what I can do. Was there anything else, Ferain?"

He flowed back into her shade. "Just one more thing."

"The dangerous part?"

"Only if you're willing. Have you ever heard of the Grateful Society?"

The morning was bright, the sunlit grove deserted. No one else would have been able to hear her shadow, but Karys still tensed. Cold fingers trailed down her spine. They had left Vuhas behind—barely escaped, committed an unspeakable crime, and nearly lost Ferain in the process, but they had gotten away with it. The next time, his lies would not be enough.

"Don't," she said.

Ilesha noted her reaction. Her gaze travelled between Karys' face and the pooled mass of her shadow.

"I'm not sure," she said. "I might have, but only in passing. Nothing that sticks in my mind."

"Will you ask around?"

Karys made a frustrated noise. "Ferain, no. Why would you want any more of their attention? Just forget them."

Her shadow grazed the side of her hand; whether in apology or reassurance, she could not tell. "Then they'll still be out there."

"Who is 'they,' exactly?" asked Ilesha.

"A cabal of very wealthy, very old skin thieves," he replied.

"Ferain."

Ilesha cocked her head. "I thought skin thieves belonged to children's stories."

"These ones tried to recruit me."

"And you want me to scope them out?"

"You would have to tread extremely lightly. Nothing that can be traced back to you."

She huffed. "What do you take me for?"

"I'm just saying be careful." Ferain's tone grew more sombre. "I don't know how deep their network runs, but they've got at least one informant in the Foreign Ministry. If you find you need to dig, stop."

"You believe they're that dangerous?"

"Yes. And vindictive."

Ilesha nodded. "The surface only. I'll watch my step."

"You shouldn't be watching anything at all," snapped Karys. "Once they hear that you're asking questions, they'll come for you. And then for *me,* just as soon as they figure out where you got their name from."

Ilesha brushed invisible dirt from the draping fabric of her shirt.

"That's assuming I get caught," she said. "I'd like to speak to Ferain alone now, please."

Karys scowled, swallowing a retort, and pushed herself up from the bench. *Fine. Stupid, arrogant reekers.* She moved past Ilesha, marching up the path toward the street. *Not my problem, anyway.* If everything fell into place, she would have disappeared to Toraigus long before Vuhas came knocking, and if matters grew worse, then the Grateful would be the least of her concerns. But did Ferain *really* think the society wouldn't catch wind of someone prying into their affairs? Ilesha had no idea what she was getting into. Yes, it was their funeral, their necks on the line—but they would both regret it once the skin thieves arrived.

A tight pain knotted inside Karys' chest as she neared the limits of her shadow's reach; the darkness stretched to a thin cord at her heels. She drew to a halt, anger fading. Behind her, the indistinct murmur of Ilesha's voice carried on the breeze. Fallen leaves stirred on the ground, brown and dry and dead. Ferain replied, and Ilesha laughed, surprised.

He missed her.

Karys dragged her fingers back through her hair. She had already known. Still, the way they spoke, the way Ferain had reached for Ilesha outside the house, their closeness . . . she had not expected it to be so obvious, or for his relief and affection to press against her like a bruise. Her future at stake, and here she stood, disappointed to discover that Ferain had a life outside of her shadow. She kicked at the wildflowers. Laughable. None of it even mattered.

Ilesha and Ferain did not speak long, perhaps for five minutes. The time dragged. Karys waited, and eventually felt the pressure inside her chest ease as her shadow drew nearer once more. She heard the leaves crunch under Ilesha's feet, and turned to face them.

"Finished already?" she asked. "If you want more time—"

Ilesha waved away the offer before Karys could even finish making it. "We're fine. I won't keep you any longer."

Ferain flowed back to his usual place, cool at Karys' side. She tried to ignore the way that his proximity caused the tension in her shoulders to unwind. "I'm sorry. The last few weeks must have been difficult for you."

"I've had better." Ilesha's gaze held an appraising light, as though she was measuring Karys in some new way, re-evaluating her. "From what Ferain tells me, so have you. Take care of him for me, won't you?"

Karys wasn't sure how to respond, so she just nodded. Ilesha seemed satisfied with that. She walked toward the street, and her arm softly—accidentally—brushed against Karys' as she passed. Up close, her perfume smelled like cedar and rain.

"I'll call again once I have something to share," she murmured.

Karys felt flustered.

"That's—yes," she said. "All right."

Ilesha laughed and continued walking, leaving Karys at the edge of the woods. Her steps were quick and purposeful, her hair bright in the sunlight. Although she must have known that Karys was watching her, she did not once look back.

Karys' shadow drifted up her side.

"What did you think of her?" asked Ferain.

"She threatened to ruin my life."

"But you liked her."

"I don't see why this is so important to you."

"Because I care what you think. And because you are blushing."

Karys rubbed her hand across her face. "No, I'm not. And you didn't have to tell her about Toraigus."

"Are you still angry?"

Ilesha reached the far end of the street, and turned west toward the bridge, disappearing from sight. Karys shook her head.

"I know that I might seem . . . irrational about it," she said reluctantly. "I just—I need to believe that Toraigus will work."

Her shadow pressed against her shoulder for a second, the drawing light.

"I know," he said. "And it will."

CHAPTER

40

When Karys returned to the house, Winola was sitting downstairs at the kitchen table eating a wilted salad, her expression unfocussed, her books stacked up on the counter. Her foot tapped arrhythmically against the leg of her chair.

Although Haeki's absence was conspicuous, Karys did not ask. So what if Nuliere's sea-blessed was upset? Was she now obliged to pretend that nothing had happened, to sit around and devise further writing exercises? No, Haeki had made her loyalties abundantly clear. What did it matter, the rush of pride Karys had felt whenever she caught Haeki mouthing the letters in street signs, on storefronts, on the spines of books? Why should she care if Nuliere's Favoured had begun to smile more often, warmed to Ferain, occasionally sang quietly to herself while she was alone? It had only ever been an illusion and an indulgence, and now it was over. Better this way—one less distraction, one less regret in the end. Karys scanned the kitchen for possible sources of salted water. She collected two teacups from the counter and emptied their dregs in the sink. Winola looked up from her meal.

"'A friend of Ferain's?'" she queried.

Karys made a noncommittal sound. The scholar returned to her salad.

"Don't take it out on Haeki," she said. "She is in a difficult position, and you know it."

Karys washed out the cups, and set them upside down on the rack. Through the kitchen window, she could see Lindlee and her friends, a group of youths in garishly dyed clothing. They lounged around on the grass, some propped up against one another; heads resting on legs or stomachs. Chewing osk, drinking from dark bottles. One of them, a boy with wavy brown hair and an unappealingly slack mouth, stood and gestured like a performer. They all looked significantly inebriated.

At least Lindlee got what she wanted. Karys leaned over the counter. A line of decorative clay gourds sat on the window sill; until now, she had not paid them any attention. She picked one up, and it sloshed with water. With a scowl, she tipped it over into the sink.

"Do you know when Rhevin might be back?" she asked, reaching for the next gourd.

"No."

Karys ran the water inside over the back of her hand, and tasted it. She grimaced. Sure enough: salt. There it was, undeniable and clear. She would have to check every room in the house, and no doubt Haeki would secrete away more vessels as fast as she could find them. Like a stupid game of catch-up.

The brown-haired boy sauntered over to where Lindlee was seated on the grass, still waving his arms around, proclaiming something. Rather comically, he tapped her on the top of her head. The others giggled, and the boy smirked. Lindlee gazed up at him wide-eyed, and blinked.

I never behaved that strangely when I was a child, thought Karys sourly. Although she supposed there had been fewer opportunities, and less intoxication. Her life at that age seemed small and confined, her idea of a thrill stealing Ané's bottle of reef-wine from the temple. In retrospect, a petty little act of rebellion—she had decanted it, replaced the contents with vinegar, and then split the liquor with Haeki and Oboro down on the beach. Back then, the gesture had seemed so important, so potent; she remembered that the silvery sweetness of the wine had been unlike anything she had ever experienced; the taste of a world beyond her reach. And they had all gone quiet, drinking it, listening to the waves on the sand, the wind through the cleft. Oboro reclined next to her, Haeki walking barefoot in the shallows. No one else had ever discovered her crime.

Well, except for Nuliere. The herald would have known. *No wonder she disliked me.*

Outside, Lindlee's friends had stopped laughing. For some reason, they were all staring, as if mesmerised, at the empty air above Lindlee's head. Karys set down the last gourd, her skin prickling. Their new stillness felt unnatural, eerie; they had gone entirely silent. At the edge of Karys' hearing was a high whining sound.

She moved without thought; she was across the room and through the back door to the garden in seconds. Winola called her name in alarm, but Karys barely heard.

Lindlee sat frozen on the lawn. Even from a distance, Karys saw her clothing darken—the girl gleamed with a rusty bronze liquid; it welled and dripped from her skin, pooling underneath her. Her posture had gone unnaturally rigid, as though her flesh was calcifying. The whining increased. Karys ripped open the Veneer.

The mangled Ephirite-derived working hovered in the air over Lindlee's head, shining like a corona, a tangle of rank light unspooling and sinking thirsty tendrils into her skull. It jittered and screeched horribly, trembling as it grew. The wavy-haired boy shouted something—a slur of syllables—and the working ballooned outward.

Karys reached her senses into the sickly shining mass and yanked it apart.

The working unravelled, lights spinning out into nothing. Lindlee keeled over, quivering, just as Karys reached her. She dropped to the ground beside the girl, hunting any further traces of the diseased light, but they winked out like falling sparks, harmless. Around her, the Veneer's chaos abated. Its colours stopped seething; it grew still and the sawing shriek fell silent.

"It's gone," whispered one of the other boys.

Lindlee moaned, and brought her hands up to clutch her head. Karys breathed heavily, her heart racing. If she had been a few seconds slower . . . She swallowed, her mind catching up with her instincts. That working could have obliterated everyone in the garden. She lifted her gaze, and found the wavy-haired boy.

"Are you," she said, in a hoarse whisper, "out of your mind?"

At the sight of her face, the boy took a step backwards. His slack, insipid lips parted like he had forgotten to close his mouth. Then his expression turned defensive.

"It was an honest mistake," he said.

"You nearly *liquefied* her!" Karys rose in a single motion, and advanced toward him. "What the fuck were you doing trying to work Ephirite derivations onto another person?"

Despite the flash of alarm on his face, the boy held his ground. He was lanky, easily a head taller than Karys, perhaps seventeen. He raised his hands in a placating gesture. "Relax. Everything was under control."

She shoved him in the chest. "You had nothing under control, you ignorant little shit. You thought you could show off to your friends? You thought it was all a joke? You don't know the first thing about what you were doing."

"Easy, now." He pushed away her hands, and tried to sneer at her. "Who are you, anyway?"

"Don't worry, Karys," said Lindlee anxiously. She had managed to sit upright, although she still cradled her head. "Quinn is actually a poet; he's really good. He got accepted into—"

"I don't need defending, thanks," said the boy.

"A *poet*?" snarled Karys.

"Yes, that's why he's so good at Ephirite workings." Lindlee sounded tearful. "Because it's all just weird poetry."

Karys sensed that she was on the verge of losing her head completely. She breathed in.

"Was that," she asked, "improvisation?"

In spite of the situation, Quinn looked quite pleased.

"Yes," he said. "All my own work."

Karys made an inarticulate noise. Behind her, Winola hurried over the lawn to Lindlee, and dropped to a crouch next to the girl.

"Are you all right, sweetheart?" she asked. "You're soaked. What happened?"

"Everything is fine," said Lindlee unsteadily. "Everything is perfectly fine. We're just having fun, please don't make a fuss."

Some of her friends had risen from the grass; they eyed Karys and Winola nervously. The atmosphere was tense. Quinn tucked his hands into his pockets, affecting disdain.

"Sorry, Linds, but I was bored in any case," he drawled.

Lindlee made a tiny pained sound, and the last of Karys' patience evaporated.

"Get out," she said.

Quinn smirked, as though he found her ridiculous. "Oh, scary. What are you going to do, huh?"

One of the girls tittered. Karys kept her gaze on the boy, saying nothing. At the edge of her vision, her shadow had gone dark. Still grinning, Quinn leaned right up close to her. He pulled a face, making his eyes bulge, taunting. Karys remained still, and kept staring. She could feel his breath. She marked as flickers of doubt, then frustration crossed his features, and gave no reaction. In the moment when he realised that his intimidation would not work, she thought he might strike her. Then he gave a forced laugh, the sound ringing loud and crass, and turned away.

"Nothing," he said. "I thought so. Like I said, I wanted to leave anyway, bitch."

He spat on the grass, and marched toward the side gate, stooping to pick up a half-empty bottle as he went. The gate creaked on its hinges, and clanged after him. For a few seconds, no one else moved.

"A real poet," remarked Karys.

The remaining teenagers hung back, uncomfortable. A few had the grace to look guilty; most just appeared awkward. None of them spoke. One of the boys collected his bag off the lawn, and moved after Quinn. The others followed him, not making eye contact. A brunette girl muttered a half-hearted apology to Lindlee as she passed.

"Oh, it's fine. Not to worry." Lindlee attempted a smile, but the girl moved more quickly, as if scared that she might be left behind. No one said goodbye. Lindlee raised her voice, calling after them. "Sorry, everyone! See you all tomorrow?"

The gate swung shut. Not a single person answered her. Lindlee's smile faltered, and her lower lip trembled. Winola rubbed her back gently.

"Are you in any pain?" she asked.

"No, no." Lindlee swallowed. She took a shallow breath, and then promptly burst into tears. "I'm fine."

"Shh."

"It was supposed to be fun. They always spend their holidays together, they've got so many stories, and I wanted . . . I just wanted . . ."

Winola put an arm around Lindlee's shoulder, giving her a hug. "You're shaken up, that's all. It'll be all right. Come on, let's get you inside."

The scholar coaxed Lindlee to the kitchen, murmuring soothingly. She sat the girl down and then heated a large bowl of water, while Karys followed Ferain's directions to the linen closet and brought out some old washcloths. Lindlee seemed drained and heartsore, but physically unharmed. She gave a sad little hiccup when Karys handed her a towel.

"Thanks," she said. "And sorry. Quinn's just sensitive."

Karys would have privately ascribed many qualities to the boy, but sensitivity was not amongst them. It seemed the wrong time to make that point to Lindlee, however. Winola placed the steaming bowl down on the counter, and patted Lindlee on the back again.

"Something warm to drink?" she offered. "If you give me a few minutes, I can also prepare you a proper bath. You should probably change out of those clothes."

"Chocolate?" Lindlee asked tentatively.

"I can do that." Winola moved to the stove. "Do you want any, Karys?"

After Vuhas, Karys was not sure she could ever drink chocolate again. She declined, and sat down opposite Lindlee. The teenager wiped the cloth over her face and neck; when she dropped it into the water, the fabric was stained dark rust-orange.

"Are you sure you're all right?" asked Karys.

Lindlee nodded, and hiccupped again. She swirled the cloth around the bowl.

"How did you do that?" she asked.

"Do what?"

Lindlee wrung the water from the towel. "Take apart Quinn's poetry. The way you untangled it? How did you do that so quickly?"

At the stove, Winola breathed in sharply. Things clicked into place inside Karys' mind all at once—the teenagers staring at the space above Lindlee's head, the boy saying *it's gone,* Quinn's obvious alarm as the working expanded and shrieked. During the crisis, she had been too focussed to spare it any attention, but now . . .

"You can open the Veneer?" asked Karys, baffled.

The girl's expression transitioned from confusion to wariness.

"Open what?" she asked, a little shifty.

Winola had gone stock still. Karys felt at a loss. "The Veneer. If you saw me take apart that derivation—"

"I don't understand. Are you talking about the Glowing?"

The Glowing? "No, I'm—you saw the working, the one that Quinn applied to you? You and your friends could all see that?"

Lindlee's shoulders bunched up as though she suspected a trap. "Well, yes. And other stuff. But if you can see the Glowing, then you're taking it too, right?"

"Taking what?" It felt like they were talking past one another. "I'm a death-speaker. I can access the Veneer whenever I want to."

Lindlee's lips parted in a soft "oh." Her eyes turned wide and dismayed, and she twined the washcloth between her hands.

"I didn't know," she said. "Karys, I'm so sorry; that's terrible. I had no—"

"Lindlee, what are you *taking*?"

The girl jumped, nearly upsetting the bowl. Her gaze automatically darted toward Winola for aid, but the scholar seemed too stricken to speak.

"Go easier," murmured Ferain. "You're scaring her."

He had not needed to say anything; Karys could see that for herself. The apprehension on Lindlee's face made her feel monstrous. She gentled her voice.

"I'm sorry," she said. "I shouldn't have snapped at you. I'm worried, that's all."

Lindlee hesitated, then nodded. She dropped the cloth in the bowl, reached into the pocket of her trousers, and drew out a small metal tin. The exterior was clumsily painted with elephants. She popped the lid open, and slid it across the counter to Karys.

"Quinn has a friend who sources it," she said.

Inside the tin were about fifty pea-sized yellow spheres. Slightly translucent, the jelly-like balls were the colour of sunshine; they could have passed for a sugar sweet or candy. Karys picked up the tin and held it closer to the light. It was heavier than it appeared, as if the spheres inside had the density of lead.

Little yellow beads, a bit like caviar. It's hallucinogenic, apparently.

"What are those?" Winola asked, hushed. She adjusted her glasses, and leaned over the table to see. "They look like the sacraments we used during ceremonies in Toraigus."

The beads gave off an unusual smell: an unfamiliar plant or spice, sharp but earthy. Karys narrowed her eyes. There was something faintly familiar about their appearance, as if she might have seen them elsewhere, just . . . different. She couldn't put her finger on the memory, but the sight of the spheres immediately made her feel queasy.

"Necrat?" she asked.

Lindlee nodded again, a tiny movement.

Karys set down the tin, and scraped back her hair. She could hear Marishka in her Psikamit kitchen, the Second Mayor saying: *that's part of the thrill, the inherent profanity of it all.* "You're taking the corpse drug, aren't you? You and your friends."

The girl studied her hands, profoundly miserable.

"It doesn't do any harm," she mumbled. "It's just . . . it's just fun. All of the others take it; they say it—"

"Corpse drug?" said Winola.

"I think you deserve better friends," said Karys.

Lindlee's eyes welled up once again. She angrily brushed away the tears.

"They're not always like that," she said. "What would you know?"

"That one of them nearly killed you today." Karys closed the lid of the tin, and sat back in her chair. "And he didn't seem all that sorry about it."

Lindlee gripped the fabric of her trousers tightly. "That's a hateful thing to say. Quinn told you it was an accident."

"I'm sure it was. I'm not trying to be unkind, Lindlee."

Winola put her hand on the girl's shoulder. "Enough of that. Karys, would you get rid of the water in that bowl? Take it outside; the effluent might interact with workings in the water system."

Karys doubted there was any real risk to Eludia's sewage works, but she rose, picking up the tin of necrat and sliding it into her pocket. Lindlee did not protest the confiscation. She refused to even look at Karys.

Outside in the midday sun, the water shone oily and slick: the colour of rotting peaches. Karys walked to the end of the garden, and emptied the liquid on the soil in the shade of a pair of old cypress trees.

"She'll have more of that stuff hidden away, you know," said Ferain.

Karys straightened up, and looked back toward the house. *How would taking necrat allow someone to penetrate the Veneer?* That was an Ephirite power, a death-speaker power. Consuming the remains of a dead Bhatuma shouldn't grant the same ability to a bunch of reckless teenagers. "Are you familiar with it?"

"Heard of it, haven't encountered it before now. You really think it lets them see through the Veneer?"

"I don't know what to think." A crowd of drug-addled would-be death-speakers, all living without the burden of a compact. Karys could not dwell on the idea too long, the possibility of Vareslian children idly buying access to the power that had cost her soul. "They saw something."

The kitchen smelled of chocolate when she returned. The pan simmered unsupervised on the stove, and water moved through the pipes overhead. Presumably Winola was drawing the bath she had promised Lindlee. Karys moved the chocolate off the heat to prevent it from burning.

The necrat felt heavy in her pocket. She thumbed the dented lid of the tin. She had taken it from Lindlee without a plan; it had seemed like the right choice in the moment. Now, however, she wasn't sure what to do with the yellow beads. Sell them, throw them away? Both options struck her as wrong; the first felt like she was simply robbing Lindlee, and the second seemed disrespectful. Karys sighed and left the kitchen, climbing the stairs to the second floor. Which was illogical. For starters, it would never make the slightest difference to whichever herald the necrat had come from; they remained dead. And she was an apostate, so she shouldn't care anyway. It wasn't like she planned to host a funeral for the beads.

Sabaster would take them, though; she knew that. Her master would be ecstatic to add necrat to his Bhatuma collection. More favour, more honour for her. Just what she needed: for the Ephirit to believe that she was presenting him with a wedding gift. One last token before their vows, before he consummated . . .

Sweat broke out on Karys' skin. *It won't come to that. Toraigus. Keep your mind on Toraigus.* Down the hallway, Winola was talking to Lindlee. Karys entered the street-facing bedroom, and quietly shut the door after her.

The room was cool and tidy, unchanged since she had left it that morning. Except, propped up against her pillow, was a little elephant statue. It was carved from yellowwood and burnished to shining; it gleamed like amber against the white linen. Karys approached the bed slowly and picked it up. The statue fit snugly in her palm, comfortingly smooth and heavy. She had seen the same elephant in Hetan's curio shop in Tuschait.

She sank down onto the bed, the gift cupped in her hand. Her chest hurt. She could see Haeki slipping into the room, carefully setting the elephant down on her pillow. For some reason, the vision made her unbearably sad. Tiny black stones marked the elephant's eyes; its trunk curled gracefully. Karys traced her finger over its face.

She had been refused the Auric's grace; the mercy of the Embrace was not for her kind. And yet there was Haeki, her hand extended. Always reaching. Haeki, sea-blessed and unstained, unaware that the elephants had turned her away. Haeki, laying out her gift for Karys to find, never knowing what it meant.

CHAPTER

41

Rhevin arrived home at dusk, stepping down from a grey awrig into the shadow of his house. Karys saw him through the window, caught him mumbling to himself. Unlike the man she had been introduced to at the station only a few short days ago, he appeared dishevelled and ill at ease. The long hours at the university seemed to have frayed him. When she met him at the front door, he was startled to see her.

"Oh," he said. "Cas Eska. Good."

The way that he spoke suggested that he felt the opposite. Since their first conference in his study, Karys had barely seen Ferain's father, but nevertheless received the impression that he disliked her. It wasn't because she was Mercian, or, at least, she didn't think that was the case; she had noticed that he remained gracious and obliging around Haeki. He appeared indifferent to Winola, mildly irritated by Lindlee—from what Karys could tell, it was only her that he was truly set against. While Rhevin was impeccably polite in all their interactions, his civility struck her as cold and false.

"I was hoping to talk with Ferain tonight," he said. His skin was sallow, his rust-coloured eyes shadowed. "There is something I must show him in the old sector."

"Of course," said Karys quickly. "Winola also wanted to speak to you. She thinks she's figured out how to neutralise the Construct's effect."

"That's fine. I'll hear her before we go."

Karys had expected Rhevin to be excited, but he scarcely seemed to register what she had said. "She thinks she knows how to fix Ferain."

"Good," he said, distracted. "Very good news. Will you be ready to leave in the next half an hour?"

"Oh, contain yourself, Father," muttered Ferain from her shadow. "You'll embarrass me."

"Yes," said Karys.

Rhevin cast an eye over her clothing, and suppressed a sigh. "You might want to dress a little tidier."

Karys glanced down at her shirt, flecked by orange stains from the work-ings' effluent. "Right."

Lindlee was sleeping, Haeki still absent. When Karys walked into the room she shared with Winola, she found the scholar hunched over on her bed, scrawling illegible workings formulations in her notebook. Deeply immersed in her thoughts, she took a few seconds to react to Karys' entrance. She low-ered her pencil.

"Rhevin's back?" she asked.

"Wants to talk to Ferain, and disapproves of my clothing." Karys moved to the wardrobe and retrieved her spare shirt. "I tried to tell him your theory about the Construct's effect, but I'm not sure he understood. He seems upset about something."

"Did you explain the urgency of the situation?"

"He wasn't listening. It might be better coming from you."

Winola tucked her book under her arm, and rose. "I'll have a word with him."

Karys waited until the scholar left before she stripped off her old shirt, lay-ing it on the shelf to wash later. The hem of her spare was coming loose, the material worn thin, faded with age. She pulled it over her head and straight-ened out the fabric. Although it hadn't seemed important before, she was sud-denly aware that all her clothing was tattered and drab. Not that she cared about impressing Rhevin; she just disliked the way that he looked at her. Like she was unclean, an eyesore, an intruder in his pristine, empty house. Down-stairs, she heard the murmur of Winola's voice. She picked up her comb from the shelf, and brushed her hair through. He never looked at the others like that.

When did I become so sensitive?

She put back her comb, and walked down the corridor to the bathroom. The air inside held the fading scent of lavender after Lindlee's bath, the mirror over the sink still fogged at its edges. Karys wiped it clear with a towel.

Her reflection greeted her. She saw herself as others must: her flat, cropped hair, her downturned mouth, the deep lines around her eyes. Nothing soft, nothing bright. She appeared older than she was, and tired, and sad. She touched her cheek below her right eye, smoothing the crease. New clothes wouldn't fix anything, because she would remain the same underneath them. This was her face, this was what the world saw. What Rhevin saw.

What Ferain saw.

It didn't even hurt, not much. Why should it? Against Ilesha, there could be no comparison—skin like silk, eyes like coal, quick and confident and effortless. Nothing about the wan, shadowed figure in the mirror measured up, and Karys harboured no illusions. Ferain had his life to return to; he would put this nightmare behind him, make amends with Ilesha, and remain in Eludia. He would be happy.

"What is it?" he asked her quietly.

She wanted him to be happy.

"Karys?"

She bent and splashed water over her face.

Rhevin was already waiting by the door when she returned downstairs, drumming his fingers against his leg. If anything, he seemed even more displeased; the conversation with Winola must have gone badly. Outside, the gloom had thickened, and the shadows drew long.

"We'll go by awrig," he said. "This won't take much time."

The wind was cool, the afternoon heat fast dissipating into the twilight. Karys followed Rhevin to the vehicle, and climbed inside after him. He sat down beside the window, body closed off to her. She settled on the other bench and interlaced her fingers over her knees. The awrig rolled forward.

Her shadow crossed the floor to meet Rhevin.

"Where are we going?" asked Ferain.

"You'll see," his father replied.

Karys kept her eyes down. Her hands were pocked with scars, creased and grooved at the curve of her wrist and between her thumbs and index fingers.

It would never matter: her feelings. She had not met anyone quite like Ferain before, that was all. Which was irrelevant; if she had any chance of a future, it lay in Toraigus; her only hope of survival hinged on never seeing him again. Difficult to imagine, but she could be practical about it. The sooner they parted, the sooner she would grow used to his absence; put this painful distraction behind her. Let them say goodbye as friends; she would shake Ferain's hand, and thank him, and be glad to have known him at all.

"You're upset," Ferain murmured. "Why? Is it my father?"

The worst and most stupid thing was that a part of her wanted the separation to fail. It ran against every rational thought, but when Winola had suggested the binding might be permanent, a tiny traitorous voice in Karys' head had whispered: *is that so bad?* For a fraction of a second, she had felt *relieved*. Then shame followed—she knew confinement caused Ferain discomfort she knew he wanted his body back, and if Sabaster were to call her while he remained bound, she would have damned them both. Not to mention the fact that the Toraigian authorities were immediately going to uncover an active binding and bar her entry, forged papers or no.

It wasn't possible. She would lose him, just as she would lose everyone else. There was no other way.

"Is it me?" asked Ferain.

His concern twisted like a barb. *Yes. It's you.* Karys turned her head toward the window.

"I'm fine," she mouthed.

"You can tell me. I wish you would."

"Fine," she repeated silently.

Although Rhevin said that the trip would be brief, dusk had deepened into night before the awrig slowed. For the full length of the ride, Ferain's father did not once look in Karys' direction or speak to her. His silence felt like censure; it lay heavily in the air. Ferain tried to draw him out once or twice, but Rhevin seemed immovable, replying flatly and in few words. When they came to a stop, it was at a park near the edge of a plateau, the valley beyond screened by a wall of tall evergreens.

Karys' travels had not taken her anywhere near this sector of the city, but Ferain clearly knew where they were. He seemed annoyed; his voice came out curt.

"Why here?" he asked.

Rhevin pushed open the door. He stepped down from the awrig, and walked toward the trees.

"A reminder," he said.

Karys trailed after him. The sounds of Eludia were strangely muted here; they had passed by a commercial district of eateries and bars only minutes previously, but in the moonlit shade of the park, the music and laughter diminished to a distant hum. Unfamiliar nightbirds called from the trees, sweet and fluting, and cicadas hissed. The footpath Rhevin followed wound through the long grass; it seemed to be made from a smooth vein of unbroken stone, deep midnight blue flecked with paler veins of translucent crystal. Through the dimness, Karys glimpsed shapes moving inside the rock, quick like darting fish in a river.

"The Night Way," said Ferain, following her eyes. "It runs all through the old sector. Ambavar made the paths from his own blood; they're indestructible. If you're lost, they'll lead you home. If two people are looking for each other, their paths will converge. That's why it's also called the Lover's Road; it takes you where you're wanted."

She smiled slightly. "Did you and Ilesha find it useful?"

"On a few occasions."

Ahead, Rhevin glanced back with a hint of impatience. Karys walked more quickly to catch up with him. The air tasted clear and sharp and cool; it smelled green like cut sap. Beyond the line of evergreens the plateau dropped steeply, and she saw into the bowl of the valley for the first time. Her breath caught.

The structure lay partially submerged in the ground, but it still rose at least two hundred feet from the valley floor, and it *sang*. Not with any audible sound, but Karys heard it all the same, a pure trembling melody reaching through the dark and into her head, not a voice, not strings or flutes or shivering keys, but music less formed, the feeling below the notes. Her hair stood on end. She didn't, for a few seconds, even know what she was looking at.

"Remarkable, isn't it?" said Rhevin.

The Singing Crescent emitted its own unearthly radiance, shedding silken light on the meadow of black flowers at its base, on the ancient dogwoods blossoming in a white ring around it. It appeared to be made of clear shining water, ever falling, and through the luminous sickle moved ghostly forms, figures not quite visible, winnowing away and reappearing. The sight filled Karys with an inexplicable longing.

"A cross section of an artery of the Embrace." Rhevin gazed down into the valley. "In the whole world, this is the closest we can come to her—Ambavar's most precious gift to us."

Karys tore her eyes away, and the singing inside her fell silent. Her body felt light and unstable. She let out her breath.

"Why bring us here?" asked Ferain bluntly.

Rhevin did not seem surprised or offended by his son's question. He walked to the edge of the plateau, and stopped. Karys' shadow closed the distance to him.

"Just tell me," he said. "Because if you want to make a point—"

"I need," Rhevin spoke with deliberate slowness, "for you to remember what you are part of."

Her shadow scoffed.

"What you scorn, what you turn your back on—"

"What drove my mother to jump off a roof." Ferain's voice was scathing, as cold as Karys had ever heard him. "You don't need to remind me of Ambavar's *gifts*. I couldn't forget them if I wanted to."

Rhevin clasped his hands behind his back. Standing alone, he appeared oddly frail.

"History has a price," he said. "We are not always at liberty to decide who pays it."

"You don't say."

"Ferain, Joselle is dead, and I mourn her—but that does not make your lineage any less of a gift. You are the living memorial of Ambavar, and of her."

The peripheries of Karys shadow deformed. "I am not a fucking artefact in your collection."

"Don't be juvenile. I'm saying you have obligations—to your heritage and to Varesli—which are more important than your personal grievances."

"Oh, *obligations?*" Ferain drew out the word. "What would those be, I wonder?"

"By virtue of your birth—"

"Maybe to expose the retinue's assassination. Wouldn't I make the perfect figurehead for your crusade? The survivor, Ambavar's own blood, returning to wreak divine vengeance on the apostates of Mercia. Is that how you thought this would go?"

His father's face darkened. "By virtue of your birth, you have responsibilities."

"You know, when I saw you waiting at the station, I actually thought: 'maybe he does care.'" Ferain laughed. "'For once in my life, maybe my father is genuinely worried about me.' I should have known. It was only ever about your stupid little imperial project, wasn't it?"

Rhevin's voice grew withering: precise, controlled, and utterly devoid of warmth.

"It amazes me that you still haven't changed," he said. "Ever since you were a boy, always demanding, demanding, demanding; never for a moment considering what your selfishness cost. No appreciation of gravity or duty or sacrifice—it's always just about you, isn't it?"

"That's not true."

Karys spoke quietly. During the course of the argument, she suspected that Rhevin had half-forgotten she was even present. His shoulders went tight at the sound of her voice, and he turned to face her. She met his stare, unflinching.

"I don't think you know your son very well," she said.

Rhevin's expression was difficult to decipher. Hostile, that much was clear.

"My son's weakness is not your concern, cas," he said. "He is meant for greater things. I only want him to remember that in the coming days."

"Don't call him weak."

Rhevin grunted, contemptuous. He turned back to the Crescent.

"I can open the Lapse," he said.

Ferain stiffened. Karys felt like the air had been knocked out of her lungs.

"You can . . . you've worked it out?" she asked.

"I studied that relic for years; no one else in Eludia knows more about the intricacies of its authorisations. Yes, I've worked it out. If cas Diasene has the means to heal Ferain, then I am ready to do my part. A relief, I'm sure, as I would imagine you're eager to be paid."

Rhevin probably intended the last part as a dig, but Karys scarcely heard him. They could do it. After everything that had happened since escaping the Sanctum, they would finally be able to free Ferain. It was real.

"You're certain?" asked Ferain. "You've talked to Winola about this?"

"Not yet. I wanted to tell you first."

The breeze picked up, rising from the valley, carrying the smell of wildflowers. Karys shook herself.

"Winola isn't ready," she said. "She needs more time. In a few weeks—"

"No," interrupted Ferain. He fell back to her feet, and spoke urgently. "Karys, no, you can't wait, not on my account. Nuliere told us that she could remove the Construct's effect. Whatever she's after, she had no reason to lie about that."

"That you know of," she murmured.

"She's protected us until now. What if Winola never finds the answer? This is too important; I can't be the reason you . . ." He stopped and took a breath. "Please. Let me make the choice. This is what I want."

It doesn't feel right, Karys almost said, but that was no excuse. Her mistrust of Nuliere was personal, and it clouded her judgement—even she could see that the Bhatuma had done everything to keep Ferain safe. In that regard, their goals aligned; she did not believe Nuliere would harm him, at least not intentionally.

And although Karys shied from the idea, she also knew that this might be their only chance. Whatever the cost, she had to free Ferain before Sabaster summoned her. *So stop stalling, and be practical.*

"How long would you need to prepare?" she asked Rhevin.

Her shadow sighed with relief, and then laughed, quick and clear. Rhevin considered. The glow of the Crescent lit the side of his face, made his features appear sunken.

"I could be ready by tomorrow evening," he said. "But I don't know how much time cas Diasene requires."

"That's long enough," said Ferain before Karys could speak. "Winola has help. I'm sure she won't need more time than that."

Rhevin nodded, accepting the statement without question. His expression had turned distant and detached once more, all traces of his earlier anger vanished. He showed no pleasure or apprehension; it was as though the outcome of their discussion had been a foregone conclusion.

"Tomorrow, then," he said.

The ride back home took an hour. When they reached the house, most of the lights had already been extinguished, and the moon hung over the roof, a pale and sickly pretender to the Singing Crescent's brightness. Rhevin stared up at the night sky, lost in private thoughts. He seemed to come back to himself when Karys closed the awrig's door; he shivered as if struck by a sudden chill, and climbed the steps. She followed him inside.

Haeki sat on the ground at the base of the staircase, her legs stretched out in front of her, her chin resting on her chest. She stirred at the sound of the door opening, and began to rise. Rhevin offered her his hand. She looked at it, confused and flustered, before accepting the assistance.

"I'm sorry," she mumbled. "I must have fallen asleep."

"No need to apologise," said Rhevin, and it almost sounded kind. "Goodnight, cas."

He passed her and climbed the stairs. His steps were heavy, the creak of his footfalls on the floorboards pronounced. He moved down the upstairs hallway; Karys heard the rattle of a key in a lock, and the click of the study door closing after him.

The house went quiet. In the kitchen, a tap dripped.

Karys forced a smile. "Strange place for a nap."

With a slow exhalation, Haeki pushed her mussed hair back over her shoulders. She avoided Karys' eyes, and turned toward the stairs.

"Well, I . . . goodnight," she muttered.

How long was she sitting there? "Wait."

Haeki stopped. Karys took a step toward her.

"Rhevin wants to separate me and Ferain tomorrow evening," she said. "Will you ask Nuliere if she's still willing to help?"

At the mention of the Bhatuma's name, Haeki winced.

"Does Winola know?" she asked.

"Not yet; I don't think Rhevin told her. But he seems confident."

"I'll ask. Anything else?"

She appeared so uncomfortable: face blank, wary like a kicked dog. Walled-off and alone, all her hurt clamped down so that no one could touch it, so that no one could look at her and see a burden. A lock of her hair had fallen in the wrong direction, and Karys longed to reach out and fix it. Instead she sighed, and shrugged.

"I'm glad you're here, that's all," she said.

Haeki's throat moved, but she said nothing.

"And you don't have to—" *Why is this so difficult?* "I reacted badly, but I know the position you are in. I understand, and it doesn't . . . it doesn't change anything. For me. I just want you to know that."

When Haeki spoke, her lips scarcely parted.

"I'm sorry," she whispered. "I didn't want to do it. I knew you would feel—"

"I understand. It doesn't matter."

Haeki abruptly turned away. She gripped the banister, knuckles white.

"I'll ask Nuliere about tomorrow," she said.

"Thank you."

A swift nod, and then Haeki hurried up the stairs. Karys waited a few seconds, standing alone in the low light of the foyer. The kitchen tap continued to drip. An old clock ticked in the living room through the door on her left.

Winola wasn't in the bedroom. Her shoulder bag and books were missing; there was a note on the windowsill, explaining that she had gone back to the library. A pity, Karys would have liked to talk to the scholar. She sat down on her bed. After a moment, she retrieved Haeki's elephant out from beneath her pillow. Ferain stretched over the wall behind her.

He is meant for greater things. I only want him to remember that in the coming days.

Karys kicked off her shoes and lay back, turning the elephant over in her hands. Who knew what Rhevin wanted. New Favour believed that Ferain could reignite the conflict between Mercia and Varesli—but, by all accounts, Varesli stood to lose that fight badly. Whatever Rhevin's convictions, he could not be ignorant of that danger. Greater things, what greater things? Despite their fractious relationship, he did seem to care about his son, even if he significantly underestimated Ferain. She ran her fingertip over the curve of the Auric's smooth yellow back. Not a pawn, and not a figurehead. Certainly not weak. Ferain would never let anyone use him to start a war.

Tomorrow, she would see him. If Nuliere agreed to go ahead with the sundering, if nothing went wrong. It was what he wanted, what she needed. The beginning of their end.

Restless, Karys rolled onto her side, and tucked the elephant under the bed. Her gaze snagged on her pack, propped up beside the wardrobe where she had left it. One of the bag's straps hung loose.

She frowned. She could have sworn that she had left it fastened. *Lindlee?*

"Something the matter?" asked Ferain.

Karys pushed herself up and walked over to the wardrobe. While they had been out with Rhevin, Lindlee would have had all the time in the world to hunt down her confiscated necrat. Unlike her to go through Karys' things, but if she was sufficiently motivated . . . Karys lifted open the flap, expecting to find the tin gone.

But no, there it was. Everything looked exactly as she remembered: the necrat, Ferain's stolen relic, her coat. All in place. The beads rolled as she lifted the tin. When she flipped back the lid, there seemed to be just as many as before. Their appearance still tugged at her, the memory drifting out of her grasp like fine grey smoke.

"Just being paranoid, I think," she said. "Nothing important."

CHAPTER

42

Rhevin's study had been completely transformed. When Karys entered, she found the floor space cleared, the desk and the workbench removed, the books and papers filed away. A sturdy table stood on the far side of the room, a large slab of bone-white stone affixed to its upper surface. How Rhevin had gotten that upstairs, Karys had no idea; it looked like it weighed a ton. Rings of chalk dust and grey paste covered the floorboards, iron workings anchors marked the compass points, precise streaks of dark blood ran at intervals along the bare walls. All very traditional, very Bhatuma, reassuringly orderly. On the floor six feet from the table, Rhevin had sketched an intricately bordered hexagon in a shimmering gold paint. The interior looked like it was filmed with a layer of black water; through the Veneer, Karys could hear it humming.

Ferain whistled, impressed.

"Watch your step, cas," said Rhevin. "Please wait on top of the cradle. In your vest, if you wouldn't mind—the binding mark needs to be exposed. I trust cas Diasene will be here shortly?"

On the surface, Ferain's father remained composed and clipped, but his tension seeped through the study. He referred to his notes, and pressed a thumbprint of blood to the northern anchor. Checked his notes again.

"By cradle, you mean . . ."

He gestured at the table. "Precautionary. There's no real danger, but if you faint while the sundering is underway, it will prevent you from disrupting the working."

Karys eyed the stone slab. "Why would I faint?"

"You probably won't. Precautionary, as I said."

That didn't strike her as a particularly reassuring answer, but Karys carefully crossed the room and sat down. Her stomach fluttered as she breathed in the coppery smell of the workings' blood. The study was very cold. She took off her shirt, and shivered as the chill touched her bare shoulders.

The day had passed at a nauseating speed, both too quick and slow. In the morning, Rhevin had sent her to purchase fresh calf's blood and silver-stem orchids before locking himself in the office and forbidding interruption.

Winola had returned home from the library at midday and headed straight to bed; Haeki had been equally scarce, leaving in the early afternoon on some errand for Nuliere. On her uncle's instruction, Lindlee went to stay with one of her friends.

With only her shadow for company, Karys had felt trapped—nothing to distract her, nothing to do but watch the hours slide away. Ferain had dictated a brief, unadorned letter for Ilesha, detailing the decision to go ahead with the separation, apologising for not informing her of it in advance, explaining that he did not have the right to cause her any more worry. If everything went as planned, Karys would never have to deliver it. If things fell apart, well . . .

"It's going to be fine," said Ferain.

She scowled. Rhevin folded his notes and retreated to the opposite site of the room, methodically checking the angles of the markings on the floor. "You are basing that assumption on . . . ?"

"Call it a hunch."

"I feel so much better."

"Ferain, I'll need you to . . . hm." Rhevin paused, temporarily confounded. "Place yourself within the containment area?"

"I don't know about this," Karys muttered, holding tight to the edge of the table. "What if Winola's theory about the Construct's effect was wrong? What if—"

She felt a light, incongruous pressure on the top of her head, as if Ferain had touched two fingers to her hair parting.

"Has anyone ever told you that you worry too much?" he asked.

Then he drew away from her, flowing over the floor to the golden hexagon. Karys' gut twisted with fear. She wanted to say more; there was a gnawing dread in the pit of her stomach, something dark and biting and cold. If this went wrong, he was lost.

"Ferain," she said, quickly and too loud.

Rhevin looked over at her.

"It's going to be fine," her shadow repeated, even more gently. "You'll see me soon."

"Is there an issue?" asked Rhevin.

She would see him soon. Her fingers pressed against the stone slab. This was what he wanted. "No."

The door swung open, and Winola walked in, looking dazed and frazzled, as if she had only woken up a few moments previously. For some reason, she was wearing her coat. Haeki followed behind the scholar, and behind *her* . . .

On first glance, the girl appeared younger than Lindlee, perhaps thirteen.

She had pale skin and a shock of storm-water-coloured hair that haloed her thin face; her eyes were sky blue except around the pupils where they gleamed vivid orange. Her smile did not belong to a child; her mouth curved with secretive, knowing amusement. She wore a simple white dress, ill-fitting: too large for her narrow shoulders and falling almost to her ankles. It should have looked ridiculous, but did not; nothing about the girl could have aroused humour in Karys. She moved, and the world seemed to pull back from her adolescent body like oil from water.

Nuliere.

Rhevin turned and froze when he saw the herald, taken aback by the appearance of the strange child in his study. Nuliere's unnatural eyes fixed on Karys.

"Hello, apostate," she said.

Winola spoke before Rhevin could raise an objection, sounding more than a little stunned herself. "This is the practitioner who will be helping me."

"She's older than she looks," added Haeki.

Nuliere glided over the floor, heedless of the careful circles of dust and blood. The markings were left undisturbed in her wake; the herald did not seem to touch the ground. She stopped before the cradle, and, in the space of a blink, her small cold hand had wrapped around Karys' left wrist.

"Much older," she said sweetly.

Karys wanted to pull away. Her body failed to respond. With an uncanny tenderness, Nuliere lifted her arm and turned it outward; exposing the binding scar on the side of Karys' chest. She lightly traced her nails over the blue veins running up Karys' forearm, a smile still playing on her lips.

It dawned on Karys, sudden and clear, that, without Ferain as a liability, the Bhatuma would probably quite like to kill her.

"Is your part prepared?"

Haeki's question broke the spell. Karys breathed out hard, and jerked her wrist from Nuliere's grasp. Rhevin started, coming awake. The Bhatuma appeared to have entranced him too.

"Yes," he said. "Yes, of course. Everything is as it should be."

Nuliere produced a low, amused noise in the back of her throat. Her smugness made Karys think of a cat with one paw pinning down a rat's tail, a predator toying with its prey. The herald glanced at Rhevin over her shoulder.

"You will open the smallest possible aperture," she said. "The window must be cracked, not thrown wide—if the binding is broken before the body is healed, all will be lost."

Perhaps it was Nuliere's air of command, but Rhevin did not question the girl. He nodded. Nuliere returned her attention to Karys.

"Lie down, apostate," she said.

Karys raised her chin. "Ask nicely."

Her body fell back against the slab, her head hitting the stone, the air leaving her lungs. Nuliere's damp hand rested on her bare shoulder. Ferain made a sound of alarm, and moved to return to her, but the herald raised a hand to forestall him. He wavered.

"Karys?" he said tightly.

Karys' ears rang from the impact. She lifted her head.

"Fine," she said. "It's fine."

Across the room, Haeki had taken a few steps forward. Her body was tense, distress written across her face. Not willing to contradict her herald, but not happy. Karys locked eyes with her, and offered a smile. *It's fine, it's nothing.* With all the disdain she could summon, she pushed Nuliere's hand away, and shifted so that she lay properly upon the cradle. Tried to ignore how vulnerable it made her feel. Nuliere leaned down close, and spoke so that only Karys would hear her.

"I heard when you cried for me in Miresse," she whispered. "Every word."

Karys stared at the ceiling.

"Bitch," she said under her breath.

Nuliere laughed. She straightened, and grasped Karys' arm again, drawing it up to expose the scar once more. Karys kept her muscles slack and unresisting, even though she hated to be lying down, hated that she was half-undressed and supine like an offering on the cold slab, hated that the herald's touch left water on her skin. She slowed her breathing, but could not stop herself from flinching when Nuliere pressed her fingers to the binding scar.

"If Rhevin is responsible for opening the Lapse, why are you in contact with the mark?" asked Winola.

The scholar sounded curious, as if the question had slipped out without her full intention. Everyone looked at her. She touched her mouth with one hand, self-conscious.

"It's just that the binding has nothing to do with displacing the Construct's effect," she said. "Two separate, unamalgamated workings, right?"

Nuliere spoke as though exercising great patience. "It is necessary to ground the process."

"Oh." Winola tilted her head sideways. "It is?"

The herald stared at her, unblinking and cold.

"Yes," she said. "Do you question me in these matters?"

"No, no, of course not. Never mind."

Karys twisted her head to the side. Ferain had returned to the hexagon, and only a thin band of shadow connected them. From the way he moved—tiny stutters at the edge of his silhouette—she could tell that he was worried. Nuliere pressed harder against the scar, nails digging in.

"Open it now," she ordered.

Wordless, Rhevin knelt. He pressed a drop of blood to his lips, and laid his palms on either side of the southern anchor, fingers stretched wide. He murmured a word deep in his throat and then, very slowly, began to curl his fingers inward over the floorboards.

Karys felt something inside her chest wrench and pull taut. The pressure burned. She heard Ferain gasp.

"What's wrong?" asked Haeki.

"If workings degradation has occurred, there might be some discomfort." Rhevin did not look up from his task. "It's to be expected. Not too much of a concern."

I guess this is why he thought I'd faint. Karys gritted her teeth. The sensation was intense, but not unbearable; it was the same overstretched feeling of dizziness she suffered whenever Ferain moved too far away from her. She could endure it. In her peripheral vision, she saw Winola sidling around the edge of the room, apparently trying to get a closer view. The scholar didn't appear concerned, only intrigued. She craned her neck to watch what Nuliere was doing.

"Fused," she murmured to herself. "All the threads are melted."

What is she talking about?

Karys reached for the Veneer, and her senses instantly hit a wall. Although she encountered the rippling surface of its fabric, there was no purchase; each time she tried to grasp it, she slid away. Standing above her, Nuliere's eyes narrowed in concentration.

"That is sufficient," she said. "No further."

Why couldn't she open the Veneer? Karys' apprehension increased. It felt as though the herald was blocking her. Simple malice? She wanted the process to stop; her instincts were screaming that something was wrong, it should not hurt like this, no one's behaviour added up—not Winola's, not Nuliere's, not Rhevin's.

With sharp and sudden intensity, Ferain drew on her. Karys made a hoarse sound of protest, and turned her head back toward him. "What are you *doing*?"

Her shadow remained within the hexagon. "Nothing. I'm not doing anything."

Rhevin, Haeki, and Winola all looked toward him simultaneously. With the Lapse cracked open, they could hear Ferain's voice. The drain of the drawing intensified; Karys' flesh crawled as the binding scar shifted sideways. *This can't be right.* She tried to sit up.

In an instant, the stone turned fluid beneath her. White bands snaked over her legs and her free arm, eggshell-thin and quick; they set hard, and locked her down against the cradle.

"Be still," commanded Nuliere.

"Stop," said Ferain. "Something has gone wrong."

The herald dripped brine; salt water ran from her in rivulets. Her expression was focussed. "Nothing has gone wrong. You will be saved."

Karys' back arched, her ears resounded with the rapid beating of her own heart. She could not draw breath, could not speak. Nuliere's fingers followed the movement of the scar. Ferain cursed and her shadow darted across the hexagon, only to come to a hard stop at its perimeter, falling back as if repelled.

"She can't sustain it," he said desperately. "You have to stop; you told us this would be safe. What are you doing to her?"

"The power to displace the effect requires a source," said Nuliere.

Ferain threw himself at the edge of the hexagon, and recoiled again. The cord of shadow between them thrashed. "You're using her to heal me? As the Son of Night, as your kin—"

The herald looked up from the binding scar, and laughed at him.

"Oh, you arrogant fool," she said. "You think I care about that? What you hold is vital, what you are is nothing."

Ferain faltered. "You never—"

"You are as much my kin as a worm crawling in the mud." The scar reached the skin above Karys' heart. Nuliere spread her small child's hand wide, and pressed it flat and forcefully to the mark. "But you will be restored."

It felt like a floodgate ripped open. Karys screamed, voiceless, as the life rushed from her body in a searing tumult. She convulsed, and through the pain she saw Haeki lunge at Rhevin. Before she could touch him, however, Nuliere gave an inhuman snarl and threw up one hand. An invisible force drove Haeki backwards into the study's wall. She crumpled.

"Do not interfere, sea-blessed," the herald hissed.

Haeki raised her head. Her mouth was bloody where she had cut her lip on her teeth.

"You swore," she whispered.

"Remember your *place*. I gave you Favour, and I can take it all away again." Nuliere's eyes burned; the air around her sheened with power. "Without me, you're worthless. I am the only one who ever wanted you."

Karys' throat was on fire, her torso locked in an airless vice. She trembled violently, but her body would not respond to any instruction. Her vision darkened at its edges. *I need to breathe, I can't breathe.* It felt like drowning. Ferain's voice echoed inside her head: raw and wild, too far away from her.

"Please, stop!" he pleaded. "Father, please help me. You have to help me."

If Rhevin replied, Karys did not hear; she could not see, could not think; her heart struggled beneath the cold press of Nuliere's hand, beating like a weak, trapped bird inside a cage, battering itself to death at the walls.

Ferain, she thought. *Ferain.*

Without warning, Nuliere's palm left her chest. The drawing ceased immediately.

Karys heaved and tasted air; it flooded her lungs in a rush, intense and sweet. Her whole body shuddered. Distantly, she heard Nuliere's voice. The world swam around her: movement and light and sound. The herald's words reached her.

"But you're not a deathspeaker," said Nuliere.

Then, out of nowhere, Winola giggled.

"Oops!" she said.

The haze receded, and Karys struggled to the surface. Nuliere was standing with one hand clutched to her chest, staring at Winola.

"Are you drunk?" the herald asked in disbelief.

The scholar held her hands behind her back, swaying, swishing her coat from side to side. She looked unaccountably pleased with herself, and completely unafraid.

"I've been such a bad girl," she purred.

Still choking, Karys reached for the Veneer, and this time it parted; it welcomed her and she fell through its light. *Ferain.* The barrier surrounding him glowed like the moon through ice; crystalline ribbons ran between them in a tangled network of veins. She found the edge of the containment working even as it slipped and shied from her, even as her mind sank toward unconsciousness. She caught the thread and pulled.

Winola laughed, delighted. "Amazing, Karys! You're so quick; how do you do that? Show me again, I want—"

Nuliere made a hard gesture, and the scholar gagged like she had been punched in the throat. "Enough with your prattling. I shall be done with this."

She pressed her hand back to Karys' heart, and the Veneer slammed closed. *No, please,* thought Karys. No more, she had no more. The drawing opened her like a wound, and then her shadow collided with Nuliere, tackling the herald to the floor.

"Haeki!" he shouted.

Nuliere's limbs lashed out, but she could not touch Ferain; her power did nothing to him. "You *dare* try to turn my Favoured against me?"

Movement to the left of the cradle; Winola staggered away from the wall, one hand clasped over her throat, the other pulling an empty phial from the interior pocket of her coat. Karys' vision blurred; Ferain was drawing on her to keep Nuliere pinned down. She saw Winola throw the phial, badly. Saw the vessel arc across the room, hit the ground, and roll.

Haeki snatched it up, ripped out the stopper, and fell upon her herald.

Howling filled the study. A net of black stars pierced Ferain and sank into Nuliere's body; the air flexed inward around the phial. On her knees, Haeki held it fast, teeth bared in a bloody snarl. Nuliere screamed in fury and pain, and the pressure of the drawing released. Karys inhaled, but this time found no air. Her heart stuttered, suffocated; the room spiralled. Ferain flew to her.

"No, no, no, Karys. Karys!" Her shadow covered her, shielding her from the rest of the room. She could see nothing but darkness. "Karys, please."

"Embrace forgive us," moaned Rhevin.

Ferain's voice cracked. "Fix it, damn you. Close the Lapse!"

"Emissary, herald, our shepherd and light. How could you? How could you all? Look what you've done."

Howling, shouting, voices dissolving into sound. Karys clung to the last shreds of consciousness, her senses receding. Then the wave bore her down, and she fell into lightless waters, and knew no more.

A dog was barking.

The noise was muffled. Distant and moving further away; after a few moments, it faded from hearing. Other sounds replaced it. Quiet footsteps. Water creaking through pipes. Shutters rattling in the wind.

A heavy, soft weight rested on top of her. Warmth. It was very important that she did not move. If she stayed perfectly still, nothing would hurt. She would not have to think. She would stay here, in this bed, and the rest of the world would cease to exist.

The only problem was that she was extremely thirsty.

Karys groaned.

"Awake at last?" asked Ferain.

She was not going to open her eyes. If she just kept her eyes closed—

"I hate to bring it up again, but you really are very boring to watch sleep."

Her lips parted, and she produced a low whisper. "Water."

"Next to you. Can you manage?"

Karys opened her eyes. Overcast light filtered through white gauze curtains; she lay in a large four-poster amidst mountains of linens and blankets. The bedroom was unfamiliar: the walls a pale peach colour, the floor covered in thick rugs. A second, smaller bed was jammed into the corner, a thick duvet neatly folded on top of it. Ferain rested on the coverlet at her side.

"Hello," he said.

She levered herself up, and reached for the glass on the bedside table. Her hand shook when she raised it to her mouth. In her haste, she spilled half the water over her chest.

"Slower, don't gulp it," said her shadow.

Karys ignored him, and tilted the glass further. She accidentally breathed in, broke into a coughing fit, and upset the rest of the water down her shirt. She spluttered.

"I told you: slower," said Ferain, exasperated. "No one's going to steal it. There's more in the pitcher."

Karys wiped her mouth with the back of her hand. She looked down at the water-soaked cotton bedclothes she was wearing, and grimaced. Cold. But her thirst no longer burned. She set down the glass. On the bedside table stood a lamp, a silver pitcher, and Haeki's elephant.

"Where are we?" she asked, her voice a thin rasp.

Her shadow flowed over to the dresser below the window. Karys felt a soft pull in her chest as he opened a drawer. "Ilesha's place. Here, she won't mind."

He picked up a long dark red shirt and carried it back to the bed, then retreated to the corner of the room. He always did that—whenever she got undressed, whenever she bathed. Making sure that she knew he wouldn't look. With shaking arms, Karys peeled off her wet bed shirt and set it down next to the lamp. A dull chill permeated her body. It wasn't just the spilled water; the cold ran deeper than that.

The Split Lapse scar sat squarely over her heart. She touched it.

"Well, that could have gone better," she said.

In the corner, her shadow sighed. Karys unfolded the new shirt and struggled into it. The fabric smelled clean, lightly perfumed. She dropped back onto the pillows.

"I'm sorry," muttered Ferain.

"For?"

"I—you were right. About the separation. I pushed you into it."

He sounded so tired, so . . . fragile. Karys shut her eyes briefly. The ghost of the drawing pressed down on her chest. "Nuliere?"

"Contained. Haeki's taking care of her."

"And Winola?"

"Still recovering. Lindlee thinks she must have taken at least four times the usual hit of necrat. Spent the first night crawling up the walls, but there shouldn't be any permanent harm."

"When you say 'first night' . . ."

"It's been two and a half days."

The words took a second to sink in. *How . . . how could I have slept that long?* Karys felt winded; the walls of the bedroom shrank around her. Although she tried to sound cheerful, her voice came out in a strained croak. "Well, I can understand why you were bored."

Ferain returned to the bed, settling at her feet.

"You scared me," he said.

Karys nodded, and forced her mouth into a smile. She found it difficult to look at her shadow. Two days. Time slipping like water from her fingers. "It's more time than I would have expected."

"Oh, but it could have been worse." Her shadow shifted, and Ferain's tone went strangely casual, conversational. "The mender wasn't sure you would wake at all. 'Complete enervation.' Even if you did regain consciousness, he thought there could be damage—your mind might be gone."

For no real reason, she nodded again.

"So, do you think you've lost your mind?" he asked, voice dropping slightly.

"It doesn't feel that way."

"Good. It's good to hear that. I was losing mine, by the way."

Karys gave another weak smile, gaze downcast. She ran her fingers over the weave of the blanket.

"What now?" she said. "With the separation, with . . . with everything."

Ferain drew closer to her.

"We try again," he said. "We do it better. Winola saw Nuliere's workings through the Veneer; she thinks she'll be able to adapt the herald's process. Make it safe. My father's contributions were nothing special, so we'll easily be able to replicate those."

Karys was quiet for a few seconds.

"How long had Nuliere been talking to him?" she asked.

"Since before we left Boäz, maybe earlier. It's hard to be sure." Her shadow flickered, a tiny movement not fully repressed. He slipped back to the foot of the bed. "I would have forced the full truth out of him, but you were . . . well. I couldn't draw on you at the time. We left him at the house, and I haven't seen him since."

There was an edge to his voice. With a wince, Karys pressed herself up straighter, sitting with her back against the headboard. "He wanted to save you."

Ferain's composure cracked. "Embrace, don't *defend* him."

"Sorry."

"No, it's—" He breathed in. "My father doesn't matter. Should never have mattered, and I was stupid to think . . . doesn't matter. The important part is that you're awake now. I don't care about him."

Karys pressed her lips together. *An excellent liar—but not quite good enough for me to believe that.* Rhevin's betrayal had cut Ferain deeply. She wondered how many hours her shadow had sat alone in this room, turning over their conversations.

"Fathers, hm?" she murmured. "No good on either side of the border."

Ferain gave a small huff. "Apparently not."

"Are you all right?"

"Yes." He shook himself. "Yes, I'm fine. And this is all just a setback. Winola's new theories really do seem promising. This morning, she spent forty minutes telling me about interdimensional overlapping."

"Then she's back to normal?"

"Almost, I think. According to her, the experience was extremely instructive—so if all else fails, we should try putting her on drugs more often."

Karys laughed. At the end of the bed, her shadow shivered, a ripple travelling through the darkened edges of Ferain's silhouette.

"It's just a setback," he repeated, softer. "There will be enough time. We don't need Nuliere and we don't need my father. Next time, it will work. I know it."

The fierceness of his quiet conviction made Karys' heart ache. She should not believe him, but she did, and she was going to miss him more than she could stand. Shake his hand and say goodbye; that was how it needed to be. The rest of her life without hearing his voice. She would be practical, she would survive as she always had, but she knew that there would never again be anyone like Ferain. There would always be an absence where only he fit.

She breathed out, and raised her gaze to the ceiling.

"Write letters," she said.

Her shadow hesitated. "Letters?"

"Once I reach Toraigus. Anything you send will probably take months to arrive, but I'll have the time to be patient." She lowered her eyes again. "Promise that you'll write to me."

There was a long pause.

"You don't speak Toraigian," said Ferain.

His response was so bewildering that, for a moment, Karys thought she had misheard him.

"Well, I'd prefer correspondence in Continental," she said, "but I *was* actually planning to pick up the language once I arrived."

He shook his head. His voice was oddly guarded. "Sure, but it will still take months before you can communicate properly."

"And?" Her face warmed. "I know a few words. It can't be that hard."

"You'd be surprised."

Karys wished that she had not started this conversation. "Then I'll pay a tutor. Look, I just wanted you to keep in touch. It isn't even that important."

Her shadow did not move.

"I can speak Toraigian," he said.

She gritted her teeth. "Yes, congratulations, that's very nice."

"Will you stop being so obtuse?" he snapped.

"*I'm* not being obtuse; you're the one making stupid comments when all I wanted was the occasional—"

"Do you really need it spelled out?" he asked, cutting her off. "Fine. Watching you die on that table was the worst moment of my life. I couldn't reach you, and I couldn't stop it, and it was happening because of me. Then you wouldn't wake up for two days, and I didn't know if you ever would."

"I don't . . . what does that have to do with—"

"Now you want to sail off to Toraigus, and leave me behind again," he said. "You'll force me to lose you a second time."

Her throat constricted. "I don't have a choice."

"No. But I do." Her shadow shrugged. "You'll need a translator. My Toraigian is perfect."

Karys shook her head, unable to speak.

"No?" he asked.

She was suffocated. "You can't."

"Oh, but I can. Ilesha made the enquiries, and my inheritance will be enough. More than enough, once I cut off my useless bastard of a father."

It was too much. Karys' hands trembled, and she buried them in the blankets. "Toraigus is a prison. You aren't going to—aren't going to—"

"Do you not want me to come?" he asked.

A sound of despair escaped her throat. "Once you reach the island, you won't ever be able to *leave.*"

"I'm familiar with Toraigus' immigration policies. Knowing them was actually part of my job description."

"Your life is here. Ilesha is here."

In the face of her emotion, Ferain remained steady. "My life is wherever I choose to live it. As for Ilesha, she has her family, friends, and ambitions in Varesli. You would have nothing in Toraigus."

"I'll be fine on my own."

"Karys, do you want me to come with you, or not?"

She was silent. Too cruel, he could not torture her like this. She had made her peace, she had laid it all to rest, and now he came along and ripped the ground out from beneath her.

"Look at me," he said. "Tell me to stay in Eludia, if that's what you really want. But look at me."

She turned her head away. Outside, thin rain pattered against the window pane.

"What I want isn't . . ." She swallowed. "I made my choices, and I'll live with their consequences."

Her shadow rolled over her legs, spreading across the blankets on her other side, placing himself within her line of sight.

"Then let me make mine," he said. "Do you want me to come with you?"

It was too much.

"Yes," she whispered.

The tension in her shadow fell away; every hard angle relaxing, softening like the mist at dawn, fading to pale translucence. Karys had never seen him respond that way before; he seemed so light. He laughed, and the hair lifted from the nape of her neck.

"Was that so difficult?" he asked.

She found her voice again. "That doesn't mean you *should*—"

"Oh, be quiet."

She sputtered. Her shadow spread out over the lower half of the bed, formless and radiating. Karys could not draw her eyes away from him.

"I take it back," she managed. "Stay here."

"Too late now. You won't get rid of me that easily."

He sounded so pleased, so infuriatingly smug. An unwilling smile tugged at the corners of Karys' mouth, and she covered her face with her hands to block him out.

"I can't stand you," she mumbled.

Ferain laughed again. His happiness felt dangerous; it had the warmth of a dream. Karys tried to imagine a future in Toraigus—not alone, but with him—and found that she couldn't; she only knew that to lose her bright, fleeting fantasy would obliterate her completely. It was wrong, it was selfish, and Ferain would resent her for it in the end, but the possibility still hung in the air, shimmering. She lowered her hands.

"You would really do it?" she asked in a small voice. "You would follow me to Toraigus?"

"To the end of the world," he replied.

The gentle, open sincerity in his voice brought Karys up short; her mind ground to a halt, thoughts evaporating. She was spared from having to reply, however, because at that moment, the door creaked open.

Haeki walked into the room, her hair and shoulders damp from the rain. "The mender was out, they told me to . . ."

She faltered, seeing Karys sitting upright in bed. Her lips parted and she made a short, startled sound.

"Told you to what?" asked Karys.

"To . . . to come back later." Haeki took a few quick steps toward her. "You're awake. Embrace, we didn't know if you—how long?"

Ferain flowed over to meet her. "About ten minutes after you left."

Up close, Haeki appeared battered and tired: the bags under her eyes heavy, her nails bitten short. She glanced toward the door. "Figures. Do the others know?"

"Not yet."

"Then I'll tell them."

"Haeki, wait." Karys wrested her legs out from below the blankets. Her muscles protested the movement, but there was no real pain, only residual weakness. She put her feet down on the plush white carpet beside the bed, and felt better. "I need to talk to you."

There was the apprehension again, the old walls rising. Haeki backed toward the door. "Later. Winola and Ilesha—"

"Don't run away."

"I'm not running."

Karys looked up at Haeki, and saw the girl she had always known: bold and wilful and reserved, burying everything that hurt, bruised by her own wanting. Fishing drowning rats out of the pool, walking through the moon-touched surf at night.

"Good," she said. "Because I'm not sure I could catch you right now."

A flicker of feeling. Haeki folded her arms.

"As if you ever could," she muttered. "Karys . . ."

"I need to make something clear, that's all."

"Then say what you have to say. The others will be—"

Karys spoke, matter-of-fact and sure. "Your herald is a liar. Your Favour is the least important part of you, you deserve so much more than Nuliere, and she is a fool to call you worthless. She was never the only one who wanted you—I did."

Silence. Haeki's face had gone rigid.

"Oboro as well, obviously." Karys ran her bare foot back and forth over the dense pile of the carpet. "I never stopped missing you. And I'll always regret leaving you behind in Boäz."

For a second longer, nothing. Then Haeki moved forward, and slowly sat down on the bed next to her.

"You should be angry," she said.

Karys wavered, before leaning sideways and resting her head on Haeki's shoulder. The way they used to sit, sometimes. On the beach, counting pearls, talking about nothing.

"Sorry," she said.

Haeki turned, and pressed the lower half of her face against Karys' hair. Her voice dropped. "I'm the one who's meant to say that."

Karys shook her head slightly. Haeki's breathing grew uneven.

"I thought she wanted you back," she said haltingly. "I thought that she would accept you in the end. So fucking stupid. I was so—"

She broke off. Her rain-damp hair was cool, and her body exuded warmth. She smelled a little like almonds. Her mouth remained set against Karys' head, hard, as if she needed the pressure to hold her words in.

"I didn't know what Nuliere was going to do," she whispered. "I swear I didn't know."

Karys sought Haeki's hand, and wove their fingers together. "Never thought otherwise."

A faint tremor. Haeki swallowed.

"Ever since I left Boäz, I've felt lost," she said. "I'm running, but you're so far ahead, and I can't catch up."

Karys made a sound of admonishment, and squeezed Haeki's hand.

"I'm right next to you, idiot," she said.

Haeki's laughter caught in her throat. She pulled away, her hair falling forward to conceal her face. "Watch yourself, Eska."

"Or what?"

Haeki stood up, her head angled to the side. "Just watch yourself. I'm going to tell Winola and Ilesha you're awake."

With that, she hurriedly left the room, her feet light on the floor. The door swung shut after her. Alone again, Karys touched her hair. Haeki's warmth lingered.

"She deserves to know about Toraigus," murmured Ferain. "You have to tell her."

Not yet, thought Karys, and let her hand fall back to her lap.

She would. But not yet.

Ilesha's house was older than Rhevin's, a double-storey building standing on top one of the city's northern plateaus. Clean and orderly, it folded around a small green courtyard at its heart, where the leaves of two crab apple trees bent under the dripping weight of the rain.

Karys found her bag beside the dresser, and pulled on her own trousers. The waistband hung looser than before; her hips protruded, and the skin of her stomach was mottled and pale. Movement revived her, however—although she felt unsteady, she sensed that the weakness was temporary. Unable to locate her shoes, she collected her wet bedclothes and padded barefoot out of the room.

Paintings decorated the walls of the corridor, intricately rendered still lifes of flowers and spooling bolts of bright cloth. A faded green runner covered the floor; at its end, the passage opened to the kitchen, where clouded grey light fell through a pair of enormous windows above a white-wood cabinet. The smell of frying garlic, spices, and meat fragranced the air.

Ilesha stood over her stove. She turned around at the sound of Karys' footsteps, and smiled faintly.

"That's my shirt," she said.

"Sorry."

"The colour suits you. I've always liked that shade."

Karys looked down at the fabric, blood red and flowing. *Sabaster's colour.* She raised the wet bedclothes. "I knocked over a glass of water. Ferain suggested—"

"Oh, did he?" Ilesha set her wooden spoon on the countertop. "Put those down by the wash basket in the corner. Haeki told me that you were awake; she's just gone to fetch Winola. Why don't you sit down?"

It felt more like an order than a suggestion. Karys placed the clothes over the side of the basket, then walked to the kitchen table and sat. Through the window, she could make out the distant peak of the Singing Crescent at the far end of the valley. Muted by the misted air, it shimmered like a mirage.

"I don't know how to repay you," she said.

Ilesha ground dark peppercorns in a mortar, and added them to the pan on the stove. She picked up a large bowl of peas from the counter, crossed to the table, and set it down in front of Karys.

"Shell these," she said. "Has Ferain talked to you about Toraigus?"

Karys nodded. Her expression must have amused Ilesha, because the corner of the woman's mouth quirked upwards.

"Don't worry," she said. "I'm not going to poison you."

Ferain slipped into Ilesha's shadow.

"She tried to talk me out of it," he said.

Ilesha snorted, and returned to the stove. "After three weeks, I'd be dying to escape you too."

"Karys expressed it slightly more tactfully than that."

"A credit to her patience."

Their shared levity made Karys feel stupid and slow, out of her depth, like they were putting on a performance to mock her. She had expected fury or coldness, but instead Ilesha acted like parting with Ferain was a joke.

"Doesn't it bother you?" she asked.

Ilesha stirred the pan. The tarnished cooking pot beside it simmered low and steady. Oil hissed; steam misted the window.

"It does," she said, not turning. "Very much, actually. I'm only human, and I'm set to lose my closest friend for the second time this month. Trust me; while you were asleep, I said things that neither of us want repeated."

She picked up a small jug, and poured its contents into the pot. The browned meat in the pan followed, alongside a bowl of diced peppers, carrots, and tomatoes.

"He actually asked me to come with him," she said. "Did he tell you that?"

"No," said Karys.

Ilesha set the lid on the pot.

"Ridiculous. As if I'd drop everything, and go live out on a rock in the middle of the ocean. More ridiculous still, I even considered it." She moved the empty jug and bowl to the sink. "And I could be bitter, but what's the point? He'll still be gone. So no, I won't stand in the way if this is what Ferain has decided. Some things matter more than our shared convenience."

Karys was silent. Ilesha glanced back.

"You're surprised?" she asked.

"I just don't know if I really understand. Shared convenience?"

Ilesha looked meaningfully at the untouched bowl of peas. Karys picked up a pod, and pulled back the husk.

"Mutual trust, sharing of information, a united front at parties." Ilesha waved her fingers. "Conversation, reliably enjoyable sex . . ."

Karys coughed, fumbling the pod and sending peas rolling over the table. Ilesha deftly caught one before it fell to the floor, and tossed it into her mouth. Her face had turned sly, her chin tilted, her eyelashes lowered.

"That sort of thing," she said, turning back to the stove. "In a word: convenience. I'll miss Ferain terribly, but what we share isn't essential. It's just . . . convenient."

Ferain lay quiet and dark on the floor. Ilesha stooped, and selected a patterned enamel bowl out of her cabinet. She ladled soup into it.

"I don't think he ever saw you as just a convenience," said Karys softly.

Ilesha gave a low *hah*. The skin around her eyes creased—a little ironic, a little sad. She set the filled bowl down next to Karys, and stretched over the table. Karys froze, but Ilesha only reached out and caressed the side of her face.

"Sometimes," she murmured, "circumstances dictate that not everyone gets what they want."

Her fingers, firm and warm, brushed down Karys' cheek, and Karys, without thought or intention, leaned into the familiar touch. It took a few seconds for her mind to catch up to her body, and then she flushed, confused, and pulled back. Ilesha smiled.

"Eat," she commanded, taking away the still-unshelled peas.

Karys ate.

The soup was hot and over-salted and greasy—the fat from the meat left a thin sheen of yellow oil over the dark liquid, the vegetables had gone limp, the meat stringy—and Karys realised she was ravenous. Until presented with food, her hunger had lain dormant, but now her body cried out for sustenance. She burned her mouth on the scalding liquid, ignored the pain, and kept eating. Ilesha poured her a glass of water, then resumed cleaning up around the kitchen.

By the time Winola appeared, Karys was already most of the way through her second bowl.

"You're looking better than I expected," said the scholar.

Karys twisted in her seat. Winola stood in the entrance to the corridor, supporting herself against the wall. Haeki hovered behind her.

"Better than me, anyway," said the scholar ruefully.

Karys began to rise, but Winola waved her back down. Her already pale face was bloodless. She wasn't wearing her glasses, and the skin around her eyes was swollen, her lips turned bluish and chapped.

"Ferain told me that you were almost back to normal," said Karys, aghast.

Winola made a dismissive gesture. "Oh, that was a few hours ago. Apparently, this thing comes and goes; every time I think I'm through with it, a new surprise crops up. I suppose that's what you get for eating dead heralds. I really am improving, though; you just mistimed your revival by about twenty minutes."

"Do you think you could manage food?" asked Ilesha.

The suggestion appeared to make Winola feel even more ill. Her cheeks gained a greenish tint. "Not . . . right at this moment."

"Just how much necrat did you *take*?" asked Karys.

"Well, I had to guess the dosage, and then doubled that. Plus one for luck."

"Embrace, why?"

Winola gave a weak grin. "Instinct, I guess. Curiosity. I wanted to keep an eye on Rhevin's workings, and I figured the higher the dosage, the better I would see. Which seemed to hold true, even if there were more side effects than I anticipated. I've already explained this to everyone else."

Karys frowned. "You suspected Rhevin?"

"Just had a bad feeling. When I spoke to him the night before the separation, he kept brushing me off like he already knew everything I was saying. Afterwards, I began thinking about how quickly his research had progressed compared to mine, like he had started his investigations before we even arrived." She shrugged. "And he was nice to Haeki. Respected her. You saw that too."

"Because he knew I was Favoured," said Haeki bitterly.

Karys snatched a glance at Ilesha, but Haeki's statement didn't seem to come as a revelation. *Ferain must have told her everything.* "Necrat really allowed you to penetrate the Veneer?"

Winola's expression gained a wistful quality. "I'm not sure. But I could see workings, and they were all . . . so precisely formed. Coherent, even if they were too complicated to be understood in their entirety. Beautiful." She shivered, and seemed to come back to herself. "It clarified a lot. I'm confident I can reproduce Nuliere's diversion mechanism using Ephirite derivations; it's just a matter of drawing power from a different source. Or a series of sources in parallel."

"Just like that?"

"Being able to see what you're doing makes working significantly easier, it turns out. No, I'm not worried about removing the Construct's effect, or holding the Lapse open. But the way that the binding has ossified? It's as though you and Ferain have . . ." She knitted the fingers of her hands together, one between the next. "Did you see it?"

The tangle of glowing crystal ribbons running through the air between them. Karys nodded. "A little."

"I don't know if separating all of that is possible, or what harm severing it might do." Winola rubbed her eyes, her mouth going thin and pained. "Of course, it might not matter, it just looked . . ."

Her voice faded. Haeki touched her shoulder.

"Are you all right?" she asked.

Winola groaned. "It's frustrating; my thoughts keep scattering. I'm so tired but I can't sleep. Even when I try, I see them through the walls. They change shape when I'm not looking."

A chill ran down Karys' spine. "Winola?"

"I hate lying there alone." The scholar didn't seem to hear Karys; her voice was fretful. "It gets so quiet. Something is watching me."

"Winola," said Haeki firmly.

The scholar snapped out of her reverie, and for a second she appeared afraid. She leaned more heavily against the wall.

"Sorry." She spoke with an uncharacteristic, childlike uncertainty. "Lindlee told me paranoia and insomnia are common aftereffects of overdosing. That and the initial euphoria, loss of inhibition and empathy, and mania. It's . . . fairly embarrassing, thinking back."

"You need more sleep," said Haeki.

The scholar nodded.

"Sorry," she said again. "I just wanted . . . well. It's good to see you awake, Karys."

A sharp pain lodged in Karys' throat.

"I think," she said, "that the day I ran into you at Psikamit College was probably the luckiest in my life."

Winola smiled, touched, and briefly looked more like herself. "I guess that makes two of us—not many practitioners can say that they've witnessed a living herald perform a working. Although you do still owe me dinner."

Haeki helped the scholar back to her room, while Ilesha finished tidying the kitchen. The rain had stopped, but the clouds remained heavy and low, piercingly white where the sun shone through them, slate grey where it did not. Karys ate the rest of her food, slower than before. She had not expected Winola to look so sick, especially not after two days had already passed. Distracted, she worried at the broken skin around her fingernails.

Haeki returned, her expression troubled. Ferain flowed over to her.

"You're concerned?" he asked.

She opened her mouth to speak, then seemed to change her mind. She shook her head, and walked over to the window. "She's tired, that's all. Nothing unexpected. Lindlee said it would take time."

"It sounds like the hallucinations are back."

A shrug. Silhouetted against the grey light, Haeki appeared faded: her skin washed out, her hair lank. "Not as bad as before. She sleeps better with someone else in the room, though. I'll watch over her tonight."

"You need rest too."

"I get enough. Besides, she'll recover soon."

Haeki's statement was pronounced with more hope than conviction. Karys got up and placed her empty bowl in the sink. *Winola must have had a really bad reaction to the drug.* In the distance, the Singing Crescent gleamed, and the faintest strains of its music echoed inside her head. She rubbed her temples.

"I need to talk to Nuliere," she said.

Silence from Haeki. Ilesha, leaning against the wall, gave a weary sigh.

Karys turned. "Ferain said that you have her contained. That you're taking care of her. Can she communicate?"

Haeki's face was blank. "She's angry."

I'm sure. "That doesn't matter."

Ilesha grunted. "You say that now. You bottled a really nasty piece of work, by the way. I suggested burying her in the yard."

"We've already tried talking," said Haeki. "She won't cooperate."

Karys shook her head. "She'll listen to me. Please, Haeki."

A pause. Then Haeki reluctantly reached inside her shirt, and drew out Vuhas' relic. The phial's exterior had been wrapped in brown cloth, and its throat was ringed in twine; it hung like a pendulum from the chain around Haeki's neck. Even covered, the bottle radiated a creeping menace; Karys could hear the glass ringing through the Veneer. Haeki passed it across. As soon as Karys touched the wrapping, her head filled with a wordless wash of whispering.

"I didn't realise you were carrying it around with you." Karys turned the phial over in her hand. "It holds her secure?"

"If she could get out, she would."

Difficult to argue with that logic. From what Karys remembered of Vuhas' account, the vessel had once confined a far more powerful Bhatuma than Nuliere. She steeled herself, and pulled back the wrapping.

Black water filled the phial, pocked with sickly pulsing blooms of sky blue and orange. The liquid spiralled slow and ceaseless, circling the interior.

"So the apostate did not die," said Nuliere.

The herald's voice had an echoing quality, as if projected through an empty hall. Karys turned the phial upside down, but the water inside remained as it had been, revolving and sedate.

"That is good," continued Nuliere. "The process should be more pain-ful. Then again, the ends I envision all pale before what your fell master has planned. Are you looking forward to his tender attentions, apostate?"

Karys' jaw tightened. "What do you know about that?"

"About his intentions for his special favourite?"

"She's bluffing," muttered Ferain. "She doesn't know anything; she just lis-tened to our conversations."

"Where there is salt in the water, so am I," said Nuliere serenely. "Hold what delusions you will, but your time runs short, apostate, and your honour awaits you. Soon, so very soon, you will get what you deserve."

Karys gripped the phial tightly. *Just bluffing.* Her voice came out rough. "What do you want with Ferain? What does the 'last harbour' mean?"

The phial made a clear tinkling noise, like a wine glass struck with a tuning fork. The herald was laughing. The sound rang through the kitchen. Haeki flinched, and Ilesha gazed at the phial with obvious dislike.

"Oh, poor apostate," jeered Nuliere. "Do you truly believe that I will tell you anything?"

"I do, actually."

The herald laughed louder, and the sound made Karys' ears ache. "Then you have deceived yourself, you little—"

"Did you never wonder," Karys interrupted, "why I chose to conceal your existence from my master?"

Nuliere fell silent instantly.

"He collects your kind," said Karys. "Your corpses, anyway. For years, I've fed his obsession; I've bribed him with Bhatuma baubles and tokens, anything to keep him from calling my compact, anything to stay in his good graces. But in all that time, I never breathed a single word about the herald still living in Boäz."

The orange and blue rings in the water darkened. Karys smiled, humourless.

"Pride," she said. "You turned your back on me, but I never wanted to be the one to forsake you, Nuliere—because you remain my herald, even if I am not your adherent. No matter how much I hate you, I would have walked straight into Sabaster's arms before ever selling you out."

"I do not require the loyalty of traitors," the herald hissed.

"Is that so?" Karys cocked her head. "Test my pride, then. Right now, you look like a wonderful parting gift for my master. Easy to carry. Bite-sized. My Lady of Brine and Urchins, you'll give me everything I ask for—because if I know one thing about you, it's that you're a coward."

A pulsing vibration filled the kitchen, heavy as a physical weight. Karys thought that the phial might shatter under the preternatural force, but it remained cool and smooth against her palm. And, in spite of the herald's fury, Nuliere spoke evenly.

"In that case, allow me to make a confession of my own," she said. "It was I who told your father that Oboro Eska intended to leave Boäz."

A second's silence. Haeki drew a sharp breath, and pressed her hand to her mouth.

"Through my Favoured, I encouraged your brother to go," said Nuliere. "I knew that there were only two ways to compel your return to Boäz—the death of Oboro Eska, or the death of Haeki Maas. Tell me, did I choose rightly, apostate? Because it was for the sake of your attention that your brother died."

Ferain drew closer to her. Karys fought to hide all feeling. *Give her nothing.* Oboro, lying in the temple, covered in coins, his face a stranger's, his skin like wax in the candlelight. Her brother, sinking into the water. *Give her nothing.*

"I wonder now," murmured Nuliere. "Whose blood would have soaked your hands more deeply?"

Oboro, pushing her backwards into the Penitence Pool, the light that shone through their father's face. Karys closed her eyes. Up on the switchback behind the boatyard, her brother's twelve-year-old fist striking her jaw, and how he had sobbed afterwards, inconsolable, and her certainty in his love.

"What is the last harbour?" she asked, voice gravelly.

The herald breathed out a single word.

"Hope."

Karys wanted to smash the phial against the wall. She shook it. "Damn you, hope for what? What was all this for? Answer me."

The black water remained undisturbed, implacable and remote as the ocean.

"The Bhatuma's revival," said Nuliere. "Your shadow harbours the last seed. The hope of our rebirth lies within him, waiting to be born."

Stillness. The herald's words were swallowed by the air; Haeki and Ilesha stood unmoving, uncomprehending. Karys felt the world slip on its axis.

"No," she said, shaking her head. "No metaphors, no more—"

"I speak plainly."

Silence again. Karys could hear her own heartbeat. At her feet, her shadow shifted.

"A . . . a physical seed?" said Ferain. He sounded disconcerted. "Are you saying there's something inside my body?"

Nuliere hummed affirmation.

"A seed, an egg—it does not signify," she said. "The matter from which we heralds arrive in this world; the potential lying dormant before formation. Yes, it is within you. It was within all those of your company, but you, alone, survived."

"Then the whole ambassadorial retinue had these . . . seeds?"

Nuliere's voice grew softer. "It had been so long awaited, so carefully planned. The remaining seeds were hidden, preserved beyond the enemy's reach until the time was right. Imagine it: a score of heralds to reclaim what was lost. And then, at the last, they were betrayed. The apostates discovered the plan; they sought out and slaughtered the seed-bearers, dashing my kin against the rocks. All but one. I could do nothing but watch."

"What will this seed do to Ferain?" asked Ilesha, speaking out for the first time. Her face was cold, her dark eyes piercing. "What happens to him when the herald is born?"

Nuliere acted as though the question was worthy of scorn. "Nothing consequential. My kin would not *harm* him; they would simply keep his body until they wished to adopt their own aspect. It is a high honour, one which would have seen his name written into history. That was why he was selected—his father wished for him to stand amongst those who restored Varesli to glory. Few could prove more unworthy of the task."

Ferain seemed too preoccupied to absorb the slight. "I still don't understand. Where did these seeds come from?"

"I have already told you—they were preserved in the one place that exists beyond our enemy's reach."

"Toraigus," muttered Karys.

"Yes. That faithless, barren rock." Within the phial, the water turned, slow and black. "There the seeds were planted within the chosen on their arrival. My kin were to be brought to Eludia, and born in the warmth of the Embrace's light."

"But the retinue never even made land," said Ferain. "And we had stringent security measures aboard our ship—when was there an opportunity . . ."

He trailed off.

"Even if they hold no true faith," said Nuliere, with a hint of satisfaction, "the people of Toraigus adhere to ritual."

Karys' shadow said nothing.

"A grand welcoming ceremony," said the herald. "All of your number included, all of them honoured—"

"The Amity Beads," said Ferain dully. "Those were the seeds, weren't they?"

Nuliere hummed her agreement again.

"It is curious, how the sacraments of the faithless so closely resemble that which births us," she said, and briefly sounded more affable. "Curious, but of great service."

Ferain uttered a vicious string of curses. "New Favour murdered the retinue because we had all been fed *parasites*?"

As quickly as it had appeared, the herald's geniality vanished again. The orange and blue lights inside the phial flared. "My kin were not parasites, you wretched, ungrateful fool, but the dormant potential of this world's salvation. You were the harbinger of dawn, and the last harbour of our hopes, and I have given you answers. Release me."

He scoffed. "After everything you've done, do you really—"

"Too much lies at stake!" said Nuliere fiercely. "I have greater concerns than vengeance, even if it is richly deserved. Enough of this. Apostate, I have given you the truth—if you have pride, then listen to me now. Your time has run out. Your master is coming, and you will not escape him. Will you drag the man you bound to the same fate?"

"Oh, don't you dare," snarled Ferain.

Karys felt small and cold. "I . . ."

"You need not both be lost to the Ephirite." Nuliere spoke quickly, no longer hostile, but urgent. "He must be severed from your shadow before it is too late. Release me now, be spared from your compact, and ensure that he lives. You still have the power to save him, if you care to. If you care for him at all."

The herald's words resounded inside Karys. She felt unsteady; the kitchen was suddenly airless, too bright, but the bottle lay solid inside her palm. Water like the sea at night, down below the surface where the light could not penetrate, deep in the swallowing dark.

The phial disappeared from her hand. Karys' head jerked up.

Haeki stood on the far side of the kitchen, the relic held protectively close to her chest. Her eyes were red-rimmed. Karys had not even seen her move; she had only felt the lightest brush of skin against her fingertips.

"She already took Oboro," said Haeki huskily. "You don't get to follow him into the sea."

Karys lowered her empty hand. *I wasn't going to,* she wanted to say, but she wasn't sure if that was entirely true. Haeki had seen something on her face; for a single moment, she had—

"You worthless traitor." Nuliere's voice sliced the air. "You stupid, pathetic, crawling insect of a woman, you are *nothing*. I will make you weep for death, I will take it all away. Everything you care for will burn. You'll never be anything but a cowering, faithless, useless—"

Haeki wound the brown cloth around the phial, sealing the herald's voice away. Quiet descended on the kitchen. Outside, the wind whistled over the plateau and down the slopes of the cliffs.

"Do you hear that all the time?" asked Karys shakily.

With care, Haeki tucked the last stretch of the cloth wrapping underneath the twine.

"I am her sea-blessed," she murmured. "She is my responsibility."

She moved to hang the phial back around her neck. Ilesha made a disapproving sound, and straightened up from the wall.

"This isn't good for you," she said. "Always having her so close. I admire your resilience, but it's gone far enough. Lock her in my safe—I'll set the working to only open to your touch."

"She is my herald. I can't—"

"Yes, you can," said Ilesha. "What you're doing right now is more dangerous than sealing her away. You're exhausted. The longer this goes on, the more likely you are to make a mistake."

Karys stared down at the floor. *Does Ilesha know?* Haeki might be too tired to realise that the safe was no defence—it could seal Nuliere away from the rest of the world, but not from Karys. If it was worked, she could unravel it. *Does Ilesha know that?* Ferain might have told her that Karys could break workings. Was that what she hoped? It was true: if Karys went away, Ferain would live, could remain in Eludia, no loss of convenience, no hidden grief, no parting. The world set right. He would not be dragged down to the desolation of Sabaster's domain, or spend his life trapped and wasting away behind the Unbroken Wall. Karys swallowed the lump in her throat. A stupid, selfish dream. And after all, what did she know? Toraigus wasn't even a guarantee.

"It would only open for me?" asked Haeki warily.

Unseen by Haeki or Ilesha, Ferain brushed against Karys' palm, questioning. She pulled away from the touch, drawing her fingers into a closed fist. What had she been thinking? What had all of this been for? Throwing everything into the pursuit of a pitiful fantasy, endangering everyone just so she could lie to herself a little longer. The money, Toraigus—it was a delusion. She had made her bargain, there was no escaping it. Either Sabaster or death, those were her cards to deal—there would be no quiet house behind the Wall, no small garden of her own, no time to read books or lie in the sun, no getting older, no learning Toraigian, no letters pressed with flowers, no future, no anything. And no Ferain, of course: there would be no Ferain. They should never have tried to stop Nuliere.

"Karys?" said Ilesha.

She turned abruptly and walked out of the kitchen, away from everyone. Her feet were quick on the floor, her eyes burning. All those years alone, grinding herself to the bone and saving for nothing. She could have lived. She could have built something—anything—that would matter now. Her life was a waste, and she had done it to herself.

She pushed open the door at the end of the corridor and stumbled out into the courtyard. The trees glittered silver and shining in the clouded light, blurring before her eyes, and her shadow rose up and caught her. The cool darkness wrapped around her; she felt Ferain's arms close over her shoulders. He hugged her, and the last of Karys' composure gave way, and she was crying.

"No one can see you," he murmured. "I won't let them."

"I tried so hard." Her voice broke. Overcome, it was all she could say. "I tried so hard."

Her shadow held her, and Karys barely felt the drawing at all. She could not hold him back.

CHAPTER

45

Karys had waited until everyone was asleep before she slipped out of the house. It was not difficult. Haeki had moved into Winola's room for the night, in the hopes that her company might finally allow the scholar to rest. She also seemed to sense that Karys wanted to be alone.

Ferain directed her to the old sector's public library. It was closed, but Karys unworked the lock on one of the side doors, and let herself in. There was a curious restlessness within her—she no longer felt remotely tired; it was as if the days of unconsciousness had filled up forgotten reserves deep inside her body. She wanted to move, she wanted to occupy herself. At the same time, a strange peace glazed her senses. She possessed no further capacity for grief or fear. The late-night silence surrounded her, and her steps were light.

The library was old and beautiful; it smelled of yellowed paper and ancient stone. Twelve-foot-high stained glass windows ran the entire western flank of the building, framed in intricate arches of interlocking grey granite. Through them, the Singing Crescent gleamed like a second moon in the dark valley below. The floor was polished redwood, and sun-faded woven rugs lay below the long rows of reading desks under the windows. During the day, the space would be bright and full of rustling steps, whispered conversations, the crinkle of turning pages. At night, empty, it still retained some of the sun's warmth. Karys touched an etherbulb resting inside the basket next to the side entrance door, and the little light awoke and shone pale orange. It floated up into the air, following her as she wandered through the long, echoing corridors of shelves.

Nothing like Psikamit's library, Karys thought, with a certain wryness. She had once been so impressed by those cobbled-together collections of manuscripts and papers; her younger self had believed that the College's meagre selection of books represented a world-spanning repository of knowledge. In comparison to this place, well . . . *it's no comparison at all.*

Still, she felt oddly protective of the smaller library. For all its size, it had given her answers when she needed them. *And this one probably doesn't have half as much material on the Ephirite.*

Karys tracked down the shelves containing books on the topic of workings entanglement and coalescence, running her eyes over the dusty leather spines, waiting for a title to jump out at her. She only held a vague idea of what information she was searching for; Winola had dropped the thread of the binding's ossification, and she felt compelled to follow it—although she wasn't certain those crystalline ribbons were part of a working at all; they seemed to be made of some different matter, both more and less solid than the rest of what lay past the Veneer.

"Nuliere was only posturing, you know," said her shadow, trailing over the books behind her. "She's been spying on us from the start; she would have heard our conversations. That's all she knows—how to scare you."

He had been quiet all evening, keeping close to her while absorbed in his own thoughts. Karys reached up and checked the cover of one of the volumes on the top shelf. Her shadow flowed past her, placing himself in her line of sight.

"'She wants something from you, and she'll spin a story to get it,'" he said. "'That doesn't make it true.'"

Karys smiled to hear herself quoted, although she stayed silent. Ferain seemed encouraged.

"Nothing has changed," he said. "We'll have enough time."

Her voice was calm. "And if we don't?"

"You can't lose your nerve, not now. We are going to fix this."

"Will you kill me?"

Her shadow recoiled, losing its shape.

"If it comes to the worst," said Karys, undeterred. "If we're still bound, and Sabaster calls my compact, will you kill me? I know you're able to. You could spare me from . . . from what would follow."

Ferain re-formed, gathering tight and dark.

"I would never let him hurt you," he said.

"Then offer me a guarantee." She returned her gaze to the shelves. "Swear that you'll kill me. I don't ever want it to come to that, I don't want you to get dragged down with me, but if it comes to the worst, if he calls—"

Her shadow grazed her left cheek, carefully lifting a loose lock of hair back from her face and tucking it behind her ear. Karys' breath caught.

"Do you still trust me?" asked Ferain.

She nodded wordlessly.

"Then know that if the worst comes, I will never allow Sabaster to claim you," he said. "I swear."

Karys believed him. She nodded again.

"Thank you," she whispered.

He slipped away from her, back down to the floor. The sensation of his fingers on her cheek remained. Karys wanted to touch the skin there, but did not. Unable to control the expression on her face, she turned her head aside.

"Are you afraid?" she asked. "About what Nuliere said—the seed, the last harbour?"

"Yes."

He spoke plainly, almost absent of feeling. Karys' heart ached.

"I am too," she said, without looking in his direction. "For you."

"Not because I might unleash a herald to destroy Mercia?"

She shook her head. "Seems unlikely."

"But what if it meant that I could 'bring glory to Varesli.'"

"That would risk pleasing your father."

Ferain made a small sound of amusement. For a little while, he was silent. Karys let him be, walking further down the shelves toward the windows, the etherbulb floating after her. She was aware that the seed must have been on Ferain's mind ever since Nuliere revealed the truth, although he seemed unwilling to talk about it. Her shadow darkened the rich brown floorboards at her feet.

"I hate it," he muttered at last. "I can't stand the idea of it growing inside me."

Karys ran her fingers over the spines of the books.

"What if it prevents me from following you to Toraigus?" he said. "What if this . . . thing never lets me go?"

A cruel joke, one herald replaced by the next—Ferain trying to escape Ambavar's legacy, only to find himself even more tightly bound to the next Bhatuma. All of it orchestrated, all of it against his will and beyond his control. And yet he still worried about Toraigus.

Perhaps sensing that she was upset, Ferain shook himself. He seemed to make an effort to lighten his tone.

"It doesn't matter right now," he said. "Forget it. It's almost morning; you should go home before anyone misses you."

It was unlikely that the others would notice her absence at three o'clock in the morning. Besides, lying alone in the dark house, Karys' thoughts had circled endlessly back to Ilesha's safe. In the kitchen, locked, waiting like a promise. Whispering: *if you care for him at all* . . . It was easier for that temptation to be out of her way. She tried to focus on the faded titles of the library books, tilting her neck back to read those on the highest shelf. *Unseen Authorities: The Disruptive Forces; Divine Accidents and Contested Workings; Ephemeral Phenomena.*

"You're the one who's always complaining that I sleep too much," she said. "I'm not tired now."

She stretched up on her toes to retrieve *Divine Accidents and Contested Workings*. In response, her shadow swept up the bookcase and pushed the volume backwards, out of her reach. Karys dropped back down onto her heels, irked.

"Don't be irritating," she said.

"It's a finely honed skill."

"You're only motivating me to stay here longer." She reached for *Ephemeral Phenomena*.

He pushed that book back too.

"Ferain."

Her shadow laughed. Karys could tell that he was trying to cheer her up— and she was annoyed to discover that it was working.

"You do realise I'm doing this for your sake too?" she grumbled.

"I know." He drifted a little lower on the shelves. "Do you really want me gone?"

"What?"

Ephemeral Phenomena slid forward into the air. Ferain held it up above Karys' head, too high for her to grab.

"Jump for it," he said.

"Yes, I want you gone."

Her shadow drew backwards toward the reading desks and the windows, still holding the book overhead. "How badly?"

Karys followed, exasperated and trying not to laugh. "Just give me the book."

"On a scale of one to ten?"

"Fifteen."

He lifted *Ephemeral Phenomena* higher still. "Oh, only fifteen?"

She pressed her lips together to stop her smile. "Ferain."

"Say please."

"I'm just going to find another book."

"But what if the answers are in this one?" He dangled it lower. "Jump."

"Not on your life."

"You drive a hard bargain, but I'll offer a compromise: close your eyes."

Karys could not keep it inside any longer; she laughed. "Why?"

"Close your eyes, Karys."

"You're impossible," she said, shutting her eyes. "There. Are you happy n—"

Ferain kissed her gently. The drawing pulled like a whisper in Karys' chest. She felt the pressure of his lips against her mouth, dry and firm; he was both there and not, and yet, with her eyes closed, he seemed much closer. Her stomach lurched; instinctively, she reached out for him. Her hands passed through empty air. His lips left hers.

Karys opened her eyes. The sound of her own breathing filled her ears. Her shadow stood before her, the light of the Singing Crescent shining through the stained glass behind him, casting a spectrum of colours across the desks and the rugs on the floor. He dropped the book softly at her feet.

"Ever since the celebrations in Miresse," he said, his voice low. "Or maybe earlier, I'm not sure. You're the only thing I've ever been completely sure of. Do you want me?"

"Ferain," she whispered, helpless.

He returned to her, swiftly dipping her backwards and carrying her down to the floor. Karys gasped, partly from surprise, partly from the exertion of the drawing; her hips met the threadbare weave of the old carpet, and Ferain kissed her neck. Her hands sought him vainly, catching nothing but shadow.

"That really won't work," he murmured, amused. His lips trailed down her throat, cool and smooth. Her clothing was no obstacle, her shadow was beneath it, through it; he moved as if it did not exist. Invisible hands glided across her waist to the curve of her hips, his mouth found the scar over her heart. Karys arched into his kiss; her whole body responding with acute sensitivity, with fluttering heat, her every nerve singing and raw, lost to him. Her eyes closed, and a soft moan escaped her.

The sound of her own voice, breathless with longing, brought her back to the world.

"Wait," she said. "Stop."

Without a second of hesitation, Ferain drew away. The lines of her shadow went sharp with anxiety.

"Not what you want?" he asked.

Karys shook her head. "I don't . . . I don't know what I'm doing. I've never—before, anyone."

"Oh." Somehow, he seemed to understand her incoherent fumbling. His tone softened. "Oh, Karys, I know that; I had sort of guessed. You're scared?"

Humiliated, she felt her whole face warm. "Ilesha."

"What about her?"

"I don't want—you were *engaged*."

"You're worried that she would be offended?"

A nod.

"For what it's worth, she won't be." Ferain hesitated, then continued. "Ilesha already knows how I feel, and she doesn't . . . disapprove. That was never how our relationship worked, even before she broke off the engagement."

"I'm sorry," muttered Karys.

"Don't be."

She looked up at her shadow, her silhouette like thin black smoke where he crouched before her. She tried to see through the darkness, to find him behind it. Ferain held out his hand.

"Come on," he said. "Let's go back."

Karys wavered, then reached out to him. Her shadow twined around her wrist, and he pulled her to her feet. The exertion caused her to sigh—but ever since the failed separation, Ferain's drawings seemed to tax her less. He released her hand, two fingers lightly tracing the delicate inner curve of her wrist as he did so, and fell to his usual place at her side. Self-conscious, she adjusted her shirt, then pushed her hair back behind her ears.

"All right," she said. "But I'm taking the book with me."

The clouds had descended while they were inside the library; it had rained again, and the sky threatened more. The streets shone wet and shimmering in the pre-dawn darkness. Lamps formed regular islands of yellow light along the verges of the deep blue road—the Night Way, one of Ambavar's old paths. The depths of the stone glittered with constellations of crystals, scattered like diamonds, like stars. It was quiet and still, as if the whole city was empty but for the two of them.

This world was never mine, Karys thought, walking slowly. A bridge arced over the road ahead, the metal fretwork of its support beams hung with flowering vines, tiny yellow climbing roses. Her shadow stretched over the ground in front of her feet. *But I don't know if I want to leave it.*

She felt a new shyness in Ferain's presence, a more pressing awareness of her movements and his. He seemed content, comfortable in the silence as he led the way home. Where his silhouette met the road, he blotted out the pale, shifting stars.

For the first time, Karys allowed her fractured dream to take on shape and colour; she let herself imagine Ferain in his own body. Had he smiled in the Sanctum? She could not remember, couldn't recollect much of his appearance at all. Taller than her. Resembled his father a little. What would he look like in sunlight? A sharp thrill ran through her at the thought, although unease quickly replaced the feeling.

He'll be like a stranger.

The idea gave her a sinking sensation in the pit of her stomach—in a crowd, would she even recognise his face? To her, Ferain was cool liquid darkness, a voice easy and laughing, familiar as her own skin. For a solid, breathing person to fill up the dimensions of her shadow seemed uncanny, even wrong.

Would he fit, would she know him at all? Karys gazed down at his silhouette. The thought of losing her certainty in him, of losing Ferain as he was now, disturbed her. And, once restored to himself, he might see her differently too—because after everything he had witnessed, everything he knew of the damage and the ugliness that she carried inside herself, how could he not? Perhaps distance would bring clarity. Apart, they might wash away like sand beneath the waves.

But even as the idea slipped into her mind, she drew back from it. No. Whatever came to pass, Ferain had marked her indelibly; she thought of him, and she ached. His careful tenderness, his curiosity, the breezy outward assurance covering his reticence, the burning intelligence he kept concealed, his self-control, his iron will, his openness and buried fragilities, his desire to be needed and useful and seen, his uncanny ability to read others, to read *her*. She knew him. She would always know him. No matter what came, her feelings would remain, true and fixed at the heart of her.

"Hurry up," he said. "It's going to start raining again."

Karys raised her head, lifting her eyes to the sky and the misted reflections of the lights all around them. She was alive, so alive, and he was here with her.

"I don't mind," she said.

Ferain huffed. "You're carrying library property. Stolen, but still."

"Arrest me, then." Her body was weightless. She laughed. "Deport me. Take me away and—"

Agony laced through her skull, blazing and white.

She felt her legs collapse underneath her, felt Ferain catch her before she hit the road. Eludia vanished like a stone dropped in a pool. Red hallways replaced the clouded night, the streetlamps disappeared, and the walls of the palace breathed rank, corrosive sweetness. A tall figure stood above her, spine curved, clothed in wings, his attention upon her. A hand emerged from the grey curtain of feathers, black fingers extended in offering.

The vision snapped out of existence, and Karys inhaled. She heard her shadow's voice; she was curled on her side on the wet road. Her skin burned.

"Come back to me," said Ferain. "Karys, I'm here."

Sabaster.

"No," she breathed. "No, not now."

She scrambled upright, her head spinning, the road veering before her eyes. Her master was coming.

Her shoes slipped on the smooth stone, and she ran. *Ferain, not Ferain.* She could not let Sabaster call her compact while Ferain remained bound. The Night Way blurred in her vision; the lamps smeared yellow as she sprinted. She did not breathe, her feet barely touched the ground, and that single thought consumed her: she could not let Sabaster have him.

Ilesha's house pulled into focus at the end of the street; the world had shifted around Ambavar's roads. Blood pounding, Karys flew up the steps and threw open the door, sending it crashing into the hallway wall. She would have almost no time—Sabaster might have offered her his welcome, but that was all the generosity she could expect; the reprieve would be temporary. She raced down the passage to the kitchen. From upstairs, she heard alarmed voices, running footsteps.

"Stop," said Ferain.

Clutching her chest, Karys tore open the Veneer. Workings bloomed to life in her senses. Even through the walls of the safe, she could see Nuliere's phial glowing an insidious yellow-green. Disregarding subtlety, she grasped the lock's simple Bhatuma-derived working, and ripped it open. The metal box made a sound like a cannon firing. Its door snapped in two, and intense heat rippled through the room. Her shadow automatically rose in front of her, shielding her from harm.

"I'm not going to let you do this," he said.

They should never have stopped the separation. "Nuliere!"

On the opposite side of the kitchen, Haeki appeared in the doorway, Winola at her back. Both of them wore nightclothes, roused from sleep by the noise. Karys lunged toward the open safe, but Haeki, with her Favour, closed the distance faster. She placed herself between Karys and the phial.

"Don't," she said, skin pale.

Karys snarled, and turned to Winola. "Open the Lapse, and get him out. Now."

The scholar clutched the doorframe. "Karys, I—I can't."

Karys reached through the Veneer, deeper, and grasped for the workings imbedded in the relic behind Haeki. They refused to yield, nothing at all like the clumsy weave of the safe; they flexed away from her senses as she struggled to grasp their threads. Bhatuma-made: too dense, too strong, too complicated. *I have to get him out!* "Haeki, move. Don't make me hurt you."

Haeki shook her head. At the corner of her eye, Karys saw the bare white kitchen walls begin to warp: the plaster sliding wetly, sweating milk. With a cry of frustration, she seized the working in the ceiling etherbulb above Haeki, and twisted.

The glass exploded. Winola screamed, and Haeki instinctively ducked, raising her arms to protect her head. Karys threw herself forward, knocking

Haeki off-balance. The safe was before her; she only needed to release the herald, she only needed—

Her shadow pushed her away, causing her to stumble. Haeki surged upright and shoved Karys backwards, driving her into the wall. The impact dazed her; for a second, Karys forgot how to breathe. Behind her head, she could feel the brickwork dissolving, hear it oozing as it melted.

"No," she wheezed.

Shards of glass glinted in Haeki's hair. Her hands were tight on Karys' arms. Too strong. *I can't let this happen.* Karys twisted, straining to shake her off. Above them, the ceiling bulged, drooping under an invisible weight.

"Nuliere!" she cried out. "Herald, help me."

The phial lay still and silent inside the safe, the Bhatuma failing Karys for one last time. A lightless circle appeared in the centre of the kitchen floor. Its darkness unravelled outward in a jagged black spiral, falling wider like stacked tiles collapsing. Karys found Haeki's eyes, saw fear reflected back at her, felt it in the bruising press of her friend's fingers.

Then the ground gave way, and the ceiling fell, and the pressure of those hands was gone.

CHAPTER
46

She landed in a deep red pool. Karys' head went under; she submerged completely and then floundered back to the surface, choking. The sky above her was fathomless black; the water deep carmine and thick, smelling of iron—unseen bodies swayed around her, amorphous and slick, moving like eels, like sliding organs. She shuddered for breath, treading through the blood, then kicked toward the side. The edges of the pool curved inward like the rim of a bowl.

Beneath the surface, her fingers snared on a clump of fine weeds. Karys jerked her hand upwards, and the material came with her, clotted and heavy, not a plant, but long matted blond hair. A face followed, rising up from below, the woman's features vivid with death, her skull half-shaven. The deathspeaker's eyes were missing.

Karys screamed.

Ferain shoved the woman away. Sabaster's vassals surrounded Karys, in pieces but not dead, undulating, mouths open, pressing against her legs, her back, tangling their bloated fingers in her clothing. She thrashed, panicked. Her shadow expanded in all directions through the red murk, and drove them backwards.

"Get to the edge," he said sharply.

Karys swam the last few feet. The wall was too high, and she had no purchase. She could taste foul blood in her mouth. The pool began to churn, the bodies within agitated and squirming, seeking her.

"Here," said Ferain.

She felt pressure under her heels as her shadow boosted her upwards, and she caught hold of the rim of the pool. Ferain swept across her back and grasped her arms, pulling her higher. The pressure of the drawing tightened within her chest. Karys scrabbled, and managed to hook her elbows over the top of the wall. Past its edge, she could see Sabaster's domain stretching out into the endless dark. The pool balanced on top of the white pyramid's pinnacle, at the centre of it all.

A cold, slippery hand fastened around her ankle, and ripped her down from the wall. She fell, and the writhing mass swallowed her again. Karys struggled wildly, but more hands found her arms, her neck—and she could hear them now, the bodies were screaming: *favour, favour, favour.* They clawed at her clothes, tore off her shoes. Her mind blank and reeling with terror, she descended through the howling press. When she met the base of the pool, it flexed like skin over muscle, resisting, then giving way in a violent rush, and disgorging her into the air.

For a few awful seconds, Karys tumbled through empty space. She saw white. Then her knees hit a soft, pliant surface, and she toppled forward in a wash of rank blood, coughing and spluttering.

"Karys Eska," said Sabaster.

Her heart hammered. The Ephirit stood a few feet away. She knelt in a posture of worship before him, folded double over her knees. Red gore dripped from her hair, running down her skin. She did not lift her head; she could only see the whispering fringe of her master's smoke-grey wings, and beyond him, a fence built out of tattered bronze skin and outsized bone. The old Bhatuma corpse, reshaped. The rest of the chamber gleamed blindingly white.

"Vassal of my will." The Ephirit's voice sighed into the air. "Your time of honour has arrived."

Karys spat out blood from the pool; it seared her throat like acid. A numb crawling pain blossomed in her shins and calves—she looked down and saw that thin strands of pale cilia had broken her skin and woven into her flesh, probing deeper, affixing her to the floor. Her throat worked in horror, her shoulders shook. She squeezed her eyes shut.

"Sorry," she whispered, faint.

Her shadow gripped her hand tightly where it lay on the ground. Shame wracked her. She had failed, and damned them both.

"The Disfavoured bore the receptacle. The receptacle has bloomed." The feathers of Sabaster's wings rustled in his eagerness, pinions quivering. "The fruit of their bodies spoiled in decay, but this I have righted and brought to new vitality. The stain and the scourge is no more—you shall bear forth our multiplication, Karys Eska."

She had wanted to save him. She had wanted to carry him from the dark into daylight. She had wanted to see his smile.

A thin trilling filled the chamber, like two metal cables sliding across each other. Karys opened her eyes and found Sabaster looming above her. His three white faces contorted hideously, expressions meaningless, mouths agape. His acrid sweetness washed over her, and the blood on the floor turned to red mist in his presence, rising like vapour. The air flickered with unnatural colour where he wore the Veneer thin.

From beneath his veil of wings, the Ephirit had drawn out a round object. He held it carefully between his long black fingers; the sphere was roughly two feet in diameter, shining and translucent, the sickly brown-yellow of decaying seaweed, the source of the trilling. It looked like necrat, only larger and diseased. Karys stared, transfixed.

"Ferain." Her mouth shaped his name, although she made no sound. "Please."

Sabaster leaned closer. The receptacle pulsed with fallow light, a slow heartbeat. She could not look away.

"Please," she whispered. "You swore."

Her shadow loosened his hold on her hand.

"Forgive me," he breathed.

"Karys Eska, vassal of my will," said Sabaster. "I call your com—"

Ferain unfolded from her body, rising over her head and crossing Sabaster's shadow. In his liar voice, effortless and nonchalant, he said: "That won't work."

Sabaster's wings flared outward in surprise. A discordant ringing rent the air of the chamber; the light bent and discoloured under the Ephirit's power, and the receptacle vanished. Karys' heart leapt to her throat.

"I greet you, Prince of Scales," said Ferain.

Sabaster hissed, his body rippling as though surrounded by a high wind. "A deception!"

"A gift," Ferain corrected. "You like gifts, don't you?"

Karys tried to rise, but the cilia bound her; she could not get up from her knees. *What are you doing?* Sick with fear, her voice came out desperate and strained. "No, stop."

"I am Ferain Taliade," said her shadow. "The only survivor of New Favour's attack on the Vareslian ambassadorial retinue to Toraigus, a massacre meant to prevent the Bhatuma's resurrection. And I hold a living receptacle within my body."

His words rang clear and calm through the room.

"No!" shouted Karys.

Sabaster's wings stilled. The Ephirit extended one grasping, long-fingered hand. He passed it across the merged spill of shadow on the smooth white floor, like a wary dog sniffing at something unfamiliar.

"That's what you want, isn't it?" said Ferain. "You've been trying to find a viable seed. New Favour misunderstood—you no longer want the Bhatuma destroyed, you want them *harvested*."

Karys struggled. The cilia dug deeper into her legs, cold as fishhooks. "Ferain, don't. Don't do this."

"A deception," murmured Sabaster, although he seemed less convinced. His fingers made a series of small, jolting movements, flexing backwards in their sockets. He circled Karys slowly.

"Yes, he lies." Karys twisted to keep her eyes on the Ephirit, breathing hard. "He is lying to you. My lord, I am the vassal of your will, I am faithful to you, *listen* to me."

"You know that your current receptacle won't work." Ferain's voice flowed smooth as glass. "The seed is corrupted. It won't grow."

"He's a *liar!*"

Sabaster searched the floor, weaving fractionally closer and then pulling back again. The face in his groin panted, its eyes screwed shut.

"I have what you need." Ferain's tone dipped low and seductive. "And you have the power to retrieve it."

Karys reached for the Veneer, and ripped it back. Immediately, agony ricocheted through her skull. Every sensation and colour flooded her; all of it molten and alive and furious, the whole domain lit up like a dying star. She fell back, gasping, and the Veneer dropped closed. This close to Sabaster, she could not endure it. Her throat was raw.

"Call my compact," she rasped. "If you want me, call it now."

Ferain tensed, a barely perceptible darkening on the floor. Sabaster's body slanted closer to her, searching. His saliva dripped onto her shoulder.

"You hold the receptacle that breeds true?" he whispered.

"Of course," said Ferain.

She would not let him do this. Karys pressed her hands against the ground, and, with all her strength, pushed upwards. The skin covering her shins tore away with a wet ripping sound. Her blood gushed over the cilia, shockingly red; pain stole the breath from her lungs. Below her, the white tendrils strained to hold fast, stretching elastic between the porous ground and her flesh. She pushed harder.

Sabaster laid a hand on the top of her head.

"It is well." The chorus of his voices blended: part scream, part whisper. "It is well."

Karys went limp. His body's workings crawled over her; she tried to speak, but her mouth failed to respond. The remaining cilia slithered out of her blood-drenched legs. Sabaster's fingers tightened; he lifted her by the head, and she hung from his grasp like a slack-limbed puppet.

"Put her down," said Ferain quickly, his perfect control breaking. "Put her down now."

Sabaster lacked the capacity to interpret Ferain's emotion, and human command meant nothing to him. With the delicate needle-point of his free hand's index finger, he sliced through the collar of Karys' shirt and found the Split Lapse scar. She recoiled with inward horror as he stroked the skin above her left breast.

"Disfavoured," he said. "It is truth. You have brought me this gift."

Ferain came between them; a thin wall of shadow pushed back the Ephirit's fingers. "Put her down *now*."

Although Sabaster maintained his grip on her head, he lowered Karys, and her feet met the blood-slick ground. One of his fingers cupped her jaw; she could taste him inside her mouth: molasses and ash. So close to her, so tightly pressed—she felt as though she was unravelling.

"I offer you a compact," said Ferain.

Despite the workings paralysing her, Karys produced an agonised sound in the back of her throat. *No, no please.* Her shadow flinched at the noise.

"There are conditions," he added.

Sabaster's feathers shivered. The Ephirit seemed bewildered.

"You are a gift of my vassal," he whispered.

"A gift with a price." Ferain drew back across the floor. "If you want me, you will separate me from your vassal without harming her. You will return her safely to where she was summoned from. And then you will release Karys Eska from her compact, after which neither you nor any other Ephirit will ever go near her again. I ask for nothing else."

Karys wanted to scream, but her nerveless body refused. From the depths of Sabaster's shroud came a harsh, repetitive clicking sound.

"A compact cannot be broken," he said, and pure relief surged through her. "My honour was given to Karys Eska."

Ferain was unyielding. "You can claim me from the moment our compact is formed, but in exchange, she is free. I will not negotiate."

Sabaster went ominously silent.

You can't, Karys urged him. *You can't, you can't.*

"Does your honour matter more than the Ephirite's future?" asked Ferain.

The light around Sabaster twisted. The blood on Karys' legs turned black and ice-cold, separating into disks like liquid scales.

"A compact cannot be broken," repeated the Ephirit.

"Why?"

The disks turned to blood once more. The clicking below Sabaster's wings resumed, louder.

"Why can't a compact be broken?" pressed Ferain.

"To break is to Disfavour," hissed Sabaster, the syllables rattling. "We treat, we offer—that is the compact. I am my honour; the compact is of me."

"Oh," said Karys' shadow softly. "I see. Well, in that case: Are *you* more important than the Ephirite's future?"

Absolute silence.

No, thought Karys. *Embrace please. Please don't listen to him.*

"Without me, you have nothing but honour, Prince of Scales," said Ferain, his words like honey, like poison. "Form the compact."

Fighting against the power of the working, Karys mouthed his name. *Ferain.*

"It is so," whispered Sabaster. "The terms are accepted."

NO!

In a fluid motion, he drew his fingers together and drove them like a stake into the binding scar over her heart. The Split Lapse broke open.

All other pain withered to insignificance. Karys lost the sense of her body; she was not made from flesh, but blinding, unending excruciation, the deepest recesses of her soul rent asunder and set alight; she came apart, she came apart from him in pieces, their spirits too entangled to unwind, she did not know if she was alive or dead, only that it had to stop, she was broken too deeply, her essence splintered and divided, Ferain, it had to stop, Ferain come back, end, please end, Ferain, let me die.

Then air.

Sabaster released her head, and Karys fell limbless to the floor. For a few seconds, the world was incomprehensible—she could see herself lying on her side, bleeding, a dark sweep of hair slashed across her face, Sabaster standing over her. She could see herself from outside of herself, and feel the weight of a different body around her. Then the room blurred, she blinked, and her view shifted.

Six feet from her, a man lay on the white ground, propped up weakly on his right elbow. Ferain clutched his wounded arm. Blood ran from his nose and ears, dripping from his face. He bared his teeth in a grin, red and savage.

"You'd better fuck me fast, Ephirit," he said. "I'm dying."

Karys caught a glimpse of the gash on his left arm, peeling apart, turning inside out and spreading, and then Sabaster swooped down on him. The Ephirit covered his body completely, wings spread in a wide tent. She heard Ferain scream in agony.

She should not have been able to move, but she did; Karys swept to her feet and threw herself at Sabaster. His body felt heavy and oily beneath her, his feathered shroud hard as chitin—and yet she sank into him, his wings sucked at her skin. She tore at the Ephirit's back.

"Don't you dare touch him, don't you dare touch him!" she snarled.

Unscathed, Sabaster rose and shook her off. Ferain lay gasping on the floor behind him, convulsing slightly, his eyes rolled back. The wound on his arm had drawn closed. The Ephirit turned his attention to her.

"First and most disgraced of my vassals," he said. "I have dishonoured you beyond understanding. The taint is mine; there will be no atonement worthy of you."

With a cry of fury, Karys punched his second face. She split her knuckle open, but the blow did not leave the slightest mark. Helpless anger emptied her mind, she struck him again and again, and Sabaster stood perfectly still, unmoved by her violence.

"You, I have cherished," he said. "You, I have stained."

His focus on Karys, the Ephirit failed to see Ferain's neck arching to breaking point. With his back turned, he missed the blue spill of light that suddenly blazed across Ferain's chest. Unearthly, the colour—like the sky cracked open.

Ferain cried out her name, and Karys' heart flew straight to him. The chamber dissolved into hallowfire.

The blast staggered her. Flames burned across her eyelids, all-encompassing and bright as the midday sun; fire roared over her body, but she felt no heat. She flung her arms up in front of her face, warding off the light. Then, as abruptly as it appeared, the Bhatuma's brilliance diminished, and the room was visible once more.

Karys lowered her arms. The fence of skin and bone had fallen flat to the ground, flickering with eddies of blue flame. Where he had lain, Ferain now hovered a foot off the floor: upright, eyes closed, his skin licked by banking waves of hallowfire, his chin tilted to the ceiling. He opened his mouth, and produced a rattling inhuman sound, a throaty noise like a ratchet turning, a crow's warning.

"Disfavoured." Sabaster spoke in reverential, whispering chorus. "The vessel bears fruit."

Ferain's head lowered. His eyes flicked open, shining with azure fire.

That's not him.

The attack was too quick for Karys to see. One moment, Sabaster stood before her, and the next he was gone—in the blink of an eye, Ferain ploughed him across the room and slammed him against the chamber wall. The Ephirit's lowest face cleaved away from his body; Ferain gripped the visage between his hands and crushed it like chalk.

"Did you think to play cuckoo, usurper," he hissed. "Did you think to supplant me within the womb?"

Sabaster's body pivoted. With a brutal wrench, reality dislocated. Gravity of the domain reversed, and the world flipped upside down.

Karys fell back to the ceiling and the pool; in midair, she twisted, landing hard on her shoulders. Her collarbone snapped—a heavy crunch reverberating through her chest—and her teeth sliced into her bottom lip. The skin and bone fence clattered as it struck the base of the pool next to her. Winded, blood filling her mouth, she rolled over and pushed herself up onto all fours. Her flayed shins seared with anguish. Through the thin membrane of the ceiling, she could see the imprints of the deathspeakers' hands as they reached for her, their fingers grasping desperately.

In a shuddering crash, Sabaster and Ferain collided with the pool beside her. The force of their impact sheared through its floor, tearing half the structure away and opening a wide abyss to the black sky. Karys scrambled back from the edge. The fence slid and fell through the hole, and she could hear screaming: the howls of Sabaster's blood-soaked vassals as they dropped down into the vast darkness. Her heart thudded.

Sabaster and Ferain rolled to the far wall and broke apart. The Ephirit thrust off from the ground, taking to the air in a rippling wave. A web of yellow fibres emerged from beneath his winged shroud, fine as spun silk. The net shot forward and enveloped Ferain. The instant that the glistening cords touched his body, he went rigid; all his muscles drew tight and still, and his face pulled into a tortured rictus. The strands drew inward, coiling close like a living creature.

Ferain flickered with blue light, and turned to shadow.

The net collapsed. A dark silhouette raced across the ruptured base of the pool; he flew along the wall, formless and quick as mercury, and climbed to the former floor of the chamber. There was nowhere to hide in the spotless white hall; Sabaster pursued him with dispassionate, singular focus, and more strands of the yellow silk reeled out from between the Ephirit's wings. The scales had shifted; where they had appeared evenly matched before, Ferain now held the disadvantage; he retreated.

Sabaster's shroud drifted wider, expanding to form an enormous mantle. He rose serenely after his prey, surrounded by his flowing reams of shining thread. His web almost reached the edges of the chamber, thick and weaving ever more densely, cornering the shadow above him. In the last seconds before the trap closed, the white surface of the floor underneath Ferain flared with blinding fire. When Karys' vision cleared, the shadow had vanished.

Sabaster had lost sight of him too. Above Karys, the Ephirit halted and hung suspended in the air. He slowly rotated in place, scanning the chamber.

When he finished his circle, he stopped. An eerie sawing groan emerged from the mouths of his two remaining faces. In response, every surface in the hall—the walls, the floor, the ceiling—turned to mirror glass.

Thousands of identical Sabasters hovered over Karys' head. Then they began to move, reflections separating and diverging. Each Ephirit hunted the hall alone, hungrily seeking Ferain.

Karys clenched her fists. Her breathing was shaky. The vast crowd of wings and white faces seemed to smear together; her mind could not make sense of the way their bodies decoupled. Every inch of the domain lay under Sabaster's control, reality itself an extension of his command. Within this place, she was the only aberration, the one thing that did not belong. The only unknown—and the only place to hide.

She scarcely moved her mouth, her words no louder than an exhalation. "Tell me what to do."

And her shadow, dark and still at her side, whispered into her ear. "Jump."

Karys shut her eyes. It was not Ferain. She knew that. Whatever lurked in the darkness, it was not the man she had bound. Her muscles tensed. *I can't do this.* She shifted her weight, rising even as her mind rebelled. *Please don't make me do this.*

She knew that it was not Ferain. But the shadow had spoken in his voice.

With a cry of despair, Karys ran forward and threw herself into the sky.

Time slowed. Ahead, nothing: no light, no sound, no end. The void sang, and she fell into it, too terrified to scream, unable to move any part of her body. Air rushed over her skin. She felt each second, each heartbeat booming inside of her chest, all of it increasing; ever faster, darker, and colder. The empty black sky yawned. Her momentum spun her downwards, cast her head-first into oblivion, and she was falling, falling, falling.

With a cruel jerk, gravity reverted. The shift hit her like a punch; her momentum expired, and for the barest instant she found herself weightless and unmoving in the air. It felt like floating—like the swell of a wave before it broke. Then it gave way. Karys dropped and the void receded above her; she plummeted back toward the pyramid.

Sabaster caught her before she reached the summit. Still descending, the Ephirit swept around her, his shroud folding over her and breaking her fall. He pulled her in close, and Karys clutched him instinctively, latching onto the only solid matter within her reach.

Her shadow struck.

The ambush tore through Sabaster, cutting wing and sinew and the unnatural pulsing organs below, splitting his highest face in two with a shower of white powder. The Ephirit shuddered. His body compacted, his feathered mantle flattening to a single plane, but he did not release Karys. They fell together through the white chamber, and hit the ground.

The impact wrenched Karys from Sabaster's grasp. She rolled across the floor, coming to a stop flat on her back. Her head rang. The rushing of air still roared in her ears; she felt her master's feverish heat on her skin. She wheezed, and turned her head. The Ephirit knelt ten feet from her, supported by one arm. His exposed organs, dark below the tattered veil of his shroud, leaked a thick milky gloss like paint. Shattered mirrors lay in fragments around him; in pieces, they quietly chanted: *new favour, new favour.*

He meant to save me.

The thought stood hideously stark in her mind. Ferain, no longer in shadow, crouched to her right. His expression was harrowed; he faced Sabaster, and reality rippled between the pair—weak flashes of blue, incongruous reflections spiralling into nothing.

With a jagged breath, Karys picked herself up. Everything hurt. She swayed, then limped unsteadily across the glittering floor. When she reached him, Sabaster tilted his last face up toward her. In isolation, his expression only looked sad.

"Vassal of my will," he said weakly. "Most honoured . . . most disgraced."

She touched his cheek, and he crooned. The white surface of his skin felt cool and smooth.

"I was unworthy of you," he whispered. "My honour insufficient. I am sorry, Karys Eska."

Karys found that she was crying. She did not know why. Before her knelt a nightmare. Her ruin, her greatest regret. Tears rolled silently down her face.

"You still have honour," she said.

The Veneer opened to her. It burned, but less brightly than before. The workings of Sabaster's body shone before her, intricate and vast; she could see into his wounds, all the broken parts amidst the glow. Too complex to be understood, aching and alive. Karys reached her senses into the deepest and brightest of the lights, and gently brought them undone.

Sabaster unravelled with a sigh. His last face dissolved into silver like moonlight under her fingers. Then he was gone.

Karys slipped to her knees. The low chanting of the mirrors faded, replaced by a deep creaking: the wind through giant trees. She looked up. Clusters of black holes had appeared in the walls and through the remains of the chamber's ceiling. They expanded slowly. Through them, she could see nothing but darkness.

Movement caught her eye—Ferain had climbed back to his feet. He stretched, then rolled his shoulders in their sockets as if to dismiss old stiffness. A glimmering brightness settled around him, a clean smell like the breeze off the sea. Without paying her the slightest attention, he rose into the air. His expression was smooth as he ascended.

Karys felt a pull in her chest.

"Ferain," she said. Her voice cracked.

A faint tremor ran through his shoulders. He hesitated, and his gaze drew back to her. Karys stared at him, unable to speak. There was nothing familiar in his face, nothing she recognised.

Come back to me, she thought.

He smiled like he could read her mind, but it was not his smile—somehow, she knew that. Sabaster's palace continued to break apart around them. The creaking grew ever louder as the darkness ate through the walls.

"Well, why not?" he said.

Shadows reared from the glass-littered ground, and swallowed Karys.

CHAPTER

47

The shore. Black sand as fine as powder, the stench of washed-up kelp. Water. Cold waves lapping at her back, and the taste of salt in her mouth. The sound of gulls, the hush of the ocean.

Karys breathed, and water filled her mouth. Her eyes flew open. Coughing, she lifted her head from the foam-flecked shallows. The sky over the sea gleamed pale orange with the dawn; the coast stretched empty and shadowed in either direction. Her legs cramped as she sat up, her skin frozen like she had been lying in the tide for hours. The flesh of her shins was whole and unmarked. All of her injuries had disappeared. She cast around, shivering hard.

"Ferain?" she croaked.

No reply. She was alone but for the seabirds drifting over the high reaches of the cliffs. No footprints on the beach, just her, washed up onto the shore like driftwood. Karys struggled to her feet, her heels sinking into the sucking dark sand, and stumbled up the bank.

"Ferain," she called, louder.

The sun had not yet appeared on the horizon, and the light remained soft, the edges of objects imprecise. The hazy outline of her own shadow extended over the ground before her, slack and lifeless. She could not stand to look at it. Karys broke into a run. The tall cliffs rose higher, curving east along the bay, and there was the alcove, the indentation at the base of the wall—the same cave she had entered with Oselaw, the passage into the Sanctum. Her breathing ragged, she dropped down before the algae-fringed hole.

"Ferain!" she shouted.

"He isn't down there."

Karys whipped around. The Bhatuma was standing on the beach behind her. He had not been there seconds before; only her own footprints marked the sand. His expression was one of mild amusement. The sleeve of his shirt had torn away; where the Construct had wounded Ferain, the skin ran with pale, pure silver. Karys' chest tightened.

"Give him back," she said softly.

"Or what?"

She pulled open the Veneer, and reached to attack. Faster than thought, the Bhatuma rebuffed her. An invisible force drove into Karys' midriff, sending her sprawling backwards on the sand. She gagged, clutching her stomach.

"Like a kitten," he remarked. "Hissing at the ocean."

She lifted her head. "Give him back."

"Can't." The Bhatuma shook his head regretfully. "He's gone, kitten. I ate him."

Karys snarled. She drove up from the ground, and grasped the fabric of the Veneer a second time. The Bhatuma made a contemptuous sound. His power collided with her once more, and he threw her back down.

"A slow learner, aren't you?" he said.

Karys gasped for breath. Her head pounded; beneath her, the black sand felt hard as tar. She fought to rise.

"Persistent, though, I'll give you that," said the Bhatuma.

She made it to her feet. When she spoke, her voice sounded unlike her own: harsh and uncontrolled. "You're a liar."

The Bhatuma gave her a look of pity, and she hated him for it, hated that he used Ferain's face that way.

"Do you really believe I'd share a vessel?" he asked. "Come, you aren't naïve. You should know better than—"

"I can still feel him!" Her voice rose to a shout, and she struck her chest hard over her heart, over the Split Lapse scar. "I can still feel him now. Don't lie to me, I know he's there!"

For a second, the Bhatuma looked startled. Karys took a step toward him.

"Part of him belongs to me." The words spilled rapidly from her mouth. "We did not break apart cleanly; part of him stayed with me, part of me stayed with him. Ferain is alive—you can't deceive me, because I can feel him."

A moment of silence.

"Well," murmured the Bhatuma, "aren't you full of surprises?"

Karys took another step toward him.

"Please," she said. "Please give him back."

Behind the Bhatuma, the first rays of light hit the sea, scattering gold over the water. He raised his right hand, examining Ferain's slender, blunt-nailed fingers in the faint glow of the sun. The edges of his body caught the light, and the shadows warped at his feet.

"My kind are not born as humans are," he said. "Our potential is held within the Embrace, fully formed; we wait for an opportunity and an affinity. And in the end, after all the long years of waiting, there was only one opportunity.

Mine. This isn't how it was meant to be, but I'm awake, and you are largely to thank for that."

He lowered his hand, and turned his eyes on her. They were a rich hazel colour, warmer than Rhevin's but with the same russet cast.

"Valaht," he said. "Ambavar is dead, but I'm of the same strain. For your aid in my restoration, I brought you out of the Ephirit's realm, and I healed your wounds. But I owe you nothing further, kitten."

Karys shook her head, struggling for words. "Whatever you want—whatever I can give you—"

"And what will you give, hm?"

It came out a whisper. "Anything."

Valaht sighed.

"Make me your Favoured," she said, increasingly wild. "Make me your vassal. I can serve you, I'll give you my life."

He raised an eyebrow. "As you did for your last master? Or Nuliere before him? If there's one thing you lack, kitten, it's fidelity. You're as faithless as they come."

"Let me be a tool, then," she said. "Use me however you want. I am begging you—please, please just let him go."

The shadows swarming at his feet drew together, and the distance between Valaht and Karys disappeared. The Bhatuma stood right before her. He lifted his hand and tenderly took hold of her chin. Her breath stopped. Briefly, Valaht allowed hallowfire to gleam behind his eyes, and they shone ice-blue with power.

She felt something move inside her: the brush of a cool, familiar weight beneath her breastbone.

"I just don't think," said Valaht softly, "that you are very useful."

Karys reached for Ferain.

The Bhatuma's fingers left her jaw; he vanished, and the shadows gathered and re-formed a few feet further away. Silhouetted against the dawn, he smiled at her.

"So long, Karys Eska," he said and then, as an afterthought, he added: "Oh, and I believe these might be yours."

He tossed a pair of leather boots onto the ground between them.

Karys' heart beat fast. She stumbled toward him.

"No, wait," she said.

Valaht laughed. The shadows bled into the black sand, dissolving in the light, and he was no more.

A cold breeze blew off the water. It traced across the shore, drawing up a stinging haze of dark powder. Over the sea, the sun touched the horizon, brilliant, blinding. Karys stood alone. Her silhouette fell long and monstrous on the ground behind her; the only sounds were the waves and her own breathing. The moment seemed to stretch into eternity, as though the Lapse had closed around her now, as though she hung suspended and apart from the world.

She could feel the place he used to occupy. Where Sabaster had divided them, she felt Ferain's absence. And there, faded and pale, the echo left behind—the faintest shadow of his presence still within her.

Karys touched the scar over her heart.

"To the end of the world," she whispered.

She picked up her boots, turned from the sunrise, and began the long walk back to the city.

ACKNOWLEDGEMENTS

Thank you to everyone at my publisher who had a hand in making this book a reality, and particularly to production editor Lauren Hougen, who ensured that a colossal number of last-minute changes were immaculately applied to the master document. *Asunder* would be a very different novel without you.

Ruoxi Chen, thank you for taking a chance on me all those years ago—and for your steadfast support ever since. You were the first editor to believe in me, and I will always treasure that.

Thank you to Jennifer Jackson for being the best agent in the business.

I owe a great debt to Clarion West. Thank you to the organizers, sponsors, instructors, and most importantly my brilliant, beloved 2022 cohort. You are all feral weirdos, and I miss you. To the Muffin Cabal—Varsha Dinesh, Steph Kwiatkowski, and Naomi Day—thank you for being the most wonderful pod-mates in the world, and for making me laugh loud enough to be heard through the walls. To honorary co-conspirator Wen-yi Lee: thank you for guarding our secrets.

When my confidence in this novel hit rock bottom, it was also my cohort who dragged me out of the ditch. I am truly grateful to Wen-yi Lee, Varsha Dinesh, Louis Evans, P H Lee, and Issa Marc Shulman for throwing a party in the Google doc. You are all hilarious, and your comments lifted me out of my despondency.

To Emma Laubscher, your friendship is a bright light in my life. You're re-markable, and I won't let you forget it, and I'm sorry that your authors always have so many feelings.

Thank you to my dad, Stephen Hall. I hope you like this one. There's slightly less cannibalism.

Thank you to my mom, Sylvia Hall—for everything.

And to Tessa, ever and always, for being exactly as you are. (Please also do think of me when you receive your engineering salary.)

ABOUT THE AUTHOR

Sylvia Hall

Kerstin Hall is the author of *The Border Keeper, Second Spear,* and *Star Eater.* She lives in Cape Town, South Africa.

kerstinhall.com
Twitter: @Kerstin__Hall